WISHDOCTOR'S SONG

HUNTER STEELE

THE WISHDOCTOR'S SONG

Futura

A Futura Book

This edition published in 1985
by Futura Publications, a Division of
Macdonald & Co (Publishers) Ltd
London & Sydney

All characters in this publication are fictitious and any resemblance to real persons, living or dead, is purely coincidental.

ISBN 0 7088 2803 5

Copyright Acknowledgements
The author and publishers are grateful to Mrs Laura Huxley and Chatto and Windus Ltd for permission to quote material from *Heaven and Hell* by Aldous Huxley

Printed and bound in Great Britain by
Collins, Glasgow

Futura Publications
A Division of
Macdonald & Co (Publishers) Ltd
Maxwell House
74 Worship Street
London EC2A 2EN

A BPCC plc Company

For everyone concerned.
And the pear tree.
With apologies to Aberdeen.

What a jovial and a merry world would this be, may it please your worships, but for that inextricable labyrinth of debts, cares, woes, want, grief, discontent, melancholy, large jointures, impositions, and lies!

Tristram Shandy

The penis does not lie.

Thomas S. Szasz

The evil doer's conscience must ne'er grow fat,
Must e'er fear that day when truth shall fly
Up from the bloody ashes of the past,
To sink eternal talons in his shame.

Shakespeare

But I have other reasons for telling
the wishdoctor's story.

Peter Squirrell

ONE

It was early in the 1970s, when most people could still remember what they were doing while Robert Kennedy and Martin Luther King were assassinated, when girls with good legs still wore miniskirts but girls with bad legs no longer had to. The place was Deenburgh, Flower of Scotland, Sparta of the North, and it was largely the architecture of the city that led to my involvement.

On the second Friday in January:

Deirdre Wishfort and I had been dining with the Tostows.

'Tell me about your brother,' said Dr Tostow (pronounced *ov*) while we waited for Mrs Tostow to bring the coffee.

Deirdre sat in a luxuriously upholstered armchair to the left of the copper-coloured stove. She smoothed her Laura Ashley dress over her knees and unenthusiastically said: 'Mallecho?'

'Do you have other brothers?'

'No, Dr Tostow. But why should you be interested in Mallecho?'

Dr Tostow was standing at the drinks trolley behind his wickerwork rocking chair. He was a short man, less tall than me, but deepchested, with breast muscles unpleasantly pronounced beneath his white poloneck sweater. He smiled his dark smile at Deirdre and said:

'Call me Ivan.'

'Ivan,' Deirdre echoed.

'Well,' said Dr Tostow, decanting tawny port into crystal glasses, 'it is an unusual name, is it not?'

'It was his grandfather's idea,' Deirdre replied coolly.

'Isn't he the chap', I asked, 'that they call the witchdoctor?'

'Some people do.'

'Yes, Deirdre,' said our host, handing me my glass, 'your brother is quite a character on Campus, you know. Up in the John Locke Tower we hear all sorts of stories about him. Some say he's the Deenburgh Mafia.' He chuckled unsuccessfully, twisting his small, cruel mouth and hooding the weak black eyes behind his spectacles.

Neither Deirdre nor I chuckled at all.

She took a driver's sip of port and looked at me aggressively, willing me to tack the conversation into a less unwelcome subject.

I found this unnerving. I have never been a maestro in social situations, and I was even less of one then. Deirdre and I were final-year psychology students at Deenburgh University, and this dinner was a warmer for our tutorials with Dr Tostow during the coming term.

The meal had been excellent: seafood cocktails; a rich variety of savoury open sandwiches made with thinly-sliced rye bread (washed down by numerous shots of aqua vitae and glasses of strong Danish lager); brandy trifle and cream for dessert, accompanied by a bottle of sweet white wine. Seldom did I dine or drink so handsomely, and what with the sherry beforehand and now the port:

'I wonder, Dr Tostow,' I tacked sluggishly, 'whether . . .'

'Ah. Coffee,' he exclaimed.

'Sugar and cream, Peter? Deirdre?' asked Mrs Tostow, entering the room like sunshine after an April shower.

'Both, please, Mrs Tostow,' I said, jumping up politely and slopping a dribble of port on the right knee of my only suit.

'You must call me Anita,' she insisted huskily as she passed me my coffee. Tall and striking, she wore a palegold satin trousersuit with flared bottoms and a yellowgold tassel round the waist. Her hair was the colour of Tasmanian honey, parted low and swept over her crown, so that when she looked down a great wave of honey hair would fall across her face. She had a habit, when this happened, of combing the hair back with the spread fingers of her right hand, thrusting her heavy breasts into a prominence that a sex-starved young man of twenty-two just had to notice noticeably.

'What were you wondering, Peter?' asked Dr Tostow from his rocking chair, when Anita had set my flesh tingling by sitting beside me on the sofa.

Holding the stem of my glass in my left hand while balancing my coffee saucer on my port-stained knee, I said:

'What do you and Mrs Tostow think of Deenburgh? Now that you've been here a year?'

'A year and a term,' Anita corrected me.

'But what about you, Peter?' Dr Tostow countered. 'How long have you been here?'

'Exactly the same time, actually. A year and a term.'

'And how is that possible if now you are in your final year?'

'I suppose,' I confessed, 'that I am what's called an Oxbridge failure.'

'Surely not,' said Anita.

'Yes. I was groomed at school for my headmaster's old college at Cambridge, but the intake standard was very high that year, and so, with no sporting achievements to make me more attractive, I just missed a place. Then, like so many in the same situation, I tried Saint Andrews. I had a great aunt who lived in the fishing village of Crail, just along the coast, and I was able to board with her for almost nothing.'

'So you didn't like Saint Andrews?' asked Anita, smiling. She had an unusually wide mouth, and the curve of her upper lip reminded me of a seagull's wings in silhouette.

'My aunt became seriously ill during my second year. She went into a nursing home, and it soon became obvious she would never come out again. The house was sold to cover nursing costs, so I ran out of cheap accommodation, and also . . .'

'You perhaps had decided,' Dr Tostow speculated, 'that the intellectual climate of that university, though no doubt cosy, somewhat fell short of your own aspirations?'

'Something like that. Everyone at Saint Andrews was very competent, of course.'

'Of course.'

'But Professor Galton had just moved to Deenburgh from Cambridge, and as I was determined to get a good degree and go back to Cambridge to do research, I got a transfer to Deenburgh.'

'And you have not regretted it?'

'Not for a moment. Although . . .'

'We believe in The Open Society here, Peter,' said Dr Tostow. 'No secrets, please.'

'It's just that I'm finding accommodation rather a nightmare at the moment. The flat I'm in is cold, damp and dirty. Two of my flatmates play in a jazz band and practise at home all night.'

'Poor Peter,' Anita exclaimed. 'You must move.'

'I'm afraid that's easier said than done, Mrs Tostow. I've fled from the frying pan several times, only to land in a louder and nastier fire!' I flushed at my drink-induced emotion. Taking refuge in the dregs of my coffee, I was surprised to hear Deirdre say:

'I might be able to help, Peter. Or at least my mother might.'

'Oh?'

'There's a flatlet in the basement of our house in Hanover Place. It used to be for our *au pair*, but she left in December and Mother's been doing it up since.'

'There you are, Peter,' Anita enthused. 'That sounds excellent, doesn't it?'

'It certainly does. But won't your mother want it for another *au pair*?'

'No,' said Deirdre. 'Rosie's old enough not to need one, and they never do any work anyway. And they often cause trouble. There was quite a fuss in our family, in fact, just before Françoise left.' She tossed her brown curls disapprovingly.

'Do tell us about it,' said Dr Tostow.

'I was an *au pair* girl once,' Anita murmured for my ears only.

'No, really, Ivan,' said Deirdre. 'I must be going. It's been very nice: that was a super meal, Mrs Tostow. Really super.'

'First class,' I agreed.

'Will you not have some more port?' Dr Tostow protested. 'Or coffee? A whisky?'

'That's very kind of you, Ivan. But I am driving, and I must get up early tomorrow to go to Glasgow. Can I give you a lift, Peter?' she offered, standing up decisively.

Deirdre Wishfort was a far from brilliant student, or even dedicated psychologist, but she was, in the idiom of the time, a very *together* person.

She was the same height as me and probably heavier, being ample though not quite plump. Her ambition was to get a Second Class degree (Division One, if possible) and work for three years as an industrial psychologist, thus acquiring enough experience to return to work easily when the youngest of her three projected children reached a sufficient age. Her wedding was planned for the first Saturday in July: the day following our Graduation. Alastair Cameron-Bell, her fiancé, whom I had met briefly at a party in her flat, was a large, coarse, rugby-playing chartered accountant who worked in Glasgow.

'They're an odd couple, aren't they?' she said of the Tostows, peering past her toiling windscreen wipers while driving me home through the sleet-swept streets of Deenburgh's New Town.

'Odd in what way?'

'There's something a bit off about him, though it's difficult to define. And I don't go for middle-aged men who wear red cord suits and white poloneck sweaters.'

'But isn't that fashionable?'

'Exactly.'

'And is he really middle-aged?'

'What do you think?'

'Maybe forty-five?'

'And his wife?'

'Thirty-five?'

Deirdre laughed.

'Come on, Peter,' she said. 'If we're going to work on the psychology of interpersonal perception, you'll have to do better than that. He's pushing fifty, and she's not a day over thirty-one.'

'How can you be so precise?'

'Didn't you notice the skin on the backs of her hands? And her neck?'

'No.'

'But I expect you did notice', Deirdre said sharply, stopping her mother's pea-green Morris Minor at a red light, 'that she's rather beautiful.'

'She's certainly striking. I'm not sure "beautiful" is quite the word. Rather heavily made up, I thought. Certainly not beautiful in the same way as . . .'

'As who?'

That's torn it, I assumed: *bang goes my chance of renting her mother's basement.*

'I was thinking,' I muttered reluctantly, 'of your flatmate Cindy.'

To my astonishment, Deirdre seemed pleased.

Turning left into Lethe Drive, the straight, wide boulevard that rolls a gentle mile from the East End down to the Docks, she said:

'So you fancy Cindy?'

'Not at all. I've hardly even spoken to her. I was merely attempting a comparison. Purely in aesthetic terms.'

'Oh yes?'

Our conversation was paused by a gaggle of drunks emerging from the Green Sea restaurant and stumbling loudly across the road. Deirdre had to swerve to avoid hitting them, which resulted in a volley of glottal obscenities and greasy chips being hurled at my side of the car. It was not yet eleven, but these were the bad old days when the pubs closed at ten.

'Have you read Tostow's novels?' I asked, steering away from my embarrassment over Cindy.

'I've read *Erewhon Three,*' said Deirdre.

'Like it?'

'No.'

'Neither did I. But then I never read fiction anyway.'

'Well I do when I have the time, and I think *Erewhon Three* is warped. All that rubbish about the Adult Mind being Guardian of the Universe. It's one of the few issues, in fact, where I agree with my brother, and it's partly why I didn't want Tostow as my tutor. I as good as said so to Galton, but he didn't get the message.'

'Next on the left, please,' I indicated.

'Why,' Deirdre inquired as she changed gear, 'should a psychologist want to write novels? If he's any good as a psychologist?'

'They must supplement his income quite nicely, don't you think? They're out in paperback here, and I believe they've sold well in America.'

'I bet Galton's textbooks bring in a lot more than Tostow's novels,' said the down-to-earth Deenburgh lady. 'Tostow hasn't produced a book on psychology in ten years.'

'He has written lots of articles, though. And . . .'

'Who hasn't? Is this it?'

'Yes. Just past the red Triumph.'

'Right,' said my together chauffeuse. 'Give my mother a ring tomorrow morning. I'll tell her to expect you.'

'Do you think,' I asked hesitantly, 'she'll want a lot for it?'

Deirdre looked at me with challenging green eyes.

'I'm sure it won't be more than you pay at present,' she said. 'If she likes you. We don't need the money, you see. But we don't need the basement either, and Mother wants it put to good use. She's like that.'

I asked her for the phone number.

She told me.

I thanked her for driving me home, and I offered to write the first essay for our tutorials with Dr Tostow.

She accepted.

I reached to open the door, but Deirdre said:

'Hang on. Better stay in the car for a moment.'

She was looking in the driving mirror.

I squinted over my shoulder and heard a sudden frantic slapping of sprinting feet on the slushy pavement. A fugitive figure flashed past and disappeared into the amber gloom down the street.

Several seconds later, heavier and less rapid steps came labouring in pursuit. A burly shape struggled past us, short of breath and weighed down by an ex-army greatcoat of the kind then popular with the more long-haired and rebellious of my student fellows. I only caught the briefest glimpse of Greatcoat's face, but it impressed itself lastingly on my mind. It was the face of a predatory brute turned vicious by unhealthy conditioning: stupid, cruel, lusting to inflict pain.

Twenty yards down the street he paused for breath, and I saw something glint sharply in his hand: a knife, or possibly a broken bottle.

'Dinny yew worry, ya *cunt*,' he bellowed after his intended victim. 'Ah'll *get* ya.'

He took off again and was swallowed up in the dark wet night.

I shuddered.

'Nice area you live in, Peter,' Deirdre said pleasantly, as I got out of the car.

'It's your town, Deirdre.'

TWO

Hanover Place, the furthest north of the classical squares and circuses in the New Town proper, is an oval squared off at the south end. At the north end the numbers stop at fourteen and begin again at twenty-one on the other side, as though there had been a great fire in between. In fact the gap has always been there. The builders began at numbers one and thirty and simply ran out of stone or finance in the middle: literally failed to make ends meet.

The result is a happy one, however, adding to the charm of the place and enabling one to look north-west to the tree-tops of Aberlethe Park and the Royal Botanical Gardens. A short grassy slope had been left in the gap until earlier in the present century, when the town council occupied most of the available space with a hideous swimming pool and public baths. But the contrast between the cool spacious elegance and clean grey stone of the four-storey terraced houses, on the one hand, and the ugly flat crouching and sandy red stone of the swimming pool, on the other, is so violently extreme that most people hardly notice it. Although:

'My poor, dear sister could remember the days when *sheep used to graze* where that monstrosity now stands,' was one of the favourite claims of Miss Moray, the octogenarian Senior Resident in number twenty-five.

I was looking for Number Ten, as I came to know it. This was on the west side, and as I approached it my heart began to pound.

What should I say if the flat was no good?

If Mrs Wishfort wanted more than I could afford?

If she *didn't like me*?

The front door and window frames were a bright clean

white, repainted recently, and the door-knocker, handle and bell-pull were of gleaming polished brass. A quick peep into the basement attracted me to a large improvised flowerpot at the foot of the steps. It was fashioned out of the lowest third of a beer barrel. The wood was painted gloss white and the metal hoops gloss black. Out of the soil in the pot grew a thriving creeper, which coiled up the railing on the inside of the steps.

I wavered between the bell-pull and the heavy brass knocker (hinged in the mouth of a snarling lion) until my reticence was swamped by a hallucination of that squalid menage in Lethe, epitomized by the Che Guevara poster above the kitchen table: faded, curling at the edges, damp from kettle steam, and poxed with yellow spots of fat condensed from countless simmering soup stocks.

I gripped the bell-pull and yanked assertively.

A distant dingling sounded within.

'Ah,' said Mrs Wishfort a minute later, holding the door open. 'Peter Squirrell? You certainly *look* respectable enough. Come along in.'

Such was her dry good humour, I soon realized. She was a tolerant lady at heart, yet professionally strict in her rôle as Head of History at St David's, the school for upper-crust Deenburgh daughters. She was forty-eight and well preserved, though her once-fair hair was streaked with grey and the smile wrinkles were many and deep in the corners of her sky-blue eyes.

Today she was wearing a fawn roll-neck jumper and navy-blue slacks.

'Now,' she said, as my tour of the house ascended to the second floor. 'That's Helen's room,' she pointed to the door facing the stairs. 'And that little one to the right used to be Rosie's. But now Rosie's got Deirdre's old room, and Deirdre uses Rosie's old room whenever she stays the night here, which isn't all that often now.'

'I see,' I said, marvelling at her energy and the trouble she was taking to make me feel at home.

'So that's Rosie's new room along at the end, where you can see the mess on the desk and the sun coming through the window, and that's Mallecho's room to the right of it. Mallecho says we're not to touch it, but we do sometimes use it as an extra guest room.'

'He won't live at home any more, I suppose?'

'No. Mallecho has his own flat now, up in Southside, but he still sleeps here sometimes. At Christmas, or if we've had a party and he's drunk too much to drive home.'

Oh Brave New Middle-class Deenburgh, where all the young natives have their own plush flats to drive home to.

'And now,' said my new landlady, 'the children's bathroom.' She opened the door in the middle of the top landing (a narrow passage railed off from a stair well that looked down to the chessboard lino of the groundfloor hall) and we stepped in.

'It's nothing special, I'm afraid,' Mrs Wishfort said truthfully, 'but my husband wouldn't like you using ours.'

'Really, Mrs Wishfort, I couldn't ask for better. You should see what I'll be leaving behind me.'

'But it is warm, and anyway you have a good sink and hot water in your kitchenette.'

I nodded appreciatively, taut with apprehension that if I said the wrong thing my good fortune might evaporate.

'There's also a toilet in the basement, beside the door to the garden – I'll show you that before you go. So it's really only baths you've to trek up here for. Now how many?'

'Sorry?'

'How many bathnights shall we give you? Françoise had a bath every night, but I don't suppose you'll want that many. Mallecho certainly doesn't.'

Not wanting to appear either dirty or extravagant, I said: 'Two per week would be very adequate.'

'Right. We'll say Monday, Wednesday and Friday, so you can take your pick.'

'I do tend to go to bed rather late.'

'That's all right, Peter. As long as you don't sing too loud. Rosie's in bed by ten-thirty, so any time after that is fine. You'll have to take pot luck with Helen, though. She's in and out at all hours – you will use your own towels, won't you?'

'Yes, of course.'

'The snib hasn't been fixed yet, I see,' she indicated. 'I'll mention it to my husband, but if you're bashful in the meantime, stick the dirty-clothes basket against the door and yell out if anyone tries the handle. That skylight,' she pointed chattily at the bathroom's only window, 'goes up to a rather nice suntrap beside the cupola.'

'Really?'

'Once,' she said, glowing with the unconvincing disapproval of a privately proud mother, as she led me downstairs, 'about ten years ago, on Guy Fawkes Night, my husband was giving Deirdre and her friends a firework display in the garden, and I came up to run a bath for Helen, and what did I find?'

'I really can't imagine, Mrs Wishfort.'

'Mallecho and Beano had got the stepladder up and gone on to the roof, and just what do you think they were doing?'

Realizing, sophisticated by my recent study of the psychology of interpersonal communication, that her apparently purposeless anecdote was secretly intended to instruct me in the basic grammar of the Wishfort family mythology, I said:

'They were pouring boiling oil on a host of Martian invaders at the front door?'

'Not quite, Peter. They were firing rockets out of a milk bottle, not into the sky but across the square at poor old Miss Moray's sitting room window. My God, was I furious.'

'Goodness.'

'Now,' she offered, when we had descended the blue-carpeted, painting-lined stairs to the hall, 'a cup of tea before you go?'

I was enjoying her company, so:

'Yes, please. Milk and three sugars.'

She smiled and said:

'Another starving student, I see. Well, we'd better not spoil Rosie's television party, so have a seat in the dining room, and I'll bring the tea through.'

The television party (four thumb-sucking thirteen-year-old girls) was sitting in the morning room glued to a BBC2 Saturday-afternoon-ancient movie. The morning room and kitchen were at the back of the house, getting the lengthening winter sunshine, and the dining room was at the front, off the hall.

I wandered contentedly round the heavy mahogany dining table, drinking in the warm, friendly atmosphere of the household and inspecting the various ornaments and paintings. One picture particularly caught my eye. It was a large palette-knifed canvas, hung commandingly on the long wall to the right of the windows. Its subject was a female nude reclining unhappily on an unmade bed.

The tips of her pendulous breasts were sharply emphasized, while her right hand rested suggestively, though not quite pornographically, on the inside of her splayed right thigh. Though her genitals were represented somewhat overmeticulously, relative to the slashing impressionistic whole, what disturbed me most was her facial expression, which seemed undecided as between: intense sexual anticipation, the explosion of orgasm itself, or the lonely torture of a young woman whose lover has deserted her for another. Still, it was a work of some power, and Mrs Wishfort caught me ogling it when she came in with the tea tray.

'Do you like that, Peter?' she asked, pouring.

'Em . . .'

'A bit shocking, you may feel, for a respectable Deenburgh dining room?'

'Not exactly shock . . .'

'Guess the artist?' She handed me my tea and plate bearing a thick wedge of fruitcake.

'Painting's not my strong point, I'm afraid. Thank you.'

'My daughter Helen,' said Mrs Wishfort, taking her matriarchal seat by the sideboard and lighting a menthol cigarette. 'She's in her second year at the Art College.'

'I see.'

'Quite new, that one. She did it a couple of months ago.'

'And is it a life drawing? Or purely a work of the imagination?'

'It's a self-portrait.'

I blinked.

'My husband says it's disgusting. But we're quite democratic in this family, in most things, and the consensus was pro Helen. Anyway,' she exhaled, 'it's not depraved, is it? Not like the *Memoirs of a Young Rakehell*, or those awful Beardsley cartoons?'

'Of course not,' I agreed, having encountered neither item. 'It looks very . . . competent.'

'Yes. Now, we've agreed the rent, and I'll expect it monthly in advance.'

'Naturally.'

'When do you want to move in?'

'Early next week? The sooner I can get on with some serious work, the better.'

'How will you shift your things?'

'One of my flatmates has a van for his jazz band. I expect he'll be glad to help me out.'

'Fine. Electricity is only lights and record players, so you can have that thrown in. Cooking is gas, and so is your fire, so you'll want a supply of shillings for the meter.'

'I'll get a bag on Monday.'

'And you will note your phonecalls, won't you?'

'I don't expect to make many, Mrs Wishfort. But I certainly will keep a careful record. I normally only phone my mother on Sunday nights, and then I reverse the charges.'

'Why not have a code?'

'A code?'

'She lets it ring three times, you ring off, then she knows to phone you. Avoiding the extra transfer charge.'

'I hadn't thought . . .'

There was an eruption of energy and noise from the morning room, indicative of credits over happiness-ever-after, and a young but heavy Dalmatian dog lolloped into the dining room and applied eager wet nostrils to my trousers.

'Good dog,' I said, tickling it behind the ears while trying to keep its saliva off my thighs.

'*Panda*,' Mrs Wishfort scolded, 'come here at once. Rosie?'

'Yes, Mummee?' called a voice from the hall.

'Call Panda.'

'Pan Da. Paaan Da. Waugh keys, Pan Da.'

The dog lolloped out.

'Don't be long, Rosie,' Mrs Wishfort instructed. 'Where are you going?'

'No, Mummee. Only up to the park.'

'All of you together?'

'Yee-es.' Plus multiple giggles.

'Well, be back by six.'

The dog-walking party departed loudly, and I relaxed. Why people in towns have to keep dogs (apart from elderly widows and the like) has always been a mystery to me. The Buttbridge area of Deenburgh, with Hanover Place at its heart, is particularly bad that way: the pavements being, literally, a foul disgrace.

But the level of civilization in the houses is high, and Mrs Wishfort insisted that I consume more tea and cake while our conversation continued. Had Deirdre and I enjoyed our dinner with the Tostows last night? Yes, very much. Did I think Deirdre would manage an Upper Second? Yes, I was confident she would. She wasn't an intellectual highflier, was she, but at least she was methodical? Indeed she was, and I envied her ability to work regardless of distractions – my own concentration was lamentably fragile and only flowered in warmth and silence. Then, as Mrs Wishfort lit a second cigarette, I threw up some honest compliments on her house and the solid, calm sanity expressed by the dining-room decor and furniture.

'Functional,' she agreed carelessly. 'But nothing special. The table's late Victorian, and just look at those dents in it.'

I inspected a rash of shallow concavities in the polished mahogany surface.

'That was Beano. Mallecho and he used to play ping-pong in here, and Beano would get in a rage when he lost, and smash his bat down on the table.'

'Goodness. Is Beano a neighbour?'

'Mallecho and he have been best friends since they were six. The Turnbulls used to live in number two, but they moved to the country years ago. You'll like Beano, I'm sure. He's great fun.'

'Is Beano his real name?'

'His Christian name's George. When he was a little boy he was fat, so they called him Beanpole Turnbull. But now he's just massive.'

'That must be rather worrying, if he still gets in rages.'

'Ah, but he doesn't. Mallecho made him do karate, so he'd learn to control his temper.'

'Do all Deenburgh boys get nicknames?' I asked, thinking that in the past few months I'd heard Mallecho Wishfort referred to as Witch, The Witchdoctor, The Man and frequently glossed as the cheapest source of the purest LSD in town.

'Most of the Academy boys had nicknames. Mallecho was Witch, George was Beano, and Alastair was Bungalow.'

'*Bung*alow?'

Mrs Wishfort's blue eyes twinkled. 'Yes. Bungalow Cameron-Bell. Rather unkind, isn't it? Actually he's not at all stupid, but he doesn't have the same sense of humour as the other boys. Doing very well for himself in accountancy. But tell me, Peter: didn't you ever have a nickname?'

This caught my guard down:

'At Junior School they called me Nutkins.'

I didn't find Mrs Wishfort's amusement at all offensive. She had a deep, earthy, rather attractive laugh, and I began to perceive her as more than just another landlady.

The telephone rang.

Mrs Wishfort went out to answer it in the hall.

Not wishing to outstay my welcome, I waited until her voice wound up the call, then went to retrieve my coat from the basement stair banister.

'Those are fascinating,' I said, as I shrugged into the brown duffelcoat I'd had since my third year at school. 'Are they butterflies?'

Mrs Wishfort followed my gaze to the ornamental case of

trophied Lepidoptera on the wall facing the foot of the stairs.

'Moths,' she said. 'Not British, as you can tell from the size of them. I really must get Douglas to replace the glass sometime. Bet you can't guess how the glass got broken?'

'No.'

'Helen's boyfriend fell down the stairs last New Year and put his head through it.'

'Goodness. Was he badly hurt?'

'Mild concussion, which was probably mainly drunkenness. And a couple of cuts on his forehead. My God, was my husband *furious*!'

'I can imagine.'

I moved in the following Tuesday and spent that week getting settled. It was like stepping ashore after months on a sickening sea. My large bed-sit had a low ceiling that was supported by two heavy beams of scarred oak. I later learned that in its youth the room was a kitchen. Hadn't I noticed the holes in the beams, where meat hooks once had lodged?

My two windows looked out to the basement steps and the railing-screened street above. In those first days I spent many hours in my deep leather armchair by the hissing old gas fire, ostensibly reading but finding my eyes irresistibly magnetized by the legs of passers-by. Old legs, young legs. Fat legs, slim legs. My vantage prevented me from seeing higher than hips unless I crouched by the lowermost panes of the window, and this my sense of proportion absolutely forbade.

Two particularly fine legs occupied my mind more than all the others put together. Having deduced from the frequency with which they went in and out of Number Ten's front door, immediately above my kitchenette, that they must belong to Helen Wishfort, I found my head buzzing like a beehive with theories as to the rest of her.

If she was in her second year at the Art College, shouldn't she be a perfect age for a presentable young man like myself?

Whose prospects were not unreasonable?

Had she, as I hoped, done herself an injustice in that cryptic self-portrait in the dining room?

Or would her face in the flesh disappoint me?

One day, while I was browsing through Dr Tostow's latest research paper (re the effects of certain psychotropic drugs on the dreaming patterns of normal postgraduate males) I heard a car draw up outside.

Helen's legs appeared in my windowscape, closely followed by a longer pair of Levi-clad legs topped by narrower hips.

This had a shattering effect on my sense of proportion.

I dropped Dr Tostow, rushed to the near window, and squinted frantically up at the Wishforts' front door.

But too late. The four legs had vanished inside.

Recalling Mrs Wishfort's story about the drunken boyfriend tumbling down the stairs and smashing the case of moths, I began to nurture a vigorous disapproval of the person in question.

Was he a pervert? Who made his girlfriend paint degrading self-portraits?

One of those despicable drop-out leeches that lived off Social Security and spent all their time taking drugs and debauching the morals of young and impressionable women?

And what kind of pitiful derelict must he be, at the least, to get so addled with drink as to fall down the stairs and pass out?

Such was the righteous rhetoric that haunted me as I:

Rearranged my furniture, placing the bed between the door and the left-hand window, and the desk against the wall opposite the windows – to avoid distractions while I was working;

Fed my books into the handsome walnut bookcases;

Heated my baked beans and poached my eggs on the small gas cooker in the kitchen;

Researched and wrote my first tutorial essay for Dr Tostow.

It was quite a good essay too, but the tutorial did not go entirely smoothly. My topic was *The International Political*

Implications of Interpersonal Speaking Distance as a Vital Subliminal Cue, and though Dr Tostow made some pertinent comments, he soon siphoned the discussion into a rather strained comparison of Scottish, English and American interpersonal speaking distances, asking Deirdre:

'Suppose you and your brother, being siblings and Scottish, are standing talking together at a cocktail party, moderately populated, where you know few of the other guests. What would you estimate to be your average eyeball-eyeball distance?'

'Eyeball-eyeball distance, my eye,' an indignant Deirdre said to me an hour later, as we sipped our chicoried coffees in the sprawling L-shaped cafeteria underneath the John Locke Tower.

'How do you mean?'

'Haven't you noticed how he's always dragging my brother into everything?'

'No.'

'Well I have.'

'His point, surely, was that American siblings in the same situation would display a significantly shorter eyeball-eyeball distance.'

'So what? Anyone in first year could tell him that. I think he's a voyeur. Kinky. Gives me the creeps. Did you know he worked for three years on the Whitman and Nixon Project – the people that wrote *The Varieties of Orgasmic Experience*?'

'No.'

'I had a flick through it in the library on Monday.' Deirdre smiled economically at Dr Tostow as he appeared through the swing-doors in the distance and made for the snack counter. 'And it's quite revolting.'

'Oh? Wasn't it said to be a major breakthrough?'

'They may have produced valuable clinical findings, but there's something very sordid about the way it's written. Stinks of bad motives.'

'For example?'

'I'd rather not go into detail,' said Deirdre primly. 'Why don't you read it yourself?'

THREE

Orgasmic experience was in demand.

The University Library stacks copy was out, and the reading-room copy was held for third-year medics *only*. In the central public library I learned, too late to withdraw my request, that *The Varieties of Orgasmic Experience* and *The Paucity of White Anglo-Saxon Protestant Orgasmic Experience*, both by Whitman & Nixon, were strictly Reserve Stock, held in The Annexe, and dispensed to serious adults *only* by an elderly lady with a glare like an outraged Pekinese.

Postponing *Paucity* until I had mastered *Varieties*, I slunk home through the yellow fog and grinding traffic of late afternoon, with my collar high and my briefcase fat with vicarious turgidity in the name of science.

What would those fresh-faced St David's girls think, prattling three-abreast down the High Street in their trim blue uniforms and licking their January ice-cream cones? If a spoiling angel whispered to them:

'Look. There. The young man in the grey flannels and brown coat. His bag is full of excited breasts, secreting penises and the clitoris in retraction. What do you think of that?'

A week of my honeymoon with Peace-to-work had elapsed, but I hadn't yet used my bath nights. This was partly because of the Strathbogle Baths (so close to Number Ten that I would walk there, on a dry day, in my bedroom slippers), where I could have a hot shower and wash my hair before my swim. But I was also shy. What if I should find the Wishforts' top bathroom occupied?

Loiter on the landing?

Or creep the three flights back to my basement and try again later?

But suppose . . .

That night, however, I stopped supposing. I went over to the pool just after seven, but it was closed for a school swimming gala. I got myself a take-away Chinese meal from the Pong On restaurant in Buttbridge Place, the local shopping centre, and as I forked my soggy chow mien and stabbed at the little brown golf balls from the sweet-and-sour pork container, I browsed jerkily through *Dumbo*, the unofficial student magazine. It was a crude but colourful effort, with obvious debts to *Private Eye*, *International Times*, *Oz*, and other contemporary purveyors of scandal and scurrility, most of them now defunct.

The Editor of *Dumbo* was Tom Redhead, a fat loose-mouthed American with fuzzy ginger hair. He was a post-graduate sociologist, aggressively and loudly left-wing, who had also managed to get himself elected as Deenburgh University's first student Rector – all previous rectors having been pensioned-off journalists, media personalities, actors, and the like.

Though he wasn't my cup of tea, it was undeniable that Rector Redhead spoke for a growing proportion of the student population when, each week, his leading articles raged purply against Vietnam, the illegality of pot-smoking, the absurdity of Deenburgh's antiquated exam system, and the fact that the Senate had forbidden him, the Rector, any access to the University's student files.

FLY AWAY DRAKE!

That was the headline this week, the reference being to Sir Gabriel Drake, the Vice-Chancellor. There was also a vitriolic attack on Dr Tostow for a piece he had published the previous week in *Scholar*, the official student paper. Dr Tostow made no secret of being a Vietnam hawk, and his article was a closely argued and thickly documented salvo in defence of Henry Kissinger.

It was greeted with howls of fury in the John Locke cafeteria, and several of my classmates got quite angry with me for refusing to refuse to be taught by such a self-confessed fascist and mass-murderer. I found that sort of thing intensely embarrassing. I *felt* the American presence in Vietnam was utterly wrong, yet I had never studied the issues in any depth. Consequently, I didn't feel entitled to take part in the debate. *Next year*, I told myself, *when Finals are under the bridge and I'm established in Cambridge: then I'll really think through the arguments.*

I left the last ounce of fried rice and went to the kitchen to make coffee. While the kettle boiled I turned on my pocket wireless and heard Radio Firth's Simon Darling interviewing Deenburgh's man of the moment, Tom Redhead.

'Right on,' Redhead was saying. 'Drake and the Senate have been told. But I will take this opportunity of warning them again. If there ain't some drastic reform, before June of this year, in the assessment methods employed by this university, we can all look forward to some *real bad trouble*.'

Nauseated by the relish with which he rolled those words round his tongue, like a mouthful of tinned potatoes, I turned him off and sat down to scan as many varieties of orgasmic experience as would not outlast a cup of coffee.

Three hours later I knew all about:

The incidence of varicosity in vaginas traumatized by childbirth;

The regrettable incapacity of the female experimental subjects to 'achieve' orgasm via fantasy alone, hence the need to provide a suitable stimulus to the imagination in the form of *suggestive material* (my italics, since the authors did not specify the said material – *Lady Chatterley*, I wondered, or *Biggles Meets Bunty Backwards*?);

The fascinating finding that no two women will attempt to 'achieve' orgasmic discharge of their automanipulatively induced sex tension increments by precisely the same automanipulative means, though the clitoris is undeniably a critical factor;

The . . . need I go on?

It was difficult to envisage Dr Tostow's part in the garnering of such wisdom, but there was his name in the Acknowledgements. Wondering if I could ever dare quiz him about it, I realized, prompted by the sickly scent of my sedentary perspiration, that I was badly in need of a bath.

It was Wednesday, and after eleven o'clock, so I collected my washbag, bathtowel and dressing gown, and ventured aloft. I had heard Mr Wishfort fetch the dog from the back garden half an hour earlier, which suggested, I hoped, that he and Mrs Wishfort might now have retired to bed.

This seemed to be the case.

Only the hall light was on, its pale nightbeams rising to the cupola eighty feet above, and I could hear Panda's snouty snoring issuing from his bed on the morning-room sofa.

On the first floor I padded past the guest room, the Wishfort Seniors' bedroom and the sitting room. Halfway up the next flight I heard strains of muted music. The local rawness of a Radio Firth jingle, from Rosie's room, and from Helen's room, facing me at the top of the stairs, an Indian restaurant atmosphere of trickling sitars.

And a sweet yellow fragrance of sandalwood.

And still I hadn't inspected Helen in the flesh above the hips.

Three steps from her door I fantasized barging in and saying: 'Terribly sorry. Thought this was the bathroom.'

When suddenly almost the opposite happened.

Helen's door opened, and a tall lithe young man stepped out. He had long fair hair, a beard and moustache, and looked surprisingly like the Dürer self-portrait of 1498 – though his hair was less rippled, his nose straighter, and there was a dynamic insolence in his eyes, almost feline in its sharpness.

He was also stark naked.

'Oh,' I apologized. 'You must be Helen's boyf . . .'

'Sssh,' he nodded, grinning, and pressing the silence finger to his lips. 'Won't be a tick.'

He went into the bathroom and relieved himself without closing the door.

I turned my back on him and sat on the top step. What was I thinking? Nothing. But my emotions had just been earthquaked.

'There,' the earthquake whispered cheerily to my shoulders,

as he returned to Helen's bedroom. 'All yours.'

I didn't enjoy my bath, and it took me a long time to get to sleep afterwards. It was damp and misty outside, I could tell by the candyfloss halos round the streetlamps, but it was also mild for the time of year. This, added to the steam in my pores, stirred up by my seismic feelings, made for many a sheetdrenching toss and rumpling turn. And at the end of each toss, and facing every turn:

The lust-frenzied image of Helen Wishfort entwined with the insolent Dürer type.

If you can't sympathize with the hot pickle into which I worked myself, you are fortunate: never having been a lonely introverted bachelor in your early twenties.

By four o'clock, soothed by a mug of milky cocoa and ten pages of *The Interpretation of Dreams*, I had cooled into shallow slumber, when:

Click.

I surfaced like a jumping salmon, with my heart two jumps ahead of me.

That click was the opening of my outside door.

Someone is in my kitchen.

For thirty seconds I lay rigid, sweating horribly with startlement as the intruder moved amid my groceries and milk bottles. What should I do?

Leap and snib my bedroom door?

But that would reveal I was on to him.

Phone the police? I could do this without moving, for the receiver was on my bedside table.

But what if he heard the bell ping? Might he not shoot me through the window?

Then . . .

My attitude swung from fear to incredulity. The kitchen marauder had stepped out into the basement, flashing a powerful torch like a stroboscope through the gaps in my curtains, and whistling softly:

We all live in a Yellow Submarine . . .

I sat up, pulled back the curtain that flanked the left side of my bed, and peered through the lace-screened window. On the basement steps I saw the donkey-jacketed back and long wavy hair of Helen's Dürer boy.

But what on earth was he doing?

Half-way up the steps was a small window which seemed to look out from some troglodyte residence entirely underneath the street. It belonged to an extra cellar that the Wishforts had considered converting into an extra bedroom. In the end, because of the damp risk, they had it walled up, so that my gas cooker now sat where the old cellar door used to be. The cellar window had been sealed open, about five inches top and bottom, and it was to the lower of these apertures that my unwelcome visitor addressed his whistling attention.

He had a heavy-duty electric cable running out from the kitchen and was feeding it into the derelict cellar as though paying out an anchor chain at sea.

I have seldom been more angry.

With a tremendous surge of assault-reprieved adrenalin, I seized my window by its ornate handles, heaved it open, and snapped:

'What on earth do you think you're doing?'

The cellar-feeder pivoted on his squatting feet, faced me, and whispered:

'Wondered if I might wake you. Sorry about that.'

'Do you know who I am?'

'Yes,' he said affably. 'You must be Nutkins.'

'*What*?'

'*Ssssh*,' he urged, exercising his silence finger once more, and beaming his torch in my bleary eyes. 'Aren't you Nutkins? That's what Helen said.'

'My name,' said its owner's quavering voice, 'is *Peter*.'

'Hi there, Pete.'

'And as from last week I live here.'

'I know.'

'Which means that this is *my* basement, for which *I* pay

rent. Especially in the small hours of the morning. So just what . . .'

'Yeah, yeah,' he said in a tone whose unconcern and impatience I found highly insulting. 'Won't happen again, Pete. Two minutes, and I'll be off. Okay?'

'What are you doing?'

'Tell you next week.' His smile stated plainly that my only way of hastening his departure was to leave him to his mysterious devices.

I closed the window on my blackest scowl and flopped back on my restless bed. For three minutes (I timed him on my luminous watch) my antagonist pottered and scraped and clunked about his business. Then he quietly closed the outside door, ran lightly up the steps to the street, and a minute later I heard the departure of a sports car.

I didn't get to sleep again until after the milkman and his horse had whistled and clinked and clopped their leisurely way round the square.

FOUR

The following Sunday morning, while the local church bells (in their apparent hundreds) were pealing their joyful injunctions, my telephone buzzed. This meant either an incoming call from my mother or that someone wanted to speak to me from the Wishfort hall, where the master telephone reposed on a carved oak bedding chest.

'Hello?'

'Pea Tar?'

'Yes, Rosie?'

'Dear Dree and Allah Stair's coming for lunch, Pea Tar. And Mummee says would you like to join us?'

'Thank you very much, Rosie. I'd love to,' I accepted instantly, banking on richer fare from Mrs Wishfort than the marmite sandwich I'd had in mind. 'What time?'

'Come up for sherree in the draw ring room at quarter to.'

'Quarter to *one*?'

'Yee-*ees,*' she confirmed in a contemptuous drawl.

'For what we are about to receive,' Mr Wishfort prayed grimly, 'may the Lord make us truly thankful. Amen.'

'Amen,' echoed unconvincingly round the table, and we all took up our soup spoons.

'That was an admirable try you scored yesterday, Cameron-Bell,' said Mr Wishfort to his intending son-in-law, seated immediately to his right.

'Thank you, sir,' said Alastair. 'A good team effort, I thought. Fine run by Miller, and Turnbull could probably have taken it over himself.'

'Ay. But the magic is in being at the right place at the right time. Success so often depends on that final pass.'

Alastair concealed his pleasure by breaking open his roll, with two vast banana-bunch hands, and scowling ferociously at his lentil soup. He was what the rugby commentators call a boiler house man: six feet four inches tall, and between fifteen and sixteen stone in weight. He couldn't have been more than two years older than me, but he looked thirty-five. His nose had been badly broken at some time, and his fleshy forehead was a permanent map of deep furrows. Asymmetrical ears stuck out from his close-cropped, receding sandy hair in a fashion that might have been comical on a skinnier person.

What could Deirdre see in him?

Financial and domestic security?

Satisfying love-making, prolonged and tempestuously brutal?

A virile father of precisely three jug-eared close-cropped baby Alastairs?

Certainly no breadth of culture or sharpness of wit.

There were eight of us for lunch that day.

I was on Alastair's right, opposite Deirdre, and next to me was an elderly neighbour called Mr Hamilton, a white-haired, weak-eyed bachelor who admired Mrs Wishfort (with whom he vaguely planned to co-author the definitive book on *The Building of New Deenburgh*) and had got himself adopted as one of the family, at least where Christmas dinners, parties and other special occasions were concerned. At the sideboard end, Mrs Wishfort sat between Mr Hamilton and Rosie. Next to Rosie, underneath her own self-portrait, was Helen.

And very attractive I found her.

Her fair complexion, mischievous blue eyes and long, wild blonde hair made you imagine Mrs Wishfort thirty years earlier. And the breasts beneath her Arran sweater were full and firm, prominent and desirable – not at all the droopy marrows of the portrait.

My principal memory of the lunch is my struggle not to be seen comparing the soup-supping Helen-in-clothes with the naked representation on the wall. So arduous was this task that I hardly spoke to anyone till after the second course, and I almost forgot to wonder why the odious Dürer character was absent. Was he still too blackly in Mr Wishfort's bad books to be invited to a family lunch?

Nor was the Wishfort brother present, and as Mr Wishfort carved the lamb he asked:

'Where, pray, is Mallecho?'

'He couldn't make it, dear,' said Mrs Wishfort, heaping sprouts, creamed carrots and roast potatoes on to meated plates.

'Did he not *say* he was coming?'

'Yes, Daddy,' said Helen. 'But he's got some recording to do. And he's going to *A Mechanical Banana* this afternoon, with Beano and Harriet. So he can't make lunch.'

'Damn thing.' Mr Wishfort frowned as his carving knife flashed. Now I knew he was a consultant neurosurgeon, I found a strange fascination in the easy dexterity with which he was slicing the meat.

'What, Douglas?' asked Mrs Wishfort.

'That damn film. It's only been here two days, and already we've got hooligans prancing about in top hats and boiler-suits, and attacking folk with hockey sticks. I saw a gang of them in King Street just yesterday, as I was driving down to Alastair's game. Six or seven . . .'

'Come *on*, Daddy,' said Helen impatiently.

'Don't you "come *on*" me, young lady.'

'But that wasn't hooligans, Daddy. That was actors doing a publicity stunt. To get people to see the film.'

Mr Wishfort's opinions on cultural matters were like handcuffs to which only Death possessed the key.

'It comes to the same thing,' he insisted. 'And next week it *will* be hooligans. What do you think, Squirrell?'

'Sorry?'

'You're a psychologist: do you think we should have young idiots allowed to watch these things – non-stop sex and violence for two hours – and then coming out and mugging old ladies on their way home?'

I was afraid I hadn't yet seen that particular film.

'And he's also afraid, Daddy,' said Deirdre, 'though he's too polite to say so, that your formulation of the problem, as usual, entirely begs the question.'

'And just what is that supposed to mean?'

The next fifteen minutes were heated by a family brouhaha hinged squeakily on cinematic violence and censorship, in the course of which:

Deirdre attacked her father for his habitual intolerance and sloppy thinking;

Mr Wishfort criticized Deidre and, for that matter, young people generally, for their impertinence and lack of respect for the experience-bejewelled opinions of their elders and betters;

Helen remarked that it was not quantity but *quality* of experience that should be respected;

Deirdre responded in knowing terms, though without looking her sister in the eye, that no one could seriously expect to get anywhere by merely parroting her brother's opinions;

Mr Hamilton ventured the view that they should all be shot, Alastair mumbled that he wasn't sure he didn't agree, and Mrs Wishfort said that if anyone should be shot it was Timothy Freeman, author of the mediocre novel from which the *Mechanical Banana* film departed;

Helen wished that Mallecho were present, so that he could explain to them all what fools they were making of themselves;

Deirdre thought it a pity that some people had to depend on their brothers to do their thinking for them, Helen made a face and stuck her tongue out at Deirdre, and Mrs Wishfort asked Helen not to do that, please, darling, especially in front of guests;

Alastair and I polished off large second helpings of roast lamb and vegetables, the frosty day outside turning sunny, and the first afterlunchers drifted past the windows on their dogwalking way to the park;

Rosie complained that it wasn't fair and why couldn't she

see the film, to which Mrs Wishfort replied that it was perfectly fair and she could see the film, having only to wait the five years till her eighteenth birthday;

Deirdre suspected that the film would be televised long before then, and Mr Wishfort stole the show with a miraculously athletic leap sideways on to his favourite hobbyhorse: the mystery enshrouding the origins of Mallecho's affluence.

He was a Scottish Scot, Douglas Wishfort – the only member of his family whose voice would advertise his nationality across the globe. It was a gentle Highland voice, but with a stony edge that sparked images of curlews crying over windswept grousemoors, solitary fishing dinghies seatrouting on wet afternoons, and perhaps a silver hipflask of neat malt whisky tucked deep in a thick tweed pocket.

'What beats me,' he told us, 'is where he got the money to buy that house. I find that very worrying.'

'You know perfectly well, dear,' said Mrs Wishfort, frowning. 'He got his inheritance when his grandfather died, and he's over twenty-one, so there's nothing anyone can do about it. He's his own master and he knows what he's doing.'

'That's all very fine, but I happen to know he bought the house before he had got that damned inheritance.'

'Jealousy will get you nowhere,' said Helen sweetly.

'Don't you be so damn cheeky, young lady.'

'How do you *know*,' asked Deirdre, 'that he bought the house first?'

'He was gracious enough, for once, to tell me.'

'Then he was probably pulling your leg.'

Mr Wishfort's dark eyes fumed behind his thin gold-rimmed spectacles. His appearance was clearly the old block from which Deirdre and Rosie had been chipped: brown hair, physically well knit, though without the rangy grace that Helen inherited from Mrs Wishfort.

'He *wasn't* pulling my leg,' he insisted. 'He even showed me the papers. And what's worse is that the sale went through *before his grandfather died*. So how did he know what he was getting? Eh? *Fifteen thousand pounds* that house cost. I find that . . .'

'Very good value too,' Mrs Wishfort interrupted decisively. 'Coffee, everybody? Or would anyone like more trifle?'

Only Helen refused coffee, saying:

'No thanks. I think I'll take Panda for a walk at Querns. If', she moued defiantly at Deirdre, 'I can have Mummy's car.'

'And me, and me,' clamoured Rosie.

'Help yourself,' Deirdre said snootily. 'We've got Alastair's father's.'

'Yes, dear,' said Mrs Wishfort to Helen. 'You can have the car, but please take Rosie with you.'

'Take Squirrell too, why don't you?' Mr Wishfort suggested out of the blue. 'Bit of clean country air on those pasty cheeks: do him the world of good.'

'That's a nice idea, Douglas,' said Mrs Wishfort. 'What about it, Peter?'

'Aaahm, yes,' I said. 'I had been thinking of going up to the art gallery in the botanical gardens, but . . .' I suddenly felt as though the concerted glare of the entire family was daring me to refuse this kind invitation, so I said:

'Yes, I'd love to.'

FIVE

Querns Mill was the Wishforts' country retreat. It was situated in the county of East Logan, on the north bank of the River Teen, about forty minutes' drive from Deenburgh. A long, low, one-storey building, it had been reconstructed out of the two original mill cottages and nestled unexpectedly in several acres of lush riverside lawns, orchids and fruit trees. When Mr Wishfort was still an impecunious junior doctor, Querns had been Mrs Wishfort's wedding present from her father, Grandfather Cunningham, some of whose distillery wealth seemed now to have passed to Mallecho.

'We lived there until Witch was eight,' Helen explained, as we drove through the dormitory town of Cockleburgh. 'Then he and Deirdre had to come into town for school, so we bought Number Ten.'

Sitting behind her in the Morris, with the dog slavering freely and smelling beside me (Rosie had insisted on the front passenger seat), I couldn't help smiling at the way her breezy diction suggested the singlehandedness with which she, Helen, had sought, selected and purchased Number Ten.

'What are you grinning at?' she inquired sharply, catching me in the driver's mirror.

'Was I grinning?'

'Yes.'

'Sorry. Only at myself.'

'Uh huh?'

'Revising my stereotypes.'

'Meaning?'

'My image of consultant surgeons. Shattered by your father.'

'What's wrong with Daddy?'

'Nothing. But I had thought of surgeons as being like airline pilots. Never touching alcohol except for a glass of port at Christmas,' I said, picturing the several generous schooners of sherry and large glasses of red Carafino that Mr Wishfort had knocked back at lunchtime.

'Yes,' said Helen. 'Daddy does like his dram. You should have seen him at New Year, Peter. But it doesn't affect his work at all. He's very puritanical that way.'

'I can imagine.'

'He's famous too, in his field. Goes on lecture tours all over the world.'

'Really?'

'Uh huh. Though you might not think it to hear him on film censorship.'

Over Panda's panting head I saw Cockleburgh race course fall behind on our left: a thin strip of hurdled green between the main road and the cold grey sea.

'. . . our very own, home-grown, electric-folk folk, folks,' piped Simon Darling, the Radio Firth disc jockey whose Sunday show was jingling quietly on the car radio, 'The *Belhaven TwangGang*.'

'That's Cindee, that's Cindee,' chimed Rosie, turning up the volume.

The TwangGang's electrified adaptation of the traditional *John Barleycorn* commenced, and our conversation paused to express respect for the cool crystal clarity of Cindy Bell's beautiful voice.

Everything about her was beautiful, I thought, and she was reigning Queen of the Squirrell Commonwealth of Erotical Romantical Phantasmagoria. Anita Tostow had a sultry, knowing sexuality that made you yearn for her to touch you, lead you on, unzip your fly and take the initiative. Helen Wishfort, by contrast, possessed a powerful but anatomically less specific sensuality, all long legs and lissomness, of the kind that girls seldom retain past the age of twenty. She made you ache to reach out and touch her. Anywhere: shoulder, breast, knee, the wild yellow curls that cascaded over the back of the driver's seat . . . it was as though every inch of her body apprehended your ache and delighted in taunting your civilized inability to give it relief.

But with Cindy it was spiritual.

I mean that my involvement with her, and the altar on which we united in my mind, were affairs of such soaring devotional purity that the earthier questions of excited breasts, secreting penises and the clitoris in retraction never arose. She was Guinevere, I was a fusion of Lancelot and Galahad, and the only unfortunate obstacle in the path of our Eternal Bliss Together was . . .

'Deirdre tells me you fancy Cindy,' Helen remarked casually, when *John Barleycorn* was over.

'Certainly not,' I protested, shrinking from her mirrored eye. 'Whatever gave her that idea?'

'Deirdre says you said you thought Cindy was beautiful.'

'Deirdre has torn what I said rather violently out of context. Which was purely aesthetic. We were discussing the definition of terms. In any case,' I said sternly, recalling the parallel case of *Nutkins*, which seemed to have swept through the Wishfort family like a flu virus, 'I've only ever met the lady for five minutes at a party. How could . . .'

'Boys,' said Helen firmly, slipping into an infuriating Womanly Omniscience, 'never tell girls they think other girls are beautiful, unless, deep down, they really want those girls to tell those other girls they think those other girls are beautiful.'

'Is that a fact?'

'You're a psychologist, Peter. You should know.'

The ignorant psychologist was annoyed, so he kept quiet. Helen went on:

'It's a pity about Othello, though. He's a cunt.'

My shock was echoed by Rosie, who moralistically cried:

'Ooooh. I'm telling Mummee, I'm telling Mummee.'

'You shut your face, Rosie Wishfort,' her sister commanded calmly. 'Or you can get out and walk. And don't be a cry-baby. Do you like Othello?'

Rosie's chastened sniff said No.

'There you are. He's a cunt. There's no better word for

him, so why not use it?'

Albert Ormrod (popularly Othello, on account of his chalk-white hair and skin) was, I had to agree, an objectively resistible person. A jumped-up entrepreneur from what, in the old days, one might have called the Deenburgh lower classes. He was thin, wiry and sharp, with the head of an acquisitive ferret. His facial skin was so pale as to seem either blue or green, depending on the light, and the dark bags of stimulated sleeplessness under his eyes appeared to contain a pair of captive earwigs, such that when he pulled a smile the earwigs would awaken, wriggle and struggle frantically to escape. Othello was guide, philosopher, friend, manager and sole creator of the Belhaven TwangGang: his human speculation on the booming folk-rock market.

He was also Cindy Bell's boyfriend.

'And then there's Alastair,' Helen continued.

'What about him?'

'If you fancy Cindy . . .'

I tutted.

'Do you also fancy being Bungalow Cameron-Bell's brother-in-law?'

I was flabbergasted.

Helen flashed a curious glance over her shoulder. 'Cindy's Alastair's sister. Didn't you know?'

'I had no idea.'

'Her full name is Lucinda, Alison, Hester Cameron-Bell. Not much of a stage name, is it?'

'I suppose not.'

'So Othello got her to drop the Cameron. She was always just Cindy at school.'

'Oh.' This was a staggering blow, and I debated my misfortune in silence. Could I really achieve Eternal Bliss Together with the sister of a jug-eared boilerhouse giant who wasn't sure he didn't agree that they should all be shot?

We were out in the country now, cruising up a long straight slope with woodland walling us in on either side. At the summit, on our left, I saw the neon yellows of a transport haven signed Jake's Cafe Petrol. Computing that we must be nearing our destination, I said:

'But Cindy doesn't . . .'

'Hellen, please can we stop at Jake's for a *look* OUT,' screamed Rosie.

'*Christ*,' screamed Helen, twisting the wheel just in time to avoid a fatal collision with an oncoming Citroën overtaking a tractor. 'My *God*, why can't they do something about this bloody road?'

'He certainly had no business overtaking there,' I said loyally.

'There's people killed on that corner every damn year,' she muttered. 'Usually tourists. They think because the slope's straight that it'll continue straight over the other side, and they don't see the Bend sign because they're looking at Jake's Cafe. And then you get lorries coming out on the corner. It's a bloody menace.'

'Hellen?'

'What?' snapped the elder sister, though the diversion helped to calm her.

'Please can we visit Mrs Em?'

'Only if they've fixed the bridge. I'm not driving round.'

'Bye now, children,' beamed Mrs Em-for-Mulligan. 'Take care.'

'Bye-bye, Mrs Em,' Rosie waved.

'You won't lose the eggs now, will you?'

'No, Mrs Em,' said Helen, her farewell smile triumphing over the irritation of a grown-up young lady being patronized like an infant.

'She's very nice, isn't she, Pea Tar?' Rosie asked, as we strolled on toward the castle. 'Mrs Em?'

'She seems very kind.'

'She used to tell us the most exciting stories. Much more exciting then anybody else's stories. Didn't she, Hellen?'

'Why don't you run on and see Panda isn't chasing Mr Em's pigs?'

'Oh Kay.' Rosie flopped ahead in her knee-length Wellingtons, the tips of her rubber-banded brown hair bouncing on her puppyfat shoulders. She would be like Deirdre in appearance, and she was at the anatomical-escalation stage when girls spend hours imagining that one of their breasts is outstripping the other.

Helen and I walked after her in silence, seeming to drink in the cool freshness of the quiet country afternoon in mature tranquillity, but actually not knowing what to say to each other.

Mr and Mrs Em were like effervescent leprechauns, with long yellow noses, darting green eyes, and maniacal Irish cackles. He was caretaker of Querns Castle, the rambling sandstone ruin now on our right. She had been Mrs Wishfort's help when Querns Mill was the young family's home, and she still did cleaning and cooking for the children during the holidays. The Ems also ran a lustily clucking, grunting and kennelled-collie-yapping smallholding, which produced such items as the half-dozen freshly laid eggs presently distorting the bosom of Helen's white quilted anorak.

Querns Castle was billed at crossroads for miles around as an Ancient Monument, and still looked imposing from the far side of the river, its north wall rising to a forbidding number of dark-red slit-windowed storeys, but once you passed the turnstiled booth where, on a summer's day, you yielded up your three shillings to Mr Em, you would soon wonder why you had bothered.

Nothing remained of the roof, little of the interior walls, and the main surviving attraction was a network of slimy pit dungeons that the public were warned not to enter for reasons of safety. Where the old cobbled courtyards and flagstoned halls had been, a carpet of thick green turf now rolled, cropped short by Mr Em's sheep. Today it was crusty with unthawed frost, which crunched beneath our feet like spilt sugar crystals on a kitchen floor.

As we looked between the black bars of a heavy iron gate, glimpsing, through the trees across the river, the green top of the car and the red-tiled roof of the cottage, Helen said:

'Witch and Beano used to come up here early in the

morning, to shoot pigeons with Witch's air rifle.'

'Why early morning, especially?'

'They're heavy then, and slow. From what they've been eating.'

'Isn't it a bit pointless and cruel to shoot them in that state?' I asked coldly. (Coming over the narrow wooden footbridge, Rosie had pointed out a cluster of holes in one of the uprights and said: 'There's where Mall Echo and Bee No used to practise with Mall Echo's air rye full', and my interest in these fabulous persons was growing increasingly finite.)

'You can't shoot pigeons on the wing with an *air* gun,' Helen said scathingly, leading me out of the castle grounds. 'And anyway they don't shoot pigeons *now.* That was when they were fourteen. Witch hasn't killed anything for years. He doesn't believe in it.'

'Why do you call him Witch?'

'All his friends call him Witch.'

'But you're his sister. I notice Deirdre and Rosie don't call him Witch.'

'I'm also his friend.'

I couldn't answer this, so I didn't.

Helen looked up the road to where Rosie and Panda were waiting in the mouth of a lane that spring would make leafy. Leaning close to me, she asked with affected sophistication:

'Like to know a secret?'

'I have a professional interest in all secrets.'

'Witch has a hundred thousand pounds worth of acid stashed in that castle.'

'LSD?'

'Uh huh.'

'Why tell me?'

'Witch says he doesn't care who knows, because no one will ever find it, and he'd like to see them try.'

This might have been true, but a deeper reason why she told me was that she hadn't got over being patted on the head by kindly old Mrs Em. She wanted respect for what she wanted me to think she was: High Priestess in an Order of

Mysteries Unknown to Squirrell.

With all due respect, I said:

'But it's hardly a secret, is it? If he doesn't care who knows.'

'He wouldn't want Deirdre to know, of course. Or the old folks. You won't tell Mummy, will you?'

'Keeping a secret, Helen, is the one thing at which I excel.'

'My, my,' she mocked. 'A modest psychologist.'

'I suppose that's where he got the money for his house?'

'What do you mean?' She looked at me suspiciously.

'Mallecho. From his drug-dealing. Wasn't your father saying . . .'

'Better ask him yourself,' she said curtly.

'We haven't been introduced.'

'Pan Da wasn't chasing Mr Em's pigs,' Rosie reported when we turned left into the lane. 'But he has been row ling. Look.'

'Filthy animal,' said Helen, surveying with distaste the brown ordure encrustments on the black and white dapples of Panda's coat. 'Get *down*,' she cursed, dancing sideways as the happy Dalmatian leapt up to punch her chest and kiss her chin.

Panda bounded on ahead, and we followed at a leisurely pace.

Through an archway of naked chestnut boughs at the end of the lane we could see, against the pale southern sky, the squat dark crown of Pratnair Law: a stony wart with a thin skin of spiky grass and patchy gorse, which, though only a few hundred feet high, is the only hill for miles around – an uncultivated sanctuary for rabbits and jackdaws in a county otherwise flat, fertile and intensively farmed.

Legend has it that Saint Maurice's unmarried mother, while carrying the saintly foetus, many and many a year ago, was hurled from the crags at the east end (long since quarried away) by her outraged father, only to be caught by the Hand of Heaven in an air current and spirited the several miles to Fairport Bay, where she touched down in ten feet of sea-water, with a gentle splash and no harm done.

'Really?' I said politely, when Rosie finished telling me

the story.

'We won't climb the Law today,' said Helen.

'Aw, *Hellen*.'

'No, Rosie. It's nearly dark. We'll walk along the road past the quarry, then back through Gables Wood.'

This caused Rosie to sulk for several minutes, which somehow braked the flow of conversation between Helen and myself. After considering a dozen puerile gambits, I tried:

'Doesn't your boyfriend come to family lunches and things?'

Helen's cheeks went the colour of tinned salmon, and Rosie gloated:

'Hellen hasn't got a boy friend, Hellen hasn't got a boy friend. Not since Grant Mac Millan got off with Jenny Fur Strachan at the Art College Freshers' *Ball*. Hellen hasn't got . . .'

'You shut your face, you nosey little bitch,' Helen snarled, seemingly at me, while jabbing a smack at Rosie's head.

Rosie dodged.

I tried to apologize:

'I'm terribly sorry if I . . . didn't . . . thought . . . but who's the person I met on the stairs? That looks like Dürer?'

'That's Mall Echo, that's Mall Echo,' crowed Rosie. 'Every body says he looks like Dew Ra.'

I gaped at Helen.

Her tinned salmon was chasing beetroot.

'When you met Witch on the landing the other night,' she informed the eastern seascape in a grudging monotone, 'he was posing for me. He's got a good body, you see, for a life-drawing subject.'

'I see.'

'I'll show you the painting sometime,' she offered carelessly.

'I'd be most interested.'

'And I suppose you'll say, Hellen Wish Fort,' Rosie accused, with all the narrow-eyed tenacity of Deirdre in a seminar dispute, 'that Mall Echo was posing for you at New Year? When he went into your bed room? At five Oh clock in the morning! I saw, I saw.'

'You sneaky little *cunt*,' Helen hissed.

Rosie gasped in horror.

I inspected the fingernails on my mittens.

'Witch got paralytic at Hogmanay,' Helen explained to me. 'And he pushed into my room after I'd gone to bed. Thinking it was the bathroom.'

I nodded understandingly.

But Rosie jeered:

'Then why didn't he *come out again*?' Evidently this was an issue on which she had been nursing strong feelings.

'*Bee coz*,' Helen mimicked, her eyes flashing sapphires of sisterly hatred, 'he passed out and fell asleep on my floor. Okay? Now you just shut your ugly little face, Rosie Wishfort. Or you'll be getting the bus back to town.'

SIX

Twenty-eight hours later:

'Peter?'

'Speaking.'

'Helen here.'

'Hello.'

'How are things?'

'Not bad, thanks,' I said guardedly, wondering what she wanted. Yesterday's Mallecho disclosures had shaken my Helen image to the roots. 'What can I do for you?'

'I want to ask you a favour.'

'Fire away.'

'I can't on the phone.'

'Is it your picture?'

'What?'

'You want to show me your portrait of Mallecho in the nude?'

'No. It's just . . . there are so many receivers in this house: you never know who might listen in. Are you busy, Peter? Couldn't I come down for a few minutes?'

'Well, I was just about to make some tea, as a matter of fact. So if . . .'

'A cup of coffee would be lovely,' she said enthusiastically. 'Milk and one sugar. I'll be down in five minutes.'

'Sorry I'm late,' she said, not sounding it. 'I got held up on the phone.'

'That's all right. I left the kettle till you arrived. Come in to my parlour. You have the privilege of being my first guest.

Or rather, my first internal guest.'

Helen's lavishly mascaraed eyes regarded me inquiringly.

'Your father,' I explained, 'comes down to his wine from time to time.' There were two large cupboards across the passage from my bedroom. One was full of trunks, suitcases and assorted junk, and the other had been racked up as Mr Wishfort's wine cellar.

When I returned from the kitchen, bearing two mugs of instant coffee and a packet of chocolate-covered digestive biscuits, Helen was sitting on my bed speaking into my phone.

'Must go now, Gordon,' she was saying. 'Someone's just come in. See you at Jerry's on Friday? Far out. Bye.'

'I'm supposed to keep a record of outgoing calls on that phone,' I said, when we had settled in the fat leather armchairs on either side of the fire. 'Biscuit?'

'Thanks.' She took two and ate them as a sandwich, with the chocolate coatings as the filling. 'I wouldn't bother,' she said airily, flicking a crumb from a magenta-sticked lower lip with a long, pointed, magenta-painted fingernail. She was really vamped up tonight, compared with the Wellingtoned country girl of yesterday. And I found the effect disturbing. Her dress, buttoned nunnishly tight at the neck, was plain black, flimsy, and flared from a St Trinian's waist just below her breasts to a breathtaking hem an inch beneath her buttocks. Leaving miles of tantalizing legs in maroon-coloured cobweb tights.

What could she possibly want from me?

'Why?' I asked.

'That phone gets used like a public toilet. A few calls by you won't hurt it much.'

Charming, I thought. *How well she plumbs my lonely depths.*

'Tell me about all these receivers.'

'There's one in the hall and one in the sitting room.'

I nodded.

'One in Mum's bedroom, one here: that's four.'

'Goodness.'

'And a fifth in Witch's bedroom. The old man got it for

his nineteenth-birthday present, 'cos he was fed up with Witch being on the phone in the sitting room all the time.'

'I can imagine.'

'So you see? If you've got anything *private* to say, you've got to watch out. People are always picking up receivers elsewhere in the house.'

'I'll bear that in mind.'

Helen uncrossed her legs and stood up to tour my furniture.

I smothered a moan as I caught a flashing triangular glimpse of her luminously white knickers. Her hair was fair, but her eyebrows dark. What colour her pubes? Suddenly it seemed important that I find out.

But not tonight.

'I like the way you've got the room,' she said. 'but why have you moved the bed beside the window? Françoise had it there.' She pointed to the opposite corner.

'I wanted my desk where I can't see up to the street. It's rather distracting: headless legs going by all the time.'

'You don't have to look.'

'One's gaze tends to wander. Especially from psychology offprints.'

'Do you like my legs?' she demanded, examining them in the mirror on the door of my wardrobe.

'They're . . . very fine legs,' I said faintly, like a punctured haggis.

'I saw you looking at my self-portrait during lunch yesterday.'

'I'm sorry . . .'

'Why should you be?'

'But I couldn't help wondering why you painted yourself as less attractive than you are.'

'That's very gallant of you, Peter.' She smiled challengingly, enjoying herself thoroughly.

'I mean it,' I said aggressively. 'Why did you?'

'You have to paint what you *see*. And that's how I saw myself at the time.'

'Are you painting Mallecho as less attractive than he is in reality?'

'What is reality?'

'Reality is normative. Don't you think?'

'I haven't the foggiest,' she said cheerfully. 'What does "normative" mean?'

I realized then how closely Helen's thinking must follow her brother's, so I rattled off a sop definition of "normative", and escaped to:

'What happened to Françoise? If you don't mind my asking.'

'Why should I mind?' She bent her head to the bookcases and scanned my titles.

I was still in my armchair. I wanted to get up and pace proprietorially around my room. But I couldn't think of an excuse for doing so.

'Deirdre said there was a fuss.'

'Don't you have any novels, Peter?'

'There are two by Ivan Tostow. On the bottom . . .'

'Who's he?'

'My . . .'

'Yes. There was quite a row. The old man came down one night for a bottle of whisky. Heard, you know, *noises*.'

'Noises?'

'Popped his head in – must have knocked, I suppose, though Witch swears he didn't – and found Witch and Françoise going at it hammer and tongs. God, was he livid?'

'Goodness.'

'So! Farewell, Françoise. She was nice, too. Quite pretty. In a bovine sort of way.'

'It seems a bit harsh, doesn't it? Sending her home.'

'Witch says it's 'cos the old man was jealous.'

I made my face suggest that surely consultant neuro-surgeons in their mid-fifties were incapable of sexual jealousy.

Helen replaced my paperback copy of Dr Tostow's *Erewhon Three*, and said:

'But it was really just an excuse. If you ask me. Mum had already decided we didn't need her any more. Fancy a smoke?'

'No thanks. I don't. I tried a cigar once, but it made me ill.'

'I mean *dope*, Peter. Would you like a *joint*? Or isn't

that your scene?'

'I'm afraid it isn't.'

'I didn't really think it would be,' she said contemptuously. 'Oh well. You won't mind if I have a roll-up?'

My alarm must have flickered, for she added:

'Just *tobacco*.'

'Please do.'

She flounced past me, trailing a wispy fragrance of incense and rosewater, flopped back into my guest armchair, and grinned at my attempt not to be caught catching another flash of those luminous knickers. Between our chairs, parallel to the hearthrug, was a long, low coffee-cum-magazine table. From it Helen took her tobacco tin. As she rolled a cigarette, freehand, she asked:

'Is that your family?'

I followed her nod to the framed photo hung above my record player.

'Yes,' I said. 'Me and my mother and sister. Taken about three years ago, before my sister went to Australia. She's married to an airline pilot.'

'Are your parents separated?'

'My father died when I was four. He had leukaemia.'

Helen said she was sorry and lit her cigarette.

I uttered some platitude about the passing of time, my eyes having fastened their apprehension on a green-streaked chocolate-coloured slab of a non-chocolate nature in Helen's smoking tin. It was the size of three fingers of Kitkat, and I had a fair idea what a whiff of it would mean to the twitching nostrils of an alert policeman. Paranoia was like dandruff in the Deenburgh student world, and my scalp itched too.

'Leukaemia isn't hereditary, is it?'

Warmed by her concern, I said:

'Not, at any rate, like baldness and bad teeth.'

'Have you got bad teeth, Peter?' she asked chattily, looking with interest at my hair.

This cooled me to a frosty:

'Few fillings, but who hasn't?' Not wishing to hear that she hadn't, or Mallecho hadn't, or somebody else more wonderful than me hadn't, I hurried on:

'Now what's this favour you want to ask me? My curiosity knows no bounds.' Although the species in me was copulating with her relentlessly, in all manner of exotic positions, the final-year psychologist in the control tower (as he then thought) could not forget the learned paper he had yet to complete for a seminar the next day. Topic? *Involuntary Pupil Dilation as a Gauge of Sexual Interest.*

Helen crossed her legs diplomatically.

'It's not really me that's asking the favour,' she told the tip of her cigarette. 'It's Witch.'

'Oh?'

'He says he's sorry he called you Nutkins and jumped into the bathroom in front of you the other night, and he'd like you to have dinner with him on Thursday.'

'He doesn't need to do that,' I said in bewilderment.

'But he'd like to.'

'Why doesn't he ask me himself?'

'He thought you might refuse.'

Very astute of him. Accepting dinner invitations from drug-dealing strangers, perfect or otherwise, was hardly an inborn Squirrell trait.

'Will you be there?' I inquired.

'Me? No. I . . .' Intuiting at twice the speed of my bad chessplayer's reasoning that her absence would dissuade me, she cornered me with:

'Yes. Why not? Witch owes me a meal anyway. That's settled then, is it? I'll tell him to expect us at seven, and we'll drive up in Mum's car.'

'Wait a minute, Helen. I think I should know a little more about my host before I accept.'

'Why?'

'I might get stuck for conversation.'

'Okay. Tell me what you know about him, then I'll fill you in.'

'Well, it's no secret, apparently, that he sells drugs . . .'

'Uh huh. But he's choosy about what he sells, and who he sells it to. No uppers or downers, and nothing hard. No H, no coke, nothing like that,' she said approvingly.

How enormously public-spirited of him.

'And your mother told me he and Beano used to fire rockets at Miss Moray.'

'Silly old bitch. Served her right.'

'But apart from that I've heard nothing but rumours.'

'Like what?'

'Like: he got a good degree in maths and physics?'

'Top of his year.'

'And a few days ago, in the John Locke cafeteria, I overheard from a first-year person that looks and smells like a scarecrow in a field of rotten cabbages, that The Witchdoctor, man, is a better guitarist than Eric Clapton. *Out of sight.*'

'That's an exaggeration,' the polymath genius's sister admitted realistically. 'But only slightly.'

'Then a couple of weeks ago I heard someone say he's queer.'

'Homosexual? *Witch*?'

'The word used was "poof".'

'Fucking hell,' said Helen. Then she filled me in.

Witch was *not* a poof, it seemed.

He was *extremely normal,* as many a St David's girl, over the past seven years, had been glad to find out. He hadn't always been a prodigy, and until he was fourteen had been in the bottom stream of his year. But then he realized that if you wanted to get ahead in This Life you had to beat The Buggers at their own game. So he zoomed up the ratings in mathematics, physics, chemistry, English, art and music – though wild horses (in conjunction with several masters at the Deenburgh Academy) had been unable to squeeze any of his attention into history, geography or languages.

When Witch and Beano were fifteen they formed a pop group called The Witchdoctor's Nosebone, which was an unabashed imitation of the Beatles and Rolling Stones, but surpassed most other schoolboy pop groups and soon was earning five pounds per Saturday night in the local youth-club dance halls. *Witchdoctor* was an in-character expansion of *Witch,* which was a junior-school corruption of the understandable *Wish.* Involvement in the Nosebone, and with the St David's girls, was presumably responsible for Witch's never quite topping his class at school – except in maths, at which he rapidly became unbeatable.

It was therefore understandable that poor old Mr Snell, the Academy's white-haired Head of Maths, should be heart-broken when Witch raised two cheerful fingers to the prospect of a scholarship to St Catharine's College, Cambridge: Mr Snell's revered alma mater and the withered breast on which his few fond memories sucked. Why the raised fingers? Because Oxbridge boys needed at least another year at school, and sometimes two. To take their *A*-Levels, Oxbridge Entrance, and *S*-Levels if necessary, which often delayed the donning of their undergraduate gowns until their twentieth years. Fuck that, Witch announced, going on to top grades in his Scottish *Highers* and a place at Deenburgh University at the age of seventeen.

During the next four years his powers matured, and, despite his cardinal rôle in a semi-pro rock band called HMS Witchcraft, he graduated in a blaze of glory the July before my transfer to Deenburgh from St Andrews. Having recently come into his legacy from Grandfather Cunningham, he decided it was then or never regarding travel (the most rewarding voyages being undertaken *in the mind*, you see), so off he went.

Europe for six months.

Winter in a hippy commune in the south of Spain, where the oranges were more plentiful than the black Labrador turds on Buttbridge pavements. North Africa next, and Helen had a postcard to say that Marrakesh was just like the John Locke cafeteria during Rag Week. From India came the news that some of the views were worth a look, but you got better curries in the Logan Restaurant in Logan Street, where all the dusky junior doctors from the Deenburgh Royal would troupe along for lunch on Fridays.

And finally America.

In New York City Witch quickly concluded that he and Woody Allen must belong to different species, and that the only way to deal with New York City was to get out immediately and never go back. In Hollywood he had, from a distance, seen Dustin Hoffman sprinting from a restaurant to a chauffeur-driven Cadillac, but he had failed to win an audience with his heart-throb, the Archetypal Lady Folk-singer, Ms Janie Carmen. Witch had few weaknesses, Helen assured me, and one of them was Ms Carmen, for whom he had even written songs especially, only to have them returned unplayed by Ms Carmen's management, on the advice of Ms Carmen's attorneys, on the ground that Ms Carmen was not at liberty to consider unsolicited material.

'Isn't that crazy?'

'It does sound rather negative,' I agreed.

In San Francisco Witch had dropped a fair amount of acid because San Francisco was a good place to drop a fair amount of acid, and formed a two-month liaison with a Beautiful Person who had a thing about oral sex. But the liaison ended one idyllic June afternoon when Witch returned from consulting a doctor (who advised that the Beautiful Person had transmitted to him a minor but unpleasant sexual infection) to find that the Beautiful Person, together with his acid stash and his moneybelt (though mercifully not his passport), had vanished without trace.

'It's all cleared up now, of course,' said Helen, as though I might be contemplating oral sex with her brother.

'I'm glad to hear it.'

'It wasn't her fault, he says. And he doesn't hold it against her.'

'I would,' I murmured.

But Helen was already telling me how Witch had enjoyed sitting in on physics classes in Berkeley, where they had a more dynamic approach to the subject. While there he spoofed politics and broke philosophical lances with the student radicals, which spawned in him a homesickness for the clipped asperities of academic Deenburgh, where he growingly felt his intellectual roots to be. After having a shoulder badly bruised by a police riot baton, during a student demonstration against the Vietnam war, he sent a telegram requesting

Mr Wishfort to pull university strings to get him on a graduate course in the philosophy department, where he proposed to research into the logic of science and the foundations of mathematics. This was arranged, and at the end of October Witch flew home to take up residence in his Southside house, which had been left in the custody of Beano Turnbull.

Beano was a student architect, and Witch had given him a budget for doing the house up, in return for which Beano and his girlfriend Harriet received a year's rent-free accommodation.

'When he saw how Beano had done the studio, he took him and Harriet for dinner in Runcornfield House!'

'Studio?'

'Recording studio. Eight-track. Only the second in Deenburgh, and it's doing quite well already. There's a lot of demand.'

Stifling an urge to inquire whether Witch also did quite well from betting shops and brothels, I asked:

'But why, if he was so good at maths, has he given it up?'

'Something to do with tautologies. Said he was tired of juggling tautologies. But I'm not sure what that means.'

She wasn't joking.

'Why don't you ask him yourself?'

'Perhaps I will.'

'Well,' she said, stubbing a second cigarette in the lid of her tobacco tin. 'Witch'll be glad you're coming, Peter. Now, I must have a bath. Where can I put my dog-ends?'

'In the . . .'

'Damn.' Helen had dropped her ashladen lid on the floor. She bent to scrape up the mess.

Suddenly anxious, I said:

'Don't bother, Helen. I'll . . .'

'Hello, hello,' she said. 'What's this?' She retrieved my *Varieties of Orgasmic Experience* from the magazine shelf under the coffee table (where I had slipped it before she came down) and thumbed the pages hungrily.

'Bloody hell, Peter,' she exclaimed, devouring a full-page diagram of a penis in pre-orgasmic erection with special attention to enlargement of the testicles and contraction of the rectum. 'I'd no idea psychologists did this sort of stuff.'

'It's purely . . .'

'Can I borrow it?'

I was aghast.

'*Please*, Peter. Just for a day or two.'

I hung in a long moment's torment.

Outside, the melted sleet drops splatted on the basement steps.

Helen probed me with arrogant teenage eyes, and asked: 'Why are you blushing?'

'I'm not blushing.'

'Then you must have a fever.'

'I just . . . wouldn't want your mother to think you had borrowed that from me. It's strictly for technical purposes.'

'I bet. Anyway, it's not Mummy that would hit the roof,' she said reassuringly, heading for the door with *Orgasmic Experience* clamped possessively under her elbow. 'It's Daddy.'

SEVEN

'Hey, Pete,' said Beano.

'Yes?'

'Humpty Dumpty *wasn't* pushed.'

'I thought he fell.'

'No,' he said ominously, as if deploring the deceitfulness of official press releases. 'He *pulled himself off*! Bet you never heard that before?' He smacked Harriet's bottom and reached to the sideboard for another can of McEwan's Export.

'More beer?' he offered me.

'I'll just nurse this, thanks. If we're having wine with the meal.'

'That *may* have been funny the first time, Beano,' said Harriet, standing at the cooker stirring the Bolognese sauce. 'But now it's a groan.'

'It's new to Pete. Isn't it, Pete?'

I nodded as I sipped my fizzy beer.

'Tell you another, shall I?'

'Please do.'

'What do you call a tomcat who eats his father?'

'A tomcat who eats his father?'

'What do you call him?'

'I give up.'

'*EatDaPuss*!' bellowed Beano. Chortling happily, he drained his Export in one prolonged swallow, crushed the empty can between his thumb and forefinger, and flipped it into the waste bucket beneath the sink.

Harriet looked round sternly. Her mass of red curls swayed on her shoulders like a pulsing jellyfish. The Glasgow in her accent strengthened as she said:

'For Christ's sake, Beano, stop buggering about. Get Nora

and Helen through, and give Witch a blow. We're ready for starters.'

Beano winked at me and then, to my surprise, knelt down by the window beside the table where I was sitting. His hairy cheeks bulged as if he were blowing a trumpet, and a few seconds later a distorted voice said:

'Southside Maternity Clinic speaking. Stand and deliver.'

'Grub up,' Beano roared back.

'Right. Down in five minutes.'

Beano left the large, bright, varnished-pine kitchen, and Harriet and I made small-talk until the other diners assembled.

Beano, I learned, had just been speaking through the grubline to Witch's apartment. The grubline was a plastic hosepipe Beano had fed down from Witch's living room to the kitchen below. It had a cork in each end, and a police whistle in the middle of the cork. To summon attention, one removed the cork and blew into the hosepipe, which produced a piercing whistle at the other end.

'Very imaginative,' I remarked.

'I expect it's been done before,' the architect's ladyfriend disparaged.

Harriet was almost as tall as Beano – a shade below six feet – and couldn't have weighed less than twelve stone. Her chest would have caused a lesser girl to topple forwards, but Harriet bore it with seeming ease.

What havoc must her couplings with Beano wreak on the springs of a normal mattress?

She was doing English literature, final year, with an emphasis on *Scottish* literature, and Beano was now in the penultimate century of his architecture training. Nora, Witch's other tenant, was an Art College crony of Helen's, and when we had arrived Helen went off to Nora's room to inspect her latest paintings. Nora could afford to live in Witch's house because she was poor, and hence got a full grant, whereas Helen got the minimum grant, which made her dependent on her parents, who refused to finance her living away from home when it wasn't necessary.

'Didn't she get any money when her grandfather died?'

'Yes. But it's in trust. She can't touch it till she's twenty-one. Like Deirdre. She got hers last April. Helen was furious,' said Harriet with evident relish.

When we were all round the table I saw that Nora was small, skinny, riddled with pimples, bespectacled, had a constant runny nose, and wore long skirts to conceal her strawlike shanks. She was the sort of ugly sister that pretty girls with desirable bodies (like Helen) often have as Best Friend, that handsome young men with sports cars and animal magnetism (like Witch) can afford to flirt with, and that nondescript young men like me detest, in case we get lumbered when the handsome young men disappear in the sports cars with the pretty girls' desirable bottoms warming up on the passenger seats.

Our starter was smoked mackerel fillets with granary bread and butter, plus lemon slices and tablespoonfuls of Hellmann's Mayonnaise – Beano's favourite food lubricant. The main course was spaghetti Bolognese with Brussels sprouts and three bottles of coarse Valpolicella.

'You don't want anything too smooth with spaghetti,' Witch explained.

'Nah,' said Beano. 'Paintstripper's the thing. Cheers.'

I don't know if subconsciously I was expecting Witch to float through the kitchen door on a magic carpet, smoking a hookah and squirting oofle dust from a hypodermic syringe, but when he eventually came down and apologized quietly for being late, having had some tape editing to finish, I was rather disappointed.

He was wearing sandals, jeans, a plain blue shirt and fawn pullover, and he looked pale and tired. If it weren't for the dominant power of his sharp blue eyes, and the reputation that preceded him round Deenburgh like a long-range weather forecast, I would have ascribed the King-of-the-Castle status to Beano.

Who fed the conversation like a stoker on an old steam train.

I mustn't worry, he informed me confidentially, if Witch fell asleep at table: the poor bugger had been up all last night recording. Furthermore and while he was on the subject, did I know the best season for a bellyache?

I confessed that I didn't, and Beano said:

'Autumn.'

'Autumn?'

'*Aw tum*!'

Witch grinned knowingly at my nonplussedness and poured me another glass of wine.

Beano ploughed on with the latest scandal from the John Locke cafeteria. *Scholar* had published another piece by Dr Tostow, in which he ridiculed *Dumbo* in general and excoriated Tom Redhead in particular, lamenting the embarrassingly high incidence, on British campussies, of American so-called Marxist theorists, who were in fact illiterate yellow-bellied draftdodgers who had never read a single word Marx wrote. (Beano, on the other hand, Beano parenthesized, *had* once read a single word Marx wrote – and it was *capital*!) In reply to this new Tostow thrust, Tom Redhead was busy whipping up a rumour that Dr Tostow was a CIA agent, prior to organizing a petition to remove Tostow from his position as a Deenburgh University Teaching Officer.

'Heady stuff,' Witch said unconcernedly, sprinkling Parmesan on his spaghetti.

'Loady shite,' pronounced Beano, who then related that there were posters up in David Square advertising a talk-in confrontation between Dr Tostow and Dr Hardy Nagil, best-selling cult-figure author of *The Economics of Consciousness*.

'When?' Witch asked.

'Middle of March.'

'What on?'

'*Hallucinogenic versus Psychedelic*,' Beano said dramatically. 'An open debate on moral issues relating to the use and legal classification of psychosomething drugs. Should be right up your street.'

'I might hobble along,' said Witch.

When I was halfway through my fruit-salad and cream, Harriet said briskly:

'Peter. Have some more?'

'I think . . .'

'Go on. Finish the bowl.'

As Harriet autocratically seized my plate and spooned into it the last of the fruit-salad, Witch leaned across the table, winked at me with the eye Harriet couldn't see, and said seriously:

'Who would think, Pete, that when Harriet was fifteen she was known as Hurry-It Harriet, the Kelvinside Chariot?'

'You'll have noticed, Peter,' said Harriet shrewishly, if somewhere there are shrews both red and huge, 'that Witch is taller than Beano?'

I nodded.

'But did you know Beano has a larger penis?'

'There's nothing wrong with Witch's penis,' said Helen.

'Not any more,' said Witch.

'Snot what you got,' Beano said generously. 'Swat it tastes like that counts.'

The roots of my hair began to pop, and I wondered if my nose would peel. There had been plenty of foul language in my Che Guevara flat, but purely affable obscenity was quite new to me. Nor was my burning soothed by Beano turning to me, his thick black brows frowning darkly and saying:

'How big is yours, by the way?'

'Peter knows all about penises,' said Helen. 'And orgasms. It's part of his subject.'

'How do you know?' asked Witch.

'He's lent me a book. It says normal women masturbate until they collapse from exhaustion.'

I protested:

'That's not quite . . .'

'Can I have it after you?' Witch asked his sister.

'*I* never masturbate,' claimed Nora.

'*Every*body masturbates,' said Harriet firmly.

'On conceptual grounds,' said Witch, 'I'm inclined to agree. The proposition "X masturbates" can be unpacked analytically from the proposition "X is a person".'

'Baaaawals,' Beano belched.

'Mind you,' said Harriet, 'if some of us blew less of our

grants on McEwan's Export, we might get our big fat pricks up more often.'

And Beano sang lustily:

Beer, beer,
Glorious beer!
If only it were not
So gassy and dear!

Harriet stood up and collected the dessert plates from the oblong pine table.

Witch said:

'Come on, Pete. Before this gets out of hand. I'd like to let you see my studio.'

'I'll help Harriet with the dishes,' Helen offered.

'You'll help *Beano* with the dishes,' Harriet accepted. 'What about coffee, Witch?'

'Got some on upstairs, thanks.'

'More coffee?'

'No thanks.'

'Whisky?'

'I don't usually . . .'

'Be a devil, Pete. Have a finger while I have a joint. Glenmorangie do? I won a bottle in the rugby club Christmas raffle.'

He poured me a finger fatter than Beano's thumb, and, rolling his reefer, asked:

'Okay if I put some songs on?'

'Why not,' I said, for the Brandenburg Concerto now playing was in my own record collection.

'You may not have heard these before,' he said, as he wound another spool on to his Revox. 'I'd be interested to know what you think.'

The music resumed.

Witch lit his joint.

I fondled my glass and sank deeper into my pile of cushions.

We veiled our gazes in the customary pretence of not continuing to weigh the other person up, and I told myself I wasn't envious of his material possessions. Not *envious.* But if Santa left Witch's flat in my Christmas stocking, I might find my pride conquerable. When we had come up the stairs I saw, on the door at the top, a boxed sign that when lit would say redly RECORDING PLEASE FUCK OFF. 'A Beano touch, that,' Witch explained, ushering me in. 'Come and have a look round.'

The entire flat was white with scarlet woodwork, but the effect was modulated in the various rooms by an intricate system of spotlights: on stands rising from floors, on bars attached to walls, even spotlights suspended from ceilings in clusters, as in a small theatre. In Witch's bedroom (over a coal fire, two large loudspeakers, a wardrobe, chest of drawers, two easy chairs and several acres of purple-duveted mattress) the prevailing hue was a warm dark blue, sweet with the scents of cannabis and incense.

His study was lit naturally: a lamp on the desk throwing light on a cassette recorder, telephone and electric typewriter. There was also a four-drawer filing cabinet, a knee-high green metal safe with a combination lock, a library of several hundred tapes in white boxes, and some two thousand books on the shelves round the walls – science books, maths books, a complete Shakespeare, the Oxford English Dictionary, Batman comics, *Mad,* the collected works of Aldous Huxley . . . I could have browsed for hours, but Witch led me on, past a small spare bedroom, into his studio.

The musician's section, where the lighting was orange, I found uninteresting. But Witch seemed pleased with it, so I made appropriate noises. It was a windowless cell, sufficiently big for a hefty upright piano not to dominate, with a drum kit in another corner, two electric guitars propped against the wall, a platoon of silver and bronze microphone and music stands in the centre, several black speaker boxes, and a fankle of cables festooning the floor.

We passed through a heavy soundproofed door to the all-purpose living area, which had an unobtrusive kitchen unit in the far right corner. Where the far left corner might have been, three steps led up to the Cockpit. 'Isn't it amazing?' Witch asked me. 'Totally unexpected,' I replied. Southside Towers was a Victorian development with a Gothick turret slapped on the south-west corner. This Beano had converted into Witch's cockpit, where he had his professional recording equipment and mixing console: a desk of VU meters, fader knobs and control switches that made him 'feel like I'm piloting the "Enterprise".'

Tapping the semi-circular Cockpit window, as the fluttering February snowflakes blew out of the black night to melt against it, he had added:

'During the day you can see over to the Freeland Hills. Only a few church steeples in between.'

'That must be very exhilarating,' I had said without enthusiasm. It was not so much his drug-vending or conspicuous prosperity that I disliked, it was the idea of him posing in the nude for Helen.

'What do you think?' Witch asked.

'Sorry?' I blinked at him over the fumes of my whisky, and was startled to see the tape rewinding. We had only heard four songs, and I was anticipating a complete album.

'Like them? Or aren't you into electric folk?'

'Very nice,' I said vaguely. 'Who are they?'

'They?'

'The group?'

Witch seemed delighted.

'That's no band,' he exclaimed. 'That's *me*.'

'Not playing everything?' I hoped.

'Everything but the drums,' he said offhandedly. 'But that's nothing. Just a few guitars and a bit of synthesizer. What I meant was: what do you think of *the songs*?'

I asked him to play the tape again.

He was pleased to do so.

This time I bolted my attention to *the songs*, and was displeased to discover that Witch had quite a good voice, similar to Kristofferson but with fewer muffed notes. As I listened, my gaze lifted from the hypnotic revolutions of the tape spools to the picture hung on the wall above the Revox: a blown-up colour photograph of Janie Carmen.

It was taken from an album cover, and showed her (rear view) standing naked on some wooded height overlooking the coast of California, with a crimson sun melting into the distant Pacific horizon. Ms Carmen's weight rested on her right foot, dimpling the above buttock, while her left leg, arms, and breeze-lifted hair were captured in a dynamic posture of wildly liberated womanhood, as if any moment the sheer force of her bodily joy might pluck her upward from the earth like a hotair balloon whose ballast has fallen through the bottom of its basket.

Perusing this pert female form, I seemed to hear the million dollar Carmen voice join Witch's singing, and I realized with surprise that two of his songs were written as by a young Red Indian girl, who said:

All through my early days
I was free as only maids are free.
I learned the age-old ways:
What may and what may not be,
While the wise men read the skies
And marked the Headman's son for me
To bear his child.

But now the Medicine Man
He wrings his hands,
I've never seen his face so long.
I believe he's saying the signs are wrong,
Yes, now he's saying the signs are wrong:
There's too many stars in the sky,
And it means somebody soon will die.
It means somebody soon will die.

When the song was over, I said to its author, singer and accompanist:

'That's very moving, Witch. But why sing with an American accent? And ungrammatically?'

He took my glass and rewarded my applause with a second fat whisky.

'It's an idiom,' he explained. 'Remember Vera Lynn?'

'Of course.'

'Imagine her singing "We love you. Yes. Yes. Yes". Wouldn't work, would it?'

I agreed.

Witch expanded:

'In any art form, the shibboleth is whether it *works.* If it doesn't work, it doesn't work. And that isn't a tautology.'

I asked what exactly he meant by 'tautology'.

He launched into a rapid conceptual monologue in the course of which I learned that he was disappointed with the philosophy department at the University (where the philosophy of science people knew nothing about science, the philosopher of religion knew nothing about philosophy, and the best teacher was the professor of metaphysics, who was a World Authority on Kant. Witch was enjoying his work on Kant (although you couldn't take Kant's ethics seriously unless you were a latent sadist with a Calvinist conscience)), and the short answer to my question was that I wouldn't really comprehend what he, Witch, meant by 'tautology' until I had grasped Kant's distinction between analytic and synthetic judgements, which grasp could be obtained by dipping into the first six hundred pages of the *Critique of Pure Reason.*

I promised so to dip when my Finals were over.

Then Witch like a nimble boomerang said:

'What do you know about the Belhaven TwangGang?'

'I've got their album.'

'Like it?'

'I like Cindy Bell's voice.'

'Wouldn't you agree,' my host asked leadingly, folding into a lotus on the cushion beside me and reaching for his Rizla papers, 'that the TwangGang is basically derivative rubbish?'

'I think that's going too far.'

'With only three things going for them: Cindy's voice,

Cindy's face, and Cindy's body? Apart from that, they're wooden, synthetic, and only in it for the money. The Belhaven *Bandwagon*, in fact, would more aptly encapsulate their aspirations. Wouldn't it?'

There was much in what he said, but I was reluctant to have my Guinevere imprisoned in a plastic castle, so I queried:

'Aren't some of their adaptations quite effective?'

'Know why they do so many traditional ripoffs?'

'No.'

'Because it's fashionable, they can't write anything decent themselves, and it's more lucrative for Othello.'

'How's that?'

'If they use other writers' songs, they don't get any publishing money. But if they fudge up some ancient folksong, with a bit of oompa and electricity, it becomes "Trad. Arr. Belhaven TwangGang". Who then pick up all the publishing money.'

'How does that benefit Othello?'

'Good question,' my music-business mentor nodded, toking on his reefer. 'Shortly before their album was released, Othello started his own publishing company. Othello Music. So, for every publishing pound the band earns, Othello gets half and Cindy and the musicians get the other half split between them.'

'But that's monstrous,' I protested, horrified to think of my Queen being milked by such an exploitative fancy man.

'All business is monstrous,' said Witch. 'And Othello's a cunt.' He used the word without malice. 'Now. Wouldn't it be better for the TwangGang, and for Cindy as an artiste, if they used more original material?'

I couldn't deny it.

'And since Cindy is their star, they should use songs that bring out the best in her?'

'Yes.'

'What about the songs I've just played you? Wouldn't they suit Cindy? Get more feeling into her singing?'

'Quite possibly.'

Before Witch could lead me round the next corner of his

maze, our sixth-floor tranquillity was shattered by the grubline whistle. This protruded beneath the curtained window to the right of the Janie Carmen blow-up. Witch rolled off his cushion, crawled to the window, plucked the corked whistle from the tube, and said:

'Whitehall 1212. Drug squad in conference. Please be brief.'

'Witch,' said Helen's piped voice, 'we've a guy down here that wants some acid. Shall I send him up?'

'Certainly not. Do we know him?'

'I don't. Says he's a friend of Kevin's.'

'What's his name? What's he look like?'

'Julian. Long hair and a beard. Looks . . .'

'No kidding?'

'He looks okay, Witch. Really.'

'See if he knows Kevin's mother's first name. If he does, get his address and his money, and his salvation will be delivered tomorrow between eleven and midnight. Two hundred mikes per cap, a quid each, and he won't get better in Deenburgh. Five quid minimum, ten quid maximum. Got that? He can take it or leave it.'

'What if he doesn't know Kevin's mum's first name?'

'Tell him to go away and find out.'

'Okay,' said the dutiful sister. Then:

'I'm going soon, Witch. If Peter wants a lift.'

'Pete'll be finished in ten minutes,' Peter's host said confidently.

'What was all that about mikes and caps?' I asked him, when he had recorked the grubline.

'Two hundred *micro*grams in each *cap*sule,' he kindly explained. 'Accurate within ten per cent.'

I tried to look impressed.

'Where do you get the stuff?' my naivety inquired.

Witch's scorching grin made me feel like Oliver Twist.

'I get it,' he disclosed, 'from the Continent of Europe. Now,' he sat down again, so close that I felt uncomfortable, as if he might suddenly caress my thighs. 'I expect you're wondering why I asked you up here?'

'I was told you wanted to make up for calling me Nutkins

and pushing into the bathroom in front of me.'

Witch blinked, and said:

'Yes, I am sorry about that, Pete. But there is something else.'

'Oh?'

'Helen tells me you're a gold medal Secret Keeper.'

'That's very flattering of her.'

'Have you told anyone about seeing me that night in your basement?'

'No.'

'Not even Helen?'

'Not even anyone.'

'If I tell you what I was doing, will you keep it a secret?'

'Of course.'

'Even from Helen?'

'Even from everyone.'

Witch regarded me speculatively. The cannabis he was smoking hadn't affected his speech, but the pupils of his eyes were swollen like ripe grapes.

'Guess?' he teased.

'I've no idea,' I said shortly. 'You looked as if you were fishing for rats in the cellar.'

'Not bad, Pete. I was fishing for dope.'

'Eh?'

'That cellar's walled up . . .'

'I know.'

'And it's about five feet down from the window to the floor. The window is sealed open, a few inches top and bottom, so no one can get in. I keep some of my dope there, in a Thermos flask, and when I want it I hoist it up with an electromagnet.'

'Hence the cable running out from my kitchen?'

'Exactly.'

'What's the point?'

'Someday this flat will get done by the pigs. So I keep less gear here than the value of a stretch in jail. See? They don't have any tape recorders there.'

'Or women.'

'Them neither,' he agreed.

'Why tell me about it?'

'I'd like to go on using the cellar – not much chance of a pig raid on respectable Number Ten, is there? But it's your basement now. So I need your permission.' He smiled pleasantly.

'Is that why you seduced Françoise?' I asked as I wondered.

And regretted it immediately.

Witch looked at me reproachfully.

'Don't be cynical, Pete,' he chided. Women *want* it.'

'Want what? Drug hoards outside their bedroom windows?'

'Women want to be touched, tickled, teased, spanked, hugged, kissed, fondled, penetrated, detonated – you name it: if it's warm, wet and intimate, they want it. So where's the shame in giving it to them?'

'I didn't mean . . .'

'Ah, but your thought was mean. Do you know: when I got back last October, Françoise had been festering in that basement since January, and she hadn't had it once. Not once, *in ten months*.'

So what? I reflected sourly. *I haven't had it since I left Saint Andrews, but that doesn't mean I need other fornicators' LSD mountains in my basement cellar.*

'When I first stuck it into Françoise,' Witch reported modestly, 'she went off like the steam whistle on the runaway train that went over the hill and she blew, blew, blew . . . *wow*. Thought I'd never get out of her alive.'

'Sounds terrifying.'

But for all my cold hostility, Witch had me on the run. And he knew it. I had been priggish and petty, which handed him the whip on a plate, and in three minutes he had lashed me into agreeing to preserve his cellar secret and allow his nocturnal visits to continue.

'Really appreciate this, Pete,' he said warmly, as I stood up to rejoin my chauffeuse downstairs.

'Don't mention it.'

'There is just one other thing.' He picked something off the knee-high cupboard shelf on which the Revox sat. 'I want you to have this.'

'What is it?'
'A cassette of the songs you heard earlier.'
'Why give them to me?'
'I'd like you to play them to Cindy for me. Will you?'

EIGHT

The hour before I was supposed to telephone Cindy Bell was the closest I have ever come to suicide.

'*Me*?' I squawked at Witch. 'Why don't you play her the songs yourself?'

'Not if you don't want to, Pete. But you did agree she should get away from electrified *John Barleycorn.*'

'But why me? Why not Deirdre?'

'Deirdre and I don't communicate.'

'What about Helen?'

'Helen and Cindy don't get on. The thing is, Pete, we want Cindy to *want* the songs. Right? They must be her own discovery. Yes?'

'No.'

'You're the only person I can think of who won't seem biased in my favour. Read *Tom Sawyer*?'

'No.'

'I'll lend you my copy. We want Cindy panting, as it were, to whitewash the fence. So we have to present the songs as if she *shouldn't* like them. And you're the ideal person to do that.'

'How?'

'Pretend it's *you* that thinks she should listen to them, but you're having to do it on the sly, because I made you promise *not to play the songs to anyone.* Because I'm worried they're not good enough, that people'll sneer. Okay? Then she'll be more receptive.'

'I don't have a cassette player.'

'I'll give you one,' he said grandly. 'Got a record player?'

'Yes.'

'What kind?'

'HMV Stereomaster.'

'Has it got a five-pin DIN input?'

'How should I know?'

'Has it,' he inquired, with the technical patience of a doctor encouraging an idiot to define his symptoms, 'got a control that says *Record, Radio, Tape*?'

'Yes.'

'Good. I'll give you . . .'

'What about Othello?'

'What about him?'

'If he's as unpleasant as everyone makes out, what on earth will he think of a stranger trying to sell his girlfriend someone else's songs?'

'You're *not* a stranger, Pete. You're Deirdre's classmate, and Deirdre's Cindy's best friend. You live in our basement, so you're an adopted Wishfort, hence a long-standing buddy of the Cameron-Bells. How can you call yourself a stranger? And besides, no one in his right mind gives a tuppenny fart what Othello thinks.'

'*I* give a tuppenny fart.'

'Waste of tuppence, Pete. Look,' he trumped. 'I happen to know that Othello is going to London on Monday and won't be back till Thursday. He's got business with his record company. You phone Cindy on Monday night, ask her down to Number Ten on Tuesday or Wednesday, and the chances are she'll be free one of those nights. She doesn't have a lot of friends, you know. Specially since she let Othello crawl into bed with her.'

'But suppose she says *No*,' I pleaded.

'Why should she?'

' "Women want it", I suppose. "Any intimate attention". Is that it?'

He chuckled omnisciently and moved to fill his electric kettle at the sink in the kitchen corner. 'Let's have some tea, shall we? If Cindy says No, too bad. We'll think again. But if you're shy, or don't have the time to lend her career a helping hand, you mustn't feel under any obligation . . .'

Witch sat me down again. We had tea. He blew down the grubline and told Helen to go home: Pete would follow later in a taxi. I told him my lifestyle didn't run to taxis. That was all right, he said, he would pay for it. Out of the question, I informed him with dignity. Surely not, he hoped, as I would be doing him a favour. We dunked ginger-nut biscuits in our tea. Witch rolled another joint. I declined another whisky. He became more vibrant, charming and informative as the night wore on. I became less so. He told me many things: about himself, his thoughts, attitudes, drug experiences, songs, family and friends.

Beano, for example, was a piss-artist only on the surface – I mustn't be deceived. Under the patter and the puns Beano was a dedicated architect, rising every weekday at half past six, to do two hours' work before Harriet served breakfast at nine. His greatest natural gifts were athletic, which was a pity. Why? Because Beano didn't take his sports particularly seriously. He'd been in the Scottish karate team, but left because of the training required and the overly solemn attitude. He was a better rugby player than Alastair, but took it with a pinch of salt and gallons of Export, so he was unlikely to make the national team, as Alastair was tipped to do the following season. Beano's ambition was to build opera houses and cathedrals, and the sorrow of his life was being bad at exams: he got nervous, went blank, that sort of thing. Witch was confident, though, that determination would carry Beano through. And he did have quite a talent for design, didn't he? Look at the way he'd done the studio, for instance.

I confessed my admiration.

Did I *like* Beano?

Who could fail to?

Even though he'd embarrassed me over the size of my cock?

I promised not to hold it against him.

Some of the other things Witch told me that night I will relate in due course. What surprised me most was a paradoxical inferiority complex. This came out when he talked about his songwriting.

'My biggest problem,' he complained, 'is that I'm good at almost everything.'

'Why is that a problem?' I asked severely.

'It levels you out. Stops you excelling at any one thing. Take Bertrand Russell and Einstein. Russell had more ammunition, but Einstein hit the bull's-eye.'

'But your songs are good, Witch,' I said obediently.

'But are they excellent? I sometimes think if I could write just one perfect song, I'd pack it all in and concentrate on something else. Know what I mean?'

He was being perfectly serious, so I suggested:

'Why not play me some more songs? I'm no judge, of course. But . . .'

He fetched his acoustic guitar from the bedroom.

Did I like it? Handmade in a little workshop in East London, by the same craftsman that made Paul Simon's guitars. In the next half-hour Witch sang me several songs he wouldn't offer to Cindy or anyone else, he said. I cared little for the traditions he drew on, but I could tell his compositions were unusual. The normal tuning for a guitar, from the lowest string to the highest, is E A D G B E. Most of Witch's 'own songs' were in deviant tunings of his devising.

Had I realized that each of the guitar's six strings could be varied by at least five semi-tones?

No, this hadn't occurred to me.

Giving a theoretically possible six to the power of six tunings. 46, 656 in all.

I blinked doubtfully.

'So it's pretty pathetic, isn't it, that most people never venture away from E A D?'

'It does seem rather unadventurous.'

'Most open tunings,' Witch said, slipping his left pinkie into a three-inch steel bottleneck, 'are variations on D. This one's a variation on C. The tuning is C G C F C E, and the song's called *Sober Serious Man*.'

It was a complex piece, in several senses, and something of Witch's attitude to life may be conveyed by the final verse:

Now I've done my best, I've sung my song
To make a slave of you,
And each in its own peculiar way

Not a word is untrue.
Thus I love you most of all the things
That live beneath the sun,
And yet I have to hope you've guessed
That when all is said and done
And underneath the agony
I say it all in fun
And I don't really care.

He laid down his guitar and offered me more tea. It was nearly four in the morning, and my eyes were squint with sleepiness. I told him his songs were strikingly *different,* yawned, and said I really must get to bed. He called me a taxi, and when I returned from a visit to the bathroom he handed me a bulging plastic carrier bag.

'What's this?'

'Couple of albums you might like. John Fahey. Leo Kottke. Open tunings, bottleneck, that sort of thing. And *Tom Sawyer* for your edification.'

'What's that bulge?'

'My dope Thermos. I'd be really grateful, Pete, if you could stick it back in the cellar. Lower it down as far as your arm can reach, then drop it. There's a pile of old coal sacks to break its fall.'

I thought of refusing, but somehow it would have seemed ungracious, and I was *so exhausted.*

'Give me a ring on Monday night,' Witch said in farewell, as I followed a disgruntled taxi driver down the first of many stairs. 'When you've phoned Cindy. About eight o'clock. If she says Yes, we'll fix you up with a cassette player. Okay?'

When I got home I found the Cindy cassette at the bottom of the carrier bag.

And tucked inside it?

A £5 note.

Phoning Cindy was no problem on Saturday and Sunday,

because there was simply no question of my doing it. I was so irritated by Witch's £5 attempt to rope me into his Tom Sawyer pantomime that I even forgot to be paranoid as I slipped his Thermos back in the cellar.

What did he take me for?

The more I chewed it over, the stronger became my feeling that Witch's spiel about benefiting Cindy's career was purely self-interested hogwash.

What was in it for him?

Either he merely wanted the TwangGang to play his songs, in which case I didn't care but why should I help him? Or he had some sinister Lancelot designs on Cindy. If so, the last person in Deenburgh to be his pander was Galahad Squirrell. The situation was hence clearcut. On Monday evening I would tell him politely to do his own dirty work: should I post the cassette back to him, or entrust it to Helen?

But on Monday morning I received a plain postcard, on which, electrically typed, I read:

> A woman (with certain exceptions which need not be mentioned) will not take the first step with a man; for in spite of all the beauty she may have, she risks a refusal. A man may be ill in mind or body, or busy, or gloomy, and so not care for advances; and a refusal would be a blow to her vanity. But as soon as he takes the first step, and helps her over this danger, he stands on a footing of equality with her, and will generally find her quite tractable.
>
> (Old Hebridean Proverb)
>
> P.S. Kisses on the bottom.

This ruined my day.

I spent the morning in the psychology library, failing to digest the latest journals. After lunch (including a pint of lager and lime – a drastic resort for me), I was unable to follow a lecture on statistical techniques in intelligence testing. I was obsessed with the idea that my weekend convictions had been mistaken: Witch had no sexual interest in Cindy. No. The entire charade was a test of my own manhood. Helen must have relayed to Witch the notion, promulgated by Deirdre, that I fancied Cindy. Being a self-styled fisher of men, Witch had hooked me in a situation where failure to contact my Guinevere would expose me as an ineffectual sexual coward and laughing stock, who might as well flee Deenburgh on the next train south.

What could be more obvious?

For supper that night I had boiled cabbage and a large Fray Bentos steak-and-kidney pie. I sweated into it a lot, and it gave me indigestion. By seven-thirty I was having trouble breathing. My heart was racing and I thought I was going to faint. I couldn't phone Cindy, and I couldn't not phone her. If I phoned her, she would laugh at me. If I didn't phone her, the rest of Deenburgh would laugh at me. I put on my scarf, duffelcoat and mittens. Out I went: pale, trembling, and determined to contemplate suicide by jumping off the Strathbogle Bridge, which crosses the River Lethe just past the bottom wall of Number Ten's back garden.

But the bridge was too low to guarantee worse than a broken leg, so I shuffled my misery another hundred yards to the Buttbridge Bar, on the corner of Strathbogle Road and Buttbridge Place.

There, among several wizened natives in shabby overcoats and hobnail boots, I sucked at a double Scotch. The natives, perched on stools at the bar, were engrossed in a comedy programme on the television above the barman's head. They were drinking halfpints of heavy and nips of *Bell's*, which was the only syllable I recognized amid the aggressive grunts and glottal cackles that periodically exploded from their toothless mouths. I knew, though, from a study I had read (on *Alcoholism in Relation to Violence as a Function of Communicative Retardation among the Lower Socio-Economic Groups in Scotland*) that I was statistically unlikely to be assaulted and that their hearts were probably in the right places, so I retired to a far dark corner to sedate my angst unmolested.

And it wasn't long before the Scotch induced in me a brainwave that would have bent the needles on an electro-encephalograph. A current fad book in the psychology department was Luke Rhinehart's *The Dice Man*. Why not? I didn't have any dice, but I had plenty of coins. And, after suicide, I only had two options. Heads: phone Cindy. Tails: phone Witch and say the deal was off. Either way I need feel no shame because *the decision wouldn't be mine*, so Cindy wouldn't be laughing at me – she would be laughing *at a random event.* I was so eager that my first toss spun out of reach and fell on the floor.

'Neh, Jimmy?' the barman quacked at me from somewhere between his dirty white coat and his mail-order toupee, when I bent to retrieve my shilling. 'Ye canny gumble in heeurr, ken.'

'Sorry.' As I departed I returned my glass to the counter: the only way I know of making a Scottish barman smile.

Behind me I heard:

'Neh. Some thick buggers dinny ken when folks is kiddin.'

'Tellin me, Jimmy. Fuckin stew dents, ken.'

'Ay. Right enough.'

Outside, in the fog off the Firth, freezing as it thickened, I tossed again beneath a streetlight.

'Phone Cindy,' Our Gracious Queen commanded me.

Back in my room, I didn't trust my voice without a warm-up, so I phoned upstairs and asked Rosie if I could speak to Helen.

'Yes, Peter?' said Helen. 'I'm watching television at the moment.'

'Sorry, Helen. I was wondering if I could have my book back.'

Ominous silence.

'Helen?'

'You don't really need it *tonight*, Peter, do you?' she asked in a tone suggesting that only a pathological masturbator could require *The Varieties of Orgasmic Experience* in what remained of the present evening.

'I do,' I said doggedly. 'I need to check . . .'

'You see, I've lent it to Witch.'

'You've *what*?'

'He was down at teatime and asked to borrow it,' she explained unapologetically. 'I can get it back tomorrow, if you like. Won't that do?'

'I suppose it'll have to.'

'Good. See you tomorrow, Peter. Bye.'

I dialled Cindy's number immediately, relying on my anger with Helen to fuel my daring. But after the second ring my nerve failed and I slammed the receiver down. Cindy's number was Deirdre's number, after all, and *suppose Deirdre answered*? Obviously she would hoot with mirth as soon as I asked for Cindy. I got my A4 narrow-feint note-pad from my desk and spent ten minutes scripting two entirely different conversations, Deirdre's being premised on a red herring about a book I'd like to borrow (*not* by Whitman & Nixon).

Armed with my scripts, I dialled again.

'Hello? Cindy Bell speaking.'

'Hello, sinned . . . my name is Peter Squirrell speaking and you probably won't remember me but we did meet once at the end of last year and I was just wondering . . .' I found myself wondering what I was just wondering and was all set to slam the phone down again.

But Cindy said:

'Why yes, Peter. I remember. You came to Deirdre's party last term, didn't you?'

'That's right.'

'And now you're in the basement at Number Ten?'

'Since last month.'

'That must be a lovely room to study in.'

'Yes. I've been very lucky.'

'Othello and I sometimes feel guilty, you know, that Deirdre doesn't get more peace up here. We're rather noisy a lot of the time. With rehearsals and everything.'

A shiver running up my spine collided with a bead of sweat rolling down it.

'Did you call ten minutes ago, Peter?' Cindy asked.

'No.'

'That's funny. The phone rang twice and then stopped.'

'Maybe someone realizing they'd dialled the wrong number.'

'Must have been. Anyway, Peter, I expect you want Deirdre. She's . . .'

'*No*,' I howled. 'It's you I want sorry what I mean is it's you I wanted to speak to.'

'Oh?'

'I hope you won't think this unforgivably presumptuous of me Cindy if I may I call you Cindy?'

'Please do.'

'But I've got some songs you see I mean songs by a friend of mine that I really think would suit the Belhaven TwangGang and particularly your own voice if I may say so and I was wondering if possibly I might be able to persuade you to let me play them to you sometime but of course . . .'

'Hang on a moment, Peter, can you?'

I heard a hand cupping her mouthpiece, and I was convinced she was summoning flatmates, guests, neighbours and strangers off the street to gather round and catch a snatch of this gabbling twit on the phone. But:

'Sorry, Peter. Just shouting. I've got someone waiting at the door. Yes, I'd love to listen to your songs. Mike and I were saying just the other day that we need some fresh material. Is it on a tape?'

'Cassette.'

'Ah. We don't have a cassette player here, Peter. But presumably you do?'

'No. I mean, yes.'

'Right. Let me see. I can't manage tomorrow – I'm going to a film with Deirdre. How about if I drop by your place on Wednesday evening?'

'Wonderful,' I gurgled. 'I'll be . . .'

'About nine? Must go now, Peter. See you Wednesday.'

'See you Cindy, Wednesday,' I croaked into the dead phone, as my eyes opened to inspect the rivers of perspiration on the landscape of my left palm.

Half an hour and a cup of coffee later, I phoned to report to Witch.

'This is Heaven. This is Heaven. We regret that none of your ancestors lives here, but by all means leave your message when you hear the groan.'

'Witch, it's Peter here.'

'Hi, Pete.'

'Why do you have an ex-directory number? I've just had to get it from your mother.'

'Try Helen, Pete. She's juicier.'

My silence expressed my disapproval.

'Okay, Pete,' said Witch. 'Sorry about that. Just been speaking to Beano on the grubline. Spills over. What news?'

I told him.

'That's great, Pete. Well done. Was she difficult? Or did she yield instantly to your urbane charm?'

'She's coming,' I said shortly. 'But I don't feel at all positive about your attitude.'

'You hate my guts, you mean?'

'That's not what I said.'

'What's the problem, Pete?'

'I agreed to do you *a favour*. And I don't expect payment for favours.'

'Meaning?'

'That five-pound note you put . . .'

'Was for the *taxi*, old son. We agreed I should pay for that.'

'That taxi cost little over a pound.'

'Jesus wept,' Witch exclaimed. 'If that's what's bothering you, you can give me the change tomorrow. But the other night a fiver was *all I had*.'

'Oh.' *You plausible shit*, I thought. *You've made me seem priggish again.*

'Thermos in the cellar okay?'

'Yes.'

'No bluebottle pigs leaning over the railings waving torches and truncheons?'

'No.'

'Fat chance these days.' He sniffed. 'Lazy buggers zoom

about all night in Panda cars and never see a thing. Petty crime's booming. Terrible business.'

'If you say so.'

'Mustn't be cynical, Pete. Doesn't suit you. Now, can you meet me under the John Locke Tower tomorrow? Half three?'

'I could do.'

'Then do do. And we'll get you a cassette player. Read *Tom Sawyer* yet?'

'No.'

'You ought to. Light-years ahead of this *Orgasmic* tripe you've been giving Helen. You should be ashamed, Pete.'

NINE

The fog cleared early next morning, and for several hours it was coldly sunny and brightly blue in that still, sharp, glinting way unique to Deenburgh in winter. It has to do with the rolling slopes the city straddles, its sprawling nearness to the sea, and the long wide north-south streets, their million windows reflecting the sunbeams into a cold gold flood that pours down to remind the arm-flapping red-nosed pedestrians below what an uplifting joy the place can be in summer, when the sun is warm and the Georgian gardens succulently green behind the pink and yellow frocks and furry white legs of those ladies who can afford the key subscriptions, to exercise their Afghan hounds and Scottie dogs.

At noon, as if a petulant angel had flicked a switch, there drifted in from the north-east sea a low and heavy sky the colour of dirty water in an old grey bath. For a solid hour a freak snowstorm fell wrathlessly in flapping flakes the size of fat white chestnut leaves. By one o'clock all motor transport had scrunched to a halt and the pubs were bursting with happily frustrated drivers exchanging headshaking climatic superlatives and wondering if the Russians weren't behind it all.

By quarter past three, when I stepped out of the University Library, it was fair again and snowblindingly white. I had been in the Social Sciences Room, checking references and wondering what conversational ground I could possibly share with Cindy Bell. Now that Guinevere was to visit me I was terrified, and I hoped renewed acquaintance would reveal her to be a bandy-legged cretin with unacceptable political opinions and halitosis, so I could retract my devotion without disgrace.

I turned right and walked east, toward the John Locke Tower. The south side had been redeveloped some years earlier, and my short walk took me past the diamond-shaped David Square Theatre (where the film club showed interminable Andy Warhol movies on Friday nights) and the Adam Smith building – a slablike modular space for the teaching of economics, sociology and linguistics.

As I trudged by the Adam Smith, a tightly packed snowball exploded on my left elbow. The storm had left a five-inch carpet across the town, and a hundred male undergraduates in combat jackets, flying jackets, donkey jackets, woolly scarves and Balaclava Helmets, were yelping and scampering about hurling snowballs at each other and any unescorted females and timid Squirrells that took their fancy. Inside the David Square Gardens a further platoon of industrious work-shirkers was rolling the belly of a vast snowman that by the morrow would have a wooden Excalibur thrust through his loins, red paint dripping therefrom, and a black bowler with a white hatband bloodily spelling D R A K E!

Walking down the tunnel to the basement of the John Locke, I wondered sadly why so little carefree japing and ribald mirth had fallen in the path of my own undergraduate career. I was a leprous loner, wasn't I? A decent chap, yes, but undeniably a tedious prune. While the Kingdom of Heaven, at whose gates the pretty girls clamoured come Saturday night, was overrun with Balaclava Helmets.

Would the injustice pursue me to my grave?

My brooding eyes scanned the poster slogans that lined the tunnel, and saw:

HALLUCINOGENIC TOSTOW
versus
PSYCHEDELIC NAGIL
All Welcome

WOULD YOU BUY A USED
CONDOM FROM THIS MAN?
Then why let him
fuck your planet?

DEENBURGH GRADS BRAINWASHED
IN DOPED SLEEP EXPTS!
Dumbo tells all

ASSESSMENT, YES.
HEART-ATTACK EXAMS?
NO!

JANIE CARMEN
IN CONCERT
Plus full supporting act

TOSS OFF TOSTOW
CIA GO HOME

MECHANICAL BANANA
(A Face Oddity)
Retained by pop demand

ACCESS TO FILES?
RECTOR REDHEAD HAS THE RIGHT!
All SECRET information
Is BAD information

IS THE NAME OF THE LAW
WORTH THE PIG IN YOUR
POCKET?
Curb Police Powers *Now!*

REBEL AGAINST REBELLION
Join Deenburgh Young
CONSERVATIVES TODAY

Scrawled across the blue background of the Young Conservatives poster was a cartoon depicting a pair of black testicles being sheep-sheared. Underneath, a scribbled caption in red said: *Algo Lagnia Rules! Ya, baas?*

Puzzling over the significance of this, I turned out of the tunnel, left past the John Locke lifts, and through the glass swing doors into the cafeteria.

The place was packed, and the disruptive snowstorm had triggered a carnival spirit in the students. Melted snow from a thousand soles had turned the floor into a shiny black rink of slippery treachery. Even as I stood in the coffee queue there was a yell of panic somewhere behind me, followed by the crashing of a body into a table and the smashing sounds of Crockery Meets Floor. Gingerly carrying my chicory brew in one hand and my briefcase in the other, I set off in search of Witch.

While I looked among the orange plastic chairs and the green formica-topped tables, with their customary litter of overflowing ashtrays, Coca-Cola tins, brown-slopped cups and saucers, abandoned clingfilm sandwich wrappings and slimy yoghurt cartons, my uneager ears recorded:

'Called me *frigid*.'

'Never.'

'So I told him . . .'

'Celtic'll annihilate . . .'

'This really far-out Red Leb, see? But . . .'

'She's gone too commercial, Janie Carmen . . .'

'So I drew a wee doodle over it, of a black man getting his balls sliced off.'

'Get away.'

'I did too. You'll see it in the tunnel when . . .'

The cafeteria was shaped like a learner driver's L, and I eventually located Witch in its toe, where the windows looked out to the lecturers' car park. He and Tom Redhead were enthroned at the head of several tables, presiding jointly over a court of a dozen yesmen, antagonists, chemical supplicants and long-haired nubile admirers.

Witch was taking orders for LSD. Tom was pounding his revelationary theory that Dr Tostow's recent experiments (conducted at the Psychology Department's Sleep Laboratory, on the effects of certain psychotropic drugs on the dreaming patterns of normal postgraduate males) were part of a CIA-funded plot to brainwash Deenburgh students into supporting American involvement in Vietnam. The antagonists were heckling Tom with 'evidence, man?', 'conspiracy-theory boogie, baby!', and other like taunts, while the nubile admirers uncrossed and recrossed their woolly-tighted legs, flexed their shoulders, lit cigarettes, and generally endeavoured to be noticed more than not at all.

'Two hundred mikes per cap,' I heard Witch chant, as I hovered outside the circle. 'A quid each, and you won't get better in Deenburgh. Accurate within ten per cent.'

'I'll take twenty, man,' said an androgynous specimen with an ashen complexion, who looked in need of vitamin injections.

'Ten maximum.'

'I've got the bread, man,' whined the androgyne, waving fivers. 'Here.'

Witch shook his head firmly.

'Take it or leave . . .'

Wondering why Witch imposed such low quotas, if he had a hundred-thousand-pound stash of LSD in Querns Castle, I was startled by Tom Redhead pounding the table with his fist and bellowing:

'The man is a mother-fuckin child-murdrin FASCIST, for Christ's sake.'

'Right on,' said a seedy yesman.

'Whose definition of "fascism", Tom?' an antagonist challenged.

'Fascism is politically motivated shit-slinging,' said a second.

'Hi, Pete,' Witch greeted me as the androgyne departed. 'Come and join us.'

I squeezed between an admirer's woolly knees and a mountain of coats, flying jackets, scarves and duffel bags piled against the wall. Feeling like a koala bear at a chimpanzee's tea party, I manoeuvred into the vacant chemical supplicant's seat on Witch's left.

'Howdy, Mr Squirrell,' he said amiably. 'What can I sell you?'

'A cassette player, please.'

'Wrong again, old son. I'm going to *buy* you a cassette player.'

'But I thought . . .'

'And if you don't like it,' he said implacably, 'you can give it to Oxfam when . . .'

'Tostow raps on about how the West must stem the spread of communism in south-east Asia,' Tom Redhead ranted like a presidential nominee, his eyebrows raised like arcs of a hairy tangerine. 'Yet who's to say he ain't a fuckin communist himself? Ah? And where's he from anyhow? Hungary? Czecho . . .'

'Cool it, Tom,' came from down the tea party. 'Either you do him for fascism, *or* you do him for communism. You can't have it every which way.'

'How would it be,' Witch asked me and the nearest admirer quietly, 'if sociology were renamed ismology, and philosophy were renamed ologyology?'

'Out of sight, Witch,' the admirer enthused.

'Good day to you, Rector,' said a new voice behind us.

Dr Tostow, Professor and Mother Galton were holding cups of coffee in the manner of lecturers disappointed not to have found a free table. Galton, large and rugged, with milky blue eyes and swept-back white hair, was in his customary tweed jacket and puffing clouds of blue smoke from his pipe. His wife, our department's Learning specialist, was known as Mother Galton partly on account of her own six children, but also because of her fussingly maternal approach to directing our studies. She was a huge, coarsely puce woman, like a mammoth fallopian tube with spectacles, on whom all garments resembled pregnancy smocks.

Dr Tostow was dressed, as almost always, in a corduroy suit, which today was dark green over a pale lemon shirt and matching green tie.

'Fuck you, Tostow,' Tom Redhead snarled stoutly.

Galton's milky eyes turned glassy.

'I think, Ivan,' he suggested, 'we might have better luck round the corner. Come along, Muriel.'

He and Mother Galton waddled away, like two fat pigeons in a garden of chattering sparrows.

Dr Tostow lingered, his cold smile playing over the tea party before fastening on Witch and myself.

Sensing more Rectorial abuse about to explode from Redhead, Witch turned and engaged Tom in diversionary conversation.

'Hello, Peter,' said Dr Tostow.

'Hello, Dr Tostow.'

'Okay for Thursday?'

'Yes. I've written my paper, and Deirdre's . . .'

'Good. Also could you stay on for five minutes afterwards? I would like to discuss your research application to Cambridge.'

'Yes of course, Dr Tostow.'

He nodded knowingly, then departed.

I finished my coffee and heard Tom Redhead protest:

'Okay, Witch. You think pig harrassment of shit-heads is a more serious problem than secrecy of information and political indoctrination, that's great. But *you* write about it, man. Not me. Write me a thousand words and I'll publish it, man. Sure thing. Okay?'

'Maybe I will,' said Witch. 'But you . . .'

Behind us a burly voice sang:

> Hail, the conquering hero comes:
> All bend over and bare your bums!
> Ho . . .
> And I'll get by with a little hemp from my friends.

'Hi, Beano,' Witch greeted him. 'Knocked off early?'

'Noman,' Beano looned, like a big black grizzly bear in a polar parka, 'has knocked me off. But the fu-fu-fu king heating in our building's broke down, ken, and in this weather *it just isn't on*!'

'No kidding?'

'And Harriet's bullied me into going for tickets for the Janie Carmen concert.'

'Now there,' said Witch, rising and rummaging in the coat mountain, 'I might save you some pennies.'

'How's that?'

'Simon Darling's doing the promotion. Should be worth a few comps.'

'Darling Simon, eh? Kiss-kiss! You sure, Witch?'

'Save your money, old son. Do me a favour instead? Take

these books back to the flat. Pete and I are off to buy toys from SuperFi.'

As we crunched along the footprinted pavement snow, me in my duffelcoat and brogues, Witch in his Afghan sheepskin jacket and fur-lined Canadian lumberboots, he said:

'That Dr Tostow?'

'What about him?'

'Bit of a weirdo.'

'In what way?'

'The author of *Erewhon Three* just has to be weird. All that tripe about the Critical Intelligence being Curator of the Universe. Sick.'

'Somebody has to care about maintaining standards,' I said coldly.

'Is he a good teacher?'

'He's all right.' Actually Dr Tostow had too many theoretical axes to grind, but I was damned if I would run him down in front of Witch.

'Isn't it hard to take someone who looks so ridiculously like Groucho Marx seriously?'

'I hadn't noticed.'

'I love this town, you know,' Witch exclaimed suddenly, indicating with a possessive wave the broad, library-lined King David Bridge, which we were following towards the High Street. 'Don't you?'

'Not particularly.'

'What do you know of its history?'

'Very little.'

'Same here. But that's excusable in me.'

'Why?'

'It's my town, Pete. To be at ease anywhere, especially in a historic city like Deenburgh, you have to *know* the place. You can either know it from the inside or the outside. Or both. I know Deenburgh from the inside, so I'm excused knowing it from the outside. You know it from neither the inside nor the outside, so you don't feel at ease here, which prevents you from loving the place. You can't love what you don't know.'

The sun had long set, but the clean white snow on the streets and rooftops was preserving a thin late daylight. The road had yet to be snowploughed, and the only traffic was the occasional adventurous taxi with chains on its wheels. My unloving gaze was arrested on the northern skyline by the Slavic dome of the Royal Bank, silhouetted against the darkening sky like a palace tower in a Grimm fairy tale.

'For example, Pete,' Witch continued, 'know what all good Deenburghers hope for when they die?'

'What?'

'A centrally-heated seaview bungalow with all mod. cons in the Church of Scotland Heaven. And to be remembered for ever on earth by donating a plaqued park bench to King Street Gardens. "Douglas Wishfort died that you might sit, dear friends. Please do not fart upon his memory." '

'And does one have to be born in Deenburgh, to attain such insight?'

'Or live there in good faith for several years. That's what's wrong with travel, Pete. Look at Kant.'

Kant was nowhere to be seen, so I said acidly:

'Your sister Helen tells me, Witch, that travel is most rewardingly done *in the mind*.'

'Can be,' he said, looking down at me curiously, as we passed the Public Library. 'Depends what you believe.'

'And what do you believe?'

He was silent for a moment, debating whether a Squirrell brain was a fit receptacle for a witchdoctor's wisdom. Then he said:

'I believe the dragon is a dancer.'

'Really?'

'That's a Wishfort variation on the Vedantic *Tat Twam Asi*.'

'Which means what, in English?'

'This is thyself. Love thy neighbour *as* thyself. Meaning, love thy neighbour because he *is* thyself. Multiplicity, individuality, personality . . . all are illusion. Not only does the bell toll for thee, but it is thyself that swingeth on the bell-rope. With me?'

Being not unaware of the Maharishi vogue, the Timothy Leary jingles and the Alan Watts industry, I said:

'But surely, Witch, these are somewhat glib and popular notions.'

He adjusted the purple woolly hat on the crown of his long fair hair, and argued:

'Take the proposition "John Lennon exists". How many people subscribe to its truth?'

'Millions. So what?'

'So some popular propositions are true. So unpopularity has no monopoly on truth. So the careless slur, Pete, that you just cast on my belief in the Vedic *Tat Twam*, outlined by me at your invitation, is not well grounded. That's what.'

Irritated, I retorted:

'And that's why you peddle drugs, is it? To fill a gap in the mystical enlightenment market?'

'Pedalling, old son, is for bicycles,' Witch said quietly. 'My merchandise is only for those I want to sell to. I never push, Pete. Be clear about that.'

'Then why sell at all?'

He smiled forgivingly.

'Because I like my image. I enjoy being in demand. In control. I get that from the old man. Terrible, isn't it? His buzz is saving the lives of his patients. Mine is saving the souls of my customers.'

'I thought multiplicity was illusion.'

'Even illusion has a language of its own. And when in Rome you speak Italian. If you can.'

'Why do you have quotas?' I asked, as we turned east down the High Street. 'If saving souls is your goal?'

'Don't take me literally, Pete. Tom Redhead's evils bag is secrecy of information. Mine is state control of consciousness. I think consenting adults should decide for themselves what they experience.'

'But wouldn't you make more money if . . .'

Witch scoffed incredulously as he ushered me into SuperFi.

'I don't make *any* money on it, Pete. I *give it away.* The five caps minimum is because most people are better not tripping alone. And the ten maximum discourages economics undergraduates from reselling at inflated prices.' He chuckled. 'Perhaps they should call me the *wish*doctor.'

'Why?'

'They come to me for the condition of their experience, and I doctor their wishes. One day, maybe, I'll grow out of it. But for now I enjoy taking the gate money. To the Circus of the Dancing Dragon! Care to enter?'

'Where does this dragon come in?'

'Tell you later,' he promised. 'Now, Pete, what can we get you? I think . . .'

The first surly youth in a creased blue suit disappeared into one back room to look for the cassette player Witch said I wanted, and a second surly youth in a creased green suit popped out like a Swiss weatherman from a second back room and said through prolapsed nostrils:

'Are youse twogethere?'

'I am, thanks,' Witch replied. 'And Mr Squirrell is with me.'

TEN

'They're beautiful, Peter,' Cindy said, when I stopped the cassette.

'Really?'

'But why didn't you tell me they were Witch's songs?'

'You recognize his voice?'

'Of course,' she said warmly. Then an ambiguous shadow passed over her lovely face. 'But the last time I heard Witch sing, he was into heavy rock. With Simon Darling. Before . . . HMS Witchcraft broke up.'

'I didn't know him then.' I perched on the arm of my host armchair and looked helplessly at Cindy's enthronement in my guest armchair. All women instinctively sense the mute worship of an ineligible male. Most women then condescend contemptuously, but a few are gracious kindly.

Cindy was one of the few.

She had a high, delicate forehead and fine shoulder-length hair, subtly tinted to the rusty hue of a robin's breast. The only feature she shared with brother Alastair was unflat ears, their pale pink tips peeping through her swirling hair when she turned her head. Her mouth was full and her lips curved outwards like the petals of an azalea, as if constantly about to blow a loving kiss to a favoured sweetheart.

'Why the secrecy?' she insisted, daintily draining her glass of the chilled Moselle that had cost me three pounds.

'Witch didn't want me to have that cassette,' I lied uncomfortably. 'And then he made me promise not to play it to anyone else.'

'Why ever not?'

'He's shy. Doesn't think the songs are good enough.'

'That's not like Witch,' Cindy puzzled. She placed her

empty glass on the coffee table and smoothed her suede skirt over her knees.

'Isn't it?' I asked chokingly, lips twitching. 'I don't know him well, but he's got some obsession about only writing one song. A perfect song. And then giving up. Some more wine?'

'No thanks, Peter.'

'Coffee?'

'Well . . .'

'*Real* coffee,' I urged. 'Not instant.'

'Yes please,' she accepted, laughing pleasantly. 'I can't drink instant, you see. It makes my tummy go funny.'

'How . . .'

'Black and no sugar, please.'

'Right. Coming up.'

'Can I hear the tape again, Peter? While you're making the coffee?'

'Yes, yes. Please do. I'll . . .'

Try not to tell you any more lies, I told the haunted reflection in my shaving mirror, which hung above the sink in my kitchenette. It had all been going so well until the lies, and I began to hate Witch again, for lumbering me with this preposterous situation.

'What am I going to *say* to Cindy?' I asked him twenty-seven hours earlier, as he connected the new Pioneer cassette deck to my record player.

'Tell her she has a lovely bum.'

'*Seriously,* Witch.'

'Get a bottle of decent white wine, and Cindy'll do the talking. Nick one from the old man's cupboard.'

'I can't do that!'

'Then buy one,' he said, grinning like a benevolent fiend in an Indian mythology poster, 'with the change from that taxi money you were so uptight about the other night.'

He also told me I must buy a potted plant for my room, and ask Mrs Wishfort for some means of making *real* coffee. 'Cindy can't drink instant,' he explained. 'It gives her a funny tummy.'

'How do you know so much about Cindy?'

'I've told you, Pete. The Wishforts and the Cameron-Bells are like Deenburghbum and Deenburghbee. Since way back.'

As the coffee filtered, and I arranged biscuits on plates, I reflected that Cindy was the second desirable young woman to visit my parlour within a week. *How long till I get one in my bed?* Earlier, I had spent one hour tidying and hoovering my room, and another hour chiselling the crusted snow from my basement steps. When eventually I heard Cindy's expensively booted feet descending from the street, I wanted to run out to the back garden and jump over the wall into the river. 'Hello,' the rational psychologist said, his tight-lipped eyes taking in the exquisite smile of the stunning young beauty in the doublebreasted Canadian beaver. 'Come along in.'

Back in the coffee-and-biscuits present:

'Shall I put some other music on?'

'That would be nice, Peter. What have you got?'

'It's mainly *B*, I'm afraid. Bach, Beatles, Beethoven. Belhaven TwangGang, would you believe?'

'No thanks, Peter,' Cindy laughed. 'Them I can hear any day.'

'Berlioz . . .'

'*Fantastic Symphony*?'

'Yes.'

'Great.'

Not until I knelt to my Woolworth's twenty-slot record rack between the Stereomaster's legs did I realize: Witch had placed the cassette deck on the lid of the record player, so I couldn't play records without disconnecting the deck.

Which I don't know how to do.

Blushing madly, I turned to my guest and said:

'I wonder . . .'

A confident knock on my parlour door interrupted me.

'Yes?'

In stepped Witch.

His abundant hair was newly washed, he was wearing high-heeled cowboy boots, flared bluejeans, a bell-sleeved chemise in gold-hemmed cream cheesecloth, and looked like a publicity photo for a million-dollar rockband.

'Hello,' Cindy said brightly, 'Witch,' she added hesitantly.

'Hi, Cindy,' Witch returned in genial surprise. 'Fancy meeting you in a place like this.'

'What are you doing here?' I asked him furiously.

He looked perplexed.

'This is my house, Pete,' he explained gently. 'My, parents, *live here*!'

'Yes, but . . .'

'And I've brought your book back.'

'What?'

'Your *Varieties of Orgasmic Experience*,' he said accusingly, pulling it out of the straw shopping basket he was carrying. 'Helen said you need it urgently. Can't think why, though. Pseudo-scientific tripe, if you ask me. But here it is.'

'Can I have a look, Peter?' Cindy requested.

'I really don't think . . .'

'And here,' said Witch, dipping again in his basket, 'is a present from Helen and me. For the inconvenience we've caused you.'

'That's really not . . .'

Witch produced a bottle of wine and, observing the nearly empty bottle on my coffee table, said:

'Ah. Moselle. Snap. Spot more?' he offered Cindy and me together.

'No thanks,' I said discouragingly. 'We're having coffee.'

'Great idea, Pete. Me too.' Then:

'Well, well, Cindy. A secret lover in the basement of Number Ten?! What will Othello say?' He spoke in fun, but Cindy sat stiffly. The flush of some emotional arousal had sabotaged her Estée Lauder cool.

'It's nothing like that, Witch,' she said tightly. 'Peter asked me down to listen to some songs. That's all.'

'Oh? Whose songs?'

'*Your* songs,' I barked aggressively, determined to explode his silly charade. 'Which you asked . . .'

'*My* songs?' he echoed, fixing me with an icy stare. 'But you promised, Pete. You *promised* not to play them to anyone.'

Words were failing me when Cindy said:

'Don't be angry, Witch. Peter thought I might like the songs for the TwangGang. And he's right. I think they're fantastic.'

'No kidding? You're not just saying that to stop me being heavy with Pete?'

'Truly, Witch,' she emphasized, her emerald eyes glowing orange with earnestness as she looked up at him. 'Specially the ones about the Indian girl. I've heard them twice now, and I'm determined to sing them.'

Witch looked pleased, puzzled and bashful.

'Well, that's different. If you're sure?' He beamed at Cindy as if his heart would break if she now changed her mind.

I couldn't bear the weight of his deceit any longer, so I said:

'I'll make some more coffee, shall I?'

'Great idea, Pete. Black with a spoonful of honey, please.'

'Not for me, Peter. But I wouldn't mind another glass of wine.'

'I'll pour it,' said Witch, dismissing me.

In the kitchen I took longer than possible over brewing the coffee. A terrible conviction was gelling in those parts of me where terrible convictions gel that there had been more previous *commerce* between Witch and Cindy than he had admitted. It was bad enough that he should pose in the nude for Helen, but if he had also bedded Cindy . . . hypothetical rage, envy and sexual hatred started steaming in my bowels.

And boiled for the next hour, as Witch and Cindy chatted in a revivingly familiar key.

While I looked on.

Witch hoped the TwangGang's datesheet was prosperously full?

Quite good, Cindy said. A two-week tour starting next Saturday, and Simon Darling had rung up only that morning to book them as supporting act for the Janie Carmen concert in March.

That was quite a score, wasn't it?

Indeed it was, and Othello would be delighted, when he returned tomorrow.

How abouts sales of their first album?

Not fantastic, but good enough for the record company to

want demos for a follow-up. That's what Othello had gone to London to discuss.

But wouldn't Othello object to the TwangGang using Witch's songs? Othello didn't like Witch very much, did he?

'It isn't that, Witch. Truly,' Cindy said anxiously. 'But he is quite possessive about Othello Music publishing all the material the band records.'

That was no problem, Witch assured her. Othello Music was welcome to publish any of Witch's songs that the Twang-Gang might record. Not only that, but Witch could also offer Othello free recording time for the band's new demos: save him a few hundred pounds, if he wanted.

Othello would be delighted, Cindy was sure.

'Like a gelded weasel,' Witch murmured to me while Cindy went to the loo. 'But he won't say No to the free demos.'

'Why not?'

'He's greedy, Pete. If I give him free studio time, he can pocket a big chunk of the advance he'll get from the record company. See? Money makes his eyes go round.'

'Why doesn't he like you?'

'I'm a better man than he is,' Witch said objectively. 'But also because, once upon a time, as I expect you've now guessed, it used to be Loins between me and Cindy. Very unnerving for a rat like Othello. Sorry I didn't explain that earlier, Pete. Read *Tom Sawyer* yet?'

'Certainly not.'

'You'll forgive me when you do,' he said confidently.

There was something irresistible about orgasmic experience that year. When Witch had helped her into her coat, before driving her home in the sports car he had parked in Buttbridge Place (the nearest street to have been snowploughed), Cindy smiled at me engagingly and, picking Whitman & Nixon off the coffee table, said:

'Do you think, Peter, I could borrow this? Just for a day or two?'

Tensing to snatch it away from her, I said:

'It is due back, actually. So . . .'

'That's okay, Pete,' Witch said opulently. 'I'll pay the fine.'

ELEVEN

Ivan Stanislas Tostowski (his wife later told me) was born in 1923 in a small town twenty miles from Warsaw. He was an only child, an identical twin brother having died at birth. By the time of his confinement and forced labour in the Warsaw Ghetto, Dr Tostow had completed the first months of his medical studies. He survived the Ghetto rebellion in 1943 (in which thousands of others, including his parents, were killed) and was held in the Dzielna concentration camp until the approach of the Red Army in 1944.

The liberating Russians kept him in an internment camp for a year, during which time he came to loathe with a fearsome intensity anything remotely associated with communism. Released in 1946, he made his way to Berlin, where he hoped to lodge with relations while completing his education. But his uncle and aunt had fled to America at the beginning of the war, and were now running a drapery business in New York. Could he join them? Yes, they would be glad to have him, provided Uncle Sam agreed. The authorities in Berlin gave him an IQ test and a political orientation questionnaire, and his performance evidently satisfied them as to his suitability for eventual American Citizenship.

Having paid his way by working part-time for his uncle, Dr Tostow was awarded his MD by Columbia University in 1951. For the next three years he served his psychiatric residency in the University of Chicago Clinics, then did research in clinical psychology at the University of California at Berkeley, receiving his PhD in 1959. In 1960 he came to England to lecture in Personality Assessment at the University of Oxford. There, in 1962, he met and married Anita Atterbom (only daughter of a wealthy Stockholm businessman), who was studying at a secretarial school.

Soon the Tostows returned to America, where he became consultant clinical psychologist to the Louisiana State Foundation For Procreational Research, under the direction of Vernon G. Whitman, MD, and Ms Ursula F. Nixon, Whitman's domestic partner and research assistant. Anita never told me precisely when and why Dr Tostow left Louisiana, only that for the following three years he remained free from formal academic ties, in order to travel, write up a prodigious flurry of research papers, and complete his two utopian novels. These were soundly reviled by the literary establishment (for their atrocious style) and by the liberal establishment (for their abominable political proclivities), but they sold well, and film rights for the second, *Erewhon Three*, fetched two hundred thousand dollars.

So it was not the lure of his Scottish lecturer's salary that drew Dr Tostow to Deenburgh, simultaneously with my own arrival, to become director of the newly built sleep laboratory at Queen's Buildings.

What then was his driving motive?

I believe that, more than anything else, it was an insatiable appetite for *control* that drove him. One always felt, talking to him, that a subtle interrogation was taking place beneath the surface of his bland remarks and seemingly innocent questions. Perhaps this began as a defence against his traumatic helplessness in the Ghetto and concentration camp, but it made one uncomfortable in his presence, and unwilling to impart any personal information that could reasonably be withheld. And what sweeter research morsel, for such a man, than the Queen's Buildings experiments on the effects of certain psychotropic drugs on the dreaming patterns of normal postgraduate males?

'Why are you so keen particularly to do your PhD at *Cambridge*, Peter?' he asked me that Thursday afternoon, when Deirdre had departed. 'And not Oxford?'

'It's always been . . .'

'My own connexions, you know, are stronger in Oxford.'

'Mrs Galton told me . . .'

'You will of course need a First,' he told me bluntly.

I nodded uneasily.

'Do you think you will get one?'

'I certainly hope so, Dr Tostow. I am going to work flat-out till Finals.'

'Yes,' drawled his naturalized American accent. 'You should be safe in most papers, but what about Statistics?'

'But I . . .!' Gaping at him in righteous anxiety, for statistical methods were my pride and joy, I saw the ridiculous resemblance to Groucho Marx that Witch had noted two days earlier.

(Nor was this the only time the Deenburgh clan's synaptic antics sabotaged my perception. One Sunday evening that spring, Rosie and I were sitting in the morning room at Number Ten, enjoying Dvorak's *New World Symphony* on the television, when Beano ambled in unwrapping a Mars Bar, listened for a moment, roared with laughter, and sang in tune to Dvorak: 'Fry's Turkish Delight. It tastes like the Emperor's . . .' 'Don't be disgusting, Beano,' said Harriet, smacking him on the back of the head as she followed him into the room.)

Dr Tostow stood up from his desk and turned to the window. His office was on the east side of the eleventh floor of the John Locke Tower, and had a soothing view over half a mile of tenemented town to the dark rocky brows of the Glastonbury Crags. By now the streets were awash with dirty slush, but the gulleys of the crags were still packed white with pristine snow.

To them he said:

'I expect though, Peter, that we should be able to push you through.'

Feeling faintly sick, I sat tight in my plastic tutee's chair.

'You need only first-class marks in five papers, after all, to be awarded on aggregate a First-Class Degree.'

I smiled understandingly till he added:

'Provided that your other three papers come reasonably close. Now,' he rested a brown corduroy thigh on the corner of his desk, 'talking of statistics brings me to another matter.

Your mathematical friend, Mallecho Wishfort?'

'He's not my friend, Dr Tostow.'

'But you do know him?'

'Hardly at all.'

'Correct me if I am wrong, Peter, but I thought I saw you talking to him in the cafeteria. Him and our aptly named Rector friend. Did I not?' His small mouth tightened. He rubbed the tip of his large sharp nose expectantly.

If only it weren't for that moustache, you wouldn't look like Groucho Marx at all. More like . . .

'Yes,' I admitted. 'But . . .'

'And I cannot believe, Peter, that a serious student such as yourself would be interested in the purchase of illegal hallucinogenic chemicals such as Mr Wishfort is a purveyor of reputedly.'

'Certainly not, Dr. Tostow. I mean, I don't know anything . . .'

'I hear he also is something of a ladies' man?'

'Really?'

'Be reasonable, Peter. You live in his mother's house, do you not?'

'If you want information about Mallecho, Dr Tostow, why don't you ask Deirdre? She's his sister.'

Dr Tostow laughed laboriously.

'I wondered when you would say that, Peter. Very well, I shall be open with you. The Open Society is my watchword, after all. Have you read Popper?'

'No.'

'Try him after Finals, perhaps. Now. My problem is this. I have a proposition to put to Mallecho Wishfort. I do not know the gentleman personally, nor does he come under my departmental jurisdiction, and my proposition requires to be put delicately in an informal social situation. Therefore am I obliged to approach him through an intermediary which means either yourself, Peter, or Deirdre.

'And I do not desire Deirdre to become involved. Particularly as she is a girl whereas the situation calls for considerable discretion. And my judgement is, Peter, that you are a man upon whose discretion I might utterly rely?'

Provided your other three papers come reasonably close.

The backs of my hands, cupped tensely round my knees, were white with bloodless nausea.

I nodded.

Dr Tostow went on:

'To invite on my behalf your friend Mallecho, and of course yourself, to dinner with my wife and I at our home on Saturday week? At eight o'clock for nine. When we can informally discuss my proposition which he may consider to his advantage. Will you ask him, Peter?'

'Think he wants to marry me?' Witch inquired on the phone.

'He already has a wife.'

'What's she like?'

'Nice.'

'Big tits?'

'Yes.'

'Okay,' Witch said affably. 'Never sniff at a free meal and big tits. Tell him I'll come. Meet me in Poldy's Bar at seven, and you can gen me up on the tits.'

'Where's Poldy's Bar?'

'Bluebell Street. Turn left at James's The Gun Shop in Castle Street.'

TWELVE

Double-basement flats are not uncommon in New Town Deenburgh. The rooftops descend in chimneyed terraces toward the sea, and in places the slope is steep enough for a south-fronting building to support an extra storey at its rear.

The Tostows' dining room was on such a floor.

It was small and intimate, converted from an original pantry. The sideboard and six-seater rectangular table were of dark oak; a pulley-lamp hung low from the centre of the gold-stippled ceiling; and tastefully framed prints of philosophical Highland cattle chewing stolidly in the mouths of misty valleys, and tweedy Victorian fishermen casting for Salmon on the Spey, and other staunchly Scottish scenes, lined the bottle-green walls.

Here was a room of subtle character, made mellow by the four ornately held candles that alone lit our magnificent dinner. Yet somehow it did not belong to the Tostows. They had taken it over, Highland cows and all, when they bought the house, and they would sell it intact when they departed, before long, to plug like an efficiently sterilized module into the next stage of his earthshrinking career.

'And do you accept, Ivan,' Witch Socratized, taking a rest from his bananas baked in rum and cream, and toying with his glass of sweet Bordeaux, 'that we never naturally use the verb "decide" in continuous tenses? We don't say, for example, "I am deciding to have a joint with my coffee". We say "I have decided to have a joint". We use a perfect tense to report what *has happened*. Right?'

'Arguably,' Dr Tostow conceded, frowning at the head of the table and running a small wrinkled finger round the neck of his white polo sweater.

'And we can't predict our decisions, can we? Not in the same way as we can predict the more obvious quotes actions unquote. Agreed? We can reasonably say "At ten-thirty precisely I will light my joint", but we can't reasonably say "At ten-thirty precisely I will *decide* to light my joint". That wouldn't make sense, would it?'

'Why not?'

'It's self-contradictory. If you *could* know exactly what you were going to decide, and precisely when, you would *already* have decided. Wouldn't you?' Witch asked Anita suddenly.

She smiled at him through her wineglass, and shrugged her bare shoulders modestly.

'Go on,' said Dr Tostow, who was following the argument but not enjoying it. 'Witch,' he added, having heard me use the nickname.

'I think, Ivan,' Witch retorted kindly, 'you'd better stick to "Mallecho". At least until we've discussed your mysterious proposition.'

'Very well,' Dr Tostow said heavily. It was clear that Witch and he detested each other, but Witch had a superior talent for expressing his detestation charmingly.

'Another important consideration,' he said, 'is that decisions happen very much faster than anything we can credibly call actions.'

'Do they?'

'Yes. They do.'

'Can you prove it? Mallecho.'

'I can strongly suggest it. Ivan. In that we can never catch ourselves *in the act* of deciding. Whereas with quotes actions unquote, even very fast ones, such as pulling the trigger of a gun, we can catch ourselves in the middle and think "Aha. Here I am pulling this trigger".

'Conscious thought, in other words, can outpace my action. Yet we're unable to stop and think "Here am I deciding to light my joint". Deciding, therefore, is faster than conscious thought, which strongly suggests it is not an action. Assuming that anything is an action, properly speaking, which it isn't. Though that's a different issue.'

'And what does all this demonstrate?'

'Merely, Ivan, that decisions – or, more accurately, *decidings* – are not events within our control. A deciding is an *accident* as far as conscious volition is concerned: a catastrophic shift from dynamic imbalance to static equilibrium. After it we feel a release from tension, so we imagine that we have *taken* or *made* a decision freely and deliberately.'

'And so we have,' Dr Tostow said pugnaciously.

'Not at all,' said Witch airily. 'Freedom of the individual will is a delusion. A fantasy. Though undeniably a useful survival mechanism. Which is why all that talk in your *Erewhon Three* about the Western World's unique privilege in possessing Freedom of Choice is, at a philosophical level, utter nonsense. If you don't mind my saying so.' Smiling evenly at Dr Tostow, Witch stroked his beard and added:

'I expect the CIA bought a copy, though. What do you think, Pete? A tightly straining condom on an enormous black man's member suddenly bursts. A moment before it bursts the condom becomes conscious. Does it, or does it not, imagine that it bursts of its own free will?'

'I'm not sure I agree with you,' I muttered hotly.

'That's the trouble with you social scientists,' Witch pronounced amicably. 'Isn't it, Anita? They're never sure. They never think. No wonder . . .'

'Psychology is *not* a social science,' Dr Tostow said thickly.

'Too true,' Witch said emphatically. 'It's highly antisocial. I was reading the other day about Watson and Little Albert: how Watson turned Little Albert's particular fondness for white rats into a pathological aversion. And it made me want to . . .'

His flow dried up as his gaze rose over my shoulder. Ingrid (the fat, button-nosed, tightly pigtailed girl who was serving us) appeared in the velvet-curtained doorway that connected the dining room and kitchen and spoke in Swedish with Anita.

'Would anybody like cheese?' Anita asked us. 'Or fruit?'

'Cheese, please,' for me.

'I might manage a tangerine,' said Witch.

For twenty minutes we picked at biscuits and Camembert, biscuits and Stilton, Satsumas and grapes, sipped the vintage Madeira Dr Tostow poured from a Tantalus decanter on the sideboard, and I made a determined effort to involve Anita in the conversation.

The meal had been superb, I assured her. Fillet steak *marchand de vin* had taken on a whole new meaning in my eyes.

It was kind of me to say so, she said.

Did she know I'd never eaten oysters before?

Then she was glad to contribute a new taste to my education, which, unlike her husband, unfortunately, she was unlikely to benefit academically.

Was Ingrid related to her, I wondered.

No, she had recruited Ingrid at the Swedish Institute, which was very active in Deenburgh. She liked to get a girl in occasionally, to help with dinner parties, especially when her dress . . .

Again she shrugged her bare shoulders.

I nodded understandingly.

She was wearing a taffeta gown of pearly white that flowed like a wedding dress from waist to ankle and flowered up and out from her bosom like the bowl of a rococo fountain. The bust looked like a chain of white roses that the slightest breeze or fondling touch would sunder and send fluttering to the ground. A necklace of beads the colour of hot blood was drawn into a V over the toast-gold skin of her breast by the weight of a pendant in the form of a silver trident, with sparkling ruby tips. Her ear-rings matched the pendant, and her hair was swept up and loosely clasped on the top of her head like the Nordic-blonde crown of a viking queen that berserker warriors would have died for a hundred times.

Personally I wouldn't have stretched to dying, but her worldly womanly beauty made the Squirrell lungs feel they had just inhaled a brace of scorpions, while the Squirrell penis retracted into a soft cocoon of castration sensations, there to nurse its felt inability to pay due homage to such a beauty's charms.

What I'm trying to convey to you, really, is the unsuitedness of Anita's revealing attire that night to the draining of new Cyprus potatoes in the kitchen.

'I think,' Dr Tostow said to his wife, when Ingrid had poured our coffee, and he had topped up our Madeira glasses, 'that Ingrid perhaps can go now.'

Anita called through to the kitchen in Swedish.

Ingrid departed.

Dr Tostow offered Witch and myself cigars.

I declined.

'Try one of mine, Ivan,' Witch invited him, producing from a breast pocket of his silver-buttoned denim jacket a hand-stitched leather cigar case. From this he took a neatly rolled four-inch reefer. He offered it benignly round the company and, meeting with universal head-shaking, said sadly to Anita:

'But you don't mind if I do, do you?'

The crimson gull wings of her upper lip arched.

'Please do, Mallecho,' she said.

'Now, Mallecho,' Dr Tostow proceeded, puffing a smokescreen out of his fat Havana corona. 'I expect you are curious to hear my proposition?'

'Not really, Ivan,' Witch said, contentedly inhaling.

'Are you not interested?'

'Not madly.'

Dr Tostow frowned.

'But how can you *know* you are not interested, in your own epistemological terms, when you do not know what I have to say?'

'But I do know.'

'Oh? What did Peter tell you?'

'He said you wanted to marry me.'

'I said *no such thing*, Witch.'

Witch said gravely to Anita:

'He did, you know. He's quite a naughty Squirrell really. His secret nickname's *Nutkins*.'

She sipped her coffee, and her chinablue eyes regarded

Witch with an intensity of puzzled interest that made my wine-numbed senses sure she was the most ravishingly beautiful woman in the world. I have often found this: that the warm propinquity of one great beauty that one must not touch will purge the mind of all the absent others – just as, listening to Berlioz, one forgets Bach and Beethoven. So, while I worshipped the pearly presence of Dr Tostow's wife that night, Helen Wishfort and Cindy Bell might just as well have been bug-eyed green monsters in the primordial slime of another galaxy.

'Of course, Mallecho,' Dr Tostow said sharply, 'if seriously you are not . . .'

'No, no,' said Witch. 'Only kidding. One of my bad habits. Comes from the company I keep. Every Christmas, at dinner, me mam reminds me of the awful fate of the boy who cried *Wolff*! Fire away, therefore, Ivan. I won't interrupt.'

'You will have heard,' Dr Tostow assumed, 'about my recent experiments at Queen's Buildings on the effects of certain psychotropic drugs on the dreaming patterns of normal postgraduate males.'

'Tom Redhead's told me all about them.'

'No doubt. And you also may know of my earlier involvement in the Whitman and Nixon Procreational Research program in Louisiana?'

'Not the Whitman and Dallas Intergalactic Communication program in . . .'

'You said you would not interrupt!'

'Just a passing cross-cultural grapnel, Ivan. Please go on.'

'We have in mind to extend both projects into an investigation into the possible use of similar psychotropic chemicals as therapeutic aids in the clinical treatment of orgasmic malfunction.'

'Which chemicals?'

'Cannabis, psilocybin, and possibly mescalin.'

'Not acid?' Witch asked nonchalantly, though I could tell his interest was engaged.

'We would not rule out that possibility,' Dr Tostow replied evasively.

‘Acid and hash I can get you,’ said Witch. ‘Top quality. Mescalin maybe, though I couldn’t vouch for the dosage. Psilocybin you’ll have to get elsewhere.’

Dr Tostow’s moustache widened in a superior smile.

‘That is kind of you, Mallecho. But obtaining the chemicals is not my problem. I have a licence.’

‘Then what do you want from me?’

‘I need a volunteer for a feasibility study preliminary to a full-scale investigation.’

‘Using dope as a treatment for orgasmic malfunction?’

‘Correct.’

‘Generous of you to think of me, Ivan,’ Witch said acidulously. ‘But actually there’s nothing wrong with my orgasms. Thanks all the same.’ He’d had a lot to drink, starting with three Pils lagers in Poldy’s, and flush patches like small strawberries had appeared on the knuckles of his cheekbones.

‘So I assumed,’ Dr Tostow said urbanely. ‘But not everyone is so fortunate, and the feasibility study will require one normal partner and another whose orgasmic achievements have so far been inadequate.’

‘Inadequate for whom?’

‘For the patient whose life thus is underfulfilled.’

‘So what you’re saying, Ivan, is that you want me to smoke dope with and then screw the arse off some orgasmically substandard female? All in scrupulously monitored laboratory conditions – of course!’

Dr Tostow’s nod suggested pain at Witch’s parlance.

‘And who,’ Witch asked curiously, stubbing his joint in the ashtray beside his host’s cigar, ‘is the fortunate floozy?’

Dr Tostow didn’t understand.

‘Who do I get to shag?’ Witch explained.

There was a high-voltage pause before Dr Tostow soberly said:

‘The orgasmically deficient partner for the preliminary study will be my wife.’

I wished I could vaporize.

Even Witch was flabbergasted. He stared at Anita incredulously.

She smiled at him with a fixed, rather doll-like smile, like a great big beautiful white rabbit in a laboratory cage.

'Is he serious?' Witch asked.

'Yes,' she replied huskily.

And if my experience of life had been broader, I would have realized she was already sexually excited.

'Anita,' Dr Tostow expanded, 'never yet has achieved orgasm during coition. Only before or after, by means of manual or . . . other forms of stimulation.'

'That's a shame, Ivan,' Witch said sympathetically. 'You should write to *Men-It-Can-Be-Done*.'

'The age-old Penile Misconception, Mallecho, definitively is now discredited.'

'Not exposed?'

'Between the size of a man's penis and the orgasmic achievements of his partner the correlation coefficient virtually is zero.'

'Wait till Harriet hears this,' Witch said to me with a wink.

'Some studies even have produced results indicative of a *negative* correlation.'

'Less cock on Beano equals more orgasms in Harriet?'

'That is the statistical position.'

'Oh, Napoleon, where art thou now?' Witch said to Anita, inspecting her with python eyes.

'Additionally is it the case,' Dr Tostow hurried on, evidently keen to withdraw his own sexual prowess from the shadow cast by Witch's doubt, 'that while a volunteer subject in Louisiana Anita repeatedly experienced relations with some dozen partners, of whom two possessed penes considerably beyond the norm. While three were female, and possessed of no penes at all.'

'This is amazing, Ivan,' Witch told him. 'Do you *like* watching other men fuck your wife?'

Dr Tostow sighed and relit his cigar. The room was blue from its smoke, and green with the sweetness of Witch's oxydized cannabis.

'Of course, Mallecho, if seriously you are not interested or do not find my wife attractive . . .'

'You knew fine I'd find her attractive . . .'

'Thank you, Mallecho,' Anita said graciously.

'But why me? Why not Pete?' Witch inquired, pointing at me like a farmer at a cattle auction.

Yes, damn it all. Why not me?

'There is no question of an undergraduate being used,' said Dr Tostow. 'We have a ruling from the Senate.'

'Then why not someone from your dreams experiments?'

'Particularly due to the participation of my wife, Professor Galton wishes the other subject to come from outside our own department. And we ideally require a male orgasmic normal with established non-aversion to the class of drugs we propose to test.'

Witch chewed on his lower lip, looked speculatively at Anita, stood up abruptly, and walked round the table to the sideboard, behind Dr Tostow.

Dr Tostow flinched as though expecting Witch to assault him.

Witch returned to his seat, sniffing at a second decanter.

'Anyone for brandy?'

We all accepted.

Dr Tostow offered to get brandy glasses.

Witch told him not to bother – the empty Madeira glasses would do.

'Where,' he then inquired, 'would these drug-crazed bouts of intercourse take place?'

'In my Queen's Buildings sleep laboratory.'

'When?'

'Two nights per week. By arrangement.'

Witch lit another reefer, leant back in his seat, balancing it on its back legs, and said to the Highland cows on the wall:

'If time is infinite, as our *a priori* intuition dictates, and if space is finite, as Einstein informs us, and if matter is finite, as it must be if space is finite, and if the possible modes of combination of matter are finite, as our present knowledge of physics suggests, then every possible configuration of matter has already occurred an infinite number of times.'

Dr Tostow frowned and said:

'What has this to do with my proposition?'

'It implies, Ivan, that you have already asked me, an infinite number of times, to jump on Anita. And that I have accepted an equal number of times, if it is possible for me to accept. And conversely, if it is only possible for me to refuse.'

I could feel that Witch's abstractions were making Anita anxious.

There was irritation and dislike in Dr Tostow's voice when he said:

'There will be a modest *payment* for your services, Mallecho. The project fund . . .'

'Fuck you, Ivan,' Witch said calmly. 'I don't know what's in it for you, but I'll smoke your dope, I'll drop your mescalin, I'll happily hump your wife if you want me to, *but I won't take a penny for it*.'

'That would be highly irregular,' Dr Tostow said obstinately. 'The normal procedure is for research volunteers to receive a payment. This helps to standardize relationships.'

Suddenly it appeared that Dr Tostow's refusal to allow Witch to have sex with Anita for free might cost him his male orgasmic normal.

Witch said:

'What's the rate?'

'One pound per hour.'

'Two pounds per hour, and a ten-pound bonus for every orgasm Anita has during copulation,' Witch stipulated. 'Payable to Oxfam.'

Dr Tostow didn't like this, but he nodded.

'Then I'll do it, Ivan. On one condition.'

'What?'

Witch's flickering eyes played over Anita as he said:

'The investigation begins tonight. Here. In twenty minutes.'

Anita gave a little gasp that was almost a moan.

'That is out of the question,' Dr Tostow snapped furiously.

'Why? The introduction to *The Varieties of Orgasmic Experience* describes in detail the informal compatibility encounters that preceded the clinical feasibility studies. Relaxed personal contacts in pleasant environments, with dim lighting and tasteful music. Well, that's exactly what we've got here – assuming you do have some tasteful music?' Witch threw at Dr Tostow, presumably as a comment on the Frank Sinatra record we heard during cocktails.

To Anita, Witch added:

'How about Ravel's *Bolero*, Mrs Tostow? That's good fucking music.'

'Quite impossible,' Dr Tostow barked.

'Take it or leave it, Ivan. I don't care.'

Occasionally, in a tense social situation, a man and woman who have lived together for many years will exchange a glance that communicates in a second more emotional information than can be found in an Irish lady's novel.

Such a glance now flashed between the Tostows.

Hooding the vitriolic displeasure in his weak black eyes, Dr Tostow declared:

'Very well, Mallecho. As you wish.'

'I will go and square up the bedroom,' Anita said nervously, pushing back her chair.

'Take it easy,' Witch directed, passing her his reefer. 'Have a drag on this first.'

When in due course the orgasmic research team went upstairs to commence their labours, I attempted to escape, pleading weariness and a heavy work schedule the following day. But Dr Tostow would not hear of it, and for what seemed like a week in an interrogation cell I sat drinking whisky with him in his sitting room, failing to feign interest in his excruciating monologue on the practical irrelevance of philosophical analysis to psychology, while booming from the hall, where Witch had placed the Tostows' hifi speakers, came the successive sounds of Ravel's *Bolero*, Rossini's *William Tell Overture*, and Beethoven's *Ninth Symphony*. I had just decided to leave the moment the *Ninth* was over, even if it did cost my First, when a naked shoulder and rumpled head of sweat-damp tresses appeared round the door.

'Hey, IVAN?' Witch bellowed through a lascivious leer.
'Uh? What?'
'You owe Oxfam twenty-two pounds.'

THIRTEEN

The next two weeks took us into the milder weather and longer days of early March, and I didn't see much of Witch during that time.

He had his business interests to attend to, the first of his recording sessions with Cindy and the TwangGang, his twice-weekly orgasmic nights with the Tostows, all on top of his work on Kant for Professor Quelch. For me such a schedule would have been impossible. One of my requirements of life is eight hours' sleep a night, whereas Witch seemed to thrive on five. He worked extremely fast at whatever he was doing, and he possessed an uncanny capacity for concentration amid distraction. He could switch and aim his attention like the beam of the torch he shone round my basement twice a week, when he came down to transact with his dope Thermos in my cellar.

One night I was still up, plodding through Freud's *Psychopathology of Everyday Life* in preparation for my General Essay Paper, so I opened my window and invited him in.

Over cocoa I asked him:

'How come you Wishforts all work so easily?'

'Eee Gee?'

'You reading Kant while listening to The Doors.'

'What about it?'

'I couldn't do that.'

'You interested in Kant, Pete?'

'Not really.'

'You like The Doors?'

'No.'

'So where's the mystery? Do you enjoy your work?'

'Yes.'

'I'm not sure you do, old son. If a man finds his work congenial, his concentration is drawn to it like iron filings to a magnet. That's a tautology, admittedly, but not an uninformative one.'

He didn't mention his orgasmic progress with Anita, so I didn't inquire. His earlier casual admission of sometime Loins between him and Cindy had so inflamed me that I couldn't bear to hear him brag about whatever genital records he was breaking with Anita. I did comment, however, on the rarity of hip jargon and obscenity in his speech, relative to most of his long-haired, switched-on and far-out contemporaries.

'Hardly surprising, Pete,' he explained. 'All that rap is just a badge. For kids to wear who feel insecure that deep down they don't really belong to the club the badge says they belong to. Like *Tune In, Turn On, Drop Your Trousers*. Yeah?'

I nodded.

'When most of the creeps that tell you to do it have never done it themselves. Whereas I've done it and I don't feel insecure, so I don't need the badge. That's not entirely true. Sometimes I *do* feel insecure, but I've learned not to mind the feeling. Satisfied?'

Not completely.

I mean that occasional immaturities would remind one that, for all the rumour-ballooning esteem in which he was held by the eighteen-year-olds in the John Locke cafeteria, Witch was not very long out of tortured adolescence himself. This was evident in his silly habit, a relic from the pimply days when he and Beano and Simon Darling were the nucleus of The Witchdoctor's Nosebone, of always answering the telephone in a disconcerting manner.

For example:

On the second Wednesday of that fortnight, I was sitting on the vast Victorian sofa in the morning room, having tea and chocolate cake with Helen, Rosie and Panda, willing Rosie to depart for a walk with Panda, so that I might fall to my knees on the heirloom Wilton carpet and protest with passion my undying admiration for Helen.

When suddenly:

We heard the front door open.

The telephone started to ring.

Panda bounded from the room, his flailing tail swiping the chocolate cake as he passed the tea trolley.

Rosie jumped up, squealing:

'I'll get it, I'll get it, I'll . . .'

'Shut your face, Rosie,' said Helen.

The receiver in the hall was picked up.

And Witch's voice said:

'Buttbridge Abattoir speaking. Whom do you wish slaughtered?'

'. . .'

'Hi there, Fuckphiz. Hammer hanging straight today?'

'. . .'

'Oh,' said Witch in a subdued tone. 'Sorry about that, Mr . . . thought you were . . . I'll just see . . . DAD?'

'He's not in yet,' shouted Helen.

'No,' Witch's voice relayed. 'I'm afraid . . . take a message?'

'. . .'

'Okay. I'll tell him. Bye.' Witch hung up and there was a pause while he scribbled on the message pad. When he arrived in the morning room he said:

'Bloody thing,' bent over the trolley and felt the teapot.

'Who was that?' Helen asked.

'Missed Her Hangus Hangusson of the Bee Bee Sea.'

'Why?'

'Wants the old man for a documentary on road accidents. Thought it was Beano arsing about with a funny voice. Hi, Pete. Rosie, dearest?'

'Yeee-es?'

'Want to make your dearest brother a fresh pot of tea?'

'No.'

'He'll give you a nife big wet kiff on the mouff if you do.'

'Don't want a nasty big wet kiss on the mouth.'

'And he won't let you watch *Blue Peter* if you don't.'

'Oh, *all right,*' the youngest sister screamed furiously.

Afternoon tea in the morning room was an ancient ritual at Number Ten, and it seemed that I was as welcome as anyone else. The first Wishfort home after four o'clock put the kettle on, and for the next hour any number of Deenburgh stalwarts, from Rosie's thumbsucking schoolchums to Mr Hamilton the neighbourly geriatric fascist, might drift in for a stimulating cuppa and chat whenever Rosie could be persuaded that Big Girls who wore bras were not supposed to watch Children's Hour.

It was a high-ceilinged, groundfloor room, of a comfortable yet cosy size. The sofa was matched by two enormous armchairs, and there were two smaller easy chairs, plus an ex-piano stool covered in tigerskin, all in a crescent round the gun-metal stove and the large colour television, which sat, to the right of the window, on a corner of the waist-high bookcasing. The window looked out to the long back garden, with the River Lethe murmuring past its bottom wall, and in summer one could lean out and pick fruit from the upper branches of a prosperous pear tree.

Surrounding the fire was a high marble mantelpiece, and on its ends sat two fat wally dugs in garish china. Between these goggle-eyed sentinels stood all the birthday, anniversary and assorted invitation cards that a popular middle-class family accumulates, and hung on the wall above the cards was a water-colour painting of Querns Mill cottage in May, as viewed from the castle across the River Teen, with blossom blazing in the garden, and four white doves on the chimney stack above the long red roof.

'Who painted that?' I asked Helen one afternoon.

She looked at me coldly, tucked her tightly jeaned legs under her bottom, opened her tobacco tin on the broad flat arm of her big brown chair, and said shortly:

'Mummy.'

'It's very good.'

'Yes. Isn't it? She's a better painter than I am. So's Witch. It's very depressing. Would you like to pour me some more tea, please, Peter?'

I'd heard from Witch that Helen and Cindy didn't get on,

and I used this to tease from Helen the first fitting pieces in my puzzle over the sometime Loins.

'Cindy's certainly *nice* enough,' Helen admitted with a sniff. 'But so's a Scotch mist.'

'How . . .'

'Thick and wet.'

'You mean she didn't go to university?'

'Cindy went to Murphy Hall College of Education. She's a qualified *primary teacher*. Nuff said, Peter?'

Cindy's mother had been schooled at St David's with Mrs Wishfort. Her father, now Sir William Cameron-Bell, was a generation older than his wife. He was a career diplomat, and spent his later years in the Far East. As soon as their son Alastair was old enough he was boarded with relations in Deenburgh and sent to the Academy. But Cindy, two years younger than Alastair, and a girl, was taken along to Sir William's final posting in Hong Kong. So she and Witch never met until the Cameron-Bells retired to Deenburgh in the early 1960s, having some years earlier invested in a desirable four-storey Georgian residence in Goldsmith Row.

Witch fell in love with her immediately.

Deirdre had brought her home from school, and they were having tea in the morning room when Witch shambled back from rugby practice with Beano and Simon Darling. He was fourteen, headstrong, with an unpredictable voice and a hundred complexes. She was thirteen, quiet, withdrawn, already pretty, with absolutely no interest in brash spotty boys whose principal expression of deathless devotion was relentless rudeness and oneupmanship.

'Bet you can't name the highest mountain in Australia, Big Bum,' Witch challenged Cindy contemptuously, secretly meaning: *Oh, most Beautiful Princess, why aren't thou enchained in the lofty turret of an Ogre's Castle, that my chivalric intrepidity might rescue thee therefrom, and grant thee succour?*

'Bet you can't either, Pluke-Nose,' Deirdre retorted protectively, in view of Cindy's silent blushes.

'Bet I can.'

'Go on then.'

'Mount Killy Man Giro.'

Cindy became a Good Girl and a St David's Prefect, specializing in choral singing, traditional folk music and country dancing. Meanwhile Witch became a Bad Boy, with special emphasis on truancy, getting drunk on McEwan's Export, and such precocious sexual exploits as befitted the star of The Witchdoctor's Nosebone.

But old family ties and the school-based structure of Deenburgh society brought the Good Girl and the Bad Boy into frequent contact, and underlying the virginal sang-froid that she maintained and the rakish disdain he affected, each was ridiculously in love with the other. He *was* her Knight in Shining Blue Denims, but he was too hog-tied in adolescent attitudes to see it. And she *was* his Perfect White Goddess In The Sky, and remained so until five minutes after she eventually allowed him to penetrate her discriminating body.

(Her actual physical impeccability had fallen when she was nineteen, to an importunate Italian ski instructor in Chamonix, but she'd only had one boyfriend since.)

This long-frustrated Union took place at midnight on the Isle of Nogg, several miles off the Scottish west coast.

Nogg is of a size suitable for purchase by retiring rock superstars or millionaire Dutch businessmen, and Deirdre and Alastair had hired a holiday cottage for the month of August. Numerous friends and relations were invited for odd weeks, contributing cash to the rent and labour to the chores: girls to shop, cook and wash dishes; boys to fetch water from the outside tap, ferry Calor Gas cylinders the mile from the post office, and empty the Elsan toilet as seldom as the girls would let them.

It so happened that Witch's condescending week fell within Cindy's recuperative fortnight. He was taking a break from rehearsals with HMS Witchcraft, prior to the Deenburgh Rock Festival in September, after which the group would disband to work for Finals the following summer. She was nursing a broken heart, since the one serious boyfriend of her life, the deputy head of a primary school where she'd done teaching practice, had emigrated to Kenya without her, to better his standard of living.

The night was warm and cloudless, and the countless stars twinkled with that merry magic unique to a West Highland sky under which one has been drinking McEwan's Export and smoking marijuana. There had been a barbecue on the famous Bleating Beach. Sausages and beefburgers had been fried, breaded, ketchupped and guzzled. Unlikely anecdotes were recounted. Cindy sang *The Great Silkie* with such heart-rending bittersweet poignancy, accompanying herself with a simple arpeggio on a Spanish guitar, while the shallow waves of the incoming tide broke expressively on the long white sands, that, immediately she finished, Beano leapt to his feet, pulled Harriet after him, and rushed into the sea for a bracing skinnydip before he wept.

Another couple followed.

Alastair and Deirdre went strolling along the beach.

Another couple vanished in the opposite direction.

Soon only Cindy and Witch remained by the barbecue fire.

He asked her to sing another song.

She sang another song.

He sang a song.

They talked.

He gently dabbed at the tears that glistened on her cheeks as she spoke of the heartless lover who had abandoned her in favour of a higher salary.

She thanked him.

He kissed her.

She did not resist.

Within minutes he was leading her to the discreet seclusion of the long spiky grass of the dunes that undulated between the beach and the cottage.

And within a month his new Perfect White Goddess In The Sky was Janie Carmen.

The relationship between Witch and Cindy in the year that

followed was very intense sexually.

She was the most beautiful girl he'd ever seduced, and his longing for her had been bottled up for six years. In the months until Christmas, after the Nogg initiation, they spent so much time in bed that even Beano was embarrassed. Not by their exertions, but by the lies he had to tell on the phone, mainly to Cindy's parents.

'Is Lucinda there, George?' her mother once demanded.

'No, Mrs Cameron-Bell,' Beano invented. 'She and Mallecho have gone for a drive in the country.'

'But it's one o'clock in the morning, George.'

'Is it? Gosh! They must have had a puncture.'

That was before Witch bought his house, and he was sharing a rented flat with Beano, Harriet, Simon Darling, and the young Greek waiter who was Simon's latest boyfriend. Cindy was still living in Goldsmith Row, and if she hadn't had to make a door-slamming show of returning home once a day, it seems probable that she and Witch would have parted sooner than they did.

For him it was an achievement.

He'd never before kept a girlfriend longer than four months.

Yet Cindy was simple in heart and mind, and rather conservative with it. She had neither the inclination nor the intellect to share Witch's theoretical interests. And, though she would happily partake of a circulating reefer, she refused pointblank to experiment with LSD. Worse than that, by the Easter before Witch's Finals, she was nagging him to give it up, complaining that it was destroying his mind and estranging her from his affections.

He would point out that she was criticizing something she didn't understand. Not only that, but her constant glum mouth and reproachful eyes were spoiling his trips. A good trip needed a warm and supportive environment, and that included a warm and supportive girlfriend.

Wouldn't she trip with him just once, if she really loved him?

No, she absolutely wouldn't.

Then how could she hope to comprehend his enthusiasm for Indian religion, not to mention his interpretation of the

Pythagorean version of the metempsychosis doctrine?

If you had to take drugs to understand something, Cindy insisted, it wasn't worth understanding.

For the two weeks before his Finals Witch moved back to Number Ten. He wanted to be alone, have maximum peace and quiet, regular meals, and practise getting up early and being alert by nine o'clock. His maths papers were on a Thursday and Friday, with his physics papers the following Monday and Tuesday. The intervening Sunday was sunny, warm and lazily inviting. Witch spent two hours reading papers on the non-conservation of parity in weak interactions between elementary particles. Then he set off for a musing saunter with his notebook.

Ambling north along Pinery Avenue, between the River Lethe and the Orchard cricket ground, he was distracted from the ethereal properties of neutrinos by taunting images of his difficulties with Cindy. By the time he lay down on the grassy slope that overlooks the Aberlethe pond and the great green square of the Academy playing fields beyond, Witch had a poem half-formed in his head, and a purpose to put it to.

He would offer it to Cindy as an ultimatum.

If, after reading it, she still refused to trip with him, depriving them both of the pure white light of the void in the perfect yinyang harmony of opposites unified in ecstasy, he would terminate the relationship and travel round the world instead.

So, as less vexed young lovers whispered and giggled and rolled on the slope beside him, with panting Labradors of every hue abounding, small boys stridently sailing their model yachts on the pond, and smaller boys rushing round its perimeter netting tadpoles into jam jars, while a pair of prudent swans kept their distance in its middle, the mystical physicist with the notebook scribed:

Pobble Cameron-Bell?

We came from the east
dressed as mages

and sages,
and priests,
and we journeyed most far
neath our guardian star
laden heavy with gifts
such as panties and shifts
and airfreshener for someone
whose grandmother rifts.

And we paused when we came
to a dwarf on a mushroom
and two of us played
at being virgin and blushgroom
and the dwarf bade us kiss
in a high squeaky hiss
and then dwelt on the joys
of exploring small boys
and how blindness results
from connubial bliss,
then he passed on the mouthpiece
and the rest went like this:

The leopard's new spots
are intensely persuasive,
by god but the bard
is intensely recursive
pray god his profusions
grow never excessive
and pray too for a choirboy
with buttocks awobble,
for you'll never break into
a windowless pobble:
Pobble Brown and Pobble Smith
are beastly boring to be with
cos Pobble Smith and Pobble Brown
are scared to let their trousers down.

So we fled from the dwarf
and his harbour of horror

and took shade neath a tree
by a magical pasture
all covered in daisies
and lush verdant moisture
and divested ourselves
of our sackcloth and ashes
and came out all over
in blushing red rashes
and disported ourselves
on the magical daisies
till our blushes abated
and our senses grew lazy.

Then we paused for a nibble
to bolster our hunger
having essence of lobster
and sandwiched cucumber
washed down from invisible
magical tumblers
by sherry from cyprus
and cider from devon.
Then we asked a brown cow
with a huge furrowed brow
about what we might hope
to encounter in heaven.

Oh the hungry will snivel
the greedy will gobble
the lovers will revel
the loveless will hobble
and philosopher kings
will beseechingly sing
about horses with wings
and similar things,
such as how to break out of
a windowless pobble.

Cindy read the poem, and asked: 'What's a pobble?'

'Trip with me on Saturday,' Witch lured, 'and you may find out.'

Cindy refused.

Witch promptly terminated the relationship, and two weeks later he set off on his fifteen-month world tour.

Cindy was so utterly amputated by this ruthless emotional surgery that she couldn't take her qualifying exams and had to be awarded her Certificate (on the strength of tutors' assessments) by a special dispensation of the Murphy Hall board of governors, of whom Sir William Cameron-Bell was one.

She spent a month on the brink of nervous breakdown, another recuperating with Deirdre and Alastair in their holiday chalet in Provence, a third back in Deenburgh, picking listlessly at the Festival and fretting at the flatness and futility of Life in Scotland, then stepped on a train to London, there to seek her fortune as a Folk Singer.

FOURTEEN

Middling March:

'Peter Squirrell speaking.'

'Hi, Pete. How's things?'

'Could be worse. I'm having supper at the moment.'

'Fancy a drink later?'

'Where?'

'Southside.'

'No thanks, Witch. I've got a tutorial . . .'

'Tomorrow?'

I was about to refuse, but I hadn't been out in the evening since he and I dined with the Tostows. My social appetite was hardly voracious, but . . .

'You can finish my Glenmorangie,' he tempted.

'What do you want, Witch?'

'Don't be like that, Pete.'

I waited.

He chuckled, then confessed:

'I want to talk about Tostow.'

'What about him?'

'I think he's round the twist.'

'Why?'

'Not on the phone, old son.'

'All right,' I said grudgingly. 'What time tomorrow?'

'About eight. We should be finished by then.'

But they weren't.

When I was ushered upstairs by the runny-nosed Nora, I found Othello squatting irritably on the cushions in the lounge, while Witch and Mike MacKay, the TwangGang's lead guitarist, were closeted in the studio, with Simon Darling at the controls in the Cockpit.

The basic recordings were complete, and Cindy and the rest of the band had been dismissed. Witch and Mike were putting some final touches on the eighth track: Witch on his synthesizer, Mike on electric violin.

I sank warily on to a cushion opposite Othello.

His suit check was so loud and large as to be almost tartan. The top button of his cream-and-silver striped shirt was undone, with his tie loosened in the style of overworked television policemen. It was a wide tie, black, with a silver fish crudely painted across the breadth of its tongue. Underneath the fish was the caption *Othello Music.*

On the floor beside him was a packet of Embassy cigarettes and a tin of Tennant's Lager, which featured the nervous grin of a plump young lady with a large red bosom. A sheaf of clipboarded papers on his knee appeared to be engrossing him so much that he hadn't noticed my arrival.

I sat quietly, listening to the jagged blasts of music that came through the speaker system as Simon Darling flicked switches and nudged faders.

Will anyone notice if I leave?

Suddenly the music was replaced by an exchange of voices through the intercom.

'HOI, PETE?' I then heard Witch boom from loudspeakers everywhere.

I looked up and saw him grinning at me through the double-glazed window. He had on heavy black headphones that made him resemble a fighter pilot in a war film.

'HELP YOURSELF TO WHISKY,' he instructed me. 'BE DONE IN TEN MINUTES. ONE MORE TIME, SIMON, PLEASE. FROM THE TOP.'

I poured a Glenmorangie from the drinks cupboard beside the fridge. When I returned to my cushion I noticed Othello's ferret eyes flash vindictively at my glass, like a covetous rodent who would much rather have been offered Glenmorangie than Tennant's Lager.

'Was your visit to London successful?' I asked, smiling appeasingly.

He glared at me nastily, as at some intruder wasting valuable studio time for which he, Othello, was paying through the nose. The earwigs twitched in his puckered eyebags, and he said:

'Who are *you*?'

I was so taken aback that I replied:

'I'm a friend of Witch's.'

Othello grimaced and went back to scowling at his papers.

For ten minutes I invented ten crushing replies that would have put him in his place, and I stoked my horror that an angel like Cindy could allow such a reptile to . . .

'Hi, Pete,' Witch greeted me cheerily, emerging from the studio. 'Okay, Simon? Let her roll.'

Simon stepped down from the Cockpit, and a moment later the environment was flooded with the integrated eight-track sound of Cindy and the TwangGang performing Witch's Hiawatha songs. The recording seemed professional enough, and it certainly tapped the richness of Cindy's voice better than the traditional songs on the TwangGang's album.

When the tape was finished, Simon went to rewind it. Witch looked down at Othello and asked diffidently: 'All right?'

'It'll do fine, Wishfort,' Othello replied with a hostility that puzzled me, his ugly accent mutating the name to *Wushfart*. 'And it would have done just as well without the eighth track. *Speed* is . . .'

'Doesn't hurt though, does it? Thanks, Simon,' Witch called to his nattily dressed, pint-sized disc-jockey chum. 'Coming for a drink? We'll mix the tape at the weekend.'

'Why not *now*?' Othello demanded angrily.

'No thanks, Witch,' Simon declined, placing his Panama hat at a jaunty angle on his shaven head. 'I'm on at ten.'

'Can't do it now, old son,' Witch said to Othello. 'Got business with Pete. Come along. Closing time soon.' He went to turn off the power in the Cockpit.

Simon departed.

Mike collected his electric violin from the studio.

As Witch herded us out, Othello complained:

'Look, Wishfort, will you sign these fuckin contracts?' His pallid skin crinkled in an attempted smile, and he thrust his clipboard under Witch's nose. '*Please*!'

'What's the hurry?'

'We're doing your fuckin songs, man.'

'But you haven't recorded them yet, have you? The record company might not like them. I'll sign them to Othello Music, with pleasure, when I hear them on an album master.'

'But we're *doing them live* at the Janie Carmen concert,' Othello argued, his voice a fusion of pleading and growling.

'So what?'

'There's PRS money for that.'

'Not much.'

'Jesus *wept*, Wishfort,' Othello whined. 'It's all *money*, man. It all adds up. *Business is business*.'

'Informative tautology?' Witch murmured to me, as we stood on the cold neon-lit street outside his house, turning up collars, kicking heels, and rubbing impatient hands.

To Othello his parting words were:

'Okay, Ormrod. You show me the programme return for the Janie Carmen show, with my songs on it, and I'll sign your precious contracts for you.'

I found conversation an effort as we whizzed down from Southside and along past the Infirmary.

'Do you mind if I wear my seatbelt?'

'Please do, Pete. I thoroughly approve of passengers wearing seatbelts.'

Clipping mine on, I asked:

'Why don't you?'

'Don't like them.'

I thought this foolish, especially for someone who enjoyed fast driving. Referring to his low-slung Lotus, which was painted in the colours of a wasp, I said:

'I expect this can reach quite a speed?'

'Pass most things,' Witch said with ironical pride. Winking over the shoulder of his thong-fringed hide jacket, he added:

'Never know who might chase you. See?'

As we purred down the Knoll and past the art galleries, I asked:

'Have you known Simon as long as you've known Beano?'

'Longer. Simon and I shared a maternity ward. The old man's his godfather. Terrible, isn't it?'

'What?'

'How cliquish we must seem. But you know what's behind it, don't you?'

'No.'

'The layout of the New Town, Pete,' he said, waiting at the King Street traffic lights. 'Seventy per cent of the old-school professionals live within walking distance of each other.'

'So?'

'All the Academy lads and St David's lasses interact more freely than they could in other cities. London, say. Everyone's been to everyone else's scrotty parties when their old folks were away, and everyone gets off with everyone else's sister. We're a frightfully incestuous lot!'

But it didn't seem to bother him.

'Has Simon got a sister?'

'Nope. Simon's a lonely only. Or was till he decided he was a poof. Now he's happy as a sandboy. You ever met a sandboy, Pete?'

'How did he become a disc jockey?'

Witch wove the Lotus along Bluebell Street and squeezed up on the pavement between a dented Mini and a Bedford van with the jaws of a horrendous Somethingosaur painted in dripping psychedelic colours along its side.

'Simon realized he wasn't a born musician,' he said, watching a pair of blotchy drunks stagger out of Poldy's, arms around each other. 'But he likes being in entertainment. Radio Firth was starting up, and Simon's old man is a director. Queue Eee Dee? He's a good dee-jay though, don't you think?'

'I don't often listen to Radio Firth.' Then, above the cackling, clinking noises issuing from the pub on a blast of hot air and the fumes of dead beer, I inquired casually:

'Is your friendship with Simon linked with the TwangGang getting into the Janie Carmen concert?'

Witch winced as if I'd accused him of stealing the crown jewels.

'Get a grip, Pete. Simon's his own man, you know. His promotions . . .'

Three men burst out of Poldy's.

Two wore belted fawn raincoats and soft felt hats. One was of average height, but burly, with a receding chin and long bushy sideburns. The second was enormous, and had eyebrows like charred doormats. With one vast paw he gripped the upper arm of the third man, a short heavily-built specimen in an ex-army greatcoat.

Greatcoat had straggling grey hair and a flat vicious face, contorted now in a yellow-toothed snarl of trapped desperation.

'Hi, pigs,' Witch said affably, standing aside to let the party pass.

'Hod yur tongue, Wishfort,' the fawn giant said dourly, in a heavy Deenburgh accent. 'Your turn will come.'

Unabashed, Witch called after the departing prisoner: 'Hey, Mack? You shouldn't have done it. It's *against the law.*'

'Ewer a CUNT, Wishfort,' screamed Greatcoat (and instantly I recalled where I'd seen him before: that foggy night in Lethe, when Deirdre took me home from the Tostows). 'An Yule git what's comin tu yuh, *dinny yew worry.*'

'That'll be nice,' Witch commented.

'Are they police?' I asked while we waited for bar service.

'Drug squad. Sergeant Anderson – the midget with the eyebrows – and Constable Calder. Pig One and Pig Two, to you.'

'Who were they taking away?'

'John James Mack, Esquire. Our local hardman.'

'Last time I saw him he was chasing someone. With a knife!'

'That's right. MackTheKnife, he styles himself. Not much good though. Stupid. Not that hard either. Wouldn't last ten minutes in Glasgow. Let's . . . squeeze in with those dollybirds in the corner.'

Bluebell Street, a narrow back alley running parallel to the world-famous King Street, was Deenburgh's traditional ghetto of the umpteen pubs. Many of the original taverns had disappeared, and most that remained were either named after some long-deceased owner or else by allusion to Sir Walter Scott. Poldy's was an exception in still being a free house, named after its present licencee, Mr Leopold Brannigan, a fat red refugee Dubliner with an infectious guffaw.

It was an unspoiled Victorian bar, with a three-sided beaten-copper counter, tables of heavy dark wood, matching chairs in scarred red leather, and dim yellow lighting that concealed the hideousness of most of the customers from most of the other customers and highlighted the colours of the two fish tanks built into the wall on the left side of the bar.

Tonight the place was seething: loud, smoky, vibrating with intoxication and itching violence.

Witch and I tacked towards a hooting gaggle of seated maenads with spiky black eyes and heavier make-up than a troupe of circus clowns.

'May we join you, ladies?' he asked politely.

'Haaaa, haa, ha . . . may . . . lay . . . haaaaaa . . .'

'Cheers,' he said when the cackling subsided.

'Cheers.' I sipped my lager and lime.

Witch glanced benevolently round the other customers, as though he were head keeper in a private menagerie.

'Mack didn't seem to like you,' I remarked.

'We once had a disagreement.'

'What about?'

'Two years ago. Othello was pushing Kiwi boot polish under the description *Amazing Nepalese.* I was selling the real McCoy at half the price, and Othello got upset. So he slipped Mack a tenner to warn me off.'

'Goodness.'

' "Ewer a *cunt*, Wishfort," Mack informed me. In this very bar. "Nam gonny carve yew hup." He hasn't progressed much, as you saw. I was with Cindy, and she was horrified. We were drinking . . .'

'So what happened?'

'I told him that if he laid a finger on me, Beano would break his arms and smash his windpipe.'

'Did that deter him?'

'Not a lot. Didn't know who I was talking about. But Beano was boozing over the other side, with the scrum, and I called him round to appraise the situation.'

' "Ewer a *cunt*, Mack," Beano told him. Got quite pugnacious. "Niff yew dinny leave this bar right now, Beano's gonny pulp ewer nozzle." Niff's the word, too. Didn't you whiff pilchards as the pigs marched him past?'

'No.'

'Neither did I. But usually he stinks of stale pilchards in tomato sauce. Lovely man.'

'Did he leave? When Beano threatened him?'

'Certainly did. Meek as an ostracized lamb. Wouldn't you?'

'I thought karate practitioners weren't supposed . . .'

'Bugger that, Pete,' said Witch. 'Who says tits like Mack are supposed to slice folk up with razors?' He looked at me virtuously over the rim of his Pils. 'Anyway. Beano likes bullying bullies. He's naughty that way. Same again?'

'Let me . . .'

'No, no. I dragged you out, old son. You sit still.'

After a two-stroke chat with some acquaintances at the bar, he returned with a duplicate round and two double whiskies.

'Do us till closing time,' he explained. 'Bar gets pretty uncivilized from now on.'

I asked if Othello was still in the boot-polish trade.

'No. Shortly after Mack met Beano, Othello got pigged with a hefty weight. They put him in Seekton for six months, and he didn't like it. Now he pursues his fortune down the straight and narrow. Most commendable.'

I inquired whether one was normally sent to prison for selling boot polish.

Witch thought this amusing.

'True enough, Pete,' he said. 'But if there'd been *less* Kiwi in it, he'd have got a lot more than six months. It's a dicey game, you know. That's why I keep my main stash in Querns

Castle.' He grinned at me, a blue-eyed sphinx with a hairy face.

'Why do you tell everyone about it?'

'I don't. Only those I love and trust. That's my meta-game. Here's to your well-earned First, Pete,' he toasted, raising his whisky.

'Hear, hear,' I muttered.

Then I asked why Othello had been so anxious to get Witch's signature.

'You're a psychologist, Pete.'

I agreed.

'You know all about Freud's orificial types: oral, anal, et al?'

I didn't disagree.

'Well, Othello's a Hoover type.'

'Really?'

'He's got the mouth of a vacuum cleaner where his arsehole ought to be.'

'I'm sure Freud would be fascinated, Witch. But you haven't answered my question.'

'Okay. Know anything about the Performing Right Society?'

'No.'

'It's an agency that collects royalties and distributes them to composers and songwriters. And, unfortunately, to their publishers. So if, for example, a Peter Squirrell symphony is played on Radio Firth, or performed live in the Lorimer Hall, then someone like Simon has to record the details on a form called a programme return, which is sent to the PRS, so that Peter Squirrell can, years later, be allocated the money due to him. Ditto for Beethoven Music, if Beethoven Music publishes Peter Squirrell's symphony. With me?'

'I think so.'

'Right. Cindy's going to sing two of my songs at the Janie Carmen concert. They aren't yet published. If they stay unpublished, I get all the money. If I sign Othello's contracts, he gets half.'

'And that's what's worrying him?'

'Yap.'

'How much is involved?'

'Less than a fiver.'

'Then why . . .'

'It's all *money*, Pete,' said Witch, mimicking Othello's humourless whine. '*Business is business*, man.'

'But you haven't signed his contracts.'

'That's right.'

'Why not?'

'I enjoy needling him. Also, if I sign them now, he might get the TwangGang to perform something else on the night: leaving me with nothing, and him owning half of my songs. Whereas once they're listed on the programme return, I'll get my money whether they're actually performed or not. And Othello couldn't bear to see me get something for nothing. Whisky okay?'

I nodded appreciatively.

'Recognize it?'

'No.'

'It's from my distillery,' he said coyly.

'What label?'

He told me.

Impressed, I invited him to tell me more about his legitimate business interests.

He was charmingly unforthcoming.

So I tried:

'How come you know so much about the business side of music?'

'I don't really, Pete. But you could say it all began . . .'

During the next ten minutes I discovered how Witch became affluent enough to buy his house *before* coming into half of Grandfather Cunningham's estate (the other half going to Mrs Wishfort and the girls). It was all because of 'my MOR song'. When he was seventeen, during the Christmas vacation after his first term at Deenburgh University, he'd been sitting in the morning room one evening, drinking cans of Export and watching television with some friends. While waiting for a film to begin they were caught by the end of a variety programme starring one of Britain's top middle-of-the-road ballad singers. Please send me your lyrics, ladies and gentlemen, the balladeer said to his ten million viewers. The songs on my next album will be written by you and me *together. You* will write the words, and *I* will write the music. (And *my* publishing company will cream up the publishing money, he tastefully did not add.)

Witch was between the Nosebone and HMS Witchcraft, and thus had composing time on his hands. Give it a try, he thought. Why not? In the first week of the following term, his Computer Science project was a program to analyse a dozen successful ballads into structural similarities. From these he composed a paradigm tune, called a schema. With the melody right, the words oozed into place of their own accord. He detached the lyric from the musical schema, typed it up, sent a carbon copy to Stationer's Hall in Ludgate Hill (to protect his copyright), lodged a second carbon copy in a sealed envelope with his bank manager (to double-protect his copyright), and then, in almost the spirit of buying tickets from Beano for the rugby club Christmas raffle, he posted off the top copy together with a pseudonym for the lyric to be published under.

By Easter that year his MOR song was on a successful album in Britain, and within a year it had, as a single, reached the top five in the American hit parade. Thereafter it was a huge success worldwide, and to date it has been covered by over sixty other artistes.

'I'm not proud of it,' Witch told me unashamedly, as a host of puke-faced Last Orderers surged frantically round the bar like a herd of pigs competing for one truffle. 'But it has made me a lot of money.'

'How much? Or shouldn't I ask?'

'So far, over fifty thousand pounds in the bank. But there's a lot more on the way. Foreign royalties can take years.'

In a daze I said:

'Does Othello know about that song?'

'Absolutely not. No one else knows except Beano and Simon. And I'd be uniquely grateful, Mr World Champion Secret Keeper, if you could keep this one from my father.'

'Why?'

'He drinks too much as it is. If he found out I'd made so much money from so little effort, he might flip completely. Beep, beep.'

'Pardon?'

Witch nodded:

'Poldy's coming to feed the piranha.'

Sure enough, the vast red Irishman was bearing down on us with what looked like a giant tea-strainer.

'Hicks queues may, Witch,' said Poldy.

'Sure thing, Poldy,' said Witch, rising.

We stood back and watched the landlord lift the lid off the fish tank above where we had been sitting. He caught a goldfish in his tea-strainer and quickly transported it to the second fish tank, which was eight feet along the wall, beside the door to the Ladies. He lifted the lid and dropped the goldfish in. An expectant hush had descended, and I realized that all the drinking-up eyes were glued to the fate of the goldfish. Suddenly:

'Wow.'

'Far out, man.'

'D'ye see that?'

A nine-inch silver streak had shot with bullet speed from the billowing green depths of the second tank, snapped the goldfish in two, and flashed back into its lair of murky fronds. It was all over in the blink of an eye, and the head half of the goldfish was left suspended in the water, goggling and mouthing as if unaware of the prettily coloured threads of guts seeping out of its severed belly.

Maybe I looked as sick as I felt, because Witch said:

'Come on, Pete. I'll drive you home.'

FIFTEEN

When I think back in global terms to that jumbled era of flower power, guru worship, the *I Ching,* hotpants and ponchos, euphoric letters ending *Yours in Love and Peace,* mammoth rock festivals, Satan's Slaves, anti-Vietnam demonstrations, big yellow taxis, brown sugar and American pie, superstars dead from overdoses, big-eyed beans from Venus and spiders from Mars, when every fourth song still extolled *Revolution* twenty-five times, I resolve not to apologize for telling another story about a talented young man with long hair and a beard, of Messianic mien, who smoked marijuana, took LSD, and channelled his artistic urges into the writing and singing of songs.

My mind gazes dreamily back at the zombie-eyed fuzzy-headed hippies who flocked to Poldy's Bar, and the bright-eyed fluffy-haired philosophers dispensing subversion and nirvana in the John Locke cafeteria, and I estimate that one in twelve of the hairier males was a songwriter of sorts. Most were uninspired, and many were embarrassing, but they did write *songs.* They had identifiable melodies, grammatically comprehensible lyrics, and subjects, such as the value of peace or the power of love, sufficiently important to human life to be deserving of exploration and celebration in even a humble medium. I mean, in a word, that the songs of those days were quite unlike the hideously tuneless confessions of worthlessness that most people haven't been listening to on the John Peel show for the past several years.

And myself:

I have always been a late developer. My hair never touched my earlobes until I was twenty-six. I have never voluntarily done anything dangerous in my life, and my artistic aspirations petered out in my fifth year at school after a short sputter of imitation-Shakespeare sonnets, which my English master pronounced irredeemably dreadful.

So you see why the star of this story is Witch.

'I'd *like* to say something in Othello's favour,' he said charitably, speeding his Lotus north down Catherine Street.

'*Tat Twam Asi*, you mean?'

'Very good, Pete. You're catching on. But the best I can think of is his loyalty to that piranha fish.'

'He owns it?'

'Poldy has it on indefinite loan. But Othello drops in now and again to see its scales are glistening. When Cindy came back from London, a year ago, she and Deirdre got that flat in Gladstone Place. It's owned by Cindy's uncle's partner, so the rent's pretty reasonable. And when Othello plugged into Cindy he wanted to move in immediately, to save on his own rent. Deirdre was hostile enough about Othello, but she categorically-imperatively drew the line at the piranha.'

'I can imagine.'

'Hence the deal with Poldy.'

'Why did Cindy leave London?'

'Too uptight for her. Too speedy. She was doing well in the folk clubs. Some cabaret. Even sniffed a recording deal. Then found out that what some slimy creep in a loud suit and a vulgar tie really wanted was to exploit her talent and jump on her lovely bum. So she came home to Mummy.'

'Just like you.'

Witch thought this observation hilarious.

'*Quite* like me,' he chortled.

'Why did she get mixed up with Othello?'

'She discovered that if there's one thing worse than a queue of creeps wanting to exploit your talent and jump on your bum, it's no queue at all. Enter Othello:

' "Please, Cindy, front the TwangGang for me, and we'll all get rich quick. Pee Ess, your knickers are superfluous.

Drop em."

'And so to bed. Most women surrender in the end. Haven't you noticed?'

'You wanted to speak about Dr Tostow,' I reminded him.

'Indeed yes. The Frankenstein of Orgasmic Achievement. What would you say . . .' he braked to avoid a tail-erect Labrador that suddenly appeared between two parked cars and sauntered carelessly across Hanover Street, 'his motives are?'

'A therapy for orgasmic malfunction.'

'You believe that, Pete?'

'Don't you, Witch?'

'It may be true,' he said, as we double-parked outside Number Ten. 'But it isn't the whole truth. He's a funny fellow, Tostow. Difficult to fathom. Usually I can see what makes people tick. But with him – Anita too . . . they're a muddy pair. Maybe just because they're foreign. Think he might be after material for another kinky novel?'

'I doubt it. He is a respected research psychologist, you know.'

'And how many such animals pay younger men, whose guts they hate, to drop free mescalin and fuck their wives?'

'You didn't have to,' I said coldly.

'Bugger it, Pete, I *wanted* to fuck his wife – she's a peach. Didn't you?'

'No.'

'I don't believe you,' he said acutely.

'Aren't you enjoying your experiments?' I diverted testily.

Witch sniffed thoughtfully:

'That first night was good fun. But it's getting a bit mechanical.'

'She isn't responsive, you mean?'

'Anita, old son, comes as easily as a pussycat purrs. Oxfam's making a fortune.'

'That must be very gratifying.'

'I don't think it has much to do with me. That sob story Tostow told about Anita never before *achieving* orgasm during intercourse . . . I don't believe it.'

'Why should he lie?'

'Throw up a challenge? Carrot for the young buck's pride?'

'Perhaps he only meant her orgasms during intercourse were *unsatisfying.*'

'Could be that. She is a bit slack.'

'What do you mean?'

'Her vagina is capacious. You have to get her really excited before she grips.'

'And how do I do that?'

'What really turns her on,' the charitably-caused lover replied, 'is the tune of the nuzzling tongue. Then she's like a bulldog.'

'You don't mean . . .?!'

Witch roared with laughter.

'Pull the finger out, Pete,' he suggested. 'If you can't get your face down south occasionally, you're wasting a girl's time. *Do as you would be done by,* more or less. No?'

'I think *Don't do as you wouldn't be done by* is more sensible.'

'And when did you last get your end away?'

I dodged this by harking to:

'In what way, then, are Dr Tostow's experiments becoming too mechanical?'

'First of all, the electrodes. He has Anita wired so he can record her Orgasmic Achievements. Makes you feel like you're humping a roll of chicken-wire. Then he's got two remote-controlled video cameras . . .'

'I simply do not know,' I exclaimed, 'how you can *bring* yourself . . .'

'That's not the problem,' he said seriously. 'Once you've *experienced the truth* that personality is an illusion . . .'

'I'm sorry, Witch,' I told him shortly, reacting against his apparent willingness to sit in the car all night. 'And I'm sure you mean that sincerely, but to me it's incomprehensible. I am one individual, you are another, and never the twain shall merge. Vedantic mysticism may live on in the Khyber Pass, but I simply cannot see its relevance to Georgian Deenburgh in the twentieth century.'

'Then for you, Pete, the best explanation is as follows. When the soft music begins to play, and the red lights mellow on the bronzed, inviting, wire-tapped body of Anita, and I hear the muted whir of the electric motors that swivel the video cameras, and I think of Tostow sitting in the control room with his eyes glued to the monitor while he jerks himself off, and I want my shy inhibitions to fall off me like dry leaves in autum, and my cock to swell up strong and hot as the morning sun in a tropical sky, do you know what I do?'

'What do you do?'

'I imagine I'm American. Look,' he commanded, pointing suddenly. 'There's the old man drinking too much again.'

Following his finger, I saw, through the dining room window, Mr Wishfort pouring himself a large Scotch.

Wasn't it hypocritical, I asked Witch, for the son to censure the father's tippling?

Why?

Because at least the father's indulgence was *legal.*

That was a short-sighted view, Witch assured me.

'Cup of tea?' I offered him, determined not to see the dawn in from his car.

'No thanks, Pete. I'm on at eleven.'

'On what?' I inquired, thinking of Simon Darling and Radio Firth.

'On Anita, old son. Got to get out to Queen's Buildings,' he said, looking at the dashboard clock. 'You coming to the Big Trip Talk-in next week?'

SIXTEEN

For an aspiring mystic to revert, in the present state of knowledge, to prolonged fasting and violent self-flagellation would be as senseless as it would be for an aspiring cook to behave like Charles Lamb's Chinaman, who burned down the house in order to roast a pig. Knowing as he does (or at least as he can know, if he so desires) what are the chemical conditions of transcendental experience, the aspiring mystic should turn for technical help to the specialists – in pharmacology, in biochemistry, in physiology and psychiatry and parapsychology. And on their part, of course, the specialists (if any of them aspire to be genuine men of science and complete human beings) should turn, out of their respective pigeon-holes, to the artist, the sibyl, the visionary, the mystic – all those, in a word, who have had experience of the Other World and who know, in their different ways, what to do with that experience.

Sir Gabriel Drake put down his copy of *Heaven and Hell* and took a sip of water from the rostrum tumbler.

'Fat lotta help ye get from the specialists in this dump,' some heckler shouted from the anonymity of the closely packed audience.

'Quack, quack,' jeered another.

'Quiet, please,' the Vice Chancellor boomed. 'The discussion will open to the floor shortly. Now. Those words were written. By Aldous Huxley. As long ago as 1956. And yet. The problems touched on. Are very much with us still. On my right, our first speaker this afternoon, Dr Ivan Tostow, well known to all of us, for his work . . .'

When Sir Gabriel eventually shut up and sat down, and

Dr Tostow came forward to the microphone, the David Square Theatre erupted, like an old-time music hall, in a deafening barrage of boos, raspberries, drumming feet, slow handclapping, and impatient calls for the topper of the bill, Dr Hardy Nagil.

It was a sunny pre-spring day outside, the last Friday before the Easter vacation, and the theatre was rank from the hundreds of pints of Export and greasy steak pies gulped and gobbled at lunchtime. Every seat was occupied, the space between the front stalls and the stage was thick with squatting bodies, and latecomers were standing in the aisles.

The hubbub subsided.

Dr Tostow spoke fluently for twenty minutes.

It was all very well, he argued, for certain privileged and extraordinarily cultivated persons, such as Huxley surely had been, to take the risk, when they reached a mature age, of experimenting with their own consciousness, in the service of art or poetry or whatever, under controlled and carefully supervised conditions, but it was quite another matter to claim, as many youthful and irresponsible elements now were claiming, that the facilitating chemicals should be legally and readily available to any young Tom, Dick or Harry who might imagine, often as a result of reading the irresponsible writings of certain academics manqué (who ought to be old and wise enough to know better, but were too enamoured, it seemed, of their cult-figure status and of the lucrative royalties accruing to best-selling paperbacks), that the swallowing of an LSD-dosed sugar cube was the instant and infallible key to that putative *Other World* where life and consciousness were infinitely richer and higher.

Through the long, narrow loudspeakers that lined the walls, his clipped tones declaimed:

'Too much sensational coverage unquestionably has been given to drug-induced psychoses resulting in, for example, attempts to fly from high buildings with fatal consequences, and to the cult killings still so hideously fresh in our memories. Yet unquestionably also such tragic incidents occur, and could be prevented, if only the unlicenced and illegal availability of the hallucinogenic chemicals could be stamped out. Thus is the issue comparable both in structure and urgency to that of firearms control in the United States, where, each year . . .'

'I don't know,' Dr Nagil confided theatrically, when the cheers and whistles were over, 'how many unfortunate persons were fatally wounded in the United States last year by a bullet from an LSD-dosed sugar cube. Do you?' he inquired of his fans, his Glasgow accent slurred by the beer he had lunched on.

No, the fans shouted. They didn't know.

Precious few, they speculated.

'Does my learned friend Dr Tostow know?' Dr Nagil turned, like a jovial balding teddybear in a leather-elbowed dog-tooth sports jacket, and smiled curiously at his adversary.

Sitting on the stage beside Sir Gabriel, Dr Tostow scowled.

Of course he doesn't, the rabble roared: *Tostow doesn't know his arsehole from his nostril.*

'Nor do I know,' Dr Nagil confessed sadly, 'how many psychedelically induced self-defenestrations take place annually . . .'

Rapturous applause . . .

'But I speculate that, when compared with the thousands slaughtered on our roads each year due to the irresponsible use of alcohol – a drug that is not only legally and readily available, but which also contributes millions of pounds to the government's coffers – the number of psychedelically induced self-defenestrations . . .'

Tumultuous approval . . .

'Resulting in fatalities will be a microscopic drop in the statistical ocean. And I put it to you, my friends . . .'

That, while we must not imagine he was advocating indiscriminate experimentation with LSD, it was nonetheless a fact that so-called *normal consciousness* had become dangerously alienated from the true fabric of existence, and that so long as it was *conceivable* that a chemical catalyst might facilitate the rediscovery of that fabric, just as a cyclotron extended the power of a physicist's observation, there would always be a minority of adventurous spirits eager to explore the possibility . . . and those friends who wished to consider more detailed arguments should (if they did not already possess a copy) rush out before the bookshops closed and buy his *Economics of Consciousness*, published by Penguin and very reasonably priced.

'. . . contributions from the floor?' Sir Gabriel invited, after his heroically short ten-minute intermezzo.

Austin Newbigging, professor of psychiatry and arch enemy to Hardy Nagil, stood up from one of the front rows reserved for senior staff. His mournful voice described several LSD-induced psychoses recently admitted to his Peter Douglas Clinic.

'Where they will be force-fed on tranquillizers and sleeping pills,' Dr Nagil counter-attacked cheerfully, 'and bludgeoned back into that false normality, that socially convenient *one-dimensionality*, from which they were bravely attempting to escape.'

Dr Nagil sat down.

A standing ovation applauded him.

The standing ovation sat down.

Mr Wishfort stood up and delivered an incomprehensibly technical homily, apparently in support of Dr Tostow, on the speed of transmission of electrical impulses in the brain.

Witch leapt up from the promiscuous slum of latecomers and exclaimed that he was unable to follow a word the previous speaker had said, and please, Mr Chairman, would the previous speaker redeliver his sermon in a semblance of the Queen's English?

Before the father-son niggle could escalate, Quentin Quelch, professor of metaphysics, spoke up, unenthusiastically, on the side of Dr Nagil. Personally he found the whole business distasteful. But liberty was liberty, was it not? And just as he could see no good argument for preventing a rational adult from committing suicide, once he was seriously bent on it, so he was unable to favour the State Censorship of consciousness in effect being advocated by his respected colleague Dr Tostow. The psychotropic chemicals *should* therefore be publicly available, he concluded, but only to persons aged thirty and over, and they should in addition be so swingeingly taxed as to discourage 'the many whose only goal is an instant kick'.

Various other speakers asked unremarkable questions from the floor and received unmemorable answers from the stage, which sparked off an epidemic of yawns, shuffling feet, and beerdrinkers glancing fretfully at their watches.

Then Tom Redhead's loud fat drawl rehearsed at length his theory connecting Dr Tostow's views on the American presence in Vietnam, his recent drug-based political indoctrination of a number of Deenburgh graduate students (who had been cunningly duped into believing they were participating in straightforward experiments on dream patterns), and his self-evident role as a CIA informer.

'Does he deny it?' Redhead yelled.

'Answer. Answer,' rumbled round the theatre.

'The question is not germane to the discussion in hand,' Sir Gabriel decreed. 'Next question, please.'

This also came from Tom Redhead, who asked The Chair if he might take this opportunity of presenting to The Vice Chancellor *Dumbo*'s petition demanding the impeachment of Dr Tostow.

'Here it is, man,' Tom shouted fiercely at Dr Tostow. Brandishing a fistful of papers, he announced gloatingly: 'We got three thousand signatures, baby, and . . .'

Permission was tersely refused by The Chair and The Vice Chancellor simultaneously.

'Any more questions?' Sir Gabriel boomed forbiddingly. 'Before . . .'

'I have a question for Dr Tostow.'

'Yes?'

A thousand eyes fixed avidly on Witch as he stepped up to the stage and approached the rostrum. He was dressed entirely in white: flared trousers, velvet jacket and silk shirt, and it was obvious to me that his seemingly impromptu performance was carefully planned.

'May I?' he said pleasantly to the flustered Sir Gabriel.

'Democratic participation?'

A roar of approval made it impossible for Sir Gabriel to refuse.

Witch leaned forward and said intimately into the microphone:

'I've heard a rumour, Dr Tostow, that you are currently testing the psychotropic drugs in the treatment of Orgasmic Underachievement. Is this correct?'

Dr Tostow came forward. He was wearing a wine-coloured corduroy suit, a white shirt and a black bow tie. Hatefully he said:

'That is so.'

'So *you* have a mandate to experiment with the drugs you want withheld from *the public?*'

'Naturally.'

'Could you tell us who is taking part in your Orgasmic Underachievement tests? I mean, that kind of investigation must involve a certain amount of taking drugs and fornicating, must it not?'

'That information obviously is confidential,' Dr Tostow replied darkly.

'BOOOO,' booed the crowd.

And:

'All *secret* information is *bad* information,' a lone theorist chimed.

'Then could you specify,' Witch inquired, 'which drugs you are using?'

'Cannabis, psilocybin and mescalin.'

'Free mescalin?' an amazed voice gasped.

'Lucky *bastards,'* another griped.

The furrows deepened in Sir Gabriel's frown.

'Dr Tostow,' Witch said kindly, 'have you ever taken psilocybin or mescalin?'

After a face-twitching pause Dr Tostow said:

'No.'

'Do you envisage *ever* taking psilocybin or mescalin?'

'No.'

'Why is that?'

'Objectivity must be maintained,' Dr Tostow said ferociously. 'The relation . . .'

'BOOOO . . .'

'Get him off.'

'Toss off, Tostow . . .'

Witch waited for the furore to simmer down.

'I put it to you, my friends,' he said, fisting a mock black-power salute at Dr Nagil, who was rubbing his pink eyes and fighting to remain awake, 'that the reason Dr Tostow will never partake of the psychedelic sacrament is this.

'*Fear.* Yes, Dr Tostow is sore afraid. Afraid that if he made the ultimate pilgrimage he would be turned away at the temple gate. That the dragon's face would sneer and say:

' "Ivan Tostow, I love you not. For ever, and ever, and ever. Unlovable Tostow without ending."

'Am I right, Dr Tostow?'

Dr Tostow bent over the microphone and shouted angrily:

'What you just have heard, ladies and gentlemen, absolutely is typical of the psychotic fantasies associated . . .'

'*Fuck you,* Tostow,' Tom Redhead bellowed, jumping up and shaking his fists. 'You ain't nuthin but a mother-fuckin shit-slingin *FASCIST.*'

'Shit-slinging fascist,' the undergraduates echoed in delight.

'Shit . . .'

'. . . for coming, ladies and gentlemen,' Sir Gabriel thundered, pushing between Witch and Dr Tostow like a portly referee between two punch-drunk boxers. 'But there we must end. Our particular thanks . . .'

'And you know what he might find, ladies and gentlemen?' Witch cried to the rising, leg-stretching, pub-destined assembly. 'That his fear was groundless. That the dragon would *open* the temple gate, and *smile,* and say:

' "Ivan Tostow, I love you too. I love you as I love myself." '

SEVENTEEN

I had no thought of going to the Janie Carmen concert until teatime on the day: the Friday before Easter. Then Helen announced casually, licking chocolate icing off her fingers, that Witch had given her a ticket for me.

'Why?'

'Why not, Peter? Don't you want to go?'

'Not madly.'

'Don't you fancy Cindy any more?'

'I've never . . .'

'There's a party afterwards in Gladstone Place,' she said persuasively. 'And Janie Carmen's going.'

'Oh?'

Eyes intent on the cigarette she was rolling, she added:

'You can be my escort, if you like.'

I mumbled how honoured I was, and what a privilege it would be to breathe the carbon monoxide Janie Carmen had exhaled.

'Come up about seven,' Helen instructed me, 'and we'll have a drink in Poldy's first. You don't mind walking, do you, Peter?'

'No.'

'Good. Then I can get pissed.'

Simon Darling's March promotions had been a great success, much helped by Simon advertising them twenty times an hour on his Radio Firth programmes. The Janie Carmen concert was the last of the series, and it was sold out weeks in advance.

The Lorimer Hall in Logan Road was Deenburgh's premier concert venue and seated several thousand people. Often these were trimly tonsured devotees of Menuhin or Barenboim, but tonight the audience ranged from fresh-faced schoolgirls in their blue St David's uniforms, to hairy-headed hippies with glazed eyes, and middle-aged arts lecturers with creases in their Levis.

Our seats were in the stalls, six rows out from the large apron stage. I was on the outside of Helen, Nora, Witch, Harriet and Beano. Witch's attire was a black velvet suit with widely flared trousers and jacket lapels like jet-fighter wings. He appeared underslept, withdrawn and distracted, and when Helen and I arrived he hardly noticed us.

There was a lurking smell in the hall, like that of old castles and damp churches, and . . . the overhead lights dimmed, the coloured spotlights focused on the stage, and a rumble of anticipation rose to the dome when Simon Darling appeared like a superball mannikin in a canary-coloured boilersuit and dark glasses like exaggerated ski goggles.

He bounced to a microphone and his singsong voice thanked us for our support this evening, thanked us for making the Simon Darling concerts such a hit (guaranteeing a second series in July), and was sure we needed no prompting to welcome:

'Our very own, home-grown, electric-folk folk, folks. The *Belhaven TwangGang*. Thank you.'

A torrent of clapping broke out as Mike MacKay led the TwangGang musicians on. Like Peter Pan pirates in heavy greasepaint, convict T-shirts, scarlet bandannas and black eye patches, they scooped up their guitars from the stands on the stage and led straight into *John Barleycorn*.

Cindy danced out to join them, and a burst of chauvinistic cheers and whistles topped the clapping. She was costumed like a gypsy queen, with flashing gold ear-rings and a long swirling dress of silver-sequined purple, and the dashing dreamlike figure whose crystal voice sang 'As I rode out . . .' made me realize for a moment how unloved men with nothing to live for can sometimes commit crazy crimes, murder, even suicide, in the hope of enlisting the affections of a goddess who exists nowhere but in their starlit fantasies.

After Mr Barleycorn came a medley of Irish fiddle-jigs, featuring the electric violin of Mike MacKay and the rhythmic handclapping of the audience, led by Cindy as she reeled across the stage. The other night I watched a television programme about the unremarkable private life of a champion jockey, who only comes fully to life under starter's orders, and he reminded me of Cindy, whom the cue to sing or dance could transform into a different person, as did a bottle of chilled Moselle.

During the fiddle-jigs I turned to glance at Witch and found Helen's taunting blue eyes scrutinizing me ironically. She had been watching me watching Cindy. I felt myself flushing, so I looked away.

The TwangGang began their *Four Maries*, another track from their album, and I wondered if Witch was wondering when his songs would come.

When all the Maries had been enumerated, and the applause was raging, I noticed Othello appear from the wings and shout something in Mike MacKay's ear. Mike looked unhappy and began to remonstrate. Othello gestured impatiently, said something terse, then vanished. The applause died down, and Mike said hesitantly into his microphone:

'I've just heard, folks, that we've to cut our spot short. This is because the White Ravens (Janie Carmen's backing band) want a warm-up before Janie comes on.'

Displeasure mixed with indifference coughed and scuffed round the hall.

Witch sat forward tensely, fists clenched whitely on his thighs.

'However,' Mike continued, 'we've just time for the two tracks – and this is the good news – that are going on our first single, out next month. When I hope you'll buy it, folks! So here goes with our A-side: *Kilgarry Mountain.*'

They they did a jerky rendition of *Worried Man Blues*, took their bow and went off.

The White Ravens came on and plunked several slick

country numbers. Musically they were streets ahead of the TwangGang, but their stage gear consisted of ordinary jeans and shirts, they smoked cigarettes and drank beer while playing, half the time with their backs to the audience, and generally gave a formidably sedative performance. Consequently, when Janie Carmen made her entry, stunning in a lace-trimmed backwoods-style pink dress over her famous bare feet, the effect was like the advent of Santa at a children's Christmas party.

'Janie,' a hysterical American cried above the general yells, 'you got more *class* than the resta Hollywood put together. You know that?'

'That sure is kinda you, fellah,' Janie replied, smiling coyly as she straightened the capo on her pearl-inlaid guitar. 'Now, a song very dear to my heart . . .'

Mr Tambourine Man.

Next: a Carmen song, pretty, ladylike, recalling a lost world of crystal fountains on distant mountains, with a tinkling harp background. Janie had less raw charisma than Cindy, but she had developed her talent to the utmost, and her audience-holding power was hypnotic. If Cindy's voice was like dancing sunlight on a frosty morning, Janie's was like the mellow warmth of a harvest evening: dusty golden, compellingly lazy, full of lotus promise.

This siren-like quality intensified as she sang *Suzanne*, making us wonder if perhaps Janie *was* Suzanne, though . . .

Helen nudged me.

Witch was coming along the row towards us.

I moved my knees to let him pass.

There were tears streaming shamelessly from his eyes, and he looked like a martyred saint walking into a Force Six gale. I think he was intending to depart without a word, but then he paused and bent to whisper in my ear:

'If you see Cindy, Pete, tell her I'm *very disappointed.*'

Awed by his grief, I mouthed compliance.

'And if you see Othello . . .'

'Yes?'

'Tell the cunt he can kiss goodbye to his tapes.'

'But why was he so upset?' I asked at the party later.

Harriet rested her glass on her enormous bosom, surveyed me maternally, and said:

'I expect, Peter, that as a psychologist you share the common prejudice that women are more romantic than men?'

'Um . . .'

'Whereas any serious student of literature will tell you that the opposite is more true.'

'I see.'

'That whereas women may be more romantic in their escapist fantasies, they are more down-to-earth about adapting to Reality. Like Belinda Drayton, who writes trash novels by the gross, and is a millionaire. While men, particularly talented men in their early twenties, are less realistic in their conduct, and more romantic in their serious expectations of Life.'

I sipped my knockout punch, moved to let someone else at the bowl, and said:

'That's interesting, Harriet. So you think Witch is a romantic? He's always struck me as rather calculating.'

'He has an analytical intellect, which helps him get what he wants. But his blood is pure romantic red. Ever since he left Cindy and went off round the world he's had this cuckoo dream that one day he would write a perfect song. Just one, but a "quintessential distillation of the spirit of the spirit of the species" [Witch's phrase, which I later used in an exam answer] . . . and that Janie Carmen would hear this perfect song, fall in love with it, record it on an album, and thereby preserve it for the edification of posterity.'

'But he hasn't written his perfect song. He . . .'

'Never will, Peter. He's too clever. His mind gets in the way, trips up his heart.' Harriet nodded emphatically, like the literature lecturer she would become. Life has taught me that there is a relation of direct proportion between a woman's intellectuality and the activity of her eyebrows. Harriet was no exception to this rule, and as she expatiated, and her thick red brows wagged up and down as if tugged by a drunken puppet master, I found it hard not to become impolitely mesmerized.

'But Witch is realistic enough,' she went on, 'to want to start somewhere. And his Indian-girl songs are better than most of the syrupy slop Janie Carmen sings.'

'So . . . all that trouble to trick Cindy into liking the songs? Just to get them to Janie Carmen's attention?'

'Looks like it to me, Peter. Witch would never admit it, of course. And you'd better not tell him I said that.'

'And that's why he was so disappointed tonight,' I mused, 'when Cindy didn't sing his songs?'

'That and this party,' said Harriet, reaching to the kitchen table for a cheese-and-cherry bonne-bouche on a cocktail stick.

'What do you mean?'

'Who do you think paid for all this?'

'Witch did?'

'Hardly Othello's style, is it?'

I looked round to see if Othello were in earshot.

'So when Janie Carmen's roadie said "Thanks for the invite but we gotta fly back to London tonight: gotta recording session in the morning", you can imagine how Witch felt.'

I supposed I could.

'Just between you and me,' Harriet confided, leaning her breasts against me, 'I think he had some wild plan to take Janie back to Southside after the party. *To seduce her.*'

'Surely not.'

'Why else did he spend the afternoon tidying his flat? Even got Nora to take his sheets to the launderette! Come on, Peter,' she switched irresistibly. 'Let's *dance.*'

The houses in Gladstone Place were the largest in the New Town, with massive façades bolstered by corrugated pillars of Samson size. Most of the houses were now offices for lawyers, architects and financial consultants, and Cindy's was the only remaining residence not occupied by an elderly professor, wealthy widow, or successful private dentist.

There were three flats.

A seldom-seen retired couple populated the ground-floor and basement, though no one could imagine what they did with all that space. An extended family of Pakistanis, with spots on their foreheads and scores of children swinging from their colourful incensed pyjamas, lived on the first floor. And Deirdre, Cindy and Othello had the top flat.

This, because of its vast rooms, was ideal for a party.

Deirdre and Alastair were in Austria on a skiing holiday, and the furniture had been moved from Deirdre's bedroom to Cindy's, to make the former into a temporary dining room. Two white-clothed trestle tables groaned under a lavish cold buffet (roast turkey in mayonnaise, smoked salmon, umpteen salads . . .) lovingly tended by a dinner-jacketed waiter from the Greek restaurant that had supplied the feast. Cindy's room was a mass of dumped handbags and coats, into which an intimately twining couple would disappear from time to time, and the living room, at the front, the biggest room I have ever seen in a town house, was a seething, prancing, whooping riot of the pounding music and epileptic strobe lighting supplied by Radio Firth Disco Services Ltd.

I danced with Harriet for twenty minutes, which made me light-headed with exhaustion as well as merrily punch-drunk. Beano had gone home at midnight. He had a rugby sevens tournament next day, and so heroically avoided the eleven-gallon keg of McEwan's Export in the hall, while others gaily kicked it even fuller of fizz with a hydraulic car-tyre pump. For an hour Beano had mooched around, sipping punch disgustedly, grumpy as a diabetic bear, until Harriet sent him home to bed.

She was easily the sharpest of the Deenburgh girls.

This was manifest in her discursive competence (not to mention confidence), also in her ability to complete the *Guardian* crossword more quickly than anyone else I know, and in the independence of thought that referred to Othello as a *prick* – as opposed, for example, to the *cunt* favoured by Helen.

Harriet had never before struck me as attractive, but as we danced that night, with her enormous proportions living life to the full beneath her sheath dress, and later again in the kitchen by the cornucopian punch bowl, Harriet explaining in depth why Dr Tostow's *Erewhon Three* was not properly speaking a novel so much as the politically motivated babblings of an illiterate anti-talent, I felt the manhood stiffening in my imagination, and even contemplated . . .

'Hope you don't mind, Harriet. But Nutkins is with me tonight. And I want him.'

Harriet and I turned to confront Helen – lithe, leggy and provocative in her St Trinian's outfit. Her campaign to 'get pissed' had reached the irrepressibly giggly stage, and she was swigging punch from a beermug.

'*Come,* Nutkins,' she ordered manically. 'I want to dance.'

'I shall be glad to dance with you, Helen,' I said with dignity. 'If you promise never again to call me Nutkins.'

'Cross my heart, Nutkins,' she chortled, fondling her left breast lewdly. 'Here.' She dragged me away, leaving Harriet smiling grimly.

I danced more that night than ever before or since.

Helen kept me at it for ages, and there was a purpose behind her bacchantic mirth. The Boyfriend, who had chucked her at the Art College Ball six months before, was present tonight, and flagrantly engrossed in the dark-eyed enchantress who had ousted Helen from his heart. Grant MacMillan was a tall, swarthy specimen, like a Latin version of Witch with more Animal and less Magnetism. One of those aggressively masculine males who love to display the coarse black matting on their wide-nippled apelike chests by jiving at parties clad only in genital-squelching jeans and frayed denim waistcoats.

'Isn't he *disgusting*?' Helen shouted above Mick Jagger's *Nineteenth Nervous Breakdown*. 'I just can't see what I ever saw in him.'

Jennifer Strachan, the dusky temptress, had been in Helen's class at St David's, which heated the bitching no end. She was undeniably pretty, in a glinting, Mexican-Indian sort of way, but:

'Look at the *moustache* on her,' Helen hooted gleefully.

After *Jumping Jack Flash* I felt cramp claw my thighs, when suddenly:

'There's Simon. Must dance with Simon. SIMON?'

As Helen swayed away to bop with the bouncy Darling, the limp Squirrell withdrew thankfully for a peaceful respite with a glass of punch amid the dumped coats and handbags.

Where Cindy found him meditating ten minutes later.

'Ah, Peter,' she said warmly, not knowing I'd been avoiding her. 'Why hasn't Witch come?'

'I don't . . .'

'Helen told me Witch said something to you. Before he left the concert.'

'Yes.'

'Can't you tell me?' Cindy pleaded, kneeling by my feet.

I was sitting on a corner of her double-bed, and, sluggishly regarding her vermilion cord slacks, her cotton-voile chemise, and her soulful green eyes, I felt suddenly cast in the mould of Ancient Sage: Moses come down from the Lorimer Hall with The Wisdom inscribed on the tablets of my mind.

'Pardon me,' I said, having belched unexpectedly. 'Witch didn't *say* he wasn't coming. But he was disappointed that you didn't sing his songs.'

'But we *couldn't*, Peter,' Cindy exclaimed.

'Why not?'

'Janie refused to go on straight after us. She said it was bad programming. So we had to give the Ravens some of our time.'

'To bore the audience into wanting Janie more?'

'Sort of.'

'Very cunning. But you could have done *one* of Witch's songs, couldn't you?'

'We weren't allowed to, Peter. The A&R Manager's up from London, and he told Othello we simply must plug the tracks on the single. So Othello told Mike, and the rest of us were taken by surprise.'

'So was Witch,' I said baldly, though it didn't bother me to see him thwarted for once.

'Was he *very* angry?' Cindy asked pathetically.

'What right has Witch to be angry?' I fumed. 'He's been manipulating people for weeks, all to get his silly songs to Janie Carmen's attention. That night . . .'

'*No*, Peter.'

I blinked.

'Witch wrote those songs for *me*.'

'How do you know?'

'I asked him. When he was driving me home from your flat. And he admitted it. He was shy at first, you see, because he thought I might not like them.'

'He didn't ask if you'd read *Tom Sawyer*, did he?'

She gave me a puzzled look, then said slowly:

'I think, Peter, that in his heart of hearts Witch is still in love with me. A little. Isn't he?'

I hurriedly confessed my incompetence to conjecture.

Cindy smiled sadly.

'He and I were once together,' she said. 'Did you know that?'

'Helen told me . . .'

'We knew each other for years before . . .'

Cindy recounted her relationship with Witch, and her eloquent body seemed to dance as she spoke. The confessional flavour of the situation appeared to cheer her, so I sat back and leant a dutiful ear, now and again shifting my legs to ward off cramp.

By the time she reached the dastardly episode of the *Pobble Cameron-Bell?* poem, my attention (several times distracted by couples prospecting for privacy in which to snog, and by girls rushing in to commune with their handbags) was half absorbed in a lurid painting hung on the wall above Cindy's dressing table.

It looked, in the dim ginger light, as if a Chinese dragon were moonwalking on a trampoline. It had a green and silver body, with a golden lion's mane, and was enmeshed in a feathery welter of loop-the-loops like the sky at a Farnborough air display. These weaving loops had an Escher-like spatial impossibility about them. They encircled the looning monster but also emanated from and interpenetrated it: frothing from its nose and into its ears, out of its erect penis and into its leering mouth.

'Witch sent me that,' Cindy suddenly said in a different tone.

I looked at her sheepishly.

'From California. It's from one of his trips.'

'Rather him than me,' I said, disturbed by the dragon's unsane snarl.

'Othello doesn't know Witch painted it,' Cindy said meaningfully.

'Didn't Witch sign it?'

'He wrote something on it. But not his signature. He said . . . Othello thinks . . .'

I sat up in consternation as my Guinevere burst into heart-rent tears. Her long white fingers rumpled the smooth sheen of her stage-lacquered hair as she buried her face in her hands, and her breast heaved with hopeless undying love for the cynical drug-fiend who had cast her off like a used paper handkerchief for the sin of refusing to trip with him.

I like to think that if Witch had been present I would have hit him. As it was, pale with terror in case Othello came in and found his woman weeping in my company, I said:

'Please don't cry, Cindy.'

'I'm *sorry*, Peter. I'm so . . .'

'Can I get you a drink?' *If only I could touch you.*

'No thanks, Peter. But . . .' She stood up, sniffing bravely, and mopped her eyes on the bell of her sleeve. 'Will you dance with me? Please?' She held out her hand. 'I'll feel better if I dance.'

'I'd love to,' I said, taking her hand. 'But isn't Othello . . .'

'Othello doesn't dance,' she explained haltingly. 'He's in his office with the A&R man.'

The disco music had slowed into a string of smooch ballads

that *required* me to lay hands on this mixed-up beautiful lady who loved me not. Cindy held me close and rested her head upon my shoulder, screening her tearstained face from the genuine smoochers, and twice a comforting Squirrell paw pressed gallantly against the forbidden fruit of a Cameron-Bell buttock.

This was heady stuff for me, and I wished it could last for ever. Paul Simon had written *Bridge Over Troubled Water*, I felt, with the sole purpose of illumining, for all the world to see, the tender, protective, futile passion that Cindy excited in me that night.

As the song cascaded to its finale an imperious finger stabbed me in the ribs, and Harriet said:

'Peter!'

'Nyee?'

'You'd better take Helen home.'

'Why?'

'She's been sick, she's drinking again, and now she's got Simon rolling joints.'

While Helen fumbled into her coat, I stepped closer to Witch's dragon painting. The inscription in the bottom right-hand corner said:

Tat Twam Asi, Mein Pobble

'Shgooed, in tit?' Miss Myrmidon Wishfort slurred loyally, pulling me away. 'Witch I could paint like Wish.'

At the door, Cindy, radiant again, thanked me for coming.

'My pleasure,' I said.

'Oh, Peter. I must give you that book.'

'What book?'

'Your . . . sex book. But it's in Othello's office, and . . .'

'Doesn't matter,' I said grandly. 'If Witch's paying the fine, I don't care if the whole world reads it first.'

'Why jew lend Cindy that orgazooms book, Petter?' Helen demanded, as we lurched with our hot jam doughnuts from

Donald's the midnight baker down to Buttbridge traffic lights, having failed to hail a taxi. The night was dark and still, chilly in the hour before dawn, and the heavy yeasty smell of busy breweries hung over the sleeping city like an invisible pungent fog.

'I didn't lend it to her. She borrowed it.'

'Think she's had one yet?'

'Had what?'

'An *orgazoom.*' Helen found this thought so funny that she heaved with helpless laughter all the way up Aden Lane and along Hanover Place to Number Ten.

'Hey, Petter!' she then hissed conspiratorially. 'Lemme cummin true debasement? Daddy ud kill miffy sawmy like this.'

'All right. Mind the steps,' I added automatically. 'They get slippy at night.'

'I *know,* Petter. Vlived here fifteen years!' This also was paralytically amusing, apparently, and Helen had to stifle hysterics that nearly put her bottom through the window of the Thermos cellar.

'Ssssh.'

'You kin make me cupuv coffee few like,' she whispered generously in my kitchen. 'Black in one cigar, peas.'

'Very well,' I said wearily. 'But just a quick one. You go through and put the fire on. Can you cope with that?'

'Muh!' she mouthed, stuck a darting wet kiss on my cheek, and stumbled down the passage to my room.

Five minutes later I followed her with two mugs of coffee and my last Penguin biscuit. She had managed to light the fire and drape her scarf round the lamp on my desk, giving the room a shadowy oriental feeling. She had also taken off all her clothes, which lay strewn across the floor, and was lying in my bed gazing at the ceiling.

'What are you doing?'

'Mmmwaiting for my cawfee,' Helen said teasingly. 'Nide like a ciggy from my bag, peas.'

'Why are you in my bed?'

'Sss comfy.'

'So are the armchairs.'

'Aw right,' she said, sitting up brightly. 'We kin sit in de almchairs.'

'Stay where you are, Helen.' I put: the telephone on the floor, the tray on the bedside table, and my sports jacket on the hanger hooked over the top of the wardrobe.

'Anna cassette?' Helen clamoured.

'I haven't got any cassettes.'

'Why jew have a cassette player den?'

'Ask your brother.' I put *Harolde en Italie* on my record player, fetched Helen her cigarettes and lighter, and sat on the bed beside her.

She was propped on one elbow, slurping coffee and infinitely unashamed of her bare shoulder and exposed right breast, whose nipple was pink and demurely pointed.

Excitedly I said:

'You can't stay there all night, you know.'

'Why not?'

'I'm tired, Helen. I want to go to bed.'

'Get in.'

'I can't.'

'Why?'

'You'd say in the morning I took advantage when you were drunk.'

'I *wouldn't,* Peter,' she exclaimed. 'I know what I'm doing. I want you to get into bed with me, and *fuck* me.'

'Why?'

'Because I haven't had it for weeks.'

'I haven't had it for twenty-one months,' I said expressively. 'I counted the other day.'

'No wonder you're out of practice,' Helen giggled fifteen minutes later, while I thrashed about on top of her, struggling to massage my penis into a presentable erection.

'I'm sorry,' I gasped, 'if I'm more of a Clark Kent than a Superman in bed. But please remember you're here entirely at your own invitation. I'll stop if you want.'

'No, no,' she cooed. 'Mmmming joying it.'

Shortly I put up a reasonable performance, I felt, and we

were lying side by side falling asleep to a Brandenburg Concerto when a haunting thought visited me.

'When,' I whispered, 'do I see your portrait? Of Witch in the nude?'

'Don't be . . . *naive*, Peter,' Helen murmured.

'In what way?'

'I wasn't *painting* Witch that night. We were having a *bang.*'

I felt like she'd snipped off my testicles with a pair of crimping shears.

'You're serious, aren't you?' I asked in agony.

'Uh huh.'

'But he's your *brother.*'

'So what?' she said calmly, inspecting my anguish with the cool, hard nonchalance of youth and energy combined with beauty and confidence. 'We're all the same Being, really,' she expounded. 'So all sex is masturbation. So what does it matter who you wank with? In an age of reliable contraception, the incest taboo is obsolete.'

'That's what Witch says, isn't it? It's not your idea.'

'Who cares?' she said haughtily. 'As long as it's true.'

'But you could get *anyone* to sleep with you, Helen. Why your brother?'

'I was very depressed when Grant left me, and I didn't want to get involved with anyone else. In case I got hurt again. When Witch got back from America he said what I needed was a good, clean, hard fuck. So I said "Okay, you fuck me". So he did. Witch says girls like me need sex regularly or we get neurotic.'

'And did he dispense this therapy before Françoise was sent home? Or after?'

She looked at me strangely, then pressed another swift kiss on my lips.

'Don't be jealous, Peter,' she said as she rolled over. '*You*'ve fucked me now.'

'Now Witch is fucking someone else, you mean?' It occurred to me that Helen's mouth tasted like a dead ashtray soaked in vinegar.

'Is he? Night-night, Peter.'

'I feel sick,' I mumbled bitterly.

From the other side of the bed, dreamily muffled, came something remarkably like:

'Then you'd better go to the bathroom.'

Two hours later I awoke in a sweating panic from a dream of being raped by a faceless woman with a vagina like the rim of a milkbottle.

The milk horse was clopping by outside, and Helen was pulling abrasively on my swollen penis, regarding me expectantly.

'What's going on?' I protested.

'Time to do it again, Peter. My turn on top.'

'Why do you want to go on top?'

'I like it better.' Rearing up and straddling me, so adroitly that my penis shot into her as if sucked, she added:

'And it says in your orgasms book that women have more on top. And I haven't had any yet. Tonight, I mean. And I want to have lots.'

EIGHTEEN

Wouldn't it be nice to truly say:

'I have never taken the initiative with a woman in my life'?

With oneself so discreetly yet compellingly attractive that women conceive such an overweening yearning for one's person as to smash through the restraints of traditional decorum in order to bask submissively in the glow of one's secured attentions?

Yet the Squirrell truth is:

That on the few occasions when I have tried to make the going with a lady, *I have never been successful.*

This, you may say, is a damaging admission, but I am sure that, for every professional psychologist with an IQ exceeding 150 from whom you could wring the truth, you could record a similar result. If people can be personality-typed by snobberies (Witch being a psychedelic snob, Tom Redhead a political snob, Mr Wishfort a moral snob, etc), psychologists are IQ snobs to a man. Professor and Mother Galton certainly were (all their children having higher IQs than their peers, as invariably emerged at department social functions), Dr Tostow was, and I was too. In my second year at Saint Andrews I had actually considered joining Mensa, but abandoned the project for fear of derision if my non-psychologist acquaintances found out.

And how, with this mentality, can one fail to either chicken out of taking the plunge at all or else dive blindly (oblivious to blatant danger signals, such as that the tide is out) and come a blushing cropper?

Helen, then, was one of those rare pieces of good fortune that even a sexual ineffectual may enjoy once or twice a lifetime: when the tide is so ripe that it knocks you off your rock and pulls you in.

She was the first objectively desirable girl I'd ever slept with.

What does 'objectively desirable' mean?

How about 'immediately desired by a hundred sexually mature males chosen at random'? In any case, you know what I mean. My few girls before Helen had been *pleasant* enough, but spotty, or dumpy, or scrawny, or in some other way a long mile wide of that *objectively desirable* bull's-eye.

Consequently, my Honourable Schoolboy Delusion (that *Guinevere* doesn't fart in bed, or have eyebrows that rasp against one's cheek like Brillo pads, or accidentally nudge one in the testicles with knees like piledrivers covered with sandpaper) was still barely dented.

Until Helen wrote it off.

She farted like a schoolboy trooper at summer camp, my left eye was nearly put out by the careless bristles of her wiry brows, and when at seven she attempted to arise and leave me, she got caught in the sheet and nearly kneed my testicles to death.

But somehow her objective desirability emerged unscathed.

Later that Saturday she asked me to spend the night at Querns with her, and I accepted like a sex-mad shot. When we stopped for ice-cream at Jake's Cafe Petrol, and the resting lorry drivers looked liverishly at Helen's legs, I felt so insanely proud and happy that I wanted to beat my chest and yell: 'Cock-a-doodle-you, you dirty-minded rascals. This lady's *mine.*'

That weekend was the most sexually active of my life.

On Monday morning I slept in by two hours and my penis felt like a frankfurter, minced and stitched back together with catgut. Helen's reading of my *Varieties of Orgasmic Experience* had stimulated an intense preoccupation with her own orgasmic 'achievements', to service which I was teased and ridiculed into a number of outré intimacies that previously I would only have believed of perverts and orgasmic research volunteers.

I knew it could never last: that I was merely a convenient tugboat for Helen to slum on until a suitable pleasure-cruiser drifted by, but that didn't seem to matter. The exercise of my reproductive parts did me a power of good, my work efficiency rose dramatically, and I regained confidence that a First was not beyond me.

'Are you busy, Peter?' Helen would ask on the phone most nights.

'I'll be finished soon.'

'I'll come down then, shall I?'

'Be my guest.'

It was rather clandestine, and we didn't behave as lovers in public. My revulsion at the incest between Helen and Witch calmed, and I couldn't deny a tingling feeling that by mounting Helen I was copulating with the entire Wishfort family, strengthening my right to participate in their mythology. My own family relationships, with my mother and sister, had always been somewhat dull, and I found a vicarious excitement in paddling on the edge of the Wishforts' unpredictable complexities and conflicts.

Apart from energetic intercourse, not a lot of interest took place in the week after Helen seduced me. I read several books, completed a long essay on *Mechanisms of Memory*, and began to apply for summer work. I anticipated commencing graduate research in October, so I wrote to all the language schools in Cambridge, offering my services as a teacher of English from July to September.

Then came Easter.

There was a big family dinner on the Sunday evening, in the course of which:

Mr Wishfort drank himself into a state of steamrolling enthusiasm for his contribution to Angus Angusson's documentary on Brain Damage in Road Accidents. This was to be recorded the following Friday, and Mr Wishfort gave a dining-table rehearsal of his projected television performance.

'Six thousand people killed in this country *every year*. Six *thousand*,' he deplored. 'And *countless* thousands seriously injured, blinded, paralysed for life. If only you young people would *realize . . .*'

Alastair mumbled unconvincingly that he *almost* always wore his seatbelt and made a strict point of never drinking more than two pints before driving.

'Can't stand the damn things,' scoffed Mr Hamilton, arguably referring to seatbelts.

Deirdre primly pointed out that Mr Wishfort often didn't wear his own seatbelt.

'*Now* I do,' he countered gloatingly. 'You wait till you see the programme, young lady, and you will too.'

'I *always* wear my seatbelt,' Deirdre said sensibly.

'And you're a hypocrite, Daddy,' Helen said accusingly.

'In what way?' her father inquired severely, pouring himself another glass of wine.

'When you drive home from the staff club, you're often way over the limit!'

'I, Helen Wishfort, am a driver of some *thirty-five years' experience.* And in that time I have never, repeat *never*, been involved in an accident.'

'Pride before a fall,' murmured Deirdre.

'You've had lots of speeding endorsements,' said Helen.

'If and when you girls reach my age . . .'

Helen hoped she wouldn't have turned into a drunken old hypocrite.

This detonated a furious blast of paternal wrath.

Alastair and Mr Hamilton looked distinctly uncomfortable, and I felt my whole body go the colour of Rudolph's nose. If mere filial insolence could make the man so angry, what ever would happen if he learned what Helen and I . . .

'Douglas, dear?' Mrs Wishfort interrupted him sharply.

'What?'

'Deirdre and I have decided. We'll have the reception in Runcornfield House.'

'Indeed? And just who do you expect is going to pay for that?'

'You are, Daddee. You are,' crowed Rosie, whose precociously lipsticked mouth was nuzzling a chicken leg. 'It's always the fa-ther that pays for the wed-ding. Mrs Beamish told us when she got married . . .'

Discussion of Deirdre's wedding led on to plans for a birthday party for her and Witch, to be held at the end of the coming week. Their births were separated by precisely a year and four days, which:

'Didn't give me much of a rest,' Mrs Wishfort agreed. 'But I think Deirdre was worth it. Don't you?'

'Just,' said Alastair, making a Herculean effort to be humorous.

'Barely,' said Helen.

Deirdre made a disparaging remark about the brains of girls who went to art college, and I asked Mrs Wishfort:

'How old is Mallecho?'

'He'll be twenty-three on Thursday.'

Only six months older than me. This seemed so incredible, and somehow *unfair,* that it shut me up for the rest of the meal.

'Where was he tonight?' I asked Helen five hours later, when she had clambered off me and was smoking a roll-up.

'Who?'

'Witch?'

'He's in Amsterdam for the weekend.'

'What's he doing in Amsterdam?'

'He's got *friends* there,' Helen said with possessive scorn, as if any twenty-two-year-old man without friends in Amsterdam were a shade less substantial than a eunuch's shadow.

NINETEEN

'Now having said all that,' said Professor Quelch, nodding benignly after having said quite a lot, '*we* once had a carving fork that to all intents and purposes *did* disappear right out of existence. Never set eyes on the blessed thing again. So what can we conclude? Do we here have an instance of the *a priori* conditions governing all thought being confounded? Or must we seek some alternative explanation?'

'Couldn't it have been stolen?' I suggested seriously.

'Might have been,' he agreed anxiously. 'I must say I hadn't thought of that. But who . . .'

'Pea Tar?'

'Yes, Rosie?' I called back hopefully. It was ten o'clock and the birthday party was in full swing. Professor Quelch had captured me by the middle window in the drawing room, where Anita Tostow had abandoned me. The house was swarming with guests that included Professors Quelch and Newbigging, Angus Angusson of the BBC, Beano and half the rugby club, the psychology Finals class and most of the department (but not the Galtons, who were on vacation in the West Indies), Simon Darling and Othello, and a bubbly bevy of Rosie's chums from school.

It was mainly a white wine occasion (though a keg of Export had been set up in the kitchen, for the rugby club), there was a cold buffet on the dining-room table (most delectably featuring Mrs Wishfort's home-made pâté and carrot pakora, and Helen's brandy-sodden brandy snaps), a background of barely audible Spanish guitar music filtered from the box record player in a corner of the drawing room, and the order of the evening was to circulate, converse, and listen obediently when captured by professors.

'Telly phone, Pea Tar,' Rosie sang.

'Please excuse me, Professor . . .'

Quelch had already captured Alastair, who looked like an uncomfortable Goliath in a brown lounge suit, sipping wine when he'd much rather be swigging Export.

My rescuer was standing by the drawing-room door.

'Who is it, Rosie?'

She smiled with an air of smug mysteriousness. She was made up with the tribal savagery of middle-class schoolgirls whose mothers allow them to arrive at good taste by a process of trial, error and gravitation, and her figure, in a hugging caftan that belonged to Helen, had come on in leaps and bounds since January. For an insane moment I determined that, as soon as Helen ditched me, I would lose no time in debauching Rosie.

'It's *Witch,'* she whispered secretively.

I went downstairs and squeezed between three of Helen's art cronies who were covened on the bottom four steps and urgently debating the wisdom of lighting a joint. Going to the phone, I finger-plugged my left ear against the babble from the dining room, and said coldly:

'Peter here.'

'Hi, Pete. How's things?'

'Could be worse. Everyone's asking after you.'

'Othello there?'

'Yes. And so's Anita.' I glanced round to make sure no one was listening.

'What's she doing there?'

'Deirdre invited all the psychology staff.'

'Good investment.' Witch chuckled. 'Think she'll get a first?'

'No.'

'Think you will, Pete?'

'What can I do for you, Witch?' I asked abruptly.

'You spoken to Anita?'

'Yes.'

'What was she saying?'

'She asked where you were. A reasonable question, really.

Since it's your birthday party. Where are you?'

'She say anything else?'

'She confided that she was disappointed', I looked round again, 'that you failed to turn up for your last week's sessions with her.'

'And what did you say?'

'That you'd been in Amsterdam.'

There was a pause, and I heard a firm palm being pressed over the mouthpiece at the other end.

'How *was* Amsterdam?' I asked frostily.

'Fine, Pete,' Witch resumed cheerily. 'Brought you back a tulip. What colour do you fancy?'

'What do you *want*, Witch?'

'How did Anita strike you, Pete? Good nick?'

'A little tense, now you mention it. She doesn't know many of the people here.'

'What's she wearing?'

'A bottomless bikini.'

'Why this hostility, Pete?' Witch said reprovingly. 'You drunk?'

'Not yet,' I snapped.

'Then what's up?'

'I don't believe in *incest*, Witch,' I hissed having relapsed to a leaping image of this tall sinewy Deenburgher stripping, penetrating and pleasuring his tall pliant sister. 'That's what's up.'

He tutted:

'Helen tells me you're quite the raging bull in bed, Pete. She says now she can't call you Nutkins, she's going to call you Peepeekins. How's that grab you?'

Sweat started spraying out of me like water from a hot shower. My hands trembled. I was unable to speak.

'Come off it, old son,' Witch said encouragingly. 'Don't take everything so seriously. Life's a holiday. Think of all the eternity during which you didn't exist, and the future eternity during which you won't exist. Why get uptight at Christmas?'

'I'm ringing off now, Witch.'

'Just a minute,' he retorted commandingly. 'Is Cindy there?'

'No.'

'Where is she?'

'I believe she's staying with relations in Perthshire.'

'Who told you that?'

'Deirdre.'

'Right,' he said, sounding satisfied. 'There's a tiny favour you could do me, Pete. Will you?'

'What?'

'Don't tell anyone I phoned, and give me a ring back when Othello and the Tostows have pissed off. Okay?'

'Where are you?'

'Southside.'

'I'll do that, Witch,' I undertook heavily, 'if you'll promise me something.'

'Uh huh?'

'Never to ask me to do you a favour again.'

'Okay, Pete. No problem.'

'Do you *promise*?'

'Cross my heart.'

I put the phone down and went into the dining room for my third brandy snap and second bowl of trifle.

It was a warm night, the windows were open, and every few minutes a startled passing face would peer in from the street for a glimpse of the inmates forking tastier morsels, enjoying more interesting conversations with more attractive women, and generally having a lot more fun than he had had this evening. A line of candles down the centre of the table provided the sole illumination, combining with the rich crimson wallpaper to create a soft, pleasant atmosphere of tongue-loosening intimacy.

Standing by Helen's revealing self-portrait were the artist herself and Mr Angusson, who was clad in the casual blazer and open-necked shirt that celebrities may wear when nonentities can't. One of Deenburgh's more famous sons, he had been in Mr Wishfort's class at the Academy: Dux while Mr Wishfort was School Captain. For years before joining the BBC he'd worked on the *Deenburgh Herald*, and he seemed to be on first-name terms with all the guests present past the age of fifty. The extravagant gestures of passionate art criticism were animating his conversation with Helen, whose docile attentiveness suggested that his comments were perspicuously fair, not to mention melodiously encouraging.

While:

Mr Wishfort told Harriet about the television recording they had made in the Infirmary that afternoon;

Harriet munched an oatcake and cheese;

Anita and Mrs Newbigging, like a swan and a melancholy turkey, were making smalltalk stiffly;

Beano, ruddy and vast in the dinner jacket he had bought from Dormie two years before (rather than admit, after hiring it for a night, that Harriet had honked on it) was siphoning Export from a litre-size German beermug and recounting a rollicking anecdote to Professor Newbigging;

Professor Newbigging was eyeing Beano with the detached interest of an undertaker regarding a comedian who doesn't know he is about to have a fatal heart attack;

Dr Tostow was standing by the sideboard chatting trivially to Othello, while no doubt speculating on the personality type of pushy young men who wear ties printed with pictures of piranha fish and captioned with the names of music publishing companies;

Professor Quelch flapped in like a bespectacled bald heron in a baggy tweed suit, poured himself a cup of coffee, and began to look predatory once more;

I finished my dessert, edged discreetly round the table, and went back up to the drawing room. There I talked to:

Mr Hamilton, about the inconsiderate young layabouts clogging the stairs with their long hair and atrocious manners;

Deirdre, briefly, about the convoluted social behaviour of social psychologists at social functions;

Simon Darling, about the lightning speed of thought,

balletically perfect timing and infinitely fertile imagination I would need if I wanted to become a disc jockey;

And Mrs Wishfort, about several things, including the psychological pros and cons of giving a child an unusual first name.

'Mallecho's argument is,' she said, puffing smoke from a menthol cigarette, 'that a distinctive name tends to foster a distinctive child. A kind of self-fulfilling prophecy, you could say.'

I blinked at her familiarity with my jargon.

'What do you think, Peter?'

'If I'd been called Mallecho, I'd probably have been bullied at school!'

'Ah,' she smiled maternally. 'But that's where mothers' intuition comes in. Your mother chose *Peter* for you because she knew it would suit you. Which it does very nicely.'

Mrs Wishfort went to check that hospitality standards were not flagging elsewhere, and I recalled my promise to Witch.

A glance over the first-floor banister revealed that the Tostows were just leaving. I waited till they'd gone, then toured the house. In the kitchen, Beano, squirting more beer into his tankard, confirmed that Othello had left.

'He didn't try to sell you one of his mackerel ties, Pete, did he?'

'No.'

'You won't buy one if he does, will you?'

'I wouldn't dream of it.'

'That's good. I told the bugger: if they're a publicity gimmick, he should be *giving* them away. And guess what he said?'

'What?'

' "*Business is business*, Turnbull. These ties dinny grow on trees, man." '

So I retreated to the basement to phone Witch from the privacy of my own room.

'Thanks, Pete,' he said. 'See you soon.'

I had no desire to see him ever again.

Suddenly I felt unbearably wretched.

Of all the sixty people gaily eating, drinking and chattering upstairs, how many would notice (never mind mourn) if they never set eyes on Peter Squirrell again? What was I to the Wishfort family but a rent-paying pet, to pat and applaud, or mock and torment, just as the fancy took them?

And they were all the same, weren't they?

Even Mrs Wishfort, who had spilled the beans over my *Nutkins* secret.

I made a cup of cocoa and once more contemplated suicide with disgust. My turbid self-pity (six glasses of wine and a surfeit of brandy snaps) found that it *did* matter that Helen didn't love me: used me like one of those battery-powered sex aids advertised in the back of Beano's magazines.

Yet who could hope for love from Helen?

Who had sex with her brother because Life was a holiday;

Fornicated me into a minced frankfurter and called me Peepeekins behind my back;

And studiously avoided me all evening, devoting herself to the erudite Mr HouseholdFace Angusson?

There is a wonderful observation in Somerset Maugham's novel *Of Human Bondage*. The grim-humoured night nurse tells Philip Carey, the young medical student, that:

. . . people don't commit suicide for love, as you'd expect, that's just a fancy of novelists; they commit suicide because they haven't got any money.

And when it *appears* that one has committed suicide for love, isn't it really that one *didn't have enough money* to do the mad romantic things and buy the outrageous sumptuous gifts that might have made the loved one love one back?

With me it was a case of trousers, and my despondency was a function of student poverty. I'd badly wanted a new pair for the birthday party (slightly flared, to suit a partner considerate enough to maximise his partner's orgasms), but I was too absolutely broke to buy them until I got my summer grant the following week.

So it was the *shame* of having to wear shiny old grey

flannels (unflared) to the party, and the perversely linked conviction that this was behind Helen's ignoring me, that were stewing away and poisoning my night with their self-deceptive fumes.

With moist eyes I finished my cocoa and took my shirt off to go to bed.

Upstairs, people were leaving the party, but it also seemed, from the traffic of car-door bangings, footsteps, guffaws and bell-ringings, that replacements were arriving.

Suppose I were a well-dressed millionaire with a Ferrari?

Would it worry me if Helen chose to flirt with older men?

That Witch took drugs and slept with his sister?

Might not the true explanation of my negative feelings be that *he had plenty of money,* owned his own house and drove a Lotus? While I had to meditate suicide because I couldn't buy new trousers?

The upstairs doorbell rang again.

Someone dropped an empty beer can into my basement, where it bounced on the flagstones with an irritating clatter.

How could I sleep through all these thoughts and noises?

I washed my face, put on a clean shirt, and selected a different cravat. (In cravats, at least, I was wealthy. My old auntie in Crail had sent me one every Christmas since I was fourteen.) Then I went upstairs to rejoin the festivities, determined not to return without Helen on my arm.

Wine and cocoa had made me thirsty, so I went first to the kitchen for a glass of beer.

Mrs Wishfort was stirring a huge cauldron of thick lentil broth that later would keep the all-night drinkers from disgracing themselves. Also present was Rosie, who, changed from Helen's caftan into jeans and a sweater, was washing dishes and complaining that the birthday cake had not been cut before her chums were parentally whisked away.

'Hello, Peter,' Mrs Wishfort greeted me. 'We'll cut it when Mallecho gets here, dear,' she said to Rosie.

'But it's after mid-night, Mummee.'

'It's Mallecho's cake, dear. And I'm sure he'll be here soon. Besides, there are still lots of other things to be eaten up.'

'Mallecho's on his way,' I offered, retreating with a half-pint of Export.

Mrs Wishfort gave me a curious look, then said to Rosie: 'There you are, dear. Peter says Mallecho's just coming. Now . . .'

The morning room was full of rugger hefties and their horsy girlfriends. Beano was swaying in front of the mantelpiece, his enormous shoulders obliterating the birthday cards, and choirmastering the jockstrap refrain:

Bungalow Bell
Made a bad smell,
All the scrum fainted
And all the scrum fell
Except Bungalow Bell
Who grabbed the ball with a yell
Bundled it over
And touched it down well,
So hip-hip hooray
For Bungalow Bell.
Hip-hip . . .

In the dining-room, the staid professorial element had given way to more cronies from the Art College, addled from several hours in a pub, some of Mr Wishfort's juniors from the Infirmary, and a batch of Deirdre's old schoolfriends, who, together with their neck-tonsured escorts, were fresh from a fund-raising do at the Young Conservatives Association. Two of the escorts had got involved in a loud political polemic with Tom Redhead, who was sharing a plateful of potato salad with a short fat woman of indeterminate age who looked like Ludwig Erhard in tattered furs and was called Haggis Annie, so I went upstairs.

The drawing room had a Victorian feel and a large china bust of Victoria herself, who crouched on the floor by the middle window, scowling whitely through the fiendish slanting eyebrows and rat-tail black moustaches that Witch had painted on to her years ago. It was a high-ceilinged rectangular room, and its length filled the width of the house. The three tall windows provided a pleasant view of the Hanover Place back gardens, where private swings and paddling pools, rabbit hutches and apple trees, sloped down to a motley line of ash and sycamore along the wall that kept the resident Labradors, Dalmatians, Red setters, Afghan hounds, Border terriers, wheezing Pekinese and younger children from falling the twenty feet into the river below.

On the blue-veined-cream marble mantelpiece a clutter of knickknacks and oval-framed cameos sat on either side of a white-faced, gold-handed carriage clock. The wallpaper was pale primrose, and above it the cornices curved into the white ceiling like an interior view of the icing on a wedding cake. The furniture included a carved Albert chair with fat cowboy legs, and a long, plush Chesterfield sofa, which divided the room in two. The floor was of varnished pine, and when I arrived with my metallic-tasting beer the usual strewage of fleecy rugs had been removed and the area behind the Chesterfield was alive with dancing.

All the electric lights were off, and candles in numerous holders round the room were flickering madly as a dozen couples bopped to up-tempo Elvis Presley.

Among the dithyrambic pairings were:

Angus Angusson and Helen (who had sold him her nude self-portrait for £200, which later made me forgive her),

Deirdre and Alastair (who either didn't know or mind about the jockstrap defamation taking place downstairs),

Mr Wishfort and Harriet (for whose ampleness he had an unconcealed soft spot),

Professor Quelch (who had removed his tie) and Nora (who hadn't wiped her nose recently),

And Simon Darling with the tongue-dribbling, penis-protruding Panda (who had been released from Rosie's bedroom following the departure of Professor Newbigging, who detested pets).

Mr Hamilton was slumped in the Albert chair and had fallen asleep over a glass of whisky that he held to his waist-coated breast with both hands, in a way that suggested he often fell asleep over glasses of whisky but had developed a reflex ability not to drop them. The windows were open, the room was hot with energy, and a kind of sludging of generations had taken place, making it possible for Mr Wishfort, when *Ready Teddy* was over, to buttonhole me where I was loitering by the door (wondering if I should insist that Helen dance with me), and say:

'I like you, Squirrell.'

'Thank you, sir.'

'You're a decent young chap.'

'He isn't,' said Helen, passing us to turn over the stack of old records on the gramophone. 'He's a filthy sex maniac.'

'Don't you be cheeky, my girl.' Her father frowned.

'With an obsession about women's orgasms,' Helen said cheekily as she swayed away in her white cashmere pullover and hugging dungarees striped like a butcher's apron.

I aborted a violent desire to rush after her, bend her over my knee, and spank her ecstatically.

As Mr Wishfort said:

'Have a whisky, Squirrell.'

'Thank you, sir,' I repeated, having observed how he gloried in *sir* from Alastair.

He went to the walnut tea table at the back of the room and returned with two full crystal glasses.

'You know, Squirrell,' he said expansively, as *Great Balls of Fire* rolled through the room and bopping resumed around us, 'You remind me very much of a young chap . . .'

So began Mr Wishfort's favourite war story, a derring-do saga set deep in the chaos of D-Day Normandy, when a dashing young British Army Medical Corps captain named Douglas Wishfort had, under a *veritable monsoon* of enemy machine-gun fire, plunged heroically into the blazing remains of a farm house to rescue a wounded American soldier, who had subsequently insisted on Captain Wishfort accepting his favourite trophy pistol as a token of his eternal gratitude. The American soldier had later been killed in Korea unfortunately, but:

'It really is a lovely gun, Squirrell,' Mr Wishfort assured me, his green eyes glazed with wine, whisky and nostalgic pride. 'In a beautiful hide holster. I must show it you sometime – would you like to see it?'

'Yes, sir. I would.'

'It's in my steel trunk, in the cupboard across from your room. I wonder . . .'

'If I were you, Dad, I'd keep quiet about that pistol. Professor Quelch has a brother in the See Eye Dee.'

Mr Wishfort turned and glowered at his son.

'Why couldn't you have come *earlier*?' he asked severely.

'Helping an old lady across the road,' Witch replied, smiling serenely, his blue eyes big with bhang. 'Hi, Pete. Here she is. Old lay dee?' he yodelled above Dave Clark's rather scratched *Bits and Pieces.* 'Where heart thou?'

In came Cindy.

Gorgeous in a jungle-blue chiffon dress.

Smiling shyly.

'Mr Wishfort,' said Witch to his sire, hooking his thumbs behind his jet-wing lapels, 'meet the future Mrs Wishfort. Miss Belll . . .'

'Hello, Cindy,' Mr Wishfort said fondly, ignoring what Witch was saying. 'I thought you were in Perth this week.'

'My parents are,' Cindy explained hesitantly. 'But,' she looked at Witch for support and he put an arm round her shoulders, 'Mallecho and I have been in Amsterdam.'

'Give Pete his tulip,' Witch scolded affectionately.

Cindy giggled and offered me two brilliant tulips – one yellow, one scarlet.

'See, Pete?' said Witch. 'You never take me seriously, do you?'

I scowled at him over my whisky, and Rosie's voice cried from the landing:

'Mah-lick-co, Dear-dree, you've to come down and cut the cake. At once. *Mummee says.*'

TWENTY

Isn't it amazing what can happen in a few days, when so much usually doesn't?

The Monday after Witch's Janie Carmen disappointment, Cindy had gone up to Southside to confront him: had he written the Hiawatha songs for her? Or for Janie?

He hadn't written them for anyone, he told her casually. They had written themselves. Fathered by his modest talent, but delivered of the spirit of the species. And she was welcome to like it, lump it, or piss off.

Didn't he feel *anything* for her any more?

Indeed: he was very fond of her. Why else did he want her to record better material than the second-rate trad vamps that were more profitable to Othello? Couldn't she see that?

Witch wasn't *angry* with her, Cindy hoped, explaining why his songs weren't performed at the concert.

Not with her, but Othello had his uppance coming.

Witch mustn't blame Othello, Cindy pleaded.

But Witch did, Witch said.

Othello hadn't planned it, Cindy urged. And he promised the programme return was unchanged, so Witch would still get his PRS money for the concert.

Witch smiled sadly and remarked that Cindy must know that Othello must know that Witch didn't give a toss about the money.

Cindy asked Witch tearfully if it could ever again make any difference that she was prepared to trip with him.

It might do, he said guardedly.

She'd like to, she said desperately.

Okay, Witch decided adaptably. He was spending Easter

with a business associate in Amsterdam. Cindy would come with him, and they'd drop a big trip together on the Sunday. Othello should be told that Cindy was going to Perth with her parents. And if things worked out, he could be given the official push when they returned from Amsterdam.

'But are you *serious* about getting married, Witch?' I asked him at the birthday party, when the furore over the engagement party had died down.

'Don't I look serious?'

'No.'

'I do love Cindy, Pete,' he said solemnly.

'But you love *everyone*, Witch. *Tat Twam Asi!'*

'That's right. But I'd go to jail if I married everyone, so I'm forced to be selective. Also, not everyone is equally desirable in bed.'

'So you *do* believe in individual personality.'

'Only as a manageable fiction. Like: everyone talks about Cold rushing in, when it's deep and dark December and someone opens the door of a warm room – whereas actually it's the heat that rushes out. The concept of a person . . .' Two minutes later he concluded with:

'However, there is a more concrete argument for me and Cindy following Deirdre and Alastair up the aisle.'

'What's that?'

'I want to ask Othello to be best man.'

'So you don't love everyone, Witch!'

' "If thine eye offend thee . . .", old son. Othello is a pluke on my arse, and I'm going to squeeze him. But that doesn't mean I don't love my arse. Get you another whisky?'

I asked if Witch's resumption with Cindy explained his recent absence from the orgasmic investigations with the Tostows.

'Partly, Pete. There are other reasons.'

'What?'

He told me, then telephoned for a taxi to take Cindy and him back to Southside.

Next morning, Mr Wishfort was up at seven and in his office before nine. He wasn't operating (I'm glad to say), but he had a lot of administration to process before a formal lunch at the University Staff Club, in honour of Mr Angusson. He didn't return to Number Ten until after four, and while changing into his gardening clothes he had a stroke and collapsed on his bedroom floor, where Mrs Wishfort found him thirty seconds later, having heard the crash of his falling body.

An ambulance rushed him to the Infirmary and he remained in intensive care for twenty-four hours. His stroke was mild, as strokes go, and he was conscious throughout. Prompt treatment minimized the danger of a sequel, and it was soon apparent that Mr Wishfort would emerge with his intellect intact and his physical powers only slightly impaired. But the damage showed most in loss of control of his right hand, making it unlikely that he would ever operate again. This caused him overwhelming depression, which kept him in hospital, under observation, for longer than would otherwise have been necessary.

On the Sunday evening I went up to the morning room (ostensibly to watch television but actually to discover why Helen hadn't come down to interfere with me on the Saturday night) and found the house deserted except for Panda on his sofa. Then at teatime on Monday, Mrs Wishfort, pale and tired but in command, explained what had happened and asked if I could take Panda for a walk later, while the family visited Mr Wishfort in hospital.

At seven on Tuesday I had washed up my supper dishes and was about to repeat my dog-walking service when I heard the distant clanging of the front-door bell.

Should I answer it?

After a pause it clanged again: two pulls, greater urgency.

I decided to lie low.

Hesitant steps came round from the front door and descended into my basement.

I was trapped: with the kitchen light on, standing behind the frosted-glass panels of the basement door, I must be visible as a human form.

Another such loomed outside.

My electric doorbell rang like a fire alarm.

Trembling with introverted loathing, I reached to open the door.

There stood Anita Tostow.

In blood-coloured high-heeled shoes, flesh tights, a silk dress, jacket and matching scarf, fawny grey with large checks formed by thin white and brown lines (so that you could have played Noughts And Crosses all over her), white gloves and a cream-coloured hat like the top half of a flying saucer. But she couldn't have flustered me more if she'd been Ursula Andress in the nude.

'Hello, Peter,' she said, an effortful smile in those china-blue eyes.

'Hello. Anita.'

'I rang the bell upstairs, but nobody seems to be in.'

'That's right. They're all out.'

'Do you think I could . . .'

'Yes I'm sorry of course, please. Do come in.'

I sat her in my guest armchair and offered tea or coffee.

She declined.

I perched stiffly and wished she would go away.

She made some polite remarks about my room, which must be a wonderful place to work in, mustn't it? There was an attractive softness to her accent, which moistened certain sibilants, producing 'upshtairs', 'mushn't', and so on. Her lips were sticked the colour of varnished poppies, and when I looked straight at her the tips of her gull-wing smile reached almost to her ears. Her appearance that day is fixed in my mind by her scent, which smelled like wet lilac blossom.

'It's about Mallecho,' she said nervously.

'How can I help?'

'What has happened to him?'

'In what sense?'

'Like I said on Friday, Peter, Mallecho has stopped coming to our experiments. And we don't know why.'

'Hasn't he been in touch?'

'Not a word. And we don't know his telephone number.'

I explained that Witch was ex-directory, corrected Anita's assumption that he and I were friends, and apologized in censorious tones for his wilful want of courtesy.

'I'm not criticizing him, you understand,' she said in a tremulous voice. 'He's a beautiful boy.'

'That hardly excuses his unreliability.'

'You know, Peter,' Anita said emotionally, and my heart sank as I realized our conversation was charged with an importance for her that I had no desire to share, 'I have never known such pleasure and satisfaction. *Never.*'

I recalled the capacious vagina Witch had glossed.

How much pleasure and satisfaction would you know with me?

'Tell me, Peter,' she begged, fidgeting with the small white handbag on her knees. 'Why did Mallecho stop coming?'

'I can certainly give you his phone number.'

'But do you *know*?'

'Something about the dosages of the drugs Dr Tostow has been testing.' *Barely enough mescalin to wobble a spider,* Witch had said. 'He's quite religious about his drug-taking, you see.'

'Why didn't he tell us?'

'But there is another reason,' I said, then bit my tongue.

'Yes? What *is it*?'

'He's getting married. To a girl he used to . . .'

Anita moaned and began to weep.

I looked at her with fascinated terror, as if she were an escaped murderer holding a gun to my head. What if Helen came down? Or Dr Tostow? Did he know Anita was here?

'I'm sorry,' I said helplessly. 'I didn't mean. I mean . . .'

Her meticulously made-up features screwed into the universally ugly mask of The Sobbing Child, doubly incongruous beneath her high-fashion flying-saucer hat.

'I'm sure it was nothing personal,' I said consolingly. 'Mallecho did say he was enjoying your experiments together. Very much! But now he's engaged . . .'

'Please forgive me, Peter,' she said between sobs, taking

a handkerchief from her handbag.

'Not at all. Can I . . . would you like a drink?'

'A little whisky would be nice.' She mopped her eyes.

'Then whisky it is,' I said hospitably.

I got two tumblers from my kitchen and a bottle of whisky from Mr Wishfort's drinks cupboard, telling myself that he wouldn't mind in the circumstances and that I would later insist on Witch buying a replacement. I poured a generous measure for each of us, closed my windows and lit the fire. Each sip of whisky took Anita closer to recovering the sophisticated poise I expected of her. Eager to nourish this trend, I let her soliloquize for half an hour about her own unhappy childhood, Dr Tostow's unhappy childhood, imprisonment, eventual flight to America and success by way of Berlin, and how the two very different owners of unhappy childhoods had met, fallen in love and got married in Oxford.

Her mother had died of lung cancer when Anita was fifteen, after an agonizing year when the family had to nurse her at home yet conceal the terminal nature of her illness – with the main burden falling on Anita herself, since her father was so busy with his business, and her brother with his studies. Four years later the brother shot himself through the mouth with a small-bore target pistol. Why? Because he'd failed his medical exams a second time. His ambition was to be a psychiatrist, but he wasn't good enough at science to qualify as a doctor first.

(Hearing this, as I topped up Anita's glass, reminded me of my own recent thoughts of suicide, impending Finals, and the menacing question-mark Dr Tostow had raised against my Statistical Methods. All at once my whisky tasted like Dettol and my stomach turned like butter in hot sunlight.)

'Then,' Anita concluded, 'when Henrik's funeral was over, my papa suggested me to come to England. To leave unhappy memories.'

'I see.'

'And I met Ivan in Oxford.'

More's the pity.

'Ivan and I love each other very much, Peter.'

'Of course you do,' I said lamely, feeling like a bush being beaten about.

'Since coming to Deenburgh we want to start a baby,' Anita said in a businesslike feminine tone. 'I would like a child, and Ivan thinks it is necessary for women to breed.'

'That's only natural.'

'And now I will have a baby.'

'Wonderful!' I exclaimed. 'Congratulations. Have some more whisky.' I seized the bottle from my coffee table.

'But you see, Peter,' she said earnestly, 'it is Mallecho's baby.'

'What?'

She nodded soulfully.

'But that's terrible,' I sympathized. 'Can't you . . .'

'No, no, Peter. We *want* to have Mallecho's child.'

'Eh?'

'Ivan cannot give me babies,' my visitor explained with industrious passion. 'The Germans, you know, did terrible things to him in . . anyway, his sperms are dead. So we needed another father for my child.'

I pulled an expressive face.

From the street came the sounds of Mrs Wishfort, Helen and Rosie returning from the Infirmary.

Would Panda blow the whistle on my failure to walk him?

'I tell you this, Peter, which is very difficult for me, because I want Mallecho to know I will have his baby.'

'You mean you've done this *behind his back*?!'

She said conspiratorially:

'Ivan wants nobody to know. But I feel,' she patted her bosom, '*deep inside*, that I must tell Mallecho.'

'Then was your feasibility study – and the therapy for orgasmic malfunction – was that all (excuse me for asking, but) a *deception*? To acquire Witch's sperm without his knowledge?'

Anita looked distressingly hurt.

'Ivan's research is perfectly *serious*, Peter,' she said sincerely. 'And we are going back to America in the summer, to start the major project. Ivan has a new laboratory in California '

'So exploiting Mallecho's fertility was just a bonus?'

'That's right.'

Right?

'Why Mallecho?'

Anita smiled.

'Ivan showed me pictures of three boys, and I choose Mallecho because he had the nicest smile.'

Oh, Life!

'Who were the others?'

'I don't know,' said Anita, as if this were the least important detail in the world. While the most important was:

'This is all confidential, Peter. Isn't it? You won't . . .'

'Not a soul,' I said blithely, thinking that if necessary I could now blackmail Dr Tostow into wangling my First. 'And you're welcome to phone Mallecho from here, Anita. His number . . .'

'Would you call him for me, Peter? Please. Ask him if he'll see me?'

I gaped at her.

She was quivering like a teenager at her first school dance.

'Yes, of course,' I said paternally, wishing I could hug her to my strong manly breast. 'I want to speak to him anyway.' I went over to the phone, sat on my bed, and dialled Witch's number.

'This is Missed Her Hangus Hangusson of the Beee Beee Seee,' his distorted voice answered. 'At the third stroke there will be a fatal road accident.'

'That's not funny, Witch.'

'What's your pleasure, Pete?'

'I've got Anita here . . .'

'Bully for you.'

'She wants to see you.'

'Bully for me.'

'Will you see her?'

'No.'

'Why not?'

'I'm busy.'

'Doing what?'

'Taking drugs and masturbating.'

'I believe you, Witch. But I think you should see the lady. She's got something important to tell you. Something *personal.*'

'Put her on, old son. She can tell me now.'

'She wants to *see* you, Witch,' I insisted, smiling supportively at Anita. 'And I wish you would. I'd consider it *a favour to me.*'

'Making us quits?'

'If you like.'

'Hang on.' He stifled the mouthpiece for several seconds, then said:

'She got Groucho with her?'

'No.'

'She got a car?'

No, she hadn't got a car.

'Okay, Pete,' Witch then agreed. 'As *a favour to you:* get her a taxi and send her up.'

TWENTY-ONE

That was the first time I encountered Anita Tostow as a person.

Until then she had either been the worldly wife of a man with the power to influence the class of my degree, or else the beautiful white rabbit in fantastic orgasmic therapy experiments forbidden to undergraduates by order of the Senate. In both these roles she had the painfully desirable, succulent perfection of a smooth ripe pear as seen by a covetous schoolboy peeping over the orchard wall.

Now it was different.

And the well-dressed lady who left my premises that night, when the black cab drew up outside, was a sad and lonely person, rather impressionable, with a ductile personality and a marriage held together by habit, fear, and self-deception. There were blemishes in her complexion that no blush powder could conceal from my matured perception, along her upper lip a sparse moustache of thick gold hairs glittered harshly, and the wetness in her smell of wet lilac blossom was the wetness of nervous perspiration.

She was, in other words, a normal woman.

More attractive than most, but with less intelligence, education and confidence than many. I've often wondered why Dr Tostow married her. He needed a glamorous wife to complete his career kit, but the world is not bereft of glamorous women with high academic attainments. Is it? Or would a spouse with a high IQ have frightened him? In any case, he must soon have realized that their marriage would fast starve to death unless he found some common ground on which to graze it.

Hence their joint involvement in the Whitman & Nixon

Orgasmic Experience project?

I don't suppose I'll ever know. But if Anita was as hard to satisfy as Witch said, and if Dr Tostow's sexual appetites correlated with his sterility (and he was twenty years older than her), then having her copulate to exhaustion with a variety of well endowed and eager young men (while he took measurements, made recordings and compiled statistics), and convincing her that these voracious couplings were a crucial contribution to a major scientific breakthrough, must certainly have made the Louisiana State Foundation for Procreational Research a rich and juicy pasture for the Tostows' private purposes.

And now, a baby.

The ultimate nuptial nutriment.

Some get maried coz they need to breed, others need to breed coz they need to stay maried, and I need a piss coz I've drunk sicks pints of piss awful beer.

I found the above wisdom chalked on a pub toilet wall some months ago, and its central pearl reflects the Tostow situation nicely. Anita did not share her husband's interests, she could not converse in any detail with him or his colleagues about their work, and her subscription to his beliefs was imitative and nominal. She had no vocation, and her only occupation in Deenburgh was a part-time job in a shop in Bluebell Street, which sold Scandinavian kitchen equipment and was run by an older Swedish lady Anita had met at the Institute.

So the time was ripe for her to bravely bear another man's child because, she said:

'Ivan and I love each other very much, Peter.'

This is why I referred to habit, fear, and self-deception, and I gave my ideas a tentative airing later that week when Deirdre and I had our first final-term tutorial with Professor Galton. After outlining an impenetrably generalized version of Anita's predicament and professed attitude, I asked:

'Wouldn't that count as self-deception?'

'Hmmmmmmmmm,' hummed Galton, tamping his pipe

with the charred remains of a matchbox. 'But a *philosopher*, you see, Mr Squirrell, might argue that the *very concept* of self-deception is, strictly speaking, a *self-contradiction*. Whereas of course Freud . . .'

At the end of the hour he pressed on me an article he had written on the subject fifteen years previously.

'Refute me for next time, if you can,' he puffed dreamily as we left. 'Two weeks from now, shall we say? I'm in Oxford next Wednesday.'

'Let me have it after you, Peter?' said Deirdre, in the lift down to the John Locke cafeteria.

Next week I would, and:

'I was terribly sorry to hear about your father . . .'

It had been on the cards, she said pragmatically. Mr Wishfort had high blood pressure, and Grandfather Wishfort had died of a heart attack at the age of forty-nine.

'So in a way it's Daddy's own fault. He's been told often enough to drink less and not work so hard.'

'Coffee?'

'No thanks, Peter. I just want . . . I need someone to replace Othello in my flat. He's driving me crazy.'

I was agog to hear more about Othello's frustration, but Deirdre rushed away to talk to a fat girl with short curly hair and spectacles, who looked like a born good cook and tidy flatmate.

I got a coffee and sat down to peruse an abandoned *Dumbo*.

Rector Redhead had now amassed *four* thousand anti-Tostow signatures, the paper said. The petition would be presented from a position of power when the *Assessment Yes, Heart Attack Exams No Action Committee* invaded and occupied the University's administration complex, which they would do within the month unless Sir Gabriel pulled the Senate's finger out.

'If there is not some drastic reform,' Editor Redhead threatened, 'in the assessment methods employed by this university *within the month*, we can all look forward to some real bad trouble.'

I pencilled *mescalin* into the first across box of *Dumbo*'s crossword, then rolled a weary eye round the cafeteria and wondered who the four thousand signatures belonged to. The tables were thinly populated (Wednesday was games afternoon) and an atmosphere of smoky lethargy and reluctant, Godot-type waiting prevailed.

'Will Life begin when we graduate?' asked the wrinkles of fact-saturated frowns.

At the other end of my table were two stodgy males in their final year of economic history. One had short hair and was picking his nose, the other had long hair and was contemplating an anaemic daffodil.

'The thing about the civil *ser*vice,' he informed the daffodil, 'is that you've no worries about yer *pen*sion.'

'Ay,' the other replied nasally. 'But the *start*ing salary's no that great. If you're wanting a deposit for yer *mort*gage.'

The hot and cold taps of all life's futile plumbing.

Full of leaden gloom, I trudged home through the clean, bright April sunshine.

To my rented basement.

At ten o'clock that night I broke off swotting and sat looking at my phone for ten minutes before buzzing Helen.

'What is it, Peter? I'm watching television.'

'I was wondering . . .'

'What?'

'How's your father?'

'Mending well, but still very depressed. Mummy's taking him down to Querns when he gets out. To convalesce. What do you want?'

'I haven't *seen* you, Helen, since Saturday morning!'

'So?'

'Well, I mean, I could quite understand, if you felt bad . . .'

'What about?'

'Your father . . .'

'Don't be soft, Peter. It's my period.'

'Oh.'

'Is that all?'

'When am I going to see you again?'

'Teatime tomorrow? Come up and watch telly now, if you like.'

'What's on?'

'Mr Angusson's documentary on poofs.'

'No thanks.'

'It says buggery gives you kidney cancer,' Helen told me in a thoughtful tone. 'I hope that isn't true of normal buggery, Peter. What do you think?'

Five hours later I was woken by the sounds of Witch in my kitchen, interacting with his Thermos. I felt so lonely, miserable and unlovably pointless that I ached to ask him in for a cup of cocoa and a chat: let him expound the secrets of the universe, so I could suck some vitality from his aristocratic confidence.

But he was gone before I made up my mind.

The following afternoon, as I was plodding upstairs for tea, the hall telephone rang. Rosie bobbed her head out of the kitchen and said:

'Can you get it, Pea Tar? I'm may king pan cakes.'

I picked up the receiver and gave the Wishforts' number.

'Is Wishfort there?' a boiling voice demanded.

'Is that Othello?' I asked mildly.

'Who are you?' he snapped back.

'This is Peter Squirrell. We met . . .'

'Well, *get this,* Squirrell. It's *Mr Ormrod* to you. *Right*?'

'As you wish, Mr Ormrod.'

'Is Wishfort there?'

'Which Mr Wishfort do you wish, Mr Ormrod?'

'Don't fuckin piss me about, Squirrell,' Othello howled. 'If that bastard's there . . .'

'Mr Wishfort Senior is in hospital, and Mr Wishfort Junior is in Timbuktu, for all I know. Have you tried . . .'

Othello slammed his receiver down on a blurred obscenity, and I went into the morning room with a nasty taste in my ear.

Helen didn't appear for tea, and when my telephone rang after supper I thought it might be her buzzing down to apologise.

But:

'Ivan Tostow here.'

'Oh. Hello, Dr Tostow. I thought . . .'

'Please tell me, Peter, if you know where my wife is. Do you?'

'Is she missing?'

'Really, Peter, I hope you will be co-operative,' he said heavily. 'I just have returned from a conference in Geneva, and I find my wife has disappeared with most of her clothes. Do you know where she is?'

'Why should I, Dr Tostow?'

'I noticed you speaking with her last Friday at the party.'

'Yes, but . . .'

'Be informed, Peter, that I will take a very serious view if I find you deliberately are withholding information.'

Provided your other three papers come reasonably close.

I had been standing by my bedside table. Now I sank on to the bed with a weak-kneed groan.

'She – your wife – did come to see me the other night,' I haltingly admitted.

'Exactly when?'

'Tuesday.'

'And precisely what did she say?'

'I . . .' allowed Dr Tostow to extract from me, like so many obstinate tapeworms, the details of my talk with Anita.

'Yes,' he commented, and I could almost hear his teeth gnashing. 'You see, Peter, I have also a preposterous note from your friend Mallecho . . .'

'He isn't . . .'

'Saying because I deliberately have stolen his seed from his loins, I thereby have forfeited possession of the vessel in which that seed is deposited.' He paused, breathing emotionally.

'Is that all?'

'He adds that I can look forward to hearing from his

solicitors shortly.'

'What about?'

'Divorce proceedings.'

'But he's marrying *Cindy.*'

'Who?'

I explained the background to Witch's post-Amsterdam engagement.

'Well,' said Dr Tostow, his voice savage with grim satisfaction, 'there we are. The fellow quite transparently is insane. The symptoms absolutely are typical . . .' At the end of a murderous diagnosis which included paranoid schizophrenia, psychotic delusions and a dozen other lunatic stigmata, Dr Tostow asked me for Witch's telephone number.

I gave it to him and added:

'His address . . .'

'I have it.'

'Perhaps . . .'

'Nobody was home, Peter.' Then he called for a redoubling of my discretion.

Which I swore upon my honour.

'Also, Peter?'

'Yes?'

'We possibly should remember that the party who introduced Mallecho Wishfort to myself and my wife was you.'

'At your request, Dr Tostow!' I protested faintly.

'And therefore any normalizing influence, Peter, that you can bring to bear upon this preposterous situation,' he warned me unpleasantly, 'hardly can count against you, can it?'

The instant he rang off, I dialled Witch.

No reply.

I continued dialling at twenty-minute intervals until after midnight. Eventually:

'Southside Seraglio. King Saud speaking.'

'What the hell are you playing at, Witch?' I shouted. 'Where have you been?'

'Take it easy, Pete. Been in Paris for the day. What's bothering you?'

'What do you mean: *Paris*?'

'The capital of France, old son. We flew there this morning. In an aeroplane.'

'What for?'

'I'm buying a farmhouse in the Dordogne, and the girls were buying clothes. We also had a shifty at the Tuileries, but we didn't eat any snails. Limit to what you can do in one day. Great place, Paris in the springtime. What's it been like here?'

'Have you heard from Dr Tostow?'

'What about him?'

I poured out the gist of my earlier conversation.

'Do *you* think I'm insane, Pete?' Witch asked gently.

'You're hardly behaving normally, are you?'

'What's so terrific about normality? Sit behind a desk for forty years? Pay off your mortgage and die?'

'Bigamy . . .'

'Bugger bigamy, Pete. Who's more insane: a man who wants to bring up his own child in his own way, or a man who burgles another man's genes because his own are no good and he's scared his marriage'll fold up?'

'Since when have you been such an ardent family man?'

'I've nothing against progeny, old son. Suffer the little children . . .' For ten minutes his irksome fluency rhapsodized about the exciting new direction his life had taken following Othello's premeditated malice and Dr Tostow's seminal theft:

Cindy and Anita got on famously, which cleared the first hurdle.

Had I ever slept with two women at once?

No, amazingly enough, I hadn't.

'Strongly recommend it, Pete. Get Rosie down some night when you're banging Helen.'

And the Dordogne farmhouse?

They were all going to retire to it after he married Cindy in July. Start a commune. Cindy would get pregnant as soon as possible, so the kids could grow up together. Sun-bronzed limbs growing sturdy, straight and true amid the vineyards of heaven-on-earth. That sort of thing.

'Fancy being a godfather, Pete?'

'You know, Witch, I'm not sure you aren't insane.'

'You know, Pete,' he mimicked gleefully, 'I'm not sure you aren't jealous.'

'Who's going to finance it all?'

'I can afford it. We'll sell up here, and my MOR song's doing well in Australia. New cover version. And Tostow'll have to pay Anita alimony.' He chuckled.

'You can't *marry* two women, Witch.'

'Might try. Maybe take a trip to Mecca. We'll work something out.'

'What about the TwangGang? And Othello?'

'That's his problem.'

'Aren't you being rather hard on him?'

'Twat Tam, old son: Othello is a bag of pus. If thy buttock boil offend thee, lance it.'

'You realize, Witch, don't you,' I asked righteously, 'that your carryings-on have become my problem too?'

'How come?'

'Dr Tostow has virtually threatened to stop me getting a First. If I don't help him get his wife back.'

'Take it to the Senate, Pete. Leak it to *Dumbo*. Did you tape the call?'

'No.'

He tutted. 'You should always . . .'

'You aren't taping *this* call, are you?'

A mirth-laden pause was followed by a high-pitched squeaking, then:

'You know, Witch, I'm not sure you aren't insane,' played back at me like an indigant plum being squashed in a garlic press.

So with a muttered oath I rang off.

On Friday the telephone spate continued.

Deirdre phoned in the afternoon to ask if I was finished with Professor Galton's paper on *Self-Deception*, my mother rang in the early evening to make sure I had received the vitamin pills she had sent to vaccinate me against plagues, floods and erupting volcanoes during my pre-Finals month, and Mrs Wishfort buzzed me later and again on Saturday morning to update my dog-minding instructions.

'And naturally, Peter, we'll forget about next month's rent.'

'No, really, Mrs Wishfort. I enjoy taking Panda . . .'

'Yes really, Peter. Now please don't argue.'

By the way, I pretended to remember, was Helen there?

No, Helen was staying the night in Glasgow. She was going to a pop concert with some friends.

This made me so ill with jealousy that I couldn't work for several hours. I'd almost recovered enough concentration to read a spot of Freud when, at about five o'clock, my phone rang again.

It was Beano.

'Okay, Pete?' he asked tentatively.

'Fine, thanks.'

'Got plans for tonight?'

'Yes.'

'Oh.' He sounded disappointed.

'I have a date with Panda. In the park.'

'Ah,' he said hopefully. 'Nothing else?'

'What are you offering me, Beano?'

'I was wondering if you'd like to save someone from dying of thirst?'

'Who?'

'Me.'

'How?'

'Harriet and Nora,' he explained disgustedly, 'are going to *The Magic Flute*. At the Queen's.'

'And you aren't?'

'And I'm not. But I would like to nip down to Poldy's for a couple of hours,' he said enthusiastically. 'Have a drink with the lads – you know?'

'What's stopping you?'

'Witch is stopping me.'

'Oh?'

In a tone suggesting patience and loyalty perilously stretched, Beano said:

'Him and his harem are tripping, and I'm looking after them.'

'And you want me to take over, while you go to Poldy's?'

'Will you, Pete?' Beano cried passionately. 'There's a *pal.* You can drink all his whiskey, and . . .'

The squashed plum in me wanted to refuse, yet what wracking agonies would I suffer if I sat in my room all night picturing Helen with her friends in Glasgow?

'Okay, Beano,' I agreed. 'I'll be there by eight.'

TWENTY-TWO

He was waiting for me at the door, elephantine in a hairy green lumber jacket, and straining with the eagerness of a trapped greyhound.

'Really appreciate this, Pete,' he beamed, patting my shoulder alarmingly. 'They're expecting you. Upstairs.'

'What's involved?' I asked uneasily. 'I've never done this sort of thing before.'

'Oh . . .' he gestured eloquently. 'Shouldn't be any problem. Witch knows what he's doing, and they're over the hump. Just, you know, *smile*! Be cheerful, supportive. Help them do anything they want that isn't dangerous. They haven't been out yet, so they might want walkies sometime, in which case take them over the golf course so they can gurgle at the moon in peace. Keep off the streets, that's the thing. Avoid the ten o'clock drunks,' he advised, nodding earnestly.

'Have they eaten?' I asked, feeling motherly already.

'Nip down to the Pride of Peking if they get peckish. Get a take-away. Here's Witch's money, and . . .' He handed me a key and a sleek leather wallet that could have starred in an American Express advert.

'Thanks.'

'*E* or *F* and an extra fried rice should do,' Beano suggested expertly, backing out. 'And take a fiver for your taxis. Help yourself to whisky. He's got wine in the fridge. Just . . . be natural, Pete,' he counselled, eyeing me with strangely disturbing amusement. 'Go with the flow. *Let it all hang out!*'

'What about . . .'

'I won't be late,' he promised unconvincingly, then

turned with a whoop and thundered down the stairs chanting a personalized version of *What Shall We Do With The Drunken Sailor?*

I closed the door and went slowly up the stairs to Witch's apartment.

What does a trainee teacher feel like just before he takes his first class?

The RECORDING PLEASE FUCK OFF door was ajar, and the flat was saturated with medieval dance music that made me think of squat Norman churches and buxom rosy-cheeked wenches prancing suggestively round maypoles. Since there were loudspeakers in every room, the music didn't tell me where my ducklings were. I tried the living room, where I saw two large spools revolving on 'my domestic tape recorder': the Revox on the chipboard shelf under the windows. But the room was unpopulated and I noticed nothing unusual except that the fridge was open, displaying three pints of milk and two bottles of white wine.

I shut the fridge and went through to the bedroom.

The door was open, revealing Witch's wardrobe and a tall loudspeaker, so I poked my head round.

It was uncomfortably hot (the windows were open at the top, but the central heating was on and the coal fire was glowing), and the pulsating atmosphere of incense, cannabis, mint tea, soap, burnt plastic, wine spilled on sheets, armpits and sex . . . brought wrinkles to my nose and a prickling to my blinking eyes.

Witch's bed was behind the door.

It had been extended by a single mattress, making a total fornicating area of some sixty square feet. This arena was sheeted in yellow, pink and white, which gave me a dizzy sensation like the stripes before a major roundabout on a fast road.

On the far wall, to the left of the fire, a painting was being screened from a slide projector. It was the fantastic shimmering image of Jean Delville's *Les Trésors de Satan*, with its intertwined host of gorgeous-coloured limbs, loins and breasts being high-jumped by a muscular demon who looks as though he's running to get a fire-extinguisher to put out his hair, which is hellishly ablaze.

Lying on the bed at right-angles to the sheet stripes, facing away from me and viewing the static picture as if it were *The Professionals* on television, was Cindy. Sitting facing each other, closer to me, were Witch and Anita. Their attention was riveted to a small circular metal tray containing a puddle of milk discoloured by a patch of the sludge brown into which my paintings always degenerated at school.

None of the trippers had a stitch of clothing on.

Hence my hot gaping, at:

Cindy's heels, knees and pale buttocks with a dark furrow between, topped by hunched shoulders and a seemingly neckless head resting on a luxurious pile of speckled duvets and striped pillows.

And:

Anita's big but disappointingly saggy breasts.

What was I to do?

I hadn't come in order to have my fantasies slaughtered, and if I . . .

Witch picked a small bottle off the floor and squeezed some colouring into an unsludged corner of the milk tray. His movement startled me, and I bumped into the door, which creaked.

He and Anita looked up, their eyes huge with childlike wonder.

I felt like an aging voyeur in a dirty duffelcoat.

'It's . . . *Pete,*' Witch exclaimed above the music, as if it were August and he were announcing 'It's . . . *snowing*'.

Cindy rolled over from her satanic treasures and sat up. Her breasts were petite and perfect in outline, but she had lumpy nipples and large dark aureoles, with an unsightly cluster of small black moles between the underside of her breasts and her navel.

My horror must have shown, for all three galactic explorers were scrutinizing me with the fascinated apprehension of eight-year-olds wondering why Teacher is angry. Overcoming a powerful desire to flee, I recalled Beano's instructions and said with a sickly smile and hollow hearty boom:

'Hello, everybody. It's me. Getting a good suntan, are we?'

I expected cynical jeers, but their faces lit up like Roman candles and they fell about the bed laughing, patting and cuddling each other and spilling the sludged milk from the tray.

This gave me confidence.

'Just forget about me,' I continued benevolently, 'unless you want something. Anyone want anything?'

'Yes, Pleatse,' said Witch. 'Can we have some clean milk?'

'Coming up.' I peeled off my coat and jacket and draped them on an easy-chair by the near window.

'And different music. Let's have . . . *Vivaldi.*'

'Yes,' Anita echoed softly. 'Vi*val*di.'

For twenty minutes I pottered about, found a tape of Vivaldi concertos in Witch's study and put it on the Revox, got a fresh bottle of Moselle from the fridge and drank most of it myself, watched Witch and Anita paint shapes in the milk tray (using bottles of food colouring catalysed by tiny drops of washing-up liquid, which made the shapes evolve and mutate like the skin of an organic kaleidoscope), and started to tidy up.

But I quickly realized my anti-entropic exertions were making the inmates uneasy.

So I left, variously scattered about the floor:

An empty wine bottle, and three crystal champagne glasses with tall hollow stems;

A tray of used tea receptacles and plates;

Witch's Paul Simon guitar, though this I moved away from the fire, in case the heat warped it;

A tin of bubble-blowing fluid, upset on the cobalt-blue carpet;

A tobacco tin containing Rizla papers and a Milky-Way-sized slab of hash;

A large ashtray full of sundry filths, including several dead reefers;

A pack of glossy brochures in French, advertising purchasable paradises in the Dordogne;

A box of coloured crayons and a sheet of cartridge paper portraying a regression of snarling mouths that became leering eyes that became mouths that became . . . not unlike the Penguin cover of William Faulkener's *The Sound and the Fury;*

A bowl of dirty water by the wardrobe mirror, with, suspended above it on a piece of string fixed to a coathanger, the smelly black burnt remains of a screwed-up cellophane bag;

And half a dozen potted cacti, borrowed from their home in the bathroom (where they thrived under the postered toilet-seat vigilance of Frank Zappa), presumably to contribute a Carlos Castaneda dimension to the vibrations.

Witch and Anita had on the floor beside them, to illumine their kinetic masterpieces in the milk tray, a multi-coloured candle the size of a small tree stump. The only other lighting came from the fire and the painting screened on the wall. The projector contained a magazine of other slides, so, after Cindy had spent half an hour ogling the lurid *Trésors de Satan,* I sat on the bed beside her, finding it easier now not to abuse my privileged propinquity to her nudity (having already abused it to saturation), and gently said:

'Wouldn't you like to see another picture, Cindy?'

Her eyes were moist with a wild, innocent, oceanic joy, as if she'd just hit the jackpot on the football pools.

'*Another* picture?' she marvelled. 'Oh, *yes.*'

I took the remote-control flex from the floor and pressed the button.

Up flashed the dark, daunting, Apocalyptic vision of John Martin's Macbeth witches on the blasted heath: tiny, pathetic abandoned figures in a wilderness of slashing reds and blacks.

'Oh,' said Cindy. Then more urgently:

'Oh, *no.*'

Witch leaned over, fondled her bottom, and said bracingly:

'It's all right, Cindy. They're *Witch's witches!*'

Cindy giggled nervously.

Witch quickly added:

'And the next one, Pleatse.'

I pressed the control.

On came a soothing squiggly-fish dream by Klee, in which all the characters look absurdly happy despite not knowing what they are.

Cindy gurgled with pleasure and settled back to watch another episode of whatever the programme was.

'Perhaps leave the fishmonger be for a while, Pete,' Witch said sagely. He began to roll a reefer, and a glint of his customary self said:

'You can take your clothes off too, if you want.'

This hilarious proposal caused Anita to laugh so violently that I began to imagine where her breasts would land if they suddenly took leave of her chest.

Witch chuckled with her.

I met his gaze seriously, and said:

'*Not* a good idea, Witch.'

'Why?'

'Someone might come to the door. Now would anyone like something to drink? Tea?'

Yes, they would like another pot of tea. Jasmine, Pleatse.

I made the tea, replaced Vivaldi with a tape of Scott Joplin rags, finished the Moselle, poured myself a generous whisky, and contemplated the icy moat that separates life's players from its shivering spectators.

And yet:

Did I really want to guddle about in the nude, blowing bubbles and spilling discoloured milk on my sheets?

I took my whisky into the bedroom.

All three guddlers had forgotten their tea and were spellbound by some epic drama taking place in the world of Klee's squiggles. I couldn't see it myself, so I watched the watchers instead.

Neither girl wore make-up, and once the novelty of their bodies wore off I regarded them almost as men without genitals (protuberant, I mean). Cindy had an unlovely covering of unwaxed black hairs on her thighs (which TwangGang audiences would never see), and Anita had a disconcerting pubic bush which bristled from the top of her legs to nearly her navel, like a crouching honeygold hedgehog.

Aesthetically, Witch had a better body than either of them: with a strong, straight back, wide shoulders, narrow hips, and a flat, taut stomach. He didn't appear magnificently endowed in the masculine appointments, but he did have an unusually long foreskin, which folded pinkly off the tip of his penis and lay wrinkled on the bed like the slumbering snout of some fly-devoured orchid. There was an angry white scar on his lower left abdomen, like a knife wound, but his soft smooth skin and long fair hair were painfully unnerving to someone who had just had his sexual identity rocked by Cindy's thighs and Anita's pubes.

So:

Guinevere had unseemly moles, the beautiful white rabbit had floppy udders, and wasn't Peter a repressed homosexual when the chips were down?

I felt I couldn't be having less fun sitting at home hallucinating Helen's Saturday night in Glasgow, so I got another whisky.

(And you may consider, if you are a devout psycho-sociologist on the eternal PhD trail, that a fertile thesis title might lie: not in the biological and personality disorders of the psychedelic voyagers themselves, but rather in those afflicting their ground control crews – with special reference to alcoholism.)

Over my third whisky, I thought:

Pooves were still people, weren't they?

Just like anyone else?

So it didn't honestly matter if I was one too, did it?

Except that I'd have to live out my life in chastity, wouldn't I?

Because I couldn't possibly bear to thrust my penis into another man's rectum or allow him to do likewise to me, could I?

This newfound tolerance perceived the Klee viewers in a different light. As the fanciful piano ragged, and Cindy, Witch and Anita oohed and wowed at the miracles amid the coloured squiggles, with tears of salty ecstasy beading from their cherubic eyes, I saw them less as statically imperfect physical appearances and more as dynamically beautiful *spiritual realities:* impish saints in the cute bodies of water babies, with myself as benevolent old Mrs Do Whatever The Hell You Want As Long As It Doesn't Damage Anyone.

'Another picture?' I asked kindly, in a break between melodies.

Witch stirred. Looking at me as though trying to remember my name, he said:

'What's it *like*?'

'What's what like?'

'Outside?'

I went to the near window, which looked over the main road to the golf course behind Southside Service Station.

'It's dark,' I reported. 'But the stars are out, and . . . would you like to go for a walk?'

Witch clenched his teeth and screwed up his eyes like I'd asked him to explain the metaphysical nature of gravity.

So I tried the girls:

'Walkies, ladies?'

'Oooooh?' said Cindy.

'Aaaaaaaah?' said Anita.

'Waugh keys?' I tempted in the manner I'd copied from Rosie for summoning Panda. 'Over the golf course and gargle at the moon in peace. How about that?'

'Walk to *the moon*?' Cindy wondered.

'Possibly, Cindy. And then a Chinese take-away. Yes?' I coaxed, for a stroll in the fresh air, followed by the Pride of Peking's *F* and an extra fried rice at Witch's expense, washed down by the last bottle of Moselle in the fridge, suddenly seemed irresistible.

My enthusiasm caught on.

Cindy stood up, smiling brightly, and said:

'Yes.'

Witch and Anita followed her, so there they all were, standing in the middle of the room, attendant upon my leadership.

'Aren't you forgetting something?' I inquired reprovingly.

They looked worried, so I quickly added:

'I mean, shouldn't you perhaps *put some clothes on*? Before we go out? Hmmnn?'

I haven't often seen adults literally fall about laughing, but that is what now happened. My three nature lovers collapsed on the bed, heaving with seismic mirth, kicking their legs in the air in delight, and gasping for breath to ventilate their cackling. It took me twenty inefficient minutes to get them dressed and presentable enough to lead down the stairs, still in fits of silly giggles, with Cindy carrying a frisbee and Witch blowing wearisome blues riffs on a harmonica.

'Ready?' I hoped, inspecting them before leaving the house.

Before I could add 'Got everything?', the doorbell sonorously dingdonged the first and third notes of Beethoven's *Fifth Symphony*. I glanced at my watch and said:

'That'll be Beano back.' Without heeding Witch's gathering frown, I opened the door.

Immediately I wished I hadn't.

In burst MackTheKnife, with Othello close behind him.

I looked at them in terror.

Mack, wearing his surplus greatcoat, shabbier and dirtier than ever, was glazed and stinking with drink. He was also brandishing an ex-army jungle machete.

'What are you doing?' I protested. 'You can't come in here.'

'Whose thus cunt?' Mack sneered, making as if to decapitate me.

Othello stepped forward.

His skin seemed a transparent green in the bright hall light, and he might not have slept for a hundred years. The weight of his earwigs had pulled the blue folds of his eyebags an inch down his cheeks, making them resemble the breasts of an ancient woman. The whites of his eyes looked painfully red, and his normally small sharp pupils were swollen with anger, malice, and probably amphetamine.

'If you don't leave immediately,' I told him desperately,

'I'll call Beano.'

Othello sneered triumphantly:

'Turnbull's getting pissed in Poldy's, Titface. Try again.'

I watched him gloat at the trio of trippers, who were standing motionless as petrified children in a fairy story. Cindy's eyes were fixed pathetically on Othello, Anita's on Mack's machete, and Witch seemed lost in a focusless slit-eyed catatonia.

'What are they on?' Othello asked me cynically.

'*Please* come back some other time. Mr Ormrod,' I tagged winningly. 'They've taken LSD, you see. This,' I whispered, 'might damage their minds.'

'Hear that, Mack?' Othello broadcast. 'These cunts are tripping. Well, that's just dandy. Now get back up that stair. Nah, nah,' he said knowingly to Witch. 'Me first. Shut that front door, Mack, and follow us up.'

Mack closed the door.

I looked helplessly at Witch, whose eyelids had sealed.

Passing Cindy, Othello suddenly slapped her viciously across the mouth and hissed:

'As for you, ya lying slut, I'll deal with you later.'

He led us into Witch's living room, with Mack at the rear, blocking my retreat like the heel of a horrible sandwich.

'It's all right,' I said to Cindy, who was weeping dismally. 'Put your arm round her,' I suggested to Anita, who obeyed.

'Right,' said Othello magisterially, nosing round the studio and remarking the whisky bottle on the fridge. 'First things first, eh? You, Squirrell, get me and Mr Mack a whisky. *Move.*'

I gave them a quarter of a pint each, vaguely hoping this might instantly knock them unconscious.

Othello tasted his, sniffed, and said:

'No Glenmorangie, Squirrell?'

'It's finished.'

Mack was standing by the door, looking violently keen to chop the limbs off anyone attempting to escape. As I handed him his whisky, not daring to meet his brutal glaze, I caught a powerful whiff as of tinned fish gone rancid.

Behind me Othello said:

'Now let's get to business, Wishfort. We've come for my tapes, and then we're taking Miss Cameron-Bell away where she belongs.'

'No, please,' I pleaded, harrowed by Cindy's wailing: 'Don't take Cindy tonight, Mr Ormrod. Not when she's . . .'

'Shut your cakehole, Titface,' Othello's thin lips snarled. 'Now where's my tapes?'

Witch was standing like a waxwork dummy by the Revox. His eyes were tight shut and he showed no sign of responding.

'Where's the fuckin *tapes, ya cunt?'* Mack shouted, rushing forward and swiping Witch across the shoulders with the blunt back of his machete.

Witch stumbled and groaned. Like a zombie in a low-budget horror movie, he said:

'It's. In. The safe.'

'And the eight-track?' snapped Othello.

'It's in. The safe. Too.'

'Where's the key?'

'There isn't a key,' I explained. 'It's a combination lock.'

'What's the numbers?' he demanded of Witch.

Witch screwed his eyes tighter and groaned again.

'Please, Mr Ormrod?' I interceded. 'Can't you see he can hardly speak? Think what this might do *to his mind*!'

'Fuck the cunt's mind.'

'Can't you just let him open the safe? Please don't make him speak.'

'Okay, Titface. You get him to open the safe. *Now.'*

'Can you do it, Witch?' I asked gently. 'Can you open the safe?'

Witch shuddered. He nodded painfully.

'Dinny let the cunt near a phone,' Mack said slyly.

So we were all herded into Witch's study, adjoining his bedroom. The desk was on the left of the window, the filing cabinet and safe on the right, with bookshelving round the other three walls. Mack guarded the door while Othello went to the desk, switched on the Anglepoise, and turned it to illumine the dials on the door of the safe.

'Right,' he said harshly. 'Move it, Wishfort.'

Witch knelt to open the safe, and Cindy, Anita and I huddled miserably in the opposite corner. The Venetian blind was up, and through the top of the window came the yellow gleam of a fattening moon playing hide-and-seek behind a skein of small fluffy clouds above the golf course.

'Don't worry,' I whispered jerkily to the girls. 'This'll soon be over.'

'SHARRUP,' yelled Mack, who had finished his quarter-pint of whisky.

Then, in the space of three seconds:

The telephone on the desk came alive with loud ringing;

Cindy screamed;

Anita screamed;

Mack roared at them to *sharrup;*

I moved mechanically to answer the phone;

Witch pulled the safe door open;

Othello flourished a meancing gesture at me, and said:

'Let it ring.'

I stepped back and was astonished to see the broken-vein skin on Mack's flat face pale with fear.

'Mother a Goad!' he exclaimed hoarsely.

'Drop the breadknife, Mack,' Witch said softly. He was standing beside the open safe. In his right hand was a slender-nosed Gestapo-type pistol. He was aiming it carefully at Mack's stomach, and his eyes were glittering with the indomitable power of someone who has no fear of the consequences of his actions.

'Drop it,' he repeated commandingly.

Mack slowly lowered his machete, causing Othello to scream:

'Don't be *daft*, Mack. That's only a fuckin *replica,* man.'

Witch turned his pistol towards Othello. His fingers tightened.

'No!' I cried. 'It *isn't* a replica. Be careful, Witch, won't you? It's *real.* It's his father's . . .'

A loud bang blotted out the ringing of the telephone, and I was sure my bowel would disgrace me. When I opened my eyes I saw that Witch had swung the pistol past Othello and fired a round through the top right-hand pane of the window, splintering the wooden upright and leaving a jagged hole in the glass about the size of a cooking apple. A short grey cartridge case had fallen by his feet and as he pointed the pistol back at Mack it trailed a sharp stench of hot oil and spent fireworks.

'Last chance, Mack,' Witch said. '*Drop* it.'

Mack dropped it.

'Get it, Pete.'

I darted forward and grabbed the machete.

'Put it in the safe,' Witch told me.

At that moment the telephone stopped ringing.

I tried to put the machete in the safe, but it wouldn't fit.

'Then drop it behind the filing cabinet.'

As I did so, the phone started ringing again.

'Can you, Pete, please?' Witch asked politely.

I answered it.

'Who is it?'

'Beano.'

Witch held out his left hand.

I passed him the receiver.

'Beano?' he said, not taking his aiming eye off Mack.

'. . .'

'Spot of bother, actually.'

'. . .'

'Othello and Mack. Been a bit naughty. Mack brought his breadknife.'

'. . .'

'Pete's just explained that the old man's Luger isn't a replica. So they've calmed down.'

'. . .'

'They'll be leaving soon, old son. But you might just get to pulp Mack's nozzle before he goes. If you hurry. See ya.'

I took the receiver and replaced it on the desk.

'Hear that, Mack?' Witch mused. 'Beano's very angry. He's racing back here.'

'Christ, Wishfort,' spat Othello. 'You're fuckin crazy,

man.' Standing by the desk, livid with furious fear, his sickly skin as white as his hair, he looked like a malignant ghost in an electric-blue suit.

'Could be,' Witch agreed. 'Pete?'

'Yes?'

'Put the girls in the bedroom, old son. Switch the projector on. Something soothing. Maybe the Turner sunset. And some music. Something cheerful. And loud. In case we need to shoot anyone. Give them a glass of wine and explain that everything's all right now. Will you? Then come back here.'

I rushed to do as he requested, putting a Beach Boys tape on the Revox, snatching a swallow of whisky from the bottle on the fridge, leaving Anita and Cindy with the last bottle of Moselle, and assuring them that:

'Everything's all right now. Okay? I'll be back soon, and so will Witch. Okay?'

They looked as bewildered as Asian refugee children in television news reports, and it hurt me to leave them. But the LSD killings in California were warm in the world's memory, and, dreading Witch's worst, I felt my first duty was to mollify the tension between him and the intruders.

He had made them take their shoes off, and a distinct offensiveness of cheesy feet had been added to the hot oil, spent fireworks and rancid tinned fish. On the wall above the safe was a poster of Bob Dylan's head wearing heavy dark glasses, like the Second Coming in a thick placenta of foaming red bubbles, and I could have sworn that for a split psychotic second I saw his nose sardonically wrinkle.

'Thanks, Pete,' said Witch, looking more himself, casual in a fawn pullover and blue jeans, with only the implacable pistol to belie normality. 'Now we'll deal with the tapes. In the safe. Two boxes marked *TwangGang*. See them?'

'Yes.'

'Right. Take them, please, to the bathroom. Put them in the bath, and fill . . .'

'*Christ*, Wishfort,' yelled Othello. 'What do ye wanny . . .'

'Shut your cakehole, Ormrod,' Witch said reminiscently. 'Fill . . .'

'For God's sake, Witch,' I expostulated. 'Why can't you just give him his tapes, and have done with it?'

'They aren't his tapes, Pete. They're my tapes. Blanks paid for by me. Recorded in my studio. In my time. Engineered by me and Simon.'

'But . . .'

'I was going to give them to him, but then he let me down. And now he's assaulted my fiancée. So fill . . .'

'I'll *pay* for the fuckin tapes, man,' Othello begged. 'I *need* . . .'

Witch silenced him with a waggle of the pistol.

'Fill the bath with hot water,' he instructed me. 'Pour in the bottle of Domestos that's behind the loo. Stir till the tapes are well and truly ruined. Then come back and tell us it's done.'

There was obviously no moving him, so I carried out my orders as quickly as possible.

'Done,' I reported breathlessly.

'Good,' said Witch. 'Want a look?' he offered Othello.

Who looked too ill to speak.

'Then it's time for our uninvited guests to leave,' Witch decided. 'Off we go.' His pistol motioned Mack and Othello to the door.

'Whut aboot owur fuckin *shoes*?' growled Mack, cross-eyed with drink, hate, and confusion.

'Buy a new pair on Monday,' Witch said constructively. 'Smells like a good idea. Now *move it.*'

As he ushered them down the narrow stair to Beano's hall, with me hovering behind him, Witch concluded conversationally:

'And you'd better believe it, Ormrod, now and for ever, that Cindy doesn't love you. She loves me, and we're getting married in July. Cindy's never loved you, in fact. You aren't lovable.

'Moreover, if you ever lay a finger on her again, old son,' he warned Othello, as the repulsive pair stood barefoot on the landing, 'or if you even *speak* to her, I'll shoot your kneecaps off. Now beat it. If you're lucky you might not meet Beano downstairs.'

Othello and Mack disappeared from view. Then a venomous howl floated back up the stairwell:

'Ewer a CUNT, Wushfart. Newall git whut's comin tea ya.'

'That'll be nice,' Witch murmured, closing the door on the sound of milk bottles being smashed below. His shoulders sagged, he exhaled mightily, grinned, and said:

'Thanks for helping out, Pete. Lucky that didn't happen while we were going up. Could have been a problem.'

'Were you acting, Witch?' I asked curiously, back in his apartment, accompanied by *Good, good, good vibrations.* 'When your eyes were shut?'

'Not to begin with, Pete,' he admitted modestly. 'Took some sweat to get back to earth. You know? To cope with the situation. Now, could you do something for me? One last thing?'

'What?'

'Phone for a taxi. Take this home with you – I've put the safety catch on.' He pressed the cool black weight of the pistol upon me. 'Wrap it in a plastic bag, and stash it in the cellar, where we keep the Thermos.'

'Why?'

He smiled ruefully.

'Because this place might get pigged tonight, old son. Othello's just the type to squeal. No point asking for trouble, is there? With an unlicenced firearm on the premises?'

'Oh, all right,' I said, regarding the gun as if it were a murdered body I had to dispose of. 'But tell me, Witch?'

'If I can.'

'Why did you make them take their shoes off?'

'Saw it in a film, Pete. Seemed sensible.'

TWENTY-THREE

My sleep that night was tortured by evil dreams.

Little pink waterbabies with cherubic wings, large breasts, horny genitals, and lecherous leers laughed at the shame of my nakedness in public. Enormous policemen in fawn raincoats, like rabid boars with deadly tusked heads, came snorting down my steps every ten minutes brandishing pistols and machetes and demanding that I open up in the name of the law and submit to my sentence of death by frenzied goring for the offence of possessing a cellar full of unlicenced firearms and dangerous drugs. While Dr Tostow sat at a roll-top desk in the distance, floating on a yellow cloud with a plutonium lining, marking Finals papers and screwing his weak black eyes into an eternity of unforgiving malice every time he wrote *Narrow Fail* on the cover of my Statistical Methods paper.

At quarter to eleven I awoke in a panic to discover that I wasn't being buried alive by mistake: it was just the lazy dinging of the local church bells summoning the Presbyterian faithful to their worship.

I got up and washed, but couldn't face shaving. Over cornflakes and Nescafé I wondered if going for a *Sunday Times* was worth the effort. And would I ever be capable of work again? A second coffee was making me feel iller rather than brighter, when sounds of a car arriving drifted down from the street, followed by footsteps entering the house above. Certain that this was Helen returning from Glasgow with two hundred muscular lovers with hairy chests and genital-squelching jeans, I lay back on my unmade bed to fester properly.

Twenty minutes later I heard four lively feet clatter down

the back staircase and thud along the wooden boards of my passageway. Simultaneously, one of the passage cupboards was unlocked and my bedroom door was lightly knocked upon.

'Come in,' I called limply.

'Hello, Peter,' said Cindy, smiling down at me like a happy sunbeam at an unforecast cloud. 'Is anything . . .?'

'No.'

'Then why . . . you haven't been . . ., have you?'

'No,' I exclaimed, blinking fiercely. 'Just a little worried about my exams. Who's out there?'

'Witch. He's getting some wine from his father's cupboard. And his rucksack from the . . . we're going for a picnic at Querns, you see. Would you like . . .?'

'You get pigged last night, Pete?' Witch asked over his shoulder, as we hugged the speed limit along the coast road from Lethe to Cockleburgh.

'Only in my nightmares,' I said sourly. 'Why? Did you?'

Yes, the pigs had come. Acting on information received, they were obliged to . . . but no, unfortunately, they hadn't been able to get a search warrant.

'Then I presume you told them to go away?'

Nothing of the sort – hadn't I read *Tom Sawyer* yet? As they'd troubled to pay him a visit, Witch invited them in for a look round, although wouldn't they first split a can of Beano's Export? And it just so happened, actually, that Harriet was getting some cheese-and-onion toasties together, so . . . after Sergeant Anderson had two cans of Export and several toasties, and a jovial debate with Beano about the pros and cons of working-class lads learning karate, it was only natural that he would feel too sheepish to take up Witch's gratuitous invitation to search the place from top to bottom if he really felt it would further The Cause of Justice, wasn't it?

'Not a bad chap, Pig One,' Witch said objectively, 'when

you get to know him. You stash that pistol okay, Pete?' he added, inspecting me in the mirror.

'Yes.'

'Good lad.'

The good lad looked out of the nearside window and saw the thin green ribbon of Cockleburgh race course pocked with thousands of newspapers, sweetie wrappers, crisp packets and drinks cans from the previous day's meeting. The blue sea beyond seemed calm as a pond, and out in the middle of the Firth was the great dark bulk of an oil tanker nosing west, upstream, to the refinery at Meadowmouth.

It was stuffy in the car.

Squashed beside me on a GT back seat hardly big enough for a midget and a chihuahua, Panda was panting and slobbering profusely. He'd matured from a lolloping adolescent into a powerful young dog, and, despite my aversion to the species, I'd become quite fond of him, except when he attempted to copulate with my legs, as had happened twice in our recent walks round Aberlethe Park.

'Do you think, Cindy,' I requested, 'you could open the window an inch? Thanks.'

I had rather hoped to sit in the front, with one of the girls cuddled intimately in my lap. But no. Anita had Cindy cuddled intimately in *her* lap, and from time to time they would murmur to each other fragmented phrases like the distant tips of massive icebergs in constant contact at a profoundly non-verbal level.

Were they still immersed in their yesterday's adventures?

I asked Witch how they were all so fresh and apparently unbothered by their psychedelic voyaging and the unpleasantness with Othello and Mack. Compared with myself, who had been badly shaken and slept like a prisoner condemned to the guillotine at dawn?

'Blessed are the pure in spirit, Pete,' he said plausibly. 'Also, we didn't drink too much. You got your bad conscience from mixing wine with whisky.'

We had left the outskirts of Cockleburgh and were accelerating like a jet on a runway up the long straight woodland tunnel towards Jake's Cafe Petrol. I was so alarmed by the crazy speed that I began constructing a tactfully irresistible sentence featuring my regrettable proneness to car-sickness. Before I got it out, however, Witch eased off and said:

'Ice-cream?'

Jake got his from Luigi's Ice Palace on the Cockleburgh sea front, and stopping for a round of raspberry-smeared cones on the way to Querns was a Wishfort Summer Must. Today it saved Witch an endorsed driving licence, since Mrs Jake warned him, thrusting the chocolate flake bar into his 99, to go slowly through Pratnair Village, at the bottom of the hill, because the police had set up a speed trap (a local child having been run over the previous week) and were nicking eastbound vehicles like swatting bluebottles.

So the laden sports car striped in nature's colours of danger proceeded at a virtuous crawl down the main road, and arrived at Querns ten minutes later.

The cottage was at the bottom of a meandering farm track, with a large steading and riding school halfway down the slope. Cow parsley was running riot, with great white heads like cauliflowers, and the may blossom, surprisingly pink, was beginning to bloom on the hawthorn hedges. As he squeezed the car on the jungly trackside, to allow three pig-tailed nymphettes on dappled nags to trot past us, Witch said:

'You ride, Pete?'

'No.'

'You should try. Great for the back muscles. But today let's climb the Law, shall we? Have our lunch on the top.'

Our walk followed the route I had taken with Helen and Rosie in January. After showing Anita the cottage and garden, where she applauded the Eden-like seclusion, the dazzling wealth of creamy cherry blossom and the idyllic charm of the doves on the rust-red roof, we crossed the river by the narrow wooden footbridge, struggled up the steep mud path on the far bank, canopied by a cool dark umbrella of sycamore and chestnut trees, and followed the single-track road along to the Em's smallholding and the rambling red ruins of Querns Castle.

We ambled on from chatting to the fiery, dwarfish Mr Em in his pay booth, and Witch remarked:

'Doesn't that castle just epitomize the futility of travel?'

'Why?' I asked.

'Your American geriatrics come to Deenburgh to follow their ancestral stream to its source before they die, they get their glossy brochures from the Tourist Board, make a special pilgrimage out here on a sunny Sunday afternoon, and then are disappointed to find there isn't much to see. Look at them,' he gestured expressively.

We gazed back at a dozen elderly persons, including several obvious Americans, mooching listlessly among the crumbling archways and ceilingless halls, sidestepping sheep droppings and perusing glossy brochures for details of architectural splendour long since vanished.

'How much more exciting would their visit be,' Witch considered, 'if they knew there was a hundred and fifty thousand quid's worth of acid stashed in the dungeons?'

'You've had a new consignment, have you? Or just a jump in the market value?'

'Six out of ten, Pete. Yet the wishdoctor's price is inflation-proof. For the time being. Two hundred mikes per cap, and only a quid each. No minimum order for you, Pete. Want one?'

'No thanks.'

'Then let's try our luck with Burnside's bull. Panda?' He called the dog to heel and we stepped over a stile into a rough grazing field full of lush green grass, clover, buttercups, giant daisies, gorse bushes, and baby rabbits startled from behind tufty hillocks that rolled like sand dunes up to the quarry road and the Pratnair Law beyond.

It was only late April but it could have been June, and the sky, the clean warmth and the hazy peacefulness (unbroken except by the cawing of irritated crows and the joyful woofing of Panda's rabbit hounding) made me think of those distant days in third-year French, when the sun blazed down on the playground outside and one began yet another stirring composition with *Le soleil brillait dans une belle ciel sans image, et Monsieur et Madame Boulanger et leur charmante fille Michel . . .*

Cindy and Anita, vegetatively passive, now and again would stop to share their unique perceptions of, for example, the miraculous perfection discernible in the head of a dandelion.

'Oh!' Cindy might exclaim. 'Isn't that . . .?'

'Yes!' Anita would echo. 'It's so . . .'

They were wearing twin garments like sexy paratrooper suits, purchased during their shopping spree in Paris. Cindy's was pale yellow, the colour of cowslips, with a broad silver belt, and Anita's was forget-me-not blue with a matching beret and a belt of almost the same honey gold as her hair. They looked feminine, innocent, vulnerable, once more impossibly desirable, and hearing the disconnected inanities of their speech made me apoplectic with indignation at Witch for the casual way he was messing about with their lives and minds. I really didn't believe he really believed his selfish, megalomaniac little love triplet could last, but the girls were behaving as if *they* believed it could, and this made me mad.

We crossed the quarry road and began our steep ascent.

'Make it to the top?' Witch inquired leadingly.

'I can if you can.'

'That's the spirit, Pete. Lay it on me. PANDA, YOU EVEN *LOOK* AT A SHEEP AND I'LL FLOG YOUR ARSE OFF.' In his tan walking boots, faded jeans and denim shirt, with his Duke-of-Edinburgh-Award rucksack bearing our picnic and rolled-up waterproofs, Witch looked every inch the professional hiker. While we followed him upward, in a laborious zigzag between the sheeptrack parallels, he plied us with diverting tales of the history of Querns and of Wishfort escapades in its neighbourhood.

Some of these stories I had already heard from Helen and Rosie: how Witch and Beano used to shoot up the footbridge with Witch's air rifle, for target practice, then steal over to the castle in the early morning to slaughter the crop-heavy pigeons; and how the legendary Saint Maurice had been wafted by the Hand of Heaven from the summit of the Law to his unscathed splashdown in Fairport Bay six miles to the north-east.

But others were new to me, such as:

How Simon Darling nearly drowned in the castle pool when, at the age of nine, he and Beano and Witch were unexpectedly let down by the raft they had built of old diesel drums, rotten planks from a demolished hen coop, and a ball of binder-twine stolen from Farmer Burnside's bailer;

And how, at fifteen, Witch had his first mystical experience in Gables Wood, when he shot a bullfinch from thirty yards. The pellet pulped the bird's right eye but didn't kill it outright, and as the marksman walked closer he saw the finch blinking at him with its remaining eye, expressing Nature's infinite surprise and sadness at the cruelty and folly of Man, while a jellied mess of blood, feathers and splintered tiny bones slopped down its faintly fluttering breast.

'In the end,' the reformed teenage gunman explained, plodding toward the triangulation monolith that marked our summit, 'the poor beast just toppled off the branch and I had to stomp him to death with the heel of my boot. Felt like I'd murdered me Ma. Sick as a dog for two days. Sold the gun to Grant MacMillan for twenty pounds. Wasn't worth it, though. Never killed anything since: would feel like suicide. Except bugs, of course,' he added realistically. 'Got to draw the line somewhere.'

'Would you have killed Mack last night?' I asked him. 'If he'd come at you with the machete?'

'Good question,' he said cheerfully, unshouldering the rucksack. 'Difficult to answer. Self-defence is something else, mind you. Might have shot the cunt's balls off for him.'

'Tat Twam Asi?'

'Ultimately, Pete, Mack's balls are my balls. So it's up to me whether I shoot them off or not. Specially if it's his balls versus my head. Now, who's for a paper-cupful of the old man's Mateus Rosé?'

For twenty minutes we reclined on a groundsheet:

Sipping wine;

Nibbling salad sandwiches, chicken legs, apples, hunks of cheese and chocolate biscuits;

Gazing pensively over the patchworked miles of green and brown arable land that separated us from the Firth, whose glacial blue supported two cargo ships heading up to the docks at Lethe, a Royal Navy destroyer cruising down from the base at Miltsickle, and a colourful confusion of racing yachts putting out from Fairport Bay;

And listening to Witch pontificating educatively about the value of tripping, styles of tripping, techniques of aborting bum trips, dosages appropriate to fun trips (like yesterday's) and seriously mystical trips (like his San Francisco dragon trip), the curious affinities that trippers often found between themselves and particular birds or animals – foxes, for example . . .

'Tell us about the dragon trip, Witch,' Cindy requested dreamily. She was lying luxuriously on her tummy, using both hands to tip her cup to her lips, making her mouth more than ever like a kiss-blowing azalea as she sipped. Her gaze was tethered adoringly to her lord-and-master's omniscient brow, and no doubt she was thinking of the extraordinary pobble painting Witch had sent her from California.

Anita, meanwhile, was lying on her back, spreadeagled in abandonment to the joy of the moment, her legs splayed in tribute to the warming virility of the sun, with a square silk scarf protecting her face from a surfeit of that same masculinity.

Witch glanced keenly from his younger concubine to the elder. Then back again.

'All right,' he said agreeably. 'Fasten your seatbelts, ladies and gentlemen, please. And I will.'

I was crashing with this weird character

(he began tautologically, uncorking the second bottle of Mateus Rosé)

in the Haight-Ashbury. Art dealer type. Great big Gothick

house like a museum. Full of spooky pictures, sculptures, oriental rugs, stuffed animals, potted plants, parrot in a cage big enough for a tiger, that sort of thing. Raving poof, but never bothered me. Very generous person, in fact. Like most Americans.

Well, one morning he woke me up with a cup of camomile tea, a hot maple-syrup pancake, and a spotted capsule like two ladybirds stuck together.

'Perfect day, Witch, baby,' he said. 'Drop this. It'll take you further out than you've ever been before. Call me at the office if you need to talk.'

An hour later I was sitting in a deck-chair under his patio parasol. Very hot day, it was going to be. I had my notebook, a sketchpad and some crayons (standard kit), a big glass of Bourbon and lots of ice (good plan to have a drink as you go up: settles any jitters), and a fascinating bowl of pansies with leaves as green as the day began and flowers like the eyes of Chinese dragons in a temper.

I'd put on a tape of Elizabethan dance music played on Spanish guitars by I can't remember who, and I was wearing headphones on an extension lead, so as not to have my magic theatre spoiled by police sirens in the distance or the angels next door tuning their bikes if I could possibly help it.

I finished my drink, sat back, closed my eyes, and for a seeming age climbed an endless stairway into the heart of the sky. Further and further into and beyond the heavens I mounted, yet seemed to be getting nowhere. Innumerable galaxies of diverse stars and other worlds I passed and left behind, having seen them all before.

No secrets here, I thought wearily. *Is this all*? And I trembled on the slippery rim of an ego-dissolving dread. There I was: unenlightened and *alone. So alone. Is this all*?

I found myself at the top of the endless stairway and about to step into the mouth of absolute nothingness. Before me? Nothing but nothing, veiled in a swirling intangible shroud of hot steaming obscurity. Less like being imprisoned in darkness, more like being suspended in a tepid state of complete colourlessness.

Ooooooh, I moaned, my anxiety untold.

Then, like a soothing spatter of baptismal drops on a fevered brow, the music resumed. A slow, stately pavane of ineffable eloquence began to dance, and the clouds of colourless obscurity surrounding me came alive in time, resolving themselves in pulsing formations of bronzed Adonises dancing courteously with their Aphrodites, all exquisite in their tawny naked beauty.

There is humour in the dance, I observed, stepping off the last rung of the everyday world. And as I floated among the supple pirouetting figures, playful hands reached out and teased away my clothes. *It is a promiscuous dance*, I noted with surprise, as flirtatious fingers and nebulous nipples brushed langorously against me. And slowly, out of the very tawny *essence* of the dance, a filmy figure of supreme significance began to crystallize.

A female form, it was. And draped. An evanescent emanation of radiant Platonic loveliness, her fiery eyes flashing the primeval promise of perfect knowledge, her sultry mouth pouting in anticipation of immaculate experience.

Aha.

Here was my destiny.

Before me, and yet in me and through me, was my archetypal Woman In The Sky, and my mission was to woo and win her, captivate and unveil her, possess and retain her. But when I had wooed and won and captured and entered her, in the very instant of cosmic consummation itself, so it seemed, the gently fornicating lilt of the pavane burst into the first crashing chord of a galloping galliard. My orgasm shot me into a higher dimension of awareness and exploded the heavenly harlot with the deceitful fiery eyes into a shimmering evaporation of vanished illusion. The hovering haze rose upward, ever higher, the tawny colours melting and refracting into delicate hues of green, and silver, and gold.

And all the while I rose also, feeling as never before the power of the amazement of creative wonder.

Yet, I remarked, *it is not complete. It is still all happening outside me, but I want to be involved.* I WANT TO BE INVOLVED, I cried from the marrow of my longings. And immediately: the droplets of green and silver and gold were no longer rising in evaporation but falling in a carefree dissipation of warming rain, as if determined to nourish the parching earth so far below, regardless of their own destruction.

Feeling the raindrops fall so selflessly, I was filled once more with foreboding. Had I offended? Why was *I* no longer rising?

Anxiety seared across my brain as if boiling vinegar had been poured into my skull through a filter funnel.

I WISH TO KNOW, cried all my aching cells in unison. I AM PREPARED TO DIE.

Instantly I rocketed beyond the rainbow clouds and warming rain. Or, to be more exact, the clouds and the warming rain were themselves rocketed out of existence, leaving me completely alone in a universe devoid of furniture.

So I thought, until, far on the periphery of my perception, I spotted a tiny dragon, no bigger than a flea, apparently dancing on a trampoline of elastic non-existence. Burning for company, I reached out to approach this dragon, leaping towards him in the great effortless bounds of an enthusiastic moonwalker.

But as I neared the dragon, I found it ever mushrooming in size and stature, its scales almost blinding in their glister of gorgeous golds and greens and silvers and . . .

What a large dragon, I exclaimed, approaching yet closer and seeing that within each colourful scale of its skin whole galaxies whirled, exploded, died and were reborn. And within each galaxy I saw solar systems, stars, planets, continents, and beyond. And all the while the dragon danced, and the faster it danced the faster the galaxies whirled.

And the faster my astonishment grew.

Hey, I shouted finally, stepping back several lightyears to peer up past the dragon's golden flowing mane and crocodile nostrils to its bulging wet pansy eyes. *Hey, you up there. This is me: Mallecho Wishfort. Late of Deenburgh*

University Physics Department.

But not for a moment did the dragon's dance falter.

And Summa Cum Laude, I yelled.

Only to see the dragon dance unconcernedly on.

I WANT TO KNOW, I howled in a paroxysm of ultimate endeavour.

BAT. I felt as if a bomb had exploded underneath my arse. The dragon had flicked me into orbit with a tweak of its forked scaly tail, like a juggler who scratches his ear for show while continuing to juggle perfectly.

WHEE, my body sang as I sailed upward through a warm plashing rain of crocodile tears.

PLOP. I realized, initially with some dismay, that I had been shied by the dragon's tail into its ear, and great waxen tentacles of darkness like amorphous mucus enveloped me.

RING-RING. RING-RING. I was vomited out of the dragon's acoustic passages into the light-speed circuitry of its brain. Round and round and round I went, like a pair of leopardskin knickers in a launderette tumbledrier. And as I whirled madly round the space lanes of thought, I was sure I would expire from the sheer energy of it all, like an overloaded fuse.

But soon:

DRIP, TRICKLE. Imagine my consternation at being shed as just one of umpteen billion salty sleepy crocodile tears, welling and pouring like wet confetti from an infinite eyelid.

Then all is lost, I thought for sure, as I cascaded anonymously downward, lonely as a sensitive country boy in Oxford Circus Station during the rush hour.

BAT. My budding despair was rudely nipped by a second spank of the dragon's playful tail. And so the cycle repeated, again and again.

BAT, WHEE, PLOP, RING-RING, DRIP, TRICKLE.

On and on, over and over.

And with each repetition I learned something about the dragon and something about myself, coming to see many similarities, many points of contact. I learned the function of rhythm in the world, and the beauty of bending. DRIP, TRICKLE. I experienced the indivisibility of Good and Bad: something I had long believed conceptually but never mastered in living life. BAT, WHEE.

And yet, as the cycle continued without apparent end, an element of jaundice arose. The more I learned, the more I inevitably forgot. Considering this made me desperately greedy, developing an escalating craving for enlightenment, like a heroin fixer building a dosage that would be fatal to you or me. Accordingly, the cycle that had seemed so luminous now reeked of the agony of eternal torture. PLOP, RING-RING, DRIP . . . on and on, over and over.

Is there no ULTIMATE TRUTH? I begged, and, because my importunity was born of anguish, the dragon obliged.

WHOOSH.

What the fuck's HAPPENING? This question burned through my brain as my flesh began to melt. For this time as I trickled tearfully from the dragon's gnarly nose, no playful tail tweaked up to bat me back. WHOOSH-WHOOSH, roared the awful inferno within the dragon's snarling jaws, its fearful fangs now bared and steamily slavering.

SNAP. And here I realized I was learning how to die, as shite-hot molars smashed together and chopped my puny mortal body into jammy fragments.

Is this all? Can this be death? My whispering curiosity continued unabated as my bleeding members swilled around the dragon's lumpy tongue and dissolved in its foaming gorge.

But no, a minced remnant of my reason called out, *this is not death. For death can never be experienced.*

GOBBLE. Now in liquid peristalsis through the dragon's heaving gizzards, I felt I was as close to death as a living man may come, and with this thought all fear lifted from me and flapped away, like a big fat frightened crow.

And I began to enjoy myself, experiencing my inviolate inmost core as a gangling tadpole slithering and squelching along the seminal shores of primeval slime that lined the dragon's bubbling intestines. *Oh, slime, slime, glorious . . .* (Beano would have sung in the same situation), when suddenly:

SPURT. I was ejaculated in joy up the flailing flue of the dragon's gargantuan tool.

And thus a new cycle began.

No sooner had I hurtled forth from the dragon's quivering tip than I began to melt once more, my wriggling tail in scorching shreds.

WHOOSH, WHOOSH-WHOOSH, SNAP, GOBBLE, SPURT. On and on and on without end. Teaching me that this dragon was the perfect unmoved mover, the laughing law-giver to whom no laws apply, at once the blueprint and artisan of its own manifestations, dancing on no surface and for no reason.

How ridiculously obvious, I gasped. THE DRAGON IS A DANCER. And then it dawned that I too was dancing. WHOOSH-WHOOSH, SNAP, GOBBLE.

How absurdly simple, I eureked: I AM THE DRAGON. *Who will ever believe it*? I AM THE DRAGON *and* THE DRAGON IS A DANCER.

'Abreactive gibberish!' the world will scream, especially Professor Newbigging.

And with the realization that ultimate realization cannot be communicated, because there is no one else to communicate it to, I began my descent back to the flickering cave-world of the mundane and the divided.

WHOOSH-WHOOSH, SNAP, GOBBLE, SPURT, BAT, WHEE, PLOP, RING-RING, DRIP, TRICKLE, then no more BAT and no more WHOOSH, but only gentle falling.

Down and down and down yet further, with all the other countless billions of warm and salty sleepy tears, following some law of lachrymose half-life, so that each tear would explode in time in a further spiral of baby dancing dragons, all weeping their own billion tears, and with each explosion and each fragmentation, I followed the syntax with one special dragon and one special tear, until tear and dragon eventually fused in the blinking form of the bodily Witch you all know and love.

Don't you?

My host had returned for lunch with some fwends, and

the rest of that day was more sociable and pleasantly shallow, like strolling up the Pratnair Law having recently returned from the Himalayas. The following day I looked at my sketchpad and found some doodles that I later worked into Cindy's painting. In my notebook were two scrawled mementoes of my journey. One said:

Such a dragon must be good, otherwise he would not create himself.

And the second:

I am that which I will soon be unable to remember, as I must now forget myself again, in order that the dance may continue.

'Oh, Witch,' Cindy murmured euphorically. 'That's really just . . . so . . .'

The sun was greying at the temples, and a hinting breeze wondered how much longer we should linger on the hill. In the watery blue distance the swarm of racing yachts had stretched into a broken line of bright triangular sails, following the coastline east. Panda, stationed at a sensible distance, was growling with savage pleasure and gnawing at the skull of a spring lamb pecked to death by crows, and Anita's complexion-protecting scarf was concaving and convexing over the outline of her mouth, as she snored in gentle rhythmic contentment.

I cleared my throat, looked Witch in the eye, and said:

'Where does *Tat Twam Asi* come in?'

'Same thing, Pete. Different trip, same insight.'

'I've missed the point, you mean?'

'I wouldn't say that,' he said politely. 'But remember the Pythagorean like-like dictum.'

'Which is what?'

'That *like* may only be known by *like*. If you're reading a newspaper in the garden, for instance, and Panda comes and sits on it, and licks your face, it's not because he wants to annoy you but because he doesn't know what you're doing:

he hasn't got the wiring. He sees the newspaper as a physical object only, not as a medium bearing coded information. Whereas an intelligence like your own would know what you were doing and hence behave appropriately: maybe ask who'd won the tennis.'

'So what *is* the point?'

Witch laughed and started tidying up the remains of our picnic.

'Yesterday, Pete, when we were having fun with the Klee picture, you were treating it like Panda treats the newspaper. And today when I told my dragon trip tale, though you didn't yawn *all* the time, you couldn't understand on an empathetic level what I was talking about. Why?

'Because you've never had a remotely similar experience yourself. Have you? You just don't know what it feels like for the brittle, one-dimensional, other-directed, hidebound ego that is the Peter Squirrell you think is all you are to take the plunge, dissolve, melt, disintegrate, like a gingerbread man dunked in a mug of hot tea. Do you?'

'Evidently not.'

'And you find the prospect disturbing, don't you?'

'Naturally.'

'Well, old son,' Witch said, with irritating generosity, 'there's a good hot dunk waiting for you whenever you want to change your mind.'

'I'll think about it.'

'On the house.'

'Thanks.'

'With me to guide you.'

'Who could ask for more, Witch?'

He answered with a genial grin, stood up, and began re-packing the rucksack.

'Come along, troops,' he exhorted energetically. 'Programme for the rest of the afternoon. We'll walk through Gables, and I'll show you where my infamous ancestor slew the bullfinch. Collect our eggs from Mrs Em, tea back at the cottage, then some of us (logically speaking) will cut the grass. So it's pretty for the old man coming out of hospital next week. Okay? How's your biceps, Pete?'

'Huge.'

'Anita?' our leader called loudly. 'Wakey-wakey.'

'Hnnneee,' that pregnant lady whinnied, stretched, and in sleepy shamelessness rubbed at a tickle between her widespread legs. 'Mnnuh?'

TWENTY-FOUR

Thursday next dawned cold, wet and miserable, as I discovered at eight o'clock when the postman summoned me to the door to sign for a recorded-delivery letter.

I put the kettle on and read with horror:

Dear Mr Squirrell,

THE VARIETIES OF ORGASMIC EXPERIENCE
By WHITMAN, Vernon G., & NIXON, Ursula F.
CAT. No. 821.43

I regret to inform you that it has been brought to my attention that the above was borrowed on one of your tickets in January and despite frequent reminders has neither been renewed or returned since.

Quite apart from the substantial fine now owing on the book you must appreciate Mr Squirrell that the above mentioned is a Reserve Stock Book in virtue of the nature of its subject matter and it is the responsibility of the Lending Library Staff to ensure that it is only issued to responsible adults requiring it for serious study purposes only. I understand from my staff that a backlog of seven Reservation Requests from such persons has now been received and I have therefore to ask you to return the book immediately or else a Senior Official of the Corporation will be visiting you to effect its retrieval and collect from you the substantial fine now owing.

Trusting you will be so good as to oblige in this matter,

Yours sincerely,

Chief Librarian

Certain that if I didn't return the book by lunchtime, the Lord Provost of Deenburgh would arrive in a horse-drawn carriage to inform all Hanover Place what a dirty-minded pervert Mrs Wishfort had lodging in her basement, I telephoned Witch's flat on the stroke of nine o'clock.

Five minutes of relentless ringing won me the sleep-stupefied voice of Anita, who told me that Witch was in France again and wouldn't be back till Friday.

'It's actually Cindy I want,' I said tersely.

Three minutes later, when I had explained the situation twice, Cindy said:

'Oh, dear, Peter, you see . . .' The orgasmic tome was still at Gladstone Place. Cindy had never got it out of Othello's office after she and Witch eloped to Amsterdam. So:

'Deirdre's probably got it, Peter. I'll ask . . .'

'Don't bother, Cindy,' I tried not to snap. 'I'll collect it on my way up town.'

Next, I dialled Gladstone Place but got no answer. I bolted a tasteless breakfast and dialled again, this time getting an engaged tone. I packed my bag in readiness for a rainy day's work in the library, then picked up the phone once more.

' . . . Grant,' Helen was saying coyly. 'Pick me up at one, and we'll have lunch . . . who's that? Mummy?'

I banged my receiver down as if it were a weapon for killing poisonous spiders. I was shaking, my Adam's apple felt like a melon, and the appalling vision of another twenty-one months of unwanted chastity rose up before me like the mushroom cloud from a nuclear explosion. For days I'd suspected Helen had been avoiding me, and here was the beastly proof. She'd resumed with the simian MacMillan and not even had the decency to tell me I was ditched.

But *why*?

Was it my *body*? Inadequate? It must be something physical, I consoled myself suicidally, because on any mental plane there was no handicap I could concede to the lout that nature had not already bestowed with a vengeance. Yet what good was my psychologist's IQ doing me now?

If I stayed in I would surely weep hideously.

The only thing was to strike out into the wet grey gloom of what the weather men call *continuous rain*, and dull my throbbing pain in the heat of action.

I put Professor Galton's *Self-Deception* paper in my bag, to give to Deirdre when I picked up Whitman & Nixon, and departed in a turmoil beneath the big black umbrella I'd bought for a shilling at a lost-property auction in Saint Andrews. As I puffed past the mews cottages of Kirk Lane, that steep and narrow short-cut to the West End, I chanted a vow never again to speak to Helen or the promiscuous brother whose corrupt example had ruined my life, and to minimize my intercourse with the other Wishforts until July, when I would move to Cambridge.

Deenburgh and I, it occurred to me (not for the first time) as my wet brogues squelched into Gladstone Place, were not well suited.

The downstairs hall of Deirdre's house was cavernous, dark, and smelled thickly of damp carpeting and curry spices from the Pakistani flat on the first floor. Round the walls were the trophied heads of numerous horned ungulates bagged in the glorious days when the sun never set on the fatuousness of the British Empire, and rearing by the foot of the wide old stairs was the gesticulating rage of a stuffed brown bear with a balding belly.

I shook my umbrella, hung it on Bruin's outstretched paw, and was about to mount the staircase. Hearing steps, I looked up and saw the descending form of a furtive person in a green raincoat (collar up) and felt hat (brim down) with an executive-style attaché-case. I had no wish . . . but suddenly:

'Dr Tostow?' I exclaimed.

'Hello, Peter,' he said with a hostile flicker of a smile. 'What are you doing here?'

I wanted to bounce the question back, but said:

'I've come to collect a book from Deirdre.'

'Deidre is not at home.'

'Then I'll ask . . .'

'Nobody is at home, Peter,' Dr Tostow assured me, staring

intently through his misted spectacles. There was a greyish tinge to his complexion, such as comes from an unhealthy diet, and his fleshy earlobes were white as milk.

'That's strange,' I said, 'I phoned less than an hour ago, and the line was engaged.'

'The person must have since gone out,' he insisted. 'I just have come myself to lend Deirdre a book I some time ago promised her.' He patted his attaché-case, and added viciously:

'Seeing as I just have been to consult with solicitors near . . . where are you going, Peter?' he demanded angrily, as though he might physically prevent my going up the stairs.

'I've also got an off-print to give Deirdre,' I explained. 'Professor Galton's paper on *Self-Deception*!', as if the professorial allusion might sanctify my presence. 'So I'll just slip it through the letter-box with a note.'

Dr Tostow scowled furiously into my mollifying smile.

'Tchaah!' he snapped, and thudded down the hall with a gait that seemed to promise me a fail in all my papers.

Feeling like a pensioner with a wooden leg and asthma, I ploughed up the two flights to the door that bore the Dymo-taped names: WISHFORT, CAMERON-BELL, ORMROD. What, I wondered, had happened to the fat girl with short curly hair and spectacles who, in the John Locke cafeteria, had looked such an ideal replacement for Othello?

I biroed a message on a scrap of paper, clipped it to the off-print, and bent to feed it carefully through the wide brass letter-box. This caused me to hear faint but unmistakable strains of a Radio Firth jingle, issuing from within.

Could someone have gone out and left the radio on?

Had Dr Tostow got it wrong?

Should I try the bell?

My finger rose to the button.

But a misgiving paralysed it.

Kneeling quietly on the doormat, I pushed the tongue of the letter-box inward and pressed an apprehensive eye between its lips. From this vantage I could see every door in the flat except that of the sitting room, which was round the corner to the left.

The Radio Firth sounds were coming from the kitchen, but also ajar was the door of the room formerly known as Othello's office. It still displayed his PRIVATE sign, painted black on green plastic, and the suspicion began to swell through my ears that . . .

Yes. In the lull between the end of a song and the resumption of dee-jay prattle, I distinctly heard Othello whine:

'Shit, man. Ye dinny have to . . .'

Another song swamped the details, though I got the impression he was on the phone.

What could this mean?

Had Othello not heard Dr Tostow's ringing?

But the doorbell could easily be heard above the radio.

Then had Othello simply declined to answer?

And why was he still here?

Maybe Deirdre was having difficulty getting him out, in which case Othello might realistically worry that any unexpected caller might be Alastair come to punch his nose.

With a dozen other *maybees* zipping round my mind like agitated gadflies, I eased the letter-box tongue back to rest and crept away, heavy with certainty that I would never see my library book again.

I walked to the West End and took a bus up the Knoll to the King David Bridge, where the public library was. I lurched into the lending room with a face like a rotten tomato and explained to the outraged Pekinese glare of the elderly maiden in The Annexe that *The Varieties of Orgasmic Experience* had regretfully been stolen by a gatecrasher during a party in my flat, and would she therefore please accept a cheque to cover its replacement?

Shortly after six that evening, tired, wet through, and poorer by eight pounds I could ill afford (since *Orgasmic Experience* came only in expensive American editions), I was slopping back through the *continuous rain* towards Number Ten, with a Fray Bentos steak-and-kidney pie and half a white cabbage in my brieface, when Mrs Wishfort's green Morris Minor pulled up in front of me.

Out of it got Deirdre, in a yellow oilskin and matching sou'wester.

'Hello, Peter,' she said, hoisting two shopping baskets full of groceries and delicatessen desirables out of the car. 'How's work?'

'Could be worse,' I said doubtfully. 'How's yours?'

'Could be better,' she said seriously, locking the car. 'Mummy's taken Daddy down to Querns today, to recuperate. She's got a fortnight off. And I can't get Othello out of my flat. There's some legal thing, and he's sticking out for his pound of flesh. So I've come back to work here until Finals and look after Rosie while Mummy's away. Would you like to come up for supper?'

'No thanks,' I croaked pathetically, blinking at her through the torrent that cascaded off my brolly like rain against the windows in the old Edgar Wallace films. 'I had something up town.'

'Lucky you, Peter. Save you from my cooking.' She heaved her bags to the front door and yanked the bell-pull.

'I'm afraid, Deirdre . . .'

'What?'

'That Galton off-print.'

'Yes?'

'I put it through your letter-box in Gladstone Place. This morning. I wanted . . .'

'Thanks, Peter, but you shouldn't have bothered,' she said unapologetically, as Rosie opened the door. 'I got another Xerox from the UL. I've been meaning to tell you.'

TWENTY-FIVE

By two o'clock that Saturday afternoon I had read the first hundred pages of the Penguin modern psychology readings on *Leadership*.

My assimilation was slowing depressingly, so I paused to lunch on a marmite sandwich and a cup of sweet Nescafé. The next forty pages took me over an hour, and when I looked at the table of *Mean 16 P. F. Scores for Leaders and Nonleaders* on page 141, and saw the statistics scampering all over the page like battling termites, I snapped the book shut in a panic and wondered what the entrance requirements were for trainee landscape gardeners.

Obviously I needed a break, but what could I do?

I would have liked to go to the cinema (*The Last Picture Show* was on at the ABC, and admiring Cybill Shepherd's body for two hours would be very acceptable). But the eight pounds I'd spent on replacing the library book had used up my entertainment budget for several weeks, and I couldn't ask Witch for a refund if I had vowed never to speak to him again.

Watching television upstairs would cost nothing but might bring me into contact with Helen, so that was out.

And further brooding over my Wishfort grievances took my animus against the family to an unparalleled zenith. The only member to escape my disaffection was the dog, so what about a walk to the park with Peter's best friend?

I buzzed Rosie.

'Pan Da's just *gone* out,' she said victoriously.

'Fine,' I said curtly. 'Just a thought. Never mind. How's your father, by the way?'

'Mummee says he's much happier at Querns, spesh lee

now he's a loud a little night cap a gain. Thank you, Pea Tar. Bye.'

What else?

I searched for free fun listings on the entertainment page of yesterday's *Deenburgh Herald*. There was a Kandinsky exhibition at the Gallery of Modern Art in the botanical gardens. Who *was* Kandinsky?

I leapt into my sports jacket and set off quivering with aimless urgency: down the dog-abused grassy slope beside the swimming pool, west over Strathbogle Bridge, then north along Pinery Avenue.

It was a fidgety day, warm but gusty.

Wheeling seagulls mewed low above me, like electrocuted cats, while the blue overhead came under threat from a multitude of colours, heights and speeds of cloud all around, including an ominous sky-high wall of rain-fat pink to the east.

As I followed the route Witch took that Sunday when he composed his *Pobble* poem for Cindy, I heard (from over the tall wall to my left) the leisurely clunking of old folk playing bowls, and saw (through the sadly un-dogproof fence to my left) the near bank of the rain-swollen Lethe being fouled by a prolific black Labrador.

After the bowling green and the Orchard cricket ground, Pinery Avenue arcs up a short slope, then broadens into a long straight boulevard that divides Aberlethe Park's football, swings, roundabouts and tarmac tennis, from the richer flora, subtler perfumes and cleaner verdures of the botanics. Halfway along, the boulevard balloons into a small metalled circus where cars may park, and as I approached the circus I saw Witch's Lotus on the far side.

Its owner was standing on the pavement between the park gate and a bickering mob not queueing at the window of the *Mr McWhipy* van. He was licking a 99, had Panda sitting unwillingly at heel, and was chatting up a pair of pretty schoolgirls in bright summer frocks.

They too were taking a Dalmatian for a walk in the park, and she too was sitting unwillingly at heel.

I might have slipped into the botanics unobserved if one of the schoolgirls hadn't noticed me scowling at Witch. She said something, nodded in my direction, Witch looked round, and I felt as if I'd been caught exposing myself on television.

'Hi, Pete,' Witch called, beckoning imperiously with his ice-cream. 'Come on over.'

Helpless as a flasher in handcuffs, I obeyed.

'Let us know if you want her pupped, won't you?' Witch was saying suggestively to the departing schoolgirls.

Blushing and giggling with delight, they promised.

'Friends of yours?' I asked.

'The brunette with the big tits is Grant MacMillan's wee sister. Going to be a peach, isn't she? What you up to, Pete?'

'I'm going to the Kandinsky exhibition.'

'Great idea. Didn't know there was one. I'll come with you.'

'You can't bring Panda . . .'

'No, but we'll . . . Hey, youse!' he roared in a terrifying accent at two wizened twelve-year-olds in the *Mr McWhipy* mob. 'Whit yese Dane?'

'Whit sit tae yew, mister?' the plimsolled leader with a leather football in a string bag sniffed defiantly.

'I'll gie yese five bob if yese walk ma dug fur a noor.'

'Ten bob, mister, in wull date.'

'Ten bob if he says you've run him off his feet,' Witch bargained, sliding into his normal voice. 'But you've not to let him off the lead: he's a very valuable dog. Cost a hundred pounds.'

'Jeez, whitta swiz!'

'And don't feed him ice-cream.'

'Dinny worry!'

'Exactly an hour. Okay? Got a watch?'

Billy Bremner The Third proudly displayed a Mickey Mouse chronometer, and said:

'Gie uz the money *now,* mister.'

'Half now, half later,' said Witch, handing over some coins and the lead.

'Whit's the dug's name?'

'Prince Philip. Mind and look after him. Right, Pete? Let's stroll round the gardens first, shall we? Before it clouds over. And I'll show you the duck-pond where MackTheKnife got pigged two years ago on Christmas Eve.'

'What for?'

Witch grinned:

'Trying to catch one of the Muscovies with a salmon net. But the curator saw his torch from the top storey of the art gallery, so he dialled blue murder and Mack got his Christmas dinner in the sty. According to the *Herald* court report, it was the considered opinion of the arresting officers that *the accused was discernibly the worse for liquor when apprehended*. If we go . . .'

He guided me hospitably: round rockeries; through mazes of all varieties of rhododendron; down grassy avenues of exotic evergreens, where blackbirds hopped and grey squirrels scampered; through a gigantic palm house that looked as if its glass roof would burst if its occupants grew another inch; fern houses, orchid houses, tropical-rain-forest houses, arid cactus houses; along a herbaceous border between a thirty-foot yew hedge and a line of twenty-five park benches generously donated in loving memory . . .

And Witch discoursed cheerfully on the incalculable value of such a wealth of botanical wonder to the aesthetics of mind-expansion in the local community, recalling an insightful experience he himself once had in the tropical aquarium, where, even as we ambled, a trio of gangling scarecrows with goggle eyes were gasping with glottal awe at the brilliant colours and darting movements of the myriad fish.

But my taciturnity advertised that all was not well in my life, and soon he was drawing out of me the fankled details of my work worries, anxieties about the future, misery over being junked by Helen despite having assured myself that I didn't mind that it wouldn't last, money difficulties, and a crippling feeling of injustice arising from my life being so hard and dull, when his seemed so easy, affluent and debonair.

'You really are a mess, Pete,' he said, when, walking past

a Henry Moore sculpture on the lawn to the south of the art gallery, I told him about my eight-pound trauma over the orgasms book. 'Aren't you?'

'Yes.'

'Why didn't you tell me?'

'I don't know.'

'Here.' He flicked two fivers out of his wallet. 'Take these. And don't argue.'

Then, concerning his volatile sister:

'You spoken to Helen about it?'

'No.'

'Why not?'

'There didn't seem any point.'

'Jesus, Pete. Those who don't ask don't get – that's Rule One. Ask, and their thighs will be parted unto you. Didn't you read my Old Hebridean Proverb?'

'No.'

'You see: Helen is very competitive. Grant chucked her, and now Jennifer's chucked Grant. So Grant's trying it on with Helen again. Helen'll set him up and then chuck *him*. Which proves she's at least as good as Jennifer. She thinks.'

'Has Helen told you this?'

'No. But you watch. Bet you fifty pounds.'

'No thanks.'

'So if you want Helen back, you get someone else in the meantime, and when Helen's chucked Grant she'll be jealous and come after you. So you'll have the whip hand!' He smiled kindly.

'Isn't that rather exploitative?'

'What isn't?'

'*Tat Twam Asi* isn't. Is it?'

'Yes.'

'How?'

'Because, Pete,' Witch sang: 'The knee bone's connected to the thigh bone, and the thigh bone's connected to the hip bone, and . . . you feeling peeved because your life's less wonderful than mine – that's priceless.'

'Why?'

'How would you describe yourself?'

'A mess.'

'That's this week. But dispositionally you're a steady, sensible, hardworking person. Who'll be a professor by the time he's fifty. Even if his psychology does have little value. You're on the way up, and your peak is still twenty years away.'

'Twenty years is a long time.'

'Ah yes,' Witch said knowingly. 'But look at me.'

I looked at him.

He had on his pullover, jeans and cowboy boots combination. His long fair hair was freshly washed and waved like a girl's in response to the breeze that eddied like a confession of nature's fickleness across the lawns rolling down from the gallery to the hot houses. The pupils in his blue eyes were narrow as sharpened match heads when he said persuasively:

'*I'm* just a gifted failure.'

'How can you say that?'

'Look at the facts. I've given up maths, I've given up physics. My mind has already been as far as mind can go. I'll never get anywhere as a philosopher . . .'

'Why not?'

'Philosophers never get anywhere. And I'll never write a perfect song. I realised that after the Janie Carmen concert. Drove down to Boonton Pier and had a value crisis. So I've stopped trying.'

'But why? What *is* a perfect song?' I expected a definition, but Witch clapped his left hand to his ear and (to the consternation of two elderly nuns walking past us with a curious dry rattling noise) soulfully sang:

Out there over the ocean
A storm is gathering.
The waves are curling angrily
And the gulls are sheltering.
And the trawlermen take
To the taverns again,
Retelling tales of old times,

And the tallest tale
That takes most ale
Is the one about me and my crime.
I don't deny my shame.

But oh what I'd give
If I only could live
My whole life over again:
I'd live it differently.

'There you are, Pete. Iain MacGinn gets the royalties, but the song popped out of the spirit of the species. Like a mushroom after rain. That do?'

'I don't think you should stop writing songs, Witch.'

'Perhaps I won't,' he conceded malleably. 'Who knows? Maybe Cindy and I will get some ethnic jugband going in France. Rewrite the *Marseillaise*, or something.

'But my serious point, Mr Squirrell, is that I am not to be envied. I've already peaked: drilled all my talents, but found no oil worth mining. Which is a terrible, tragic realisation for an honest young trooper of twenty-three to live with.'

'Yes. Clearly a great burden.'

'So now there's nothing left, except to be a good husband and father.'

'Good husbands don't have two wives!'

'In some places they do. Not still envious, are you, Pete?'

'No.'

'Glad to hear it. Wouldn't want you coveting my one consolation.'

'You do have your private income, Witch. And your drugs business.'

'I don't make a penny out of dope.'

'Then how can you deal in such bulk?'

'What bulk?'

'Your hoard in Querns Castle, which you . . .'

'Ach,' he scoffed impatiently. 'There *isn't* any hoard in the castle.'

'Then why . . .'

'It's a red herring. Wishfort roulette. See who betrays me first. Keep the pigs away from the Thermos in the cellar.'

'So the Thermos is all there is?'

'Right. Five hundred doses is my maximum stock. Just a hobby, see?'

'With no profits?'

'I've told you before, Pete: any profits go to Oxfam.'

'And you feel like Robin Hood?'

'And you'd like to feel Maid Marian?'

I was too angry to answer.

'Aren't those amazing?' Witch said appreciatively. We were weaving along a narrow path through a glass-house that reproduced the steamy humidity of the Amazon jungle with sufficient accuracy to make me remove my tie and undo the top two buttons of my shirt.

Witch had paused in front of me to examine a formation of giant lilies floating on the skin of a small pond full of dirty green water. The daylight that filtered through the overhanging foliage was a vile shade of pink, and combined with the soaking hot air to remind me unpleasantly of the marmite sandwich I'd had for lunch.

'Are they?' I queried irritably.

'What do you see in them, Pete?'

'Mildewed omelettes.'

'Not stepping stones to the gates of Paradise?'

'No.'

Sighing as he walked on, Witch asked:

'Doesn't the superficiality of your perception bother you?'

'No.'

'It does, you know.'

'How?'

'It makes you envious.'

'I thought we agreed I'd stopped being envious.'

'But you still feel, deep down, that my life is an unmerited sinecure, while yours is one long exam – silver spoon versus congenital limp. Don't you?'

'If you say so, Witch.'

'Let me give you an example . . .'

'Please do.'

'When you saw me leap on the stage to hassle Groucho, at the Hardy Nagil show, what did you think?'

'I can't remember.'

'You thought: "What an arrogant, attention-seeking bastard Wishfort is!" '

'Did I?'

'Yet part of you wished it could have been *Squirrell* up there grabbing the limelight.'

'Quite untrue.'

'While none of you saw that I was nearly sick with stage-fright.'

'How can I deny it?'

He agreed that I couldn't, then confessed two other lapses from perfection in the Mallecho ontogeny:

In the first few months of his travels round the world he'd become so obsessed with the idea that he had skin cancer, and that every tiny mole, birthmark or freckle on his body was a malignant tumour escalating daily, that he'd come within a tremble of writing to Professor Newbigging for a psychiatric diagnosis;

And in his second undergraduate year he'd been (that most abominable of all human derelicts) *a McEwan's Export alcoholic* – pursued down corridors and into lecture halls, the morning after, by horse-sized rats with the heads of pigs and blood streaming out of their eyes like the foam from fire extinguishers.

'How did that come about?'

'Trying to keep up with the rugby club's drinking, without keeping up with the rugby club's rugby.'

'So what did you do?'

'Gave up Export. Then,' he confided, as we circled back towards the art gallery, under an increasingly bellicose sky, 'when I was sixteen, shortly after I'd become what you social scientists call *sexually active*, I woke up one morning with a big fat varicocele.'

'What's that?'

'An explosion of varicose veins in your scrotal sac. Usually on top of the left ball. Feels like a pouch of lumpy worms.'

'It sounds disgusting.' I shuddered.

Witch smiled.

'First it was Nature's revenge for me shooting the bullfinch. Then it was God's punishment for shagging Haggis Annie without a rubber. And after three months of no sleep thinking I'd have to have both balls cut off to stop the cancer spreading, I went to the doctor and owned up.

'Into Southside General for a week, and by Christmas I'd enough confidence back to ask a girl to dance. Met a sex maniac in hospital, incidentally, who was having a vasectomy 'cos he'd got too many kids. Bumped into him in a pub, later, and he said:

' "Dinny believe what they tell yuh, pal. Ye canny get as good a stand efter as ye could afore." So there you are, Pete. Mustn't swallow everything you find in women's magazines.'

'But you didn't have your . . . testicles cut off?'

'Not quite. They make a slit in your groin, pull your balls up inside you, cut the varicose veins off, and push the balls back down to the scrotum. Very nifty. Didn't you see my scar?' He generously pulled at his shirt, but I said:

'No thanks.'

'Your funeral, Pete.'

'So,' I educed from his revelations with a glimmer of glee, 'life *isn't* all a holiday.'

'Wrong again, old son. But when it rains, put your Wellies on. Your holiday's what you make of it.'

'I remember you saying, Witch, when we went to dinner with the Tostows, that freedom of the will is a fantasy.'

'Freedom of the *individual* will. Yes.'

'Then how can life be what one makes of it? If one isn't free?'

'*Twat Tam*.'

'I don't get it.'

'Take a trip.'

'No thanks.'

'Please yourself,' he said amiably, as we walked past a

blast of hot scones and pancakes wafting from the bustling tea room, which was situated in an outbuilding beside the grey four-storey villa that housed the gallery. 'Some people like package coach tours. I don't. Let's see if Kandinsky did.'

We had both viewed the permanent exhibits before, so we went straight up to the special exhibition on the top floor. For fifteen minutes we browsed round three large white-walled rooms containing some fifty pictures, ranging from marginally representational ladies with fans against menacing Russian nightscapes to wholly unrepresentational assortments of blobbed spheres and rectangles. These Witch seemed to find particularly instructive, while I tried to work out from which window the curator had spotted MackTheKnife's torchlit assault on the Muscovy ducks.

Also, to allay the scowling suspicions of the black-suited security men (that Witch and I were gaping acid freaks incapable of coherent conversation), I worked up enough pluck to tell my companion I was sure his projected *ménage à trois* wouldn't last a year, and not only was he mad to try it, but wouldn't the attempt constitute a serious danger to the long-term happiness of all concerned, especially Cindy?

'Cindy's happy *now*, Pete. Why take that away from her?'

And while I could understand, in the light of her previous involvement in the Louisiana orgasms experiments, how Anita might fall with relative ease into her place in Witch's sexual triangle, how could he possibly have persuaded Cindy, a well-bred Deenburgh lady, out of St David's, to whom he was *already engaged*, that she should share him with Anita?

'Told her to give it a try or piss off. Taken to it well, too. Like a lamb to gambolling. There's a strong Lesbian latency in all women, Pete. Look at the way they're always going to the loo together.'

And was Cindy pregnant yet?

'We're working on it.'

Didn't it worry him that his sons and heirs might be born deformed, if he kept plying his pregnant concubines with psychedelic drugs?

'You examined the evidence for chromosome damage, Pete?'

'No.'

'Neither have I.'

'Then for heaven's sake . . .'

'There isn't any. Next question, please.'

Flak from Dr Tostow?

Yes. Groucho had telephoned abusively several times. He had also visited the kitchen equipment shop in Bluebell Street (which Anita was managing while the owner took a fortnight's holiday) and molested his wife while she was working. Witch had had to inform him that any repetition would result in tape recordings of their telephone conversations being played on the *Win £5 For The Funniest Story Of The Week* spot on Simon Darling's Saturday Requests Show. Divorce proceedings (premised on Dr Tostow's infertility and associated mental cruelty) were in hand, and Witch had also issued a summons in virtue of Groucho's failure to honour his agreement to make payments to Oxfam in proportion to Anita's orgasmic achievements under Witch's tutelage.

'Might have to call you as a witness, old son. Hope you don't mind.'

'As long as it's after my Finals results.'

'Talking of Oxfam,' he said, glancing at his watch, 'did you ever use that cassette deck I gave you?'

'No.'

'Sold it?'

'No.'

'What's going to happen to it?'

'I don't know.'

'That's *pitiful*, Pete,' Witch said paternally. 'If you've no use for it, selling it would have eased your money worries, and you could have spent this afternoon admiring Cybill Shepherd's body in the ABC. You must be more enterprising in future.'

'I'll try.'

'Now: back to Number Ten. Cindy'll have the kettle on,

and it's time to rescue Prince Philip from the republicans.'

As we left the gallery, Witch bought a dozen assorted Kandinsky slides from the gift counter, and a postcard for Dr Tostow. It showed a little green man on horseback, staring into the sun (as far as my superficial perception could see) and trying to pull his hair out.

TWENTY-SIX

Cindy had been buying food for the evening meal.

Then she spent an hour helping Anita in Bluebell Street, and came down to Number Ten to join Witch for tea. Anita was to follow when she shut up shop at five, and she and Cindy were going to prepare a big dinner in Mrs Wishfort's kitchen. Beano and Harriet would be guests of honour, I would be guest of habit, and Simon Darling might call by for a glass of Mr Wishfort's port when he'd finished his requests show. Deirdre was in Glasgow for the day, Helen was elsewhere with Missing-link MacMillan, and Rosie had gone out leaving an important message for Cindy to pass to Witch.

Bold purple on a torn leaf of St David's jotter said:

TELL DEIRDRE I'LL BE BACK BY MIDNIGHT MALLECHO. GOING TO A PARTY AND DEIRDRE KNOWS SO IT'S ALRIGHT. PANDA'S NEW RUBBER BONE COST £2 ON MUMMY'S ACCOUNT AT THE PET SHOP AND HE'S BERRIED IT IN THE GARDEN AND I CAN'T FIND IT SO PLEASE WILL YOU LOOK FOR IT MALLECHO. R.

Witch chuckled and said:

'Wish I was young. Don't you, Pete?'

'Why?'

'Might be going to a party tonight.'

'Roast beef and Burgundy will do me beautifully, thanks.'

Cindy smiled at my premature compliment, Witch rolled a reefer, we finished our tea and lapsed into watching the sports results and Saturday children's hour. The day outside had darkened into a dirty, sullen breathlessness. The morning room window was open wide, and even the pear-tree blossom smelled sweaty and eager for a shower of refreshing rain. It was fifteen minutes later, when Witch and Panda went to answer the telephone in the hall, that things began to go wrong.

'Tardis Exterminations Bureau,' we heard Witch bark in a Dalek monotone. 'You are surround. . .'

'. . . . . .'

'Yes, that's him. When?'

'. . .'

'Where are you now?'

'. . .'

'No. Don't tell anyone. Especially not the police. Go . . . shut up and *listen*, will you? Get a cab to Southside and stay there till I call you. Tell Beano dinner's off.'

'. . . . . .'

'I know, love,' Witch said, suddenly tender. 'But it's over now. Just sit tight, and I'll see you later. Okay?' He put the phone down gently, then muttered:

'Bastards,' and came back into the morning room looking pale, worried and angry.

'What's wrong, Witch?' Cindy asked fearfully.

'I've got to go to Querns.'

'Why?'

He took a deep breath and said rapidly:

'Mack's nobbled Anita in Bluebell Street. Ran up behind her and whipped a bag over her head . . .'

'How does she know it was Mack?' I asked.

'The stink of him. Hustled her into a doorway and said he'd slice her face if she didn't tell him where I keep my acid. So she said Querns Castle and I've got to get down there pronto.'

'But you said there *isn't* any acid in the castle.'

'Right, Pete,' he said impatiently, picking his car keys off the tea trolley. 'But either Othello and Mack will try to steal what they *think* is there, or else they'll clipe to the pigs again. Could be a big hassle for the old man, see? If wankers go sniffing round the cottage. I'll call you . . .'

'Let me come, Witch,' I offered, though I was very frightened. 'You might need help.'

'Okay, Pete. Thanks.'

'Oh, Witch!' Cindy cried petulantly, jumping up from the sofa. 'I'm not staying here on my own.'

'All right, we'll all bloody go. But let's *get a bend on,'* he urged, turning off the television and curtly cuffing Panda, who was jumping up at him in excitement.

'Shouldn't you take your pistol, Witch?' I suggested anxiously, as we poured into the Lotus.

'Get a grip, Pete. What am I to do with a gun, if Pig One turns up in a squad car? Anyway,' he added grimly, 'there's an entrenching tool in the boot. Beat a breadknife any day.'

Seven minutes later we were screeching along the coast road at a speed that made me fear we'd be stopped by traffic police.

I was in the back, with the dog, and Cindy was in the front passenger seat. Her shiny blue trousers, tunic-shaped silver shirt and clicking tangle of multi-coloured bead necklaces made her look like a gypsy vampire. Her flaming hair tint, pouting scarlet lips and heavily painted eyes offended me. I felt that since Amsterdam she'd regressed eight years and was *playing* at being an adult, in a fashion more appropriate to Rosie.

'What are we going to do, Witch?' Cindy asked, watching Cockleburgh racecourse whiz by in a blur of epileptic green.

'Whatever is necessary.'

Beyond the racecourse was a mess of clashing greys.

The sky looked as though it would melt and collapse downward, the sea as if it might boil and steam upward, and the half dozen boats in view seemed like insects trapped between two hot cobwebs.

We accelerated into the country, and as we shot up the Jake's Cafe hill at a hundred miles an hour I decided not to attempt a tension-easing joke about stopping for an ice-cream. A recent accident had left a scatter of broken glass and debris on the road, and ten seconds after the cafe the car began to judder violently, skid, and I thought we were done for.

'Bugger,' said Witch when he'd fought it back under control and slowed round the brow of the hill.

'What is it?'

'Puncture.' He pulled in to the near verge forty yards down the slope towards Pratnair village. Further down, to the right, over the flanking fir trees, I could just see the top of Pratnair Law.

We were four miles from our destination.

Witch was white from intensity of emotion. Without another word he got out to inspect the damage. What happened next has occupied my mind so often, like the crucial wrong decision or failure of nerve that one most bitterly regrets in life, that I only have to think of any part of it and the rest plays itself, round and round, like a tape loop, until I am able to trick my attention away from it by means of alcohol, engaging company, or preoccupying work.

Witch shouts that we'll have to change the wheel. He moves to open the boot. Cindy opens the passenger door. Panda suddenly whines with pleasure, jumps between the two front seats, trampolines off Cindy's thighs and is out on the verge wagging his tail with cocky delight. The boot is open, so I can't see behind us, but my body senses the approach of a heavy vehicle. I shout at Panda, but it is too late. He trots round the front of the car, sees something on the far side of the road, steps out, and is run over by the inside front wheel of a Scottish & Newcastle beer-tanker.

The tanker's back wheels pull the dog several yards down the road and then leave him in a convulsing heap. His jaws are working as if he has a bone stuck in his throat, but he makes no sound. Cindy screams, I shake her shoulder and tell her to get out of the car. Witch curses, runs towards Panda, and I call out:

'Be careful, Witch,' for there is a line of traffic coming up the hill from Pratnair, including a leapfrogging Jaguar, which looks highly dangerous.

'Can't leave the poor brute like that,' Witch calls back.

He bends to take hold of Panda's collar, but the dog snaps at him in an unrecognizing frenzy. Its jaws clamp tight on his wrist. He pulls to free himself. I am out of the Lotus and running to help, but a third car comes hurtling over the summit behind us at an unforgiveable speed. The driver is busy trying to avoid the Lotus in time not to collide with the Jaguar, so he doesn't see Witch and the dog. In the time it takes my mouth to open in despair, the black Triumph Herald, Othello's car, has smashed into Witch head-on.

Witch's body folds like a slow rugby player tackled by a very fast opponent. His trunk slaps down on the bonnet of the Triumph, his head whips down like a hammer to shatter the windscreen, his legs somersault over him and he ricochets several feet over Othello's roof, lands on the metalled road like a baby rabbit killed and tossed by a powerful tomcat, and bounces to rest on the soft green verge.

Meanwhile Othello has zigzagged crazily down the road, almost hits the oncoming Jaguar, veers too wildly, rockets off the road to the left, rips through the woodside fence as if it were tissue-paper and crunches his car into the base of a fir-tree. The body of the Triumph crumples catastrophically, a splash of glass explodes out of it like a bucket of water poured from a height, and the tail lifts high in the air before dropping to the ground with a sickening shudder.

How many seconds have passed?

I can't say. This is my first serious accident, and I feel as I once did when I got an electric shock from a faulty reading-lamp.

Cindy's moaning sets me in motion.

She is standing by the Lotus, her arms clasped across her stomach, heaving as if about to be sick. I rush to Witch's side. He looks strange and twisted, like a mutilated rag-doll. His legs are wrong, his left arm seems unhinged at the elbow, and his face might have been severely beaten in a fistfight. He is deeply unconscious; dark brown blood is seeping in a fan shape from his nostrils; it is clear he is close to death.

'*Is* he dead?' someone asks. It is the driver of the Jaguar, which is parked at the top of the hill. He looks like a successful bookmaker.

I beg the bookmaker to not let anyone move Witch until help comes. Then I turn and run to Jake's Cafe to phone for an ambulance. And as I run that furlong, each sob for breath a prayer for Witch's life, the promised rain begins to patter, and soon is pouring, as from a burst main in the sky.

The next hour was a streaming torture of torrential rain, ambulance men with luminous orange coats and blood-smeared hands, policemen in yellow plastic jackets, flashing blue lights, nurses uniformed in various shades of blue, all with white hats, doctors in white coats, most with Asian accents, and the offensive wet stench of soused herring that emanated from MackTheKnife in the ambulance that took him, Witch and myself, to the cottage hospital in Diddington, the county town of East Logan.

Othello had been killed outright, his unseatbelted chest impacted horribly on the Triumph's steering column, but Mack had catapulted through the windscreen and, apart from mild concussion, facial lacerations and a broken collar-bone, seemed to have got off lightly.

He was treated in the cottage hospital, while Witch was sent straight on to the Deenburgh Royal with a suspected fractured skull. I went with him, leaving Cindy under sedation in Diddington. I asked the local police to contact her parents, then worried about what to tell Mrs Wishfort. Should I phone immediately? Or wait for a diagnosis? Suppose Mr Wishfort answered the phone?

'Tell the police escort: *as quickly as you can,*' the Diddington doctor had gravely instructed the ambulance driver.

My main memory of that journey is the obscenely red plastic covers on the ambulance seats, as if they'd chosen the colour so it wouldn't matter if you bled on them, and the ghastly transparent tubing they had forced into Witch's mouth and down his throat to keep him breathing. Soon we were in the Emergencies intake bay in the underbelly of the Infirmary, the stretcher was unloaded and wheeled away by two male nurses who looked like convicts, one of them whistling cheerily, I was questioned again and then told to wait.

The casualties lounge was a dismal place, and Saturday nights were a busy time. Footballers with kneecaps dislodged by other footballers competed for priority over football supporters with noses broken by other football supporters. An old man who'd been knocked off his bicycle by a motorbike was in a pitiful state. A ten-year-old boy had stuck his forefinger between the mangle rollers of an antediluvian Hotpoint washing machine, his mother had managed to spring the safety release before the mangle pulled his finger off, but the skin had snapped over the join of his finger and hand, and the flesh of his palm was torn right through to the bone.

His life was in no danger, but he was bleeding all over the place, having already bled all over his mother's knees, and his piercing howls of rage, pain and fear were extremely disturbing. But worst of all were the ants. I thought I was hallucinating, but no. On the rippled green linoleum floor beneath the corner bench where I was slumped head-in-hands, several dozen black ants were manoeuvring with terrific energy. I'd just brushed two off my shoe and was considering reporting the matter when I was summoned to speak to a Dr Wilcox.

He was a sharp-featured thinly blond person in his mid-thirties, one of Mr Wishfort's juniors, whom I recognized from his brief appearance at Witch and Deirdre's birthday party.

Mallecho's life was in the balance, he told me. His skull was fractured in several places and the X-rays and other tests showed he had a blood clot on the brain that would have to be operated on immediately. Had I been in touch with the patient's mother? No?

'I'll phone her straight away, of course. I just didn't know, you see. Whether to . . .'

'That's all right, Mr Squirrell. Quite understandable. If you happen to know where Mrs Wishfort is at the moment, I'll telephone myself. Then, if you could wait till she arrives, you will have done all that anyone could do.'

Before Mrs Wishfort left Querns she phoned across the river, ostensibly to ask Mrs Em if she'd mind coming over to wash up the supper dishes, but actually to ensure that Mr Wishfort wasn't left alone for too long. Mallecho had broken his leg in an accident, she bravely informed both her husband and the old Irish lady, and she didn't know when she would get back.

Immediately his wife departed, Mr Wishfort telephoned Mrs Em again and told her to stay where she was. He was perfectly all right, thank you, the dishes could wait till the morning, and if he felt need of assistance he would call her. Then he dispensed himself a large Scotch and switched on Radio Firth to listen to his godson's Saturday requests show. Perhaps he was hoping Simon might read a get-well-soon-Mr-Wishfort card.

The seven-thirty news headlines included the flash, just phoned in by an *Evening News* cub reporter, who'd got it off an obliging nurse while chasing the latest on an injured soccer star, that local character Mallecho Wishfort was critically ill following a road accident in which one other victim had already died, and was at that very moment undergoing major brain surgery of a type normally carried out by his father, eminent neurosurgeon Mr Douglas Wishfort. While Mallecho's chances of survival were said to be fifty-fifty, the possibility of his sustaining permanent brain damage could not be ruled out at this stage.

By nine o'clock Mrs Em was terribly worried.

She'd rung Querns cottage five or six times, but always got an engaged tone – as though Mr Wishfort had taken his phone off the hook. But why should he? She scolded Mr Em into walking over the bridge with her to check that all was well. In the sitting room they found the radio still merrily playing, and Mr Wishfort's body lying on the floor beside the fallen telephone.

He had died of a heart attack.

TWENTY-SEVEN

The operation to remove the blood clot from Witch's brain was successful, but further complications and cerebral haemorrhaging developed on the Sunday afternoon. He was operated on again that evening and kept alive on support systems in the intensive therapy unit until four o'clock on Monday morning, when he died without regaining consciousness.

He and Mr Wishfort were buried the following Thursday in Whitefriars Graveyard (a noted tourist draw on account of the remains of Whitefriars Willy, the most famous faithful friend in Deenburgh's doggy history). It was a Wishfort tradition that women did not attend burials, and this gave the burial a surrealistic uniform blackness, with a hundred sombre-suited men, of all ages and persuasions, gathered together to pay their last respects.

In the professorial ranks I recognized Galton, Quelch, Newbigging, several professors of medicine, and even Sir Gabriel Drake. Also mourning Mr Wishfort was Angus Angusson, whose documentary on road accidents would receive its first showing in two weeks' time. Those specifically grieving for Witch ranged from Tom Redhead on the political front, through Poldy of Poldy's Bar, Sergeant Anderson and Constable Calder, several vitamin-deficient scarecrows, many old school friends, most of the rugby club, to a couple of wild-looking villains with short necks and thick shoulders, whose transparent hardness made MackTheKnife seem like a ball of wet cotton-wool.

It was a warm and sunny morning, with millions of daisies shining brilliantly white between the lowhanging greens of the ash trees and the yellowing laurel bushes, yet the dreamlike morbidity of the occasion was intensified by a horrendous cacophony of drumming, droning and skirling coming over the wall from Goldsmith College, where a schools pipe-band competition was in progress, and by the spotty pale flesh of some early-lunching office workers who had crept into sheltered corners of the graveyard to sunbathe.

As I looked over the double grave and allowed the purple-robed minister's solemn words to sink beneath the wailing of the bagpipes, my drifting gaze espied the tears streaming freely from Beano's big dark eyes, a scowl of unhappiness between Alastair's scrubbed jug ears, then a grin of hooded derision from Grant MacMillan, and I speculated frantically on the cruelly hyperbolized details that Helen's earthy cynicism must have whispered to my enemy, concerning my sexual shortcomings.

Forgive the dead their sins is surely a laudable maxim where practicable, and even cantankerous old Miss Moray, at whose windows Witch and Beano had fired their Guy Fawkes rockets, sent Mrs Wishfort a generous wreath and condolence card. There were handsome obituaries in the *Deenburgh Herald*, for Mr Wishfort, and in *Dumbo* for Witch, whom Tom Redhead epitaphed as a:

'. . . fearless pioneer of the frontiers of the spirit. *Long live the revolution.*'

Soon after that there was an inquest into the fatal accident, necessitated by Othello and Mack being 'known to the police'. I had to give evidence, and during my attendance I learned two facts that so badly aggravated my insomnia that I feared I would be unable to take my exams.

On Mack's person had been found, besides an illegal flick-knife, three hundred pounds in new five-pound notes, which he swore Othello had given him to pay off gambling debts. And in the boot of Othello's car was a sawn-off twelve-bore shotgun and a box of cartridges. Mack testified on oath that he knew nothing about the gun, and as no fingerprints of his were found on it, he was eventually let off with a fine in respect of the flick-knife.

Leaving me in an agony of *ifs.*

'Good morning, Peter. Please come in. How can I help you?'

'I hear you and your wife are reunited, Dr Tostow?'

'We never were apart, Peter.'

'That's not how I saw it.'

'We had just a little hiccup in our enduring relationship. These things happen.'

'I didn't see you at Mallecho's funeral.'

'Nobody invited me. And besides: pressure of work, Finals coming up, my new laboratory in Calif . . .'

'I know what you were doing, Dr Tostow.'

'Doing?'

'In the Gladstone Place flat. When I met you coming down the stairs.'

'What was I doing?'

'You had been in the flat. Conspiring with Othello. Conspiring to have Mallecho *murdered.* Weren't you?'

'Forgive me for not laughing, Peter. But your joke not only is not funny but also insulting. I told you at the time: I had meant to leave a book for Deirdre, but I found nobody was at home.'

'I don't believe you. When I went upstairs Othello was *in.*'

'Did he answer the door?'

'No.'

'So how do you *know* he was in?'

'When I put Deirdre's off-print through the letter-box I heard him speaking on the telephone.'

'And did you then ring the doorbell?'

'No.'

'Why not?'

'I think you know why not, Dr Tostow.'

'But I do *not* know, Peter. And also I cannot explain the motivations behind your preposterous accusations. Precisely how, in your theory, am I supposed to have conspired to have murdered your friend?'

'Anita had been tripping with Witch and Cindy. Othello knew this. So you and he worked out that Anita might know where Witch kept his LSD. You got Mack to attack Anita and scare her into giving him that information, reckoning that she would immediately tell Witch what had happened. He would then rush to protect his acid stash, you hoped, and Othello and Mack would follow him there and kill him with the shotgun later found in the boot of Othello's car. Quite ingenious, I must say. And I don't believe Othello could have worked it out on his own. Do you deny it?'

'In what way would this hypothetical homicide have afforded profit to Mr Othello and myself?'

'You've got Anita back, haven't you? And Othello might not have got Cindy back, but he would have had his revenge for being humiliated, having his band broken up and losing his demo tapes.'

'Mrs Tostow would have soon returned to myself in any case. This is not the first time she has had such a little adventure. As for broken bands and lost tapes, I absolutely have no idea what you are talking about. You perhaps have been reading John Le Carré, have you, Peter? Particularly before important exams has it often been found . . .'

'Look, Tostow, maybe you won't admit it, but I can easily get the truth out of Mack.'

'Who is this Mack?'

'I'll get Beano Turnbull and Alastair Cameron-Bell to help me. We'll haul him out of Poldy's, march him round the back, and *beat* the truth out of him. If necessary.'

'You perfectly are welcome, Mr Squirrell, to beat the gentleman to *death* for all I care. But you will not extract from him even the suspicion of a fact in the slightest embarrassing to myself. I indeed find it most distressing of all that you should imagine that even supposing a man of my intelligence were to involve himself in a crime of the order you are inventing, he could be foolish enough to allow his involvement to become known to a common hoodlum.'

'How do you know Mack's a hoodlum?'

'According to you he is capable of murdering a fellow human being with a fire-arm in exchange presumably for money. The probability therefore is that the appellation "hoodlum" would be warranted.'

'You Tostow, are a devious, murderous, cold-blooded *reptile*, and . . .'

'Clearly, *Mr* Squirrell, you are suffering from acute hypertension and concomitant paranoid delusions of a persecutive nature, which as I said is a syndrome not infrequently found in students working intensively for examinations the results of which will be vital to their subsequent careers. Allow me therefore to fix you an appointment to see Professor Newbigging who hopefully . . .'

'Put the phone down, Tostow. And listen carefully. Maybe I can't *prove* your involvement. *Conceivably* I'm doing you an injustice. But if I suspect for one moment that the class of my degree fails to reflect the quality of my exam papers, I'll go straight to the Senate, the police, the press . . .'

'That is *quite enough*, young man. Providing that you leave here at once and henceforth keep your slanderous fabrications to yourself, there is a *possibility* that I shall consider not reporting this present disgraceful outburst to Professor Galton. *Good day* to you.'

Changes rung on that dialogue slopped through my mind all night every night until I was forced to consult Mrs Wishfort's GP to request a supply of sleeping pills.

'Do you ever drink tea or coffee in the evenings?'

'Yes.'

'How much?'

'Five or six cups, I suppose. Sometimes . . .'

'Laddie, laddie,' Dr Dalgleish clucked dourly. 'Have some common *sense*. Cut out stimulants after seven o'clock. If you need a beverage, drink hot Bovril. Or blackcurrant juice and honey. Maybe one wee whisky before you turn in. If that doesn't work, come back and see me again.'

I stuck to hot Ribena, and it worked like a charm.

After all, this was not Los Angeles but *Deenburgh*, where one didn't so much have one's enemy assassinated as incite one's Labrador to foul his doorstep. And wasn't it perfectly reasonable that Othello shouldn't have opened the door to Dr Tostow? He'd been on the phone, and was possibly worried about Alastair coming to heavy him out of the flat. Then the shotgun. Why not? It was Witch who'd first pulled a gun on Othello, and even threatened to shoot his kneecaps off. So it was natural that Othello should take some protection along when bent on pirating Witch's fabulous LSD stockpile. Wasn't it?

Within two days I was sleeping, if not quite like the proverbial baby, at least a lot less like a haunted Miss Marples. My work picked up, and, on the strength of two offers of interviews for summer teaching jobs in Cambridge, I invested in a dozen cheap cassettes and began to use my Witch-given tape recorder as a swotting aid.

During the day I would read and make notes, in the early evening I would speak an abstract on to a cassette, and finally, in the hour before midnight, when my eyes were too weary to function, I would play the cassettes back to myself, sipping my steaming Ribena as I reinforced the packages of tedious theories and facts in the pigeonholes of my medium-term memory.

So things went with sedative smoothness until the last Monday of May, just three days before my Finals began.

That afternoon saw the boiling over of the undergraduate discontent that had been bubbling, apparently harmlessly, since Christmas. The east wing of Assembly Court, which contained the University's administrative offices, was besieged and occupied by the hard-case shock-troops of the *Assessment Yes, Heart Attack Exams No Action Committee*, supported by jubilant hundreds of first- and second-year students who hadn't done any work all year and here saw a slim chance of not being found out.

If it had only been a question of exams versus continuous

assessment, news of the sit-in would barely have made the *Herald*, never mind the national press. But the political activists behind it all, while rifling filing cabinets in the Bursar's office, unearthed evidence of the University's extensive (and hitherto secret) investments in South African gold and diamond mining. This disclosure incensed many of the academics just as much as the students, causing some of the younger lecturers to swab their consciences by joining the *Exams No* sit-in.

Tom Redhead, encouraged by this unexpected publicity and support, took a hand-picked team of campus guerillas down to the John Locke Tower to indulge in an orgy of axe-grinding. They broke down the door of Dr Tostow's office, ransacked his desk and files, and discovered that yes Dr Tostow *was* a CIA agent. Not a dirty trickster, or a cloak-and-dagger hitman, or anything romantic like that, but simply an intelligence liaison officer.

He had files on every American student at Deenburgh, including copies of their matriculation photographs, files on all the Iranian students, many other foreign students, some British undergraduates, and a puzzling subsection of three files on Scottish postgraduates (Witch being one) who had nothing in common other than having scored unusually high IQs (for non-psychologists) in a vocational-guidance test battery administered to Finals students two years previously.

This all hit the daily papers on Tuesday, was interminably documented in a special edition of *Dumbo* on Wednesday, and made me feel like a Wimbledon finalist presented at noon with a telegram saying his mother is dying. If Tostow was mixed up with the CIA, however passively, then maybe my earlier Miss-Marplings were not so outlandish? But what could I do? If I made my thoughts public I might be accused of bandwagoning, or merely ridiculed, or possibly subjected to lengthy questionings, which would hardly bolster my chances of a First.

Yet might I not be shadowed to my grave by a private conviction of moral cowardice, if now I held my peace?

On Wednesday evening I walked my quandary round to

the Buttridge Bar and bought it the big brother of the wee whisky Dr Dalgleish had sanctioned. Together we decided to let matters rest until the morning after my final Final, when I would seek out Mother Galton, confide my conspiracy theory, and thereafter act according to her counsel.

This new fixity of confessional purpose enabled me to sail through my exam papers with a zealous ease that astonished me. One after another my well constructed answers raced across the page, pertinent and slick, taking not a minute over the allocated time – while all around me others sighed, groaned, scribbled, crossed out, rushed away to the toilet, and wished they had joined forces with the *Exams No* children in Assembly Court.

What an easy ride through life the Catholics must have, I mused, as I lovingly placed my last completed paper in the *S*-for-Squirrell tray at the back of the exam hall. I knew I had done the best of which I was capable, and within an hour I was convinced I would fail anyway.

In the evening there was a celebration party given by one of my classmates. We drank a lot, but it was a gloomy and maudlin affair, full of self-reproach, self-pity, reciprocal commiseration and (with the exception of Deirdre, who left early) despair for the future. The Galtons and all our lecturers had been invited, but not one of them turned up, which was generally construed as proof that our performances had been too abysmal for them to look us in the eye socially.

As I got drunker and more despondent, the prospect of relating to Mother Galton in the morning (with what would surely be taken as a smear campaign against a fellow member of her department) became impossibly daunting, while the attractions of moral cowardice multiplied like galloping cancer cells.

So taut with alcohol-catalysed self-poison had I become that I was almost sick with relief when my throbbing eyes took in the next day's *Herald* headline:

CIA ACADEMIC RETURNS TO US

Dr and Mrs Ivan Tostow, the front page told me, had brought forward by a fortnight their scheduled departure from Deenburgh. This was said to be emphatically *not* because of embarrassment resulting from the present student unrest: it was solely due to the demands of his new position in California, where . . .

The following week I visited Cambridge to attend my summer job interviews. I was offered a post starting in the first week of July, and I accepted immediately. This meant missing the pompous plumage and unction of Graduation, and the champagne and smoked salmon of Deirdre's wedding reception in Runcornfield House, but I felt I'd had enough of Deenburgh to last me a century, and I was eager to build a new life down south.

In due course I was awarded my First, but I didn't get the class prize I'd secretly coveted, and nor did I get a postgraduate place at Cambridge University. I didn't even get an interview there, for some reason I've never been able to fathom, and had to settle for my second choice, which was Birkford College, London.

This inexplicable institutional snub was a great blow to me, and one from which, in some ways, I don't suppose I'll ever recover. If I had been accepted by Cambridge, I sometimes think, I might not have grown so impatient and dissatisfied with the academic life. Amid the excitement and stimulation of sharper and livelier minds, might I not have gone on to convert my M.Phil thesis on *Self-Deception* into a more exhaustive PhD, and thence to a research fellowship, so that today I might be a tenured university lecturer, instead of a humble and insecure music publisher?

TWENTY-EIGHT

Most times I can't speak to you,
I wear a mask all day.
So heed me now, if you ever will,
I've shed my mask to say:

Light a candle to the lonely,
Act to harm no man,
Light a candle to each
And every beating heart,
Pass by no outstretched hand.

I have no power to confess you,
To clear you of your crimes,
Just the echo of a sympathy
That sings in me sometimes:

But I do not dare to ask you more
Than you may ask of me,
In precious moments when the masks are down
We share our sympathy:

That seemed to me the closest Witch ever got to his perfect song.

I found it five years ago when, contemplating writing this book, I asked Mrs Wishfort for permission to look through his papers. It was untitled (though pencilled on the back was the note: *poss. tit. Hell Is Where You Take It*), numbered 83, and filed under LYRICS TO FUCK ABOUT WITH. I listened to all his tapes but discovered no hint of an intended melody, so, in a fit of guilt at not having loved its author in life, I sent the lyric to Janie Carmen in California, enclosing biographical details and suggesting that she might like to set the words to music.

In a few weeks my communication returned from America with a covering circular from Ms Carmen's management, explaining that regretfully on the advice of Ms Carmen's attorneys Ms Carmen was not at liberty to consider unsolicited material. Thank me for my interest. A year later my own music publishing company was beginning to crawl, and I decided to attempt a second assault on Ms Carmen's elusive attention, this time supported by my lavish headed note-paper, which proudly advertised my two degrees and my membership of the PRS.

Before I got round to it, however, my intention was withered by chancing to hear on the radio a track from the latest album by Ms Carmen – who, some might say, has come sadly down market in the last ten years. It was Witch's pseudonymous MOR song, of all his compositions the one he least valued – though it still earns Mrs Wishfort over a thousand pounds a year.

She has sold Number Ten and Querns Cottage, and retired to a modernized fishing lodge in a beautiful setting overlooking a West Highland sea loch. There she divides her time between supervising a small market garden belonging to her property, landscape painting, and research for a projected definitive history of the House of Canmore.

Deirdre and Alastair, with their son and two daughters, live in a village at the south end of Loch Lomond, from which Alastair commutes to Glasgow. Helen, who ditched Grant MacMillan the day after Deirdre's wedding, now makes a lot of money as a commercial artist in Montreal, where she is married to an advertising agency executive. Rosie Wishfort graduated from Cambridge University two years ago with an Upper Second in Anthropology, and she now teaches English in Madrid.

The Tostows are still in America somewhere, and last year I saw a small photograph of Ivan Tostow in a current-affairs magazine. He was grouped with several other minor presidential advisers and appeared not to have found whatever he wanted from life. His hair and moustache had turned white, and he had the eyes of a man who worries every night about dying. In 1976 a film loosely based on his *Erewhon Three* was released and instantly buried beneath a landslide of critical ridicule and public disinterest. As far as I know he hasn't published a word since that time.

And what about me?

I'm sure that since I ceased to be a psychologist my testable IQ has atrophied by at least ten points, but I have the compensation of being rather more literate than I was a decade ago. I have read *Tom Sawyer*, Somerset Maugham, several other novels, and even a hundred pages of Martin Bunbury. By my twenty-eighth birthday I had acquired a reasonable familiarity with the character I must live with till I die, and the past four years have brought refined techniques of making life with that character tolerable.

I'm still a loner, but I no longer feel leprous. And when I think back to the ribald yells of the Balaclava snowball hurlers in David Square, whose carefree japing had filled me with despair, I am moved less to envy than compassion. For many of the snowman rollers now have wives, children, mortgages, troublesome used cars acquired through injudicious hire-purchase agreements, and stomach ulcers – while I have none of these things.

If you press me to impart the greatest wisdom I possess, honestly clawed from the salt mines of my own experience, I cannot astound, confuse or enrage you with esoteric pinnacles of mystical insight such as Witch's *Tat Twam Asi*. Rather will I diffidently suggest:

Keep yourself in good physical condition:

Don't drink too much (on consecutive nights);

Never eat more than five eggs per week (free-range if possible);

Don't smoke cigarettes;

Take enough exercise (but please don't jog – swimming is much healthier);

Etc;

And refrain from intercourse with any partner who

conspicuously fails to observe more than two of the above imperatives, for the chances are his sexual palatability will be low.

A person *is* his body, I believe, and moral qualities are a function of physical wellbeing. It does not follow, unfortunately, that a healthy body guarantees a healthy mind, for some are innately evil. But certainly, for a given person, a less healthy body means a less healthy mind.

To review my own case:

If I drank as much as some music publishers drink, I would inevitably become less scrupulous, and my writers (if not my personal bank balance) would suffer as a result. That's not to say I've never been involved in a deal that afterwards caused me qualms, but then anyone in business who says he's never had a bad conscience can safely be dismissed as a liar or a psychopath.

My safari through the jungle of pop music was first suggested and is still supported by Simon Darling, who, now based in London, is one of the rising stars in the British media firmament. Apart from that work connection with Simon, the only contact I've really kept up from my Deenburgh days is my friendship with Cindy Bell.

She too has led a solitary life since then, and her numerous travels and jobs abroad have combined with the strength and humour of her matured personality to make her one of the most attractive women I know – especially since I learned the hard way that no member of either sex is ever physically ideal. At present Cindy teaches in Switzerland, at possibly the most exclusive boarding school in the world. Her pupils are the twelve-year-old sons of film stars, Mafia bosses, Saudi oil sheikhs, and refugee Iranian millionaires. 'I can now put fifty boys to bed in quarter of an hour,' she said in a letter last February. And:

'Roger Connery *does* wear make-up in real life! I met him in the Co-op this morning.'

Last summer I went up north for a feast of nostalgia and a week of the Deenburgh Festival. The senior Cameron-Bells were on holiday in Sutherland, so I stayed with Cindy at Goldsmith Row. On my last evening we had an early meal with Beano and Harriet, who own the converted ground floor and basement of the late Miss Moray's house in Hanover Place, opposite Number Ten.

Beano still plays rugby but each year has to struggle harder to get his weight down. He has his own architect's practice, which is already prosperous enough to perk him with a company Volvo. Harriet is lecturer in Scottish Literature at Deenburgh University. Her PhD thesis was entitled *An Examination of the Supernatural in the Writings of James Hogg* and is presently being revamped as a book commissioned by an American publisher. The Turnbulls have a mortgage that doesn't worry them, a yellow Citroën Dyane for Harriet, an au pair girl, and a strapping three-year-old called Mallecho, whose highest linguistic achievement that evening was the incessant repetition of:

'I don't like Peter.'

After dinner Beano drove us up to the Synod Hall, and we ate Black Magic chocolates through a passable production of *A Midsummer Night's Dream.* By midnight we were in the Cameron-Bell drawing-room, drinking Sir William's port and malt whisky while we talked over old times and lapsed into an Ain't-It-Awful? lament about what the past ten years had given us.

'Streakers. And Taurus Action Spray to increase sensitivity and promote a full strong erection,' said Beano, who always had a soft spot for men's magazines. 'Discover the satisfaction of your total masculinity.'

'Free love,' said Cindy.

'An *end* to free love,' said Harriet diacritically.

'Free love, Pete,' said Beano, ferrying my glass to the cornucopian drinks cabinet, 'and what happens?'

'I give up.'

'It flies away!'

'Red Rum,' said Harriet.

'Bjorn Borg,' said Cindy. 'I still say he's got the nicest legs.'

It was my turn, so I said:

'Pocket calculators and digital watches.'

'Kung Fu,' said Beano. 'And Wombles.'

'Vietnam Boat People.'

'The Queen's Silver Jubilee.'

'A fat dead Elvis.'

'Kerry Packer.'

'Gary Gilmore.'

'Edward Wilson and Harold Heath.'

'Butter mountains.'

'Quangos.'

'Camp David.'

'Roddy Llewellyn.'

' "Thank you for sticking up for me," said Florence,' said Beano.

'Jaws,' said Harriet.

'Didn't *Star Wars* make more money?' asked Cindy.

'Rod Stewart's *Sailing* must have made a lot,' said Harriet.

I pointed out that the song was written by Gavin Sutherland, and quoted a music-trades magazine estimate as to the fortune it had grossed to date. This caused Beano to sing:

'Mull off Argyll, Oh wind rifting out from The bums in the I . . .'

'Don't be disgusting,' said Harriet.

'What about the revolution in Iran?' I suggested.

'They'll need another one soon,' Harriet said confidently.

'The biggest change I notice in Deenburgh', said Cindy, 'is the health-food shops. They're all over the place.'

'What about the Chinese take-away boom?'

'And the plague of Pak grocers?'

'I think the new licencing hours are a great improvement.'

'That they are *not*, Pete,' Beano thundered, the unhairy parts of his face afire with cultural conservationism.

'Why not?'

'Bah! Dirty ashtrays all afternoon. No sense of urgency about getting the pints down at lunchtime, no spirit of reincarnation when they open again at five. Believe you me,' he said passionately, 'there is a conspiracy afoot to turn the Scottish pub into a filthy continental café, and it must be resisted with the utmost vigour. Vigilance is essential.'

Dr Turnbull suggested that Mr Turnbull should write to the *Herald* on the matter.

Mr Turnbull growled that he had, but the:

'Buggers never printed it.'

'The English people in Number Ten,' Harriet remarked to Cindy, 'have cut the pear tree down.'

'Why?'

'To stop the Buttbridge schoolkids stealing the pears.'

'Labradors seem to be declining,' I noted with satisfaction. 'But the upturn in setters is simply staggering.'

'Yes,' said Cindy. 'The whoopsies are worse than ever. Would anyone like some tea?'

'I think we'd better be going,' said Harriet.

'No hurry,' said Beano. 'Sunday tomorrow.'

So we drank tea, munched biscuits and cheese, ignored the Mozart symphonies in the background, and talked for another hour.

Had I noticed Poldy's had been taken over by one of the fucking breweries? Why had it? Because Poldy lost his pub licence: got done for drunken driving. What about Othello's piranha fish? Beano didn't know. Eventually he and Harriet lurched away in a jovial daze, leaving the Volvo till the morning, and Cindy fetched a bottle of chilled Moselle from the kitchen. She was achieving a state of charmed determination, and later she took me to bed with her.

Her room, on the second floor, overlooks the prestigious Goldsmith Row Gardens, where the setters with the finest pedigrees can often be seen defecating behind the holly bushes. With its framed prints of Byzantine mozaics, photographs of the Belhaven TwangGang on stage, Witch's pobbly dragon painting, jumbo coloured candles and crimson velvet curtains impregnated with the scent of sandalwood, that room endures as a shrine where Cindy can always take refuge for a month, when the rest of the world has let her down.

Though what will happen when her parents die?

After making love we lay side by side for some time without speaking, our bodies pressed in intimate contact by the narrowness of the bed. Candlelight from the mantelpiece threw fantastic shadows round the big square room, while tiny faults in the curtain fabric began to leak grey from the dawning south. *You and the Night and the Music* was schmaltzing quietly from a radio on Cindy's desk. A song which I co-publish with another company had just been played, and my mind was awash with a sleepy computation of my share of the royalty allocation, when Cindy said:

'Peter?'

'Yes?'

'Kiss me again.'

I obeyed.

'Didn't you want to sleep with me?'

'Yes.'

'Why didn't you ask me?'

'I didn't think *you* would want to sleep with *me*.'

'Thank goodness all men aren't like you.'

'Are you thinking of Witch?'

'Partly.'

'When did he ever *ask* you to sleep with him?'

'That's not the point, Peter.'

'What is the point, Cindy?'

'Witch always did everything he could to get what he wanted.'

But did he want to die?

I stroked a brown spill of hair away from her disturbingly earnest eyes, shared another kiss with those sweet azalea lips, felt unbelievably happy for ten seconds, then said:

'Is that such a noble quality?'

'It's quite a handy quality in a man, if you happen to be the girl who would like to be got.'

'???'

'!!!'

Later she reflected on her childhood flirtations with Witch; and their eventual midnight consummation among the sand dunes of the Isle of Nogg. We talked over the incidents that had led to his death, and wondered what might have been, if only . . . if only . . .

'What did you do with the pistol?' she asked.

'I posted it to Sergeant Anderson at the CID. Anonymously.'

'And the Thermos?'

'Dropped its contents in the river.'

'Oh, Peter, isn't life *strange*?'

'In what way?'

'Well, I haven't, you know, slept with many men . . .'

'*How* many?'

She giggled. 'That'd be telling. But isn't it amazing that two of them should be music publishers?'

'What's wrong with sleeping with music publishers?'

Cindy's reply was surprisingly cogent, considering what she had drunk and the sleep she hadn't had, but it belongs more properly in another story, and I want to end this one with the conclusion of the last essay Witch wrote for Professor Quelch:

> Kant's three problems are: God, Freedom and Immortality. His three questions are: What can I know; should I do; may I hope? Multiplying out gives us nine problem-questions, beginning with: What can I know about God? Each of these problem-questions begs the question of the signification of *I*. Now, the foregoing arguments, given the postulates stated at the outset, prove conclusively the truth, when sincerely uttered by a self-conscious subject, of the statements *I am the Dragon* and *The Dragon is a dancer.*
>
> Such a subject (and this is offered not as a demonstrated result, but as a hypothesis testable only by such subjects) will find, in the fleeting eternity during which he can make his utterances sincerely, that his state of consciousness transcends the personal to enable him to read off (from that state itself) the solution to Kant's nine problem-questions *and* the proper signification of *I* (as if he had become a self-informing bus timetable), together with the insight that when he falls back into being a mere person he must forget what he cannot remember, though he should remember *that there were* solutions (as a business executive can remember that once he knew the times of

buses to Glasgow), while the quality of his life *may* be improved by having known those solutions, and it always remains open to him to attempt their rediscovery (just as, in principle, there is nothing to prevent a business executive from travelling by bus again), which is to say: for one more fleeting eternity, to cease to be a person.

Below, in neat Pentel red, the kindly Quelch had commented:

Jolly imaginative, Wishfort.
But this sort of stuff won't go
down very well in Oxford, you know.

At the bottom of the page Witch had memoed:

Try tuning E G C G C E. *Harmonics*?

And smeared across it is a faded brown stain, which, to this day, if pressed to a reminiscing nostril, smells faintly of the John Locke cafeteria's chicory coffee.

Cambridge, 1983